LEGENDS OF DOMSTRIA
GUARDS VESTIGE

LEGENDS OF DOMSTRIA
GUARDS VESTIGE

ALEXANDER ADAMS

STOREHOUSE
Entertainment Group

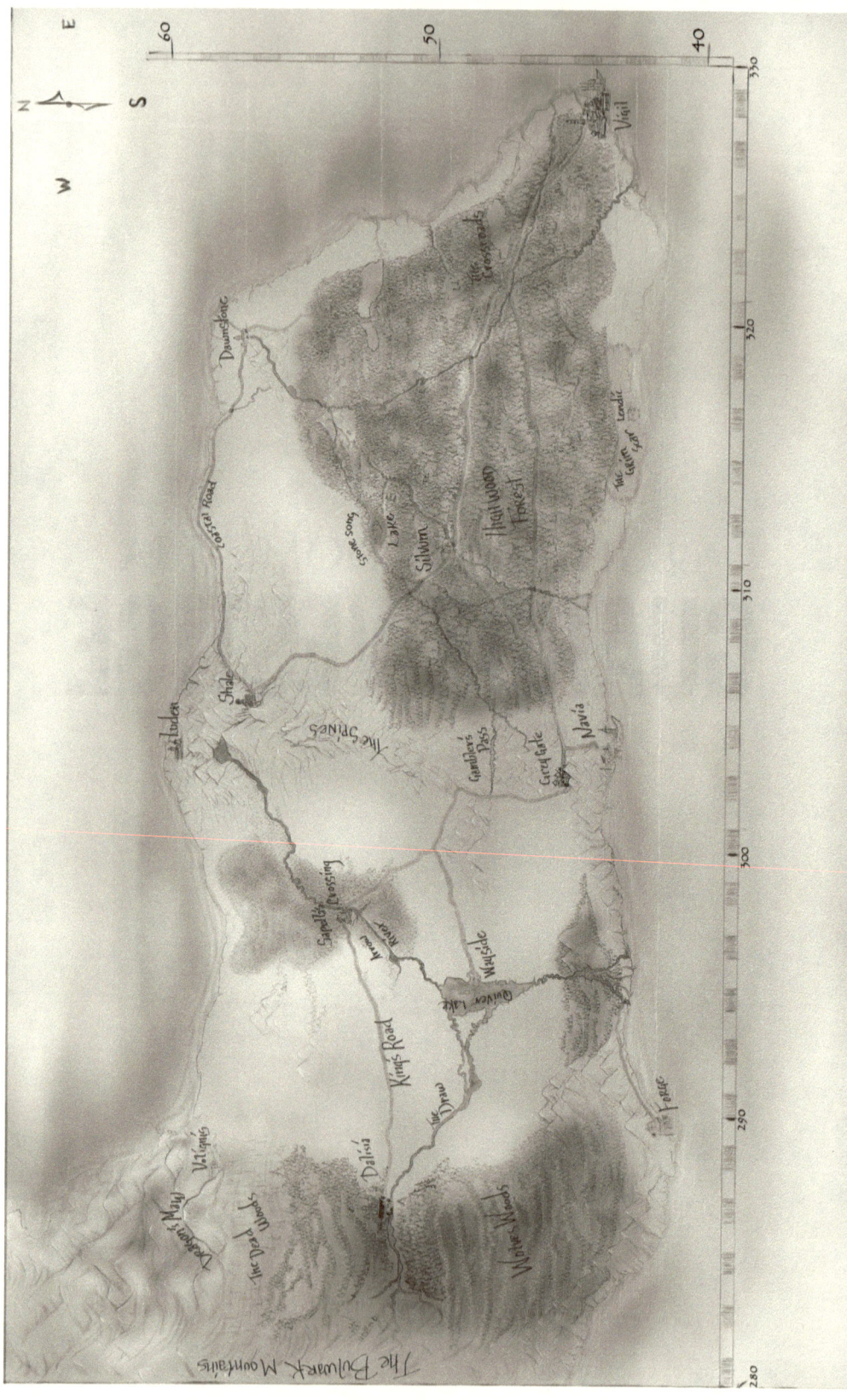

ACKNOWLEDGMENTS

FIRST AND FOREMOST I have to thank my parents. My mother, for putting up with me long enough to allow me to accomplish this and helping me work towards it. My father, for always being willing to help me flesh out ideas and inspiring me to follow through with this. Thank you both, without you there is no way I'd have ever made it this far. I can never truly repay either one of you. I have to thank my friends for being honest with me as my proof readers and focus groups. For always being happy and eager to hear any story I was able to make up for them to enjoy. Thank you to my artist, Will Stinnett, you took the images I had in my head and made them even better than I had ever hoped. Lastly, I have to thank the authors of every fantasy and sci-fi book I ever read growing up, for filling my head with a love of stories and giving me the mindset of a story teller.

PROLOGUE

3,766th year of the First Age.

THE DEAFENING DIN of steel striking steel rang out over the open coastline a thousand times over. The smell of blood hung thick in the air. Screams and wails of dying men and monsters joined together in the chorus of war. The Dragon Guard and the army of the Left Hand battled one another for the fifth consecutive day, scarring the terrain with blood, bodies, and dragon fire. The land would never fully recover from this battle. It wasn't the first area of the world to be broken beneath the feet of the two armies, and Marcus was sure it wouldn't be the last.

Marcus Prim, commander of the southern forces of the Dragon Guard, stood at the edge of a tree line overlooking the battle. He ran a hand over his balding head, feeling the last few whisks of hair as he closed his dull green eyes and took a deep breath. When he opened them again he could see everything unfolding before him. The leather-clad Dragon Guards were fighting an uphill battle against the twisted forces of Cadent the Left Hand, a fallen High Dragon who had rebelled against his siblings to enslave and rule humanity under the tutelage of a still-darker force. Across the mass of bodies and writhing monsters was the fortress of Lendic, one of the greatest feats of Dragon Guard architecture. It had been taken from them three months ago and had since been used as a staging ground for the Disciples of the Left Hand.

The castle towered over the land, its shadow stretching far into the ocean beyond. It was the second-largest fortress the Dragon Guard had possessed with the largest port on the continent allowing them to ferry troops in and out of the area with ease as well as storing some of their most vital supplies. Marcus and the bulk of his forces had been beyond the Bulwark to the west and had been alerted to the loss of the fortress only when their supply line had been cut off, which forced them to retreat from one battle and begin another. Thankfully, the Left Hand troops beyond the mountains hadn't pursued them this far. If they had, Marcus's army would have been caught between the two and slaughtered.

He took his eyes off the castle and turned them to the forces on the ground. His soldiers fought vigorously against warped creatures and their masters. They battled monsters with the visage of wolves and countless other animals from around the world, all perverted into something dark and wrong.

"Commander!"

A female voice snapped Marcus out of his trance. He turned to see a young woman clad in ranger leather a few feet away.

He motioned her over. "Report?"

The ranger handed him a folded paper. He quickly broke the wax seal when he recognized the symbol of the scholar sect. It was a battle report from Eliza, his captain currently commanding the north flank of the battle. He was disappointed to find the news as he had expected, and feared. They were being pushed back with heavy losses. He folded the paper again and looked at the broken seal, pondering his next move.

For the time being he had no way to break through the Disciples' defenses. The keep was too well fortified for a frontal assault. Even with the aid of dragons, they had no way to safely advance—which begged a question: How it was taken to begin with? Marcus chose to leave that topic for another time. Right now he simply had to figure out how to proceed. Even if they did manage to secure the fortress this night, he worried their remaining numbers wouldn't be enough to hold it against a counterattack, which he was sure would come from beyond the Bulwark.

Marcus hadn't noticed that the ranger was still standing to one side, waiting for her next order.

He waved her away. "You may return to your other duties."

She saluted him by bringing both arms up across her chest, letting the steel around her wrists *clink* together. "Yes, commander."

As she left, he lifted his hand and looked at the band around his own wrist. Steel covered in orange veins, much like a stone etched with quartz. It was the badge and the burden of a Dragon Guard, something he had worn for as long as he could remember. With a furrowed brow he turned on his heel and walked into the tree line. He only went about two dozen feet before he broke through the other side and into the thick of their western basecamp. Tents extended in a line to the horizon, with Dragon Guards running every which way, attending to a countless number of duties.

It didn't take Marcus long to stride to the command tent. Even before he reached the entrance, he heard his advisors arguing inside. With a quiet sigh he stepped past the two wardens guarding the entrance. He was greeted inside by Nadine, his commander in training, who seemed to be getting ready to storm out of the tent and nearly ran into him. The first thing he noticed was her irritated expression and the blinding white blonde hair currently braided into a tail and hanging down to her lower back.

"Commander, finally, you're here!" she said. "We can't do this much longer. If we're going to make our move to take the castle we have to do it now. Call in the reserves and make a full offensive."

Marcus stepped to the square table in the center of the tent and handed Nadine the report as she made her way to the other side. "Eliza agrees," he said. "They're being pushed back, as is Darrius on the eastern front, if his last report still holds true. Eliza believes the only way to secure her position is to sacrifice it, to send her men to reinforce his then push back even harder. Catch her attackers between Darrius and us and hopefully cutting a portion of them off, forcing them to the outskirts of the battle without reinforcements."

Nadine read through the report before passing it to Samuel on the other side of the table. He read it over and ran a hand across the black stubble on his chin and cheeks as if checking its growth.

"Something unsettles me, commander," Samuel said as he placed the report on the table. "The creatures here, they fight with a vigor we haven't seen in a long time. Blows that would normally kill only maim and enrage. In addition, it seems the Disciples have greater power than we have previously seen."

Marcus looked up from the map spread across the table at his captain. Samuel led the ranger sect of the Dragon Guard and was a rather small man. His armor like all rangers was sparse, covering only his chest, lower legs, forearms and shoulders. He was short at five feet with a thin body and small amount of muscle tone. In contrast there was Nadine, the woman who would take Marcus' place in just a few years' time. She was thirty years young compared to Marcus' seventy eight. A giant of a woman, standing at six and a half feet she was the epitome of strength with the thick heavy leather plating of her warden armor only adding to the image.

Marcus knew he could trust their judgment. This caused Samuel's words to concern him all the more. "Please elaborate," he said.

"The only other time we've seen Disciples with this much power," Samuel said, "was when one of the princes was present."

Nadine rolled her eyes. "You aren't seriously suggesting," she said, "that one of the seven is hiding nearby?"

Samuel shrugged. "It's not so unlikely. Cupi was last seen in the swamps near here a dozen years ago. Luxsus was last reported beyond the Bulwark and Furoret's personal fortress rests on the western coast of the continent."

The certainty in Samuel's eyes was chilling. It was more than enough to cause Marcus to at least entertain the idea. Even if it proved to be false, it was better to act on the assumption of a greater danger than to ignore it entirely.

"Which one would be most likely?" Marcus asked.

Samuel tapped his chin thoughtfully. "If I had to guess, it would be Luxsus. Furoret would be on the field if he was here, and as I said, Cupi has not been seen for years."

Nadine crossed her arms and scowled. "If it's really one of the princes," she said, "we don't stand a chance."

Marcus sighed and was about to speak when a commotion outside caught all their attention. The three exchanged a look and started for the door. Before they were even outside, Marcus knew a dragon was landing in the camp. The walls of the tent billowed under the wind of its wings. Once outside, they were greeted by a growing cloud of dust it as the dragon folded in its bat like wings and dropped the last few feet causing the ground to shudder under its weight.

Marcus bowed and said, "Forus, what news do you bring?"

Like all dragons, Forus was two-toned in coloration. His primary scales, which covered the majority of his body, were a deep, sapphire blue that faded into his chest and underbelly's secondary scales, which were a lighter, sky blue. The membrane of his wings shared the same color as his secondary scales. His body was nearly thirty-five feet from the tip of his tail to his snout, while his wingspan nearly doubled that. Now solidly on the ground, he stood at his full height of fifteen feet.

Forus' voice was deep and guttural: "Belladux and his forces are crossing through the woods to the northeast. They will arrive by daybreak."

Nadine suddenly stood straighter. "Belladux?" she said. "He's coming personally? Why would he concern himself with this battle?"

Forus dug his claws into the dirt and growled low. "Ocudai has discovered the Left Hand resides here."

Marcus tensed. "He's here, truly?"

Forus lowered his head to look Marcus in the eyes. His head was adorned with two curved, ivory horns resembling a ram, while at the back of his jaw he sported two much-shorter spikes jutting downward.

Forus hissed his next words, "We believe he hides within the halls of Lendic."

He lifted his foreleg and handed Marcus a bag he'd clutched in his claws. Marcus quickly opened it and read through the parchment inside. It was a report from Belladux. Cadent had been injured in a battle with his sibling Lestice, just across the sea in the tundra. The idea that Marcus had nearly tried to take the fortress with the High Dragon inside was a frightening one. He would have sent his entire army to their deaths.

The dragon's voice rumbled with irritation. "He has eluded us for centuries, but finally we have a chance to end this war. He is weakened and because of this we can finally take him for the judgment he deserves."

When Marcus finished reading, he nodded. "I'll order a full withdrawal and prepare for a final assault at daybreak when Lord Belladux arrives."

Marcus raised his shield and let the creature's claws scrape harmlessly along the shield's length before he pushed forward and brought his broadsword up and into the wolfish beast's gut. He twisted the blade until it was flat. Planting his shield against the edge, he pushed as hard as he could, wrenching the sword out through the beast's ribs. It howled in fury before stumbling off the edge and into the mass of fighters below.

Marcus had no moment to rest, however. Another of the hulking beasts lunged for him. Marcus leapt to the side, letting it fly past him before it landed and skidded across the wall, leaving scratches in the stone where it dug in its claws. The beast readied itself and charged for him again, swiping at Marcus's head, then at his midsection. Marcus ducked the first blow and blocked the second with his shield. The strike sent vibrations down his arm.

Before the creature could react and lash out again, Marcus lifted his sword and swung it down hard into the beast's skull. When the creature fell back, the implanted sword was ripped from Marcus's grip. He quickly glanced around the wall of the fortress readying himself for another attack but was thankful to find his immediate area clear, allowing him a moment to breathe as he wrenched his sword free.

The commander looked out over the battle being waged in the light of the rising sun. At midnight, Marcus had withdrawn all his soldiers into the tree line, where they regrouped and patiently waited for Belladux's arrival. The Disciples knew better then to pursue them into the forest and had taken the time to reinforce their own position. Belladux's personal legion had arrived just before daybreak. They were quickly integrated within the forces already present to fill in the gaps left by their losses. The moment the sun crested the horizon, they had charged in.

Under the cover of dragon fire directed at the walls, they had managed to close the gap to the wall quickly. Then they employed battering rams to whittle down the gate. It took two hours of nonstop pressure, not counting the additional two hours of stalls they'd faced from the walls' defenders and opposing dragons. When the gates had finally been thrown open, the fight had tipped drastically in favor of the Dragon Guard.

Most of the Disciples and their nightmarish creatures that had been protected by the walls had retreated into the fortress itself before closing it off and leaving the rest of their army to fend off the Dragon Guard. In spite of the Dragon Guard's success, Belladux had yet to reveal himself. Presumably he was waiting for Cadent to emerge from the fortress, which as of yet seemed impervious to all attempts to enter. Every door remained unscathed by both flame and steel.

Marcus had never seen the High Dragon firsthand, but had been informed by his predecessor of Cadent's powers as The Left Hand of Wisdom. He was one of four who'd been created to guide and teach mankind. Now he was a betrayer and usurper to Verhova the creator.

"Commander!"

Marcus turned to see Samuel walking toward him along the length of the wall. He was flanked by two hooded rangers with empty quivers.

Samuel smiled at his commander. "The battle has turned in our favor. The field is nearly ours."

Marcus shook his head. "This is a battle of attrition. While the majority of the Disciples themselves have fallen, their beasts seem to have no end. I will not call this for our side until the Left Hand falls from the sky."

Samuel nodded. "Of course, commander. Surely Cadent will emerge soon. He will have no choice soon."

Marcus raised an eyebrow at his captain. "How so?"

"Nadine has taken the battering rams to the walls of the fortress itself rather than the doorways. Whatever magic kept them standing does not do the same for the walls; it will only be a matter of time."

Marcus smiled. Nadine was shaping up to be a wonderful commander. "Let us hope we can manage whatever we find within. If we—"

There was a deafening grinding. The wall they stood upon shook violently. Marcus and the three rangers dropped to one knee to ensure they wouldn't fall until the shaking subsided. Then a heavy and enfeebling chill settled over them. The sounds of battle all around them slowed until they seemed to stop entirely. Dragon Guards stared in confusion as the twisted creatures they were fighting moments ago hunched down and cowered while the few Disciples remaining threw themselves to the ground and began to pray or outright flee.

Marcus felt heavy, as if there were weights strapped to his body that he was barely strong enough to lift. He struggled to rise. When he finally managed to stand straight, he turned his eyes to the towering castle of the fortress across the courtyard. Everything was still. Then the roof of the castle burst upward and apart as the titanic form of Cadent emerged, sending the remains of the towers and roof outward to rain down upon the armies in the courtyard, crushing both sides as the chunks of stone rolled. The mighty dragon spread his wings the moment he was clear of the castle and hovered in the air for a moment before beating his wings to stay aloft.

Cadent's primary scales were the purest white Marcus had ever seen, while his secondary were a shade of brilliant silver. His body was enormous, at least seven hundred feet long and three hundred tall. The morning light shone over his scales, giving him an ethereal glow. He ceased beating his wings for a moment and let himself fall onto the castle. Upon landing, the castle's upper half crumbled beneath him until he settled on the rubble. Cadent lifted his head high and looked out over the battlefield before him. How he had been able to hide within the confines of the castle was impossible for Marcus to understand.

Cadent steadied himself by wrapping his tail, which was proportionately longer than any other dragon, around one of the towers of the castle that still stood. He pointed his snout to the sky and his neck flared with light. A moment later, he lowered his head and let loose a stream of scorching white fire at the courtyard below.

Marcus ducked behind his shield but he wasn't able to evade the heat. He felt his skin bubble on his face and he cried out in pain until the flames subsided and he knelt on the broiling stone. He was crippled, unable to move, his body charred where the leather didn't protect him and cooked and boiled where it did. The breeze that passed over the coastline was torture against his skin. The courtyard had been filled with Dragon Guards and forces of the Left Hand. Now Marcus could barely see anything more than discolored blurs in front of him.

When his vision cleared, he looked around the wall and could no longer see Samuel or his rangers. He had no idea where they had gone. When he looked over the edge of the wall, he saw nothing but a sea of ash. The High Dragon's neck flared a second time as he prepared to wash the battlefield across the wall with fire.

Then something broke through the clouds above Marcus. The hulking, red form of Belladux barreled through the air and collided with Cadent. The white dragon released his flames harmlessly into the air as Belladux dragged him clear of the castle. Both roared furiously until they crashed into the ocean, sending towering waves onto the shoreline and washing away countless Dragon Guards and Disciples.

The two titans thrashed against one another as they rolled in the depths and breached the surface again and again. Belladux finally threw Cadent off and settled just off shore. Both stood and stared at one another, Cadent partially submerged in the deeper water. Belladux was half again larger than Cadent and where the latter was thin and slender, Belladux was wide and muscular. His primary scales were a deep scarlet; his secondary scales faded to a light gold. His coloration mixed with the water below him made it appear as if he stood in a pool of liquid fire. They stood nearly a hundred feet apart and waited for the other to make the first move.

It was Cadent who chose to speak first. His voice was smoother than Marcus would have thought: "It has been far too long, brother."

Belladux's voice thundered across the water making it ripple as he snapped his response: "Do not call me that! You lost that right when you started twisting humanity into puppets."

Cadent gestured to the army gathered on shore: "Puppets? If anything, I have cut their strings. Freed them from an authority that hides the truth from their eyes."

"The only thing you have done is place them in shackles and chains! You are deceived by shadows."

"The only shadows in our world are the ones cast by the false stories and teachings you spread. I have freed them from their lives as slaves and brought them out of bondage to serve the one true ruler of creation."

"This bondage you claim to have seen is nothing more than an illusion made by your own arrogance and lies fed to you to fuel it."

"The only illusions I remember," Cadent spit out, "were those shown to us at the start of our lives, and the lies told to us to ensure our obedience. I will stand for no such deceit and will see all life freed from the false light with the revelation of truth, with freedom."

Belladux lowered his head again. "What you claim is freedom is slavery. All the 'truths' you tell are lies." He took a step forward, making waves in the water. "I had hoped you would see the failings of your actions, but I see Lestice was right. You are blinded by pride and a desire for what was never yours."

Cadent was shouting furiously now. "What I *want* is what I *earned*— a place befitting the power I wield and deeds I have performed, a throne worthy of my stature in the halls of godhood alongside the true power of our world as his right hand."

"Enough!" Belladux's voice boomed with authority only Verhova could match, making even Cadent take a step back. "I see now that in spite of your title you lack wisdom. Reason is lost on you."

Cadent sighed and seemed to calm himself. "If you will not see the truth of my words, then so be it. You will fall into his shadow. Come, brother."

The two titanic dragons stared at each other for only a moment longer before charging toward one another, causing the surface of the water to crash and part before them. When the two collided, they were engulfed in their own fire.

CHAPTER ONE

4th of Horace, 26th year of the Fourth Age

"I JUST CAN'T FIGURE out how to ask her without it turning into an argument again."

"So you don't think she's changed her mind?"

"No, I don't. But I'm going to ask anyway. I'm running out of time."

Daniel Summers and Connie May sat on the bank of the Arrow, a river less than a five-minute walk from Sapella's Crossing. The river ran from a spring in the mountains all the way to Quiver Lake at the center of Edaren. Daniel picked up a pebble next to him and tossed it in. He watched the ripples spread along the water until they lapped against grass-covered banks. He glanced at Connie, who sat next to him with a hint of a smile on her face. She was as tall as he, just less than six feet. Her obsidian hair lay over one shoulder. She brushed bangs away from ocean-colored eyes as she watched the river gently flow by.

This was one of the few sections of the Arrow calm enough to swim in, though the autumn cold made that an absurd thing to consider at

1

the moment. Farther down the river was a pair of waterfalls that flowed into dangerous rapids that, if you weren't careful, would take you all the way down to the lake far beyond the forest.

Connie sighed and picked at the grass. "It didn't go well last time, did it?"

He threw another pebble. "It went about as well as the time before that, and the time before that. Almost feels like there's a pattern forming."

She shrugged. "Have you ever thought of just, you know... leaving anyway?"

"You know I couldn't do that to her."

"It's just a thought. This is your only chance, after all. You'll be too old by the time they're recruiting again."

He knew she was right. The Dragon Guard had begun recruiting at the start of the year, something they did only every five years. Those between the ages of thirteen and nineteen were eligible as long as they made it to Vigil before winter and the start of the New Year. Daniel had turned sixteen four months ago, so this was his first and only chance to join. He had tried to talk his mother into letting him go at the beginning of the year. She hadn't even stopped to consider it.

Daniel had made more attempts several more times since, without success. Now winter was fast approaching. He had only two months to make the journey, and on foot it would take all of that. Connie had offered to lend him her horse several times and he had declined several times. But Connie was used to getting her own way. He had finally given in to the idea.

Connie gently poked him. "Do you want me to talk to your mother? Maybe she'll listen to me."

"You're more than welcome to try, but I don't think it will do any good."

They sat quietly for a while and watched the river flow by. Daniel knew Connie hated prolonged silences so he wasn't surprised when she broke this one. "Have you got your route planned out? Like where you'll stay or camp, and which roads to take?"

"Most of the farms along the way are rumored to take in travelers for a night. Even if that doesn't work out, I'm fine with camping. There's a cross castle between here and Grey Gate where I can resupply and stay, but once I'm on the other side of the Spines I'll mostly be in the forest on my own. If I'm lucky I'll find a trader traveling the same way, safety in numbers right?"

Connie sighed. "You know it won't be the same here without you."

His face flushed. "We don't even know if I'll be able to go yet."

She nudged him with her elbow. "You will. I've got a good feeling about today."

He smiled shyly. "Don't, uh, don't you have to go help your father with some of the new foals before it gets any later?"

"If I said no, would you still make me leave?"

"Yes."

"What if I said maybe?"

"You better get going."

"Right." She stood and slipped on her boots and leaned in and kissing him on the cheek making his face flush even darker, before quickly making her way downstream towards the narrow bridge. He watched her long hair sway behind her and thought about how long they'd known each other, and how much they cared for one another. They had plans for their future, most of them revolving around Daniel's eventual move to Vigil. She supported his dream like no one else did; he felt indebted to her every day because of it.

Daniel sat by the water a little longer before standing and putting his own boots back on. He grabbed a handful of pebbles from beneath the water and began walking downstream, absentmindedly tossing them into the river as he went.

He crossed the rickety wooden bridge, stepping over missing sections of wood, and made his way down the winding forest path, taking in his surroundings as he had thousands of times before. The dirt path was wide and made its way through tall pine trees and thick undergrowth. Just past the trees, the view included the shapes of farmhouses that sat outside the edge of town where the forest had been logged away for the sake of open fields for crops and pastures for livestock.

After a short walk, the trees receded and the dirt path gave way to smooth cobblestone, marking the beginning of Sapella's Crossing. Daniel passed homes and a few people who greeted him with a smile, a wave, or a nod. As he neared the center of town, the homes gave way to storefronts, the occasional inn, and many bars. Posts lined the streets with sconces at their tops that would be lit by the town militia at nightfall.

From the corner of his eye, Daniel noticed movement on his right. A woman with short, greying hair was waving him over. "Mr. Summers!" she called. "Get in here!" She turned and disappeared inside the store.

Curious, he followed her into the small building. The inside was filled with jewelry and small metal figurines tucked into glass cases and lined up neatly on shelves.

He called out to the door behind the main counter: "Ms. Nilia?"

Evelyn Nilia stepped out with a wide smile spread across her face. "Mr. Summers! It's finished. I was just putting the chain on."

She walked up to him and handed him a pendent, a silver mayflower with a small sapphire at the center hanging from a thin, silver chain.

He was breathless for a moment. "It's beautiful," he whispered.

"I'm sorry it took me so long. I wanted to make sure it was absolutely perfect."

"It's incredible. The detail is amazing. I can see why it took you as long as it did."

"Well, as I said, I wanted it to be perfect."

"Thank you so much," Daniel said. "But this is worth so much more than I paid. The sapphire alone..."

She smiled. "You paid for a necklace, I made you a necklace. Don't worry about what's on it."

"It's just...this must have been expensive. Are you sure?"

"If it makes you feel any better, think of it as a gift."

He laughed. "It doesn't, but thank you. Really, I don't think I can ever repay you for this."

She clasped her hands in front of her. "Well, it looked like you were going somewhere before I distracted you, so off you go. I don't want to keep you any longer."

With that, she pushed him out the door and onto the street. He smiled and stuffed the necklace into his pocket before starting back down the road. Just past the shop was an open stone courtyard with an ornate fountain in the middle. The rim was adorned with carvings of ancient dragons in flight over a range of mountains. The spout itself was a statue of a slender dragon with scales speckled with gold flakes. The statue sparkled in the sunlight as it shot water into the air while perched atop a sword pommel. The blade was wide and exaggerated in size and took the place of the podium in the center of the water. The fountain was extravagant but beautiful nonetheless, and served as a visual reminder of the legend of the town's founding.

According to the story, an old Dragon Guard warden had come to the area when she heard of a dragon terrorizing the countryside and farmlands. When she arrived, she found the dragon attacking a farm and fought a terrible battle with the beast. During their conflict, the dragon burned away a section of the forest next to the river. When the Dragon Guard finally felled the foul creature, it crashed into the water, while the woman died from her wounds in the new clearing. The fountain now sat on the site of that supposed clearing as a memorial to the brave woman. It was an interesting story. Daniel always wondered how much of it, if any, was true.

He watched a group of children play in the fountain while parents sat and observed from a distance. On the far side of the fountain, a woman stood with her eyes closed and her hands clutched to her chest. She muttered something before tossing in a silver mark and watching it sink to the bottom. Daniel walked around the fountain before turning to his right and making his way down a narrow alley that opened onto another main road. At the far side of town, he entered another residential area before stopping in front of a small, single-story home. He made his way up crooked, weak wooden stairs to the door.

Rusty hinges screamed when he opened the door and stepped inside. The house was sparse and simply furnished. A small stone fireplace surrounded by mismatched and poorly made chairs was set in the far wall. On the other side of the room, a doorway led to a small kitchen. Next to that was another was a hallway connecting two bedrooms and a water closet.

"Mom?" Daniel called. "Are you home?"

His mother came out of the hallway, her face and clothing dotted with flour. She brushed a lock of gold hair behind her ear, revealing a large spot of flour over one of her pine-green eyes. "Hi, honey," she said. "Did you enjoy your walk with Constance?"

"Yeah, it was fine." He pointed at her face. "What happened to you?"

She shrugged. "I dropped a bag at the bakery. You should have seen it. Covered everything and took most of the afternoon to clean. Came back to grab a change of clothes. So where'd you two go?"

"Just down to the river. She had to leave to help her father with something before dark." Daniel took a deep breath. "There's something I wanted to ask you."

She frowned. "What's wrong?"

"Nothing's wrong. I just wanted to ask you again...about going to Vigil."

His mother's face fell. She shook her head. "No."

"Mom, just hear me out." She started to turn away, but he grabbed her shoulder. "Just listen. Please."

"No. I need you here."

"Why can't we just talk about this?"

"There isn't anything for us to talk about." She pulled away and walked toward the hallway.

"Why are you so against this?" Daniel said. "I'm not like Dad. I'm not just running off for no good reason."

She stopped in front of her bedroom doorway and turned to look at him. A twinge of sadness crossed her face, then her eyebrows knotted. "I said no. That's final!"

"You need to talk to me about this. You can't just shut me out every time I bring this up!"

"I said no. We aren't going to talk about this and you aren't going anywhere." His mother turned, stormed into her room, and slammed the door.

Daniel ran his fingers through his shaggy, copper-brown hair and sighed. He hadn't wanted to fight with her again but it always seemed to turn that way. Inevitably, she would walk away from the conversation and he would stand there frustrated. He shouldn't have mentioned his father. That had been the tipping point where it went from conversation to argument, like every other attempt when he'd brought him up. He walked to her door and lifted his hand to knock, but hesitated. Trying to talk to her now wouldn't do any good. He turned and walked into the room he shared with his brother at the other end of the hall. Daniel fell onto his bed with a sigh. Several strands of straw jabbed him through the thin linen.

The room was small. Two beds sat against opposite walls with a window and single nightstand between them. A simple dresser was positioned at the foot of each bed, both of which were basically empty. Daniel lay there a moment before rolling over and opening the only drawer in the nightstand. He placed the silver necklace inside and grabbed a thin, leather-bound book titled *Hidden Efforts: A Recount of History*. He flipped through a few pages, pausing occasionally to read a line. It wasn't an old book, but Daniel had handled it so often that the parchment was torn and faded, and the leather binding was discolored where he'd placed his hands over the years.

The book contained short stories about various Dragon Guards and their adventures. One was about a woman saving the city of Dawnstone from a cultist manipulating the citizens' king when it was still the capital of Prect. Another was about a man finding monsters in Wolves Wood and sparing them in the end after learning more about them. The story he enjoyed the most was about the Dragon Guard being infiltrated by a group of cultists and a civil war that broke out in Vigil. A coup was thwarted by a servant girl acting as a spy within the cult, allowing her to destroy it from the inside. What he liked most about the book was the style—it was written in a series of journal entries. It made the stories seem almost real.

The door suddenly opened and Daniel's brother, Jeremy, entered the room. He was short and stocky for an eight-year-old. His hair and emerald-green eyes mirrored Daniel's own, though Jeremy's hair was far more unruly at the moment.

"Daniel!" Jeremy flashed a smile that quickly faded when he saw Daniel holding the book. "What's wrong? Did you and Mom fight?"

Daniel rubbed his temples as he spoke. "How could you tell?"

"You always read that book after you two fight," Jeremey said. "She still doesn't want you to leave?"

"No, she doesn't."

Jeremy sat on the edge of the bed. "Why do you want to go so badly anyways?"

"Kind of hard to explain."

"Well, I want you to go too."

Daniel glanced at him. "Oh, yeah?"

"Yeah. If you go then I get the room to myself."

Daniel gently pushed his brother off the bed with his foot. "Well, at least you're on my side," he said with a smile. "Where were you, anyway?"

"At the Creeks' house. They needed help loading some boxes into a wagon so they could finish moving to a farm outside of town. I got two silver marks for helping."

There was a light knock on the window. They both turned to see Connie waving at them from the alleyway. Daniel unlocked the window and pushed it open.

Connie leaned on the windowsill. "Hey. So Daniel, how'd it go?"

He shrugged.

"Same as the last time?"

"They had another fight." Jeremy remarked.

Daniel glared at him before turning back to Connie. "So what's up, I thought you had to help your father?"

"We were supposed to separate the foals from the mother so they could start weening but by the time I showed up he'd finished. They were way more cooperative than the last group and went right into the other pen so he didn't actually need me. But Serena and Alphonse were heading down to the falls to do some fishing. I figured if your talk with your mother went well we could celebrate, or if it went badly you might want to go and take your mind off things."

"Don't see why not."

Jeremy tugged at Daniel's sleeve. "Can I go too?"

Daniel glanced at Connie, who shrugged.

"Uh, sure," Daniel said. "I guess you can come."

They hopped through the window and pulled it shut before heading down the alley, back toward the fountain, and then down the street to the river. Evelyn Nilia waved at them from her doorway and winked at Daniel as they passed. When they reached the narrow bridge they turned to follow a dirt path heading downstream. As they walked through the silent forest, Daniel thought about how he could convince his mother to let him fulfill his hope of leaving for Vigil before the end of the month. He wished she could see the difference between what he wanted to do and what his father had done to them years ago.

Jeremy had been only a year old when their father had left them. He simply walked out the door one day and never came back. Their mother wouldn't talk about it, but she had been broken for a long time. More often than not, just the mention of their father would make her retreat to her room for hours without a word. Then she would pretend it had never been brought up at all. His father hadn't hinted at trouble or acted out of the ordinary as far as Daniel could recall. He'd just left. The shock had been especially devastating for Daniel's mother. She'd thought everything was fine and then suddenly, it wasn't.

The last thing his mother wanted was for her sons to disappear the same way her husband had, leaving her to believe it was somehow her fault. So whenever Daniel brought up the subject of going to Vigil, she shut down and walked away. But this was different. Daniel wasn't going to abandon his family. He wouldn't be gone forever. If he'd wanted to vanish from their lives he never would have asked for his mother's blessing to go, he would have simply walked out the door.

Daniel's train of thought was broken by the sound of the first of two waterfalls just ahead of them. He could see it cresting over the edge as they turned and headed down a steep path so they could stand beneath it.

The two falls outside the town were unofficially known as "Sapella's Tears". The smallest was the first and fed into a pool at the base of the path from atop the hill, while the larger one sat just beyond a thin tree line down another short span of river. The area around the pool had been cleared of trees and undergrowth, making it a favorite location of the locals for a countless variety of celebrations or relaxation. The pool also had several deep holes where fishing was simply a matter of throwing a line in and pulling it back out.

Serena Baker and Alphonse Cane now sat at the edge of the pool with a fishing pole propped up between two large stones just in front of Alphonse. Serena had long, chestnut hair tied in a tail that reached to her mid back. Her matching chestnut eyes were smiling as much as she was. She nudged Alphonse, who was short and muscular, with curly, sandy-blond hair.

Serena moved closer to Alphonse, allowing space for everyone to sit together. "Hi Daniel," she said. "Constance told us you were going to try again to convince your mother to let you go to Vigil. Did it go well?"

He sat next to them and began picking at the grass. "I brought it up, she said no, we fought, she walked away."

Alphonse patted him on the back and pointed at him with his other hand. "You should listen to her," he said. "What good have the Dragon Guards ever done anyway? They sit in their fancy keep all day, ignoring the rest of the world and the problems it has."

Daniel shrugged. "They used to hunt dragons and monsters."

"Used to," Alphonse said. "Haven't heard of a Dragon Guard killing no dragon for ages. Now they're just living in the past, rambling on 'bout cults and all sorts of nonsense and fairy tales."

Connie shook her head. "If they're anything like those stories and legends say they were, then I think they're worth joining. It's wrong to let something like that die out."

Serena bit her lip. "What about the rumors of them killing councilmen and their aides? Doesn't seem like the stuff of legends."

Daniel rolled his eyes. "There's no proof of that. Like you just said, those are only rumors."

Alphonse shrugged dramatically. "Well, rumors or not, I'm talking facts. They wouldn't know great if it kicked 'em in the head."

Connie glared at him. "Oh? So what's great in your eyes?"

He grinned and put a hand over his heart. "The Edaren Royal Guard, protecting the king and his family in Dalisia. There ain't any greater calling than serving royalty."

Daniel turned to see Jeremy walking down the river near the edge. He was clearly bored of the conversation and was off to find his own entertainment. "Jeremy," he said, "don't go too far."

Jeremy called back without looking: "I won't."

Connie raised an eyebrow and chuckled at Alphonse. "You want to be a royal guard?"

"Course I do," he said. "It's one of the greatest honors in all Edaren. I'm going to Dalisia next year to join the Royal Army so I can work my way up the ranks."

"Plan on living in that big castle?"

"As only the royals and their guard can."

Connie laughed and shook her head.

Alphonse glared at her. "What's so funny?"

"Oh, nothing," she said. "It's just you talk about the Dragon Guard ignoring the world's problems by sitting in their 'fancy keep' and then you compare them to a group that sits on the sides of a throne all day with their swords up their— "

A loud splash followed by a scream cut her off. Connie and Daniel jumped up instantly and ran downriver toward the sound. They broke through a wall of underbrush that surrounded a clearing and froze in their tracks. Jeremy had his back to a tree. About a dozen feet in front of him, a valgret stood in the flowing water.

The muscular, wolf-like creature was on its hind legs. Though hunched over, it was still six feet tall and would have been more than eight if it stood straight up. Its skin was dark and covered in patches of matted black fur. Its arms were as long as it was tall, letting it balance itself on its knuckles. Blood poured from open wounds on its side. A broken arrow shaft stuck out from its shoulder and two more from its chest.

Jeremy was frozen in place, his face reflecting his fear as the creature stared at him with fury.

The sight was otherworldly. Daniel had never seen a valgret before but had been told stories about them when he was younger. Now that he'd actually set eyes on one, he realized the stories never truly expressed how horrifying they were. Its fingers were boney, with claws at least an inch long. The creature's lips poured saliva and foam as its breath fogged in the cold. Even so, without a second thought, Daniel ran to his brother and stood between him and the valgret. It hadn't noticed the new arrivals before. Now it reared back and curled its lips, showing rows of sharp, yellow teeth. A moment later it took a step towards them.

"Hey!"

A rock hit the valgret squarely in the jaw, causing it to flinch. It jerked its head toward the source and saw Connie standing defiant, fifteen feet away, another rock in hand. She hurled it and again struck the monster in the face. The valgret took a step toward her placing a single hand on the riverbank before another; much larger stone struck it in the shoulder, causing it to stumble sideways. The source this time was Alphonse with his leggings dripping water as he stood closer to the wall of underbrush on the other side of the twenty-foot-wide river. Alphonse's face paled when the beast turned its gaze toward him and uttered a low growl.

Daniel looked for anything he might use as a weapon. He glanced up and saw a long, partially broken branch hanging from a tree. Reaching for it and pulling as hard as he could, he found it wouldn't break free. He tried again and heard the strain of wood as it started to split, but it still held in place. He glanced back at the valgret as it crouched low and tensed its muscles while continuing to stare down Alphonse.

Daniel gave one last, hard pull. The branch broke free with a cracking sound, causing him to stumble backwards. He managed to stay on his feet before turning and charging at the beast, the branch raised high. He swung hard, striking it on the ribs across its multiple open wounds. The creature howled in fury and stumbled in the water. It lifted a clawed hand to grip its side. Shards of wood were now embedded in the open wounds. The valgret lashed out with its other arm and struck Daniel across the chest, knocking him toward Jeremy and sending the branch flying into the water.

Daniel hit the ground hard. He struggled for breath and his vision blurred. He'd never been struck so hard in his life and was surprised it hadn't knocked him unconscious.

"Daniel!"

Connie attempted to run to him but the valgret regained its composure and jumped onto the shore between them. It snapped its teeth at her, forcing her back, before it turned again to Daniel and growled. Jeremy helped him to his feet and stood behind him as they both began backing away. Behind them and to their side, the second waterfall roared. They were trapped. If they waded into the river on their left, they'd never be able to move fast enough to escape the creature, while the forest on their right was too thick to penetrate. Directly behind them was a rocky ledge they'd never be able to make it down in without injury. The valgret continued to advance as they backed away. Daniel could swear he heard it laugh as they neared the edge of the small cliff next to the falls. Then he had an idea.

"Jeremy, get in the water." Daniel pushed his brother gently toward the river and into the shallows along the bank.

If they could get near the falls crest, they could jump to the rapids below. They had done it dozens of times over the years at the shorter waterfall. Daniel knew there was a fishing hole at the base of this larger one. He knew it was at least ten feet deep but wasn't sure exactly how far from the base it was. He just hoped they could leap far enough to avoid the rocks but not so far they overshot the hole.

"Hey, mutt!" Alphonse shouted. Another large rock struck the creature on its back haunch.

It stumbled again but didn't seem to care. It was too focused on Daniel and Jeremy as it continued its slow trek toward them. The valgret finally stepped back into the water and bared its teeth in what resembled a smile.

Daniel placed a hand on his brother's shoulder. "Get ready to jump as far as you can," he said. "We'll be fine."

Jeremy's voice cracked as he looked at the drop behind them. "I can't. It's too high."

"Yes, you can. We'll jump together."

The valgret narrowed its eyes and tensed its muscles. It was preparing to pounce.

"Jump!" Daniel yelled. He grabbed his brother and leapt as far as he could.

Alphonse threw another stone that struck the valgret in the head as it leaped after them. The creature, off balance and howling with pain missed them by only inches. Daniel caught a glimpse of it falling against the rocks at the base of the falls as he and Jeremy crashed into the cold water just beyond. For a brief moment, Daniel saw the valgret beneath the water, but he quickly lost sight of it as he sank into the depths.

CHAPTER TWO

4th of Horace, 26th year of the Fourth Age.

THE CURRENT WAS far stronger than Daniel expected. He surfaced, then struggled desperately to keep a tight hold on his brother by wrapping his arm around his chest as they were dragged away in the rapids. If there was one thing Daniel knew, it was that he wouldn't let go, no matter what. They were again dragged under the water. When they breached the surface again, Daniel pushed Jeremy as high as he could to allow him time to breathe freely. It wasn't nearly enough. The moment they took a deep breath, they were both pulled back under the water. The cycle repeated over and over, never allowing them time to get their wind.

Daniel couldn't see anything but the white of the water as it splashed around him and the green of the trees above as they whipped past. He attempted to find purchase on the slick stones of the riverbed but found none. He tried to kick and swim toward shore but the current kept dragging them to the center of the torrent. Several times they almost barreled headlong into rocks that jutted from the water. Thankfully they were just far enough to one side that the worst of it was a blow to Daniel's shoulder.

Again and again they were pulled under. Daniel gave up trying to swim to shore with one arm, and instead wrapped both around Jeremy to keep him close. He let the water take them where it willed. He looked around as best he could, hoping to see a low-hanging branch he could grab to pull them free. But for what seemed like an eternity, Daniel saw nothing. Finally, through splashing white waves, he spied a tree that had fallen on shore, the trunk's upper half just above the river, its limbs pointing down and into the water. If he could just get farther to that side he could pull them out, or at the very least get Jeremy out.

Daniel tried again to swim but made little progress. Jeremy must have seen the tree as well and figured out what Daniel was doing, because now he felt his brother trying to kick along with him. With Jeremy's help, they started to move through the current. When they neared the tree they both kicked harder. It seemed as if they had a chance. Daniel reached out and caught a branch, but it was brittle and snapped the moment tension was applied. As they washed under it, the tips of broken branches struck him across the face. He closed his eyes, blindly reached out again, and caught hold of a thicker limb. Their sudden halt strained his arm and threatened to dislocate it, making him cry out and swallow water.

Jeremy grabbed another branch and with Daniel's help from below, pulled himself onto the trunk. After Jeremy was safely up, Daniel lifted himself out of the water and sat next to his brother. He was exhausted, but they weren't safe yet, not until they were on shore. He nudged his brother and nodded toward the rocky bank. They crawled over the trunk and jagged spikes of wood until they both fell off the tree and onto the shore. They lay there, the only sounds being their ragged breathing and the rushing water.

"That was awful," Jeremy finally said through heavy breaths.

Daniel couldn't help but laugh. "Yeah, it was."

He sat up and looked around. The shore was mostly river rock, barren of trees and undergrowth. They seemed safe for now. Daniel wasn't sure if the valgret had died, but after seeing its wounds and its fall to the rocks and the water, he chose to hope it had. He didn't want to even think about the idea of it coming back.

Daniel slowly stood and looked at the tree line. "Come on," he said. "We need to find a place to rest for the night."

Jeremy looked concerned. "We aren't going back?"

"Not right now. Look." He pointed at the sky. "It's getting dark and we can't walk back until it's light out. Come on, it won't be so bad."

Daniel led a hesitant Jeremy into the forest, keeping the river within earshot so he wouldn't lose his bearings. He found an old, dead tree with half of its roots jutting out of the side of a small hill, which made an overhang inside the tree line. It was just large enough that Daniel barely had to crouch to avoid hitting his head against the roots. Once inside the hideaway, he felt an immediate rise in temperature since the ground insulated the small area. He led Jeremy underneath the roots. His brother sat with his back against the dirt, pulled up his legs, and silently buried his head between his knees.

"We need a fire," Daniel said. "Don't move. I'll be right back."

Daniel left a silent Jeremy as he strode into the forest and began scavenging for tinder. He soon returned with an armful of twigs and broken branches that he stacked just outside of the overhang so the smoke wouldn't choke them out or set the remains of the tree aflame. When that was done, he walked into the forest again to look for kindling that would easily light take flame. He found a cluster of cattails where they had climbed out of the river and grabbed about a dozen. He broke apart the soft cotton on the top of the plant and filled his pockets with down. While scouring rocky areas of the bank, he also found two flat, light red porous stones, each one roughly fist-sized.

Spark stone, perfect. He smiled as he held one in each hand. Striking two of these together made starting a fire easy work even in the most unfavorable circumstances, though they were brittle and stones of this size were good only for a few attempts. Daniel grabbed as many as he could carry. He walked back feeling grateful to Connie's father for teaching him as much as he knew about the forest. Without the knowledge he'd been given, he was sure he and Jeremy would freeze in the autumn night chill.

When he returned, Daniel struck the stones together; causing sparks to fly toward the plant down. It didn't seem to take long, but by the time the fire was roaring and the warmth was spreading through his wet and chilled body, the forest was black and he'd used nearly every stone he'd gathered. Jeremy had fallen asleep, his head listing to one side. Daniel sat next to his brother and checked his brother's forehead and clothing. Thankfully, the clothes had mostly dried and he wasn't too cold. Daniel sighed happily, pulled his knees to his chin, and stared at the fire as he thought on the day.

No one had seen a valgret in the forest surrounding Sapella's Crossing since before Daniel was born. As far as he knew, valgrets never ventured beyond the mountains. They usually stayed near the Bulwark in the west and The Spines to the east, where travelers were a rarity and they had free reign in the area. According to the stories he'd been told, they were vicious animals and highly territorial. Why one was here, and why it had been shot and wounded, made no sense to him.

His thoughts were interrupted by a groan from Jeremy. "Daniel?"

"What is it, bud?"

"What if that thing comes back?"

"I'll stay awake and watch for it. I'll keep you safe."

Daniel sat sleepy-eyed with his back against the dirt, and watched the forest grow brighter. As the sun rose, rays of light pushed through the treetops, cutting through the gaps like golden blades. He'd struggled to keep his eyes open but had managed to keep his promise and stay awake through the night, peering into the forest the entire time. The fire had gone out hours before and was now nothing but glowing coals and smoke. Daniel had debated going for more wood while it was still burning but had decided it was better to let what little was left burn out and stay with Jeremy. He also considered letting Jeremy sleep a little longer but decided against that as well.

Daniel shook his brother awake. "Hey bud," he said, "let's go. We've got a long walk ahead of us."

Jeremy groaned and rubbed sleep from his eyes. "My clothes are still soaked."

They were hardly damp, but Daniel smiled and humored him. "Yeah, mine too. Come on, we need to get going."

Daniel kicked dirt onto what remained of the coals, more out of caution than necessity, before leading Jeremy back to the river. They started their long walk upstream, climbing over fallen trees and pushing their way through undergrowth. Thankfully, close to the bank it was relatively clear, and for several spans they walked unhindered. Daniel had never been in this part of the forest before. Though the unfamiliarity didn't bother him thanks to the guiding river next to them, he was still concerned about the valgret. The more he thought about it, the more he believed that it had survived the fall. Meaning, it would be between them and home.

"Do you think the monster is gone?" Jeremy's question in the silence startled him.

Daniel lied. "Of course it is. If it wasn't, it would have found us by now."

"What if it comes back?"

"Then you run upriver toward home and I'll try to lead it into the forest."

"What if it's faster than you are?"

"Then I'll go for a swim in the river again." He smiled at his brother to reassure him but clearly failed.

Jeremy's face still wore a sour and worried expression.

They kept walking, stopping occasionally to listen to the sounds of cracking branches or birds taking flight in the distance, always keeping an eye out for black fur and grey skin. Daniel thought back to the scene at the falls. The valgret had zeroed in on him after he had struck it along its wounded side. It had completely ignored Connie and Alphonse as he and Jeremy backed away. It was like it had been toying with them. He was sure it had even smiled, and possibly laughed at them. Which was impossible, he knew that. None of it made any sense.

After several hours of walking, Daniel glanced up and saw the sun was directly above, signaling midday. The journey home was taking longer than he'd expected. The speed of the rapids had carried them farther than he would have guessed. He just hoped they wouldn't have to spend another night in the forest. If he had been alone he would be moving faster, but with Jeremy he had to slow his pace. His brother wasn't the most graceful person. He tripped over his own feet more often than not.

The air around them grew eerily quiet. Daniel was uneasy. The forest was always full of sound. But now there was nothing. He felt as if they were being watched. Suddenly a loud *crack* came from the tree line, quickly followed by another, and then another and the sounds grew steadily louder.

"Daniel?" Jeremy gripped his brother's arm.

He gently started to push Jeremy behind him as the sound from the trees grew louder still. Soon the sounds were near enough he could make out an occasional grunt or curse mixed in. Daniel's tension eased. This wasn't the valgret, he was sure of that at the least.

In the next moment, a large man burst through the trees and tripped on an exposed root, causing him to stumble forward into the open. "Verhova save me," the man grunted, "I hate the bloody forest."

The stranger was taller than Daniel by several inches. He was wide and muscular, with golden blond hair and a thick beard, both trimmed short and slightly unruly, with several pine needles sticking out of them. He wore bulky, heavy leather armor dotted with orange-tinted steel studs. Slung across his back was a large kite shield with orange veins running across it, much like the studs that dotted his armor. At his waist was a sheathed broadsword, black leather wrapped around the hilt. The sword's pommel and guard were made of the same veined metal as the shield. It was a peculiar coloring Daniel had never seen before. Yet, he was sure he had seen, or at the very least heard of it before. But he couldn't quite place where. It reminded him of water reflecting firelight or a stone etched with a jewel vein.

The stranger regained his balance and looked around. When he spied the brothers, he pointed at them with an armored hand and said, "Are you Danny?"

The question made Daniel uneasy. He kept his brother behind him since the man clearly had an idea of who he was. "I'm Daniel," he answered. "Who are you?"

The man approached them with an outstretched hand and a massive smile. "My name is Kenneth. I've been looking for you two all morning."

"Who are you?"

"I'm Kenneth. Weren't you listening?"

"No, I mean—" He was cut short by another figure breaking through the wall of underbrush, though she did so with far more grace. She rushed over and placed a hand on the man's arm and said, "Kenneth!"

This woman was short at five feet and rather thin. Her cropped black hair was matted with sweat, as were her clothes—loose-fitting black, with a skirt in addition to trousers. Her armor was thinner and sparser than Kenneth's, covering only her chest, lower legs, and forearms. She gripped a short sword that was etched with orange. Slung over one of her shoulders was a rather plain, large bag.

"Where is Mila?" she asked.

Kenneth looked back at the trees before answering. "She caught sight of it when you split off and went after it. If we're lucky it will lead her straight to the rest of the pack. It seems like we finally caught up with them. Just in time too."

The more Daniel looked at them, the more something nagged at him about their appearance.

Kenneth glanced at the brothers. "We have to get them out of here," he said. "Take them upriver, back to Sapella. I'll find Mila and the two of us can deal with the pack."

"Are you sure?" the woman sounded concerned.

"We'll be fine, there were only a few left and they were injured. Should be no problem," Kenneth said, before he pointed at the brothers. "Just get them out of here."

The woman nodded and began pushing Daniel and Jeremy with firm but gentle hands. Daniel glanced behind and saw Kenneth disappear into the trees, already grumbling about the density of the forest. Once he was gone, Daniel dug his heels into the dirt, making them stop in their tracks.

"We're not going anywhere with you," he said to the woman, "until you tell us who you are and what you're doing out here."

She sighed and nodded. "I'm sorry. You're right; I can't expect you to tromp through the woods with a stranger." She smiled and reached out her hand. "I'm Claudia Wells."

Daniel shook her hand hesitantly. "Daniel Summers and this is my brother, Jeremy."

Claudia's smile disappeared. "I know this must be rather frightening for you, but we have to get out of the forest as soon as we can. It's not safe here. I promise I'll explain on the way. But we have to keep moving."

Daniel considered for a moment. It wasn't as if they really had a choice at the moment. They were heading the same way, after all. Claudia stepped up to walk beside instead of behind them as they resumed their trek.

"You boys are lucky Kenneth found you when he did," she said. "There was one just through the trees watching you, but Kenneth's so loud it heard him coming a mile away and ran off."

"There was one what?"

She looked at him as if he were joking. "A valgret of course."

His heart skipped. "It was watching us? Just watching?"

"They tend to do that."

Daniel glanced at Jeremy, who suddenly looked very frightened. He changed the subject. "So, uh, how did you find us?"

She laughed softly. "A lot of stumbling around trying to keep up with Mila, the stumbling being quite literal for Kenneth. We might have passed you had it not been for him scaring it off like that."

"How did you know we were out here in the first place?"

"Your friends were looking for you around the falls yesterday evening. We ran across them while we were tracking the pack. They told us what happened. We sent them back to town and started searching for you ourselves. But it got dark on us and we couldn't keep stumbling around blind with valgrets in the area, so we made camp next to the river and started looking again at first light."

Daniel noted the plural. "You said valgrets. How many are there?"

"There's more than one?" Jeremy asked. He gripped his brother's arm tighter.

Claudia saw the fear on Jeremy's face. "Oh, uh, there's only a few," she said. "Don't worry. Mila and Kenneth can handle them just fine."

Daniel glanced at Claudia's armor again. Suddenly it dawned on him: tracking valgrets, orange-etched steel, and the leather.

He thought he knew who they were now, but he had to be sure: "So who are you people, are you apart of a mercenary band?"

"I'm a scholar with the Dragon Guard."

Daniel simply stared. He'd known the answer was coming, but it stunned him all the same.

When Claudia noticed he hadn't replied, she turned and looked at him inquisitively. "Are you all right?"

"You're really a Dragon Guard..."

"Yes." She stopped walking. "Is that bad?"

"No, it's just, uh..." He felt foolish. He didn't know what to say.

"He wants to be one," Jeremy answered for him.

Claudia's gaze swept to Jeremy and then back to Daniel. A smile spread across her face. "Is that so?" she said. She lightly pushed Jeremy along and kept walking, forcing Daniel to come out of his stupor and follow.

"Yeah," Jeremy said, "he's wanted to be one for as long as I can remember."

"That's quite a long time," Claudia said. She glanced behind her at Daniel. He knew his face was flushed.

"He even has a book of stories about Dragon Guards," Jeremy continued. "He reads it all the time."

"That's interesting. What kind of book?"

Jeremy shrugged. "I've never read it because I don't know how, but it's real small and the stories are really short. He read it to me a couple times before."

Claudia smiled as she glanced back again. "Very interesting...I might have to read this book myself."

Daniel's face felt like a fire as he whispered to his brother, "Please shut up."

Jeremy either didn't hear him or simply ignored him. "He was even reading it yesterday."

"Well, he's very lucky then. We can take him with us to Vigil after we've dealt with the pack. The Dragon Guard would love to have him."

Daniel's heart skipped. Did he hear that correctly? They were going to take him with them?

Jeremy sounded sad: "He can't go."

Claudia glanced at Daniel. "Why's that?" she asked.

For a moment he'd completely forgotten about why he hadn't already left. "I can't go," he said, "without my, uh, my mother's blessing."

"Why not? I left without my parents' approval when I was around your age."

"I just can't leave her like that." He sighed. "It's complicated."

"I see. Well, I hope it becomes less so."

He desperately wanted to steer the conversation away from him. "So, what exactly is a scholar? I've read about the different sects in the book but it's not really very detailed."

"We're mainly diplomats, historians, medics, and so on."

"How many different sects are there, anyway?"

"Well, there's scholars, there's—"

A loud *crack* from the tree line cut her off.

She whirled at the noise and drew her sword in a blur of motion while placing the brothers behind her. For a long moment the only sounds were their breathing and the wind whipping through the trees. Not once did Claudia move while focusing on a single point ahead of them. She never averted her gaze as the seconds dragged on.

All at once, a growl broke the silence and a blur of fur and teeth barreled toward them. A valgret leapt at them.

Claudia reacted quickly. She crouched and swept her foot out, knocking both brothers' legs out from under them and sending them to the ground. The creature's momentum carried it over the three of them.

It tried to grab them as it sailed past, flipped end over end, and splashed into the river behind them.

"Run!" Claudia shouted as she helped Daniel and Jeremy to their feet.

They started upriver. Daniel risked a glance behind them and saw the valgret slowly clawing its way out of the water. Once on land, it started after them without hesitation at an alarming speed.

Claudia too saw it gaining on them and hurried them on. They dodged low branches and jumped over rocks and roots. Jeremy stumbled and started to fall but Claudia grabbed him by the tunic and threw him over her shoulder with surprising ease for her size. They ran as fast as they could but Daniel heard the valgret getting closer. He forced himself to keep his eyes forward.

Ahead of them, a woman in black suddenly emerged from the trees. She lifted a longbow and drew back the string as she aimed right for them, pausing for a moment before she released the arrow, seemingly sending it straight at them. Daniel heard the *whoosh* and felt the wind as the arrow passed by his head.

The valgret howled with pain. The arrow had clearly struck its mark. With incredible speed, the woman grabbed another arrow from the quiver hanging from her belt and fired again. They slid to a stop next to her as she readied another arrow. Daniel looked back at the creature as it slowed, then came to a stop a dozen feet away from them, clearly more cautious after its injuries and their swelling numbers.

Claudia gripped the stranger's shoulder. "Mila!" she said. "Thank Verhova you're here. Did you find the rest of the pack?"

Daniel took a moment to look the woman over. She was as tall as Daniel and almost as slender as the longbow in her hand. She wore nearly the same style of armor as Claudia, though with added protection along her shoulders and biceps as well as her thighs. Beneath it she too wore plain black, along with a ragged black scarf wrapped around her neck and pulled over her head like a hood, obscuring her face in shadows.

A soft voice spoke from beneath the hood: "They've moved on."

"Then why is this one still here?"

Mila turned toward Daniel. "From the story told to us, I would guess it wants him."

Daniel was confused until he looked back at the creature. Now that he could see it clearly, he realized it was in fact the same one from the falls. It still had the broken arrows in its shoulder and chest, which were now accompanied by two more in nearly the same spot on its breast. It locked its gaze on Daniel and crouched low to the ground. Mila and Claudia immediately stepped in front of the brothers, sword and bow at the ready. The valgret reared back slightly before growling again and starting forward at a careful pace.

Before it completed a second step Mila fired another arrow into its chest, causing it to stumble backwards. In the same instant Claudia lunged forward and slashed at its outstretched right arm. She cut deep, making the beast flinch and back away. Claudia ran past and to its side. The valgret swung its left arm at her head, the clawed hand spread wide. She ducked low and backpedaled out of its reach, her back now to the raging river.

The valgret lunged for her again but was pushed back by another Mila arrow, which embedded itself in the beast's chest at an angle. It howled and jumped at Claudia, who rolled forward and underneath it. She rose and spun with amazing speed to drive her sword into its back, burying half the blade.

This time the valgret didn't just howl. It screamed in rage as it whirled and caught Claudia in the stomach with its forearm, sending her backwards into a tree and to the ground.

Mila fired again, but the creature turned its back, hiding the spot Mila had been aiming for. The valgret walked awkwardly, keeping its back to Mila but advancing toward Claudia. Mila fired two more arrows, planting them next to each other at the nape of the beast's neck. She was clearly trying to get through the thick hide and cause lethal damage but to no avail. The valgret raised its arm over its head and flattened its hand, preparing to drive its claws into Claudia's chest.

But Kenneth barreled through the brush, roaring, his shield lifted in front of him like a battering ram. He slammed into the valgret, breaking the arrows off in its chest and driving the arrowheads deeper. He churned his legs forward and slammed the creature's back into a tree along the shoreline. Pine needles and loose branches fell around them. The valgret screamed again as the sword in its back was driven through, only to stop against the shield at its chest. It clawed furiously at Kenneth's armored arms and shoulders, unable to find purchase on the leather plates. Kenneth raised his other arm, the one holding his heavy and wide broadsword, to level the tip at the valgret's mouth before driving it through and into the tree behind it.

The valgret thrashed wildly before its arms fell at its sides. It was finally still. Kenneth backed away with his shield still raised. He let the valgret hang from the tree by the thick blade for a moment to ensure it would remain still. Mila ran to Claudia while Kenneth removed his sword and allowed the valgret to slump to the ground. He flipped the creature over and bent down to withdraw Claudia's sword as well, then walked to the river and began washing the dark blood from the blades.

Claudia, after catching her breath, turned to the brothers: "Are you two all right?"

Speechless, they each simply nodded.

Claudia smiled and sighed as she rested her head against the tree. "Now I remember why I like being a scholar so much," she said. "Books don't try to kill you."

Kenneth laughed deeply and nudged Daniel with his elbow before handing Claudia her sword. "That was quite the show, wasn't it?" he said.

"We should go," Mila said. She helped Claudia to her feet and kept a hand on her shoulder to steady her.

"What about the rest of the pack?" Kenneth asked with a frown.

Mila shook her head. "No sign of them," she said. "This one must have gotten separated between here and the spring. Even if we double back and try to find where they split, we'd never catch them again."

Claudia seemed disappointed but nodded. "Hall won't be happy, but all right. Let's head for town."

The sun was setting as they made their way up the dirt path back into Sapella's Crossing. Kenneth had led the way, with Claudia and Mila at the back and Daniel and Jeremy walking between them, until they were on the cobblestone streets. Mila had said the pack was gone but Kenneth hadn't wanted to take any chances, so they had moved slowly, their weapons drawn and ready.

"Lovely little town," Kenneth said as he took in his surroundings, a light smile on his face.

All the shops were closed and locked. The homes were likewise silent, with only a few windows lit by candlelight. Along the streets, light posts gave everything a comforting and warm glow.

Mila turned down an alley without a word, stopping only when Kenneth called out to her: "Mila! Where are you going?"

She half turned but started walking away again as she spoke: "To see an old friend."

"She's always so cheerful," Kenneth said with a sigh. He turned to the brothers. "I assume you can make it home safely from here?"

"Yeah," Daniel said, "we'll be fine. It's not far."

"Which way is the nearest inn?" Kenneth asked.

Daniel pointed the opposite way Mila had gone. "Two streets down and farther into town."

"Splendid," Kenneth said. "We'll speak again in the morning, I'm sure. Come along, Claudia, a nice warm meal would suit us both."

She waved him off. "Actually, I think I'll go for a quick walk. Take in a little night air."

He raised an eyebrow. "Suit yourself. A hot meal is calling my name."

After he rounded the corner, Claudia gently pushed Daniel and Jeremy down the street. They started for their home with the Dragon Guard scholar in tow. No one spoke. Jeremy was dreary eyed and yawning, while Claudia seemed cheerful. But Daniel was in a daze about the whole situation. He still couldn't believe what had happened to them. A valgret attack followed by a trip down the rapids and a night in the forest, then meeting three Dragon Guards who were, from what he gathered, doing exactly what he had read about them doing hundreds of years ago: hunting monsters and saving others in the process. His mind raced as they reached their home's front door and stepped quietly inside. In the front room, his mother had fallen asleep in front of the fireplace, an open book in her lap. All that remained in the hearth were a few glowing embers and ash.

Daniel walked over, placed a hand on her shoulder, and gently shook her awake. "Mom, we're back," he said. "We're okay."

She opened her eyes slowly. When she saw Daniel and Jeremy in front of her, she started shaking. She pulled them both in and squeezed them tight. Tears ran freely down her face.

She leaned back to look at their faces and gripped their shoulders. "Oh, my boys, I was so worried! If I'd lost you two I don't know what I would have done." She pulled them in again, tighter this time.

Once she let go again, Daniel backed away and motioned behind him. "Mom," he said, "this is Claudia. She helped us get back."

His mother stood, looked Claudia up and down for a brief moment, then pulled her into an embrace. "Thank you," she said. "Thank you so much for saving my boys."

Claudia seemed surprised and a little uncomfortable at the physical contact. "Oh, uh, you're welcome," she said. "Really, it was nothing." She awkwardly patted their mother on the back and seemed grateful when the hug ended.

Daniel's mother picked up the book that had been in her lap. "I started reading this last night," she said, "when I heard what happened." She smiled and handed it to Daniel. It was the book from his nightstand. "Why don't you two head to bed, you look exhausted. We can talk in the morning and tell everyone you made it back. I'm sure Constance is still worried sick about you."

Daniel stared at the book for a moment, then nodded. He gave his mother another hug before heading for their room, Jeremy right behind him.

CHAPTER THREE

6ᵗʰ of Horace, 26ᵗʰ year of the Fourth Age.

SEVERAL HOURS PASSED with Daniel lying in bed, unable to sleep. Jeremy, meanwhile, snored from the other side of the room. Daniel wished he could sleep like that now. He felt exhausted. But he couldn't sleep when his mind raced like this. Claudia had said he could leave with them, but if he couldn't convince his mother to let him go, it wouldn't matter. He rolled over, opened the nightstand, and pulled out the necklace he'd gotten for Connie. He looked at the silver flower for a while, then threw off his blanket. He was careful not to wake his brother as he dressed and slipped on his boots.

Daniel opened the window to the alley and carefully climbed out. He picked up a small, loose stone from the house foundation and placed it next to the hinge of the window so it couldn't be closed completely while he was gone. Once he was sure it was stuck in place, he turned toward the main road and made his way to the outskirts of town. The moonlight was bright and lit the way as he walked down the wide dirt road that went out of town to the farms.

Sapella was located in the middle of a forest on the northern edge of Edaren. It wasn't an ideal location for growing fields of crops or even raising livestock, but the people here managed well enough. He passed a couple of smaller homes before making his way to a two-story house with a large field stretching out behind it and an impressively sized stable located on the fence line near the road.

Daniel quietly made his way around the back and over the fence into the yard. He dug in the dirt to pick up a couple of small pebbles and looked up to the window of the house he thought was Connie's, counting the ones adjacent to it to ensure it was the correct one. Then he lightly tossed the stones against the glass until the window opened and Connie peaked out. He waved to her and smiled timidly. Seeing him, she put her hands to her mouth and went back inside. She was gone for only a few moments before she came out the backdoor.

Connie ran to him and threw her arms around him. "I'm so glad you're okay!" she whispered.

He laughed softly. "I am too."

She let go of him and backed up. "What about Jeremy, is he all right?"

"Yeah, he's fine. He fell asleep as soon as he was in bed."

She grabbed his wrist and led him to the far side of the yard, away from the house. She spoke a little louder now: "So how did you make it back?"

"The Dragon Guards found us as we were making our way upriver. They said you told them what happened."

"Alphonse and I did. Just after you and Jeremy disappeared downriver, they came out of the woods. The big guy asked who we were looking for. After we explained what happened, he offered to look for you. We wanted to stay and help but they made us go home." She sighed before continuing. "What about the valgret? Did they find it? They said they were hunting it or something."

"It was incredible, Connie. The valgret from the waterfall showed up again. It came after us and Mila, the one with the hood. She said it wanted me for some reason. They protected us from it. I've never seen anything like it before." He thought back to the encounter. "The way they fought was amazing. Claudia moved so fast I could barely keep up. Mila had a bow and shot arrows so close I could hear them go by my head, then Kenneth showed up and pinned it against a tree."

"They killed it?" Connie sounded just as amazed as he still was.

"Yeah, they did. Said it was part of a pack but that it had gotten split from them at some point." He sat on the ground and leaned against a fencepost.

"Well, I'm glad to have that thing out of the area. What was it even doing here? I thought they lived in the mountains?"

"I don't know. I didn't think to ask. I just hope I never see another one again."

Connie sat next to him and laid her head on his shoulder. "You know," she said, "when it had you and Jeremy cornered at the waterfall, I swear I could hear it laughing. It was terrifying. I thought I was going to lose you."

His heart began beating louder at hearing her words. *She heard it too.* He thought as his heart continued to pick up its pace, it was so loud that he had no doubt she must have heard it too.

He decided to change the subject. "They said when they leave for Vigil that I can go with them."

She shot up and beamed at him. "Daniel, that's great!" Her smile slowly faded. "What about your mom?"

He shook his head. "I'll have to talk to her tomorrow. I'm not going to let her walk away again. She has to talk to me this time. She has to understand. This is the best chance I'm going to get and I won't waste it."

They sat in the night air, simply enjoying each other's company as they watched the stars and listened to sounds of the nearby forest and the horses in the stables.

After a few minutes, Daniel reached into his pocket. He hesitated. Even before he spoke, he felt his cheeks start to burn. Before he could talk himself out of it, he pulled the necklace out. "I almost forgot. I got you this." He held it out to her by the chain.

Her mouth agape, Connie gently reached out and took it. "It's beautiful!" she said. She held it in her palm and ran her fingers over the pendant.

"Ms. Nilia made it."

"A mayflower…it's perfect. Thank you so much, Daniel." She slipped the chain over her head before leaning toward him and kissing him on the cheek before she rose and started walking toward the house. "Goodnight, Daniel," she said. "I'll see you tomorrow."

She kept walking until she disappeared inside and closed the door behind her. He breathed a sigh of relief and leaned his head against the fencepost.

A soft voice spoke from behind him.

"She's a pretty girl."

He stood, turned, and scanned the trees, but saw no one.

A light laugh echoed from above. "If you're going to be a Dragon Guard, you'll need to learn to look up more often."

He lifted his eyes. Sitting halfway up a pine tree was a woman with long blonde hair tied back in a tail. He knew it was Mila by the loose black clothing and the scarf around her neck. She jumped out of the tree and walked over rather unsteadily to lean on the fence next to Daniel.

"Mila," he said, "What are you doing?"

She lifted a large bottle to her lips and took a long draw. When she was done, she nodded toward the house. "Pretty girl with a pretty necklace."

"How long were you up there?"

She smiled. "Long enough." She laughed softly and took another drink.

She smelled terrible. Daniel took a step back and lifted a hand to his nose. "You're drunk."

"Only a little bit." She laughed before taking another drink.

He shook his head. "What are you even doing out here?"

She hopped over the fence and leaned against a post. "I saw you," she said, pointing at him dramatically, "walking down the street and out of town. Wasn't going to let all my hard work go to waste if another valgret wanted a meal."

"I thought you said they were all gone."

"I did. But you can never be too careful!" She again lifted the bottle to her lips, then looked at him and shrugged before whispering, "You're rather interesting as well. Remind me of someone."

Confused, Daniel laughed to himself. She seemed so distant and reserved before. He wasn't sure if he preferred sober Mila or not. "Well," he said, "we should go. If her parents wake up and find me outside their house in the middle of the night, then I'll end up buried out here."

Mila mumbled something incoherent as she followed him past the house. She continued to mumble to herself for a few steps, then went silent. He turned to see what she was doing, only to find she had vanished. He looked around frantically for several moments before deciding it would be better he didn't know. Daniel walked back home in silence and climbed through his window into bed.

In spite of his intentions, Daniel hadn't slept at all. He had laid in bed and watched the night give way to day. After a while he'd heard neighbors opening their doors and starting their days. When he heard his mother's door open, he sat up in bed and readied himself to confront her. Hopefully this would be a very different conversation. He dressed, grabbed his book from the nightstand, and walked to the door, placing a hand on the handle. He took a deep breath and pulled it open. When he walked down the hall, he saw that the house front door was open. His mother sat outside on the steps. Daniel sat next to her, placing the book between them.

His mom was the first to break the silence. "I'm sorry," she said.

"You don't have to be."

She sighed. There was a noticeable tremor to her voice. "No, I do," she said. "You tried so many times to talk to me, and I always just brushed you off. I ignored you. I refused to listen because…" She wiped at her eyes. "Because I was scared that I would never see you again if I let you go."

"I'm not abandoning you," Daniel said softly. "I would never do that to you and Jeremy."

"I know. I always knew that. But I just kept thinking about your father. How he told me he would never leave us. How he loved me. How he loved us. Then how he left... it was all I could think about."

"What about now?" Daniel asked.

His mother thought for a moment before speaking. "I think about how, last night, I thought I had lost you and your brother. I thought that the last words we would have ever said to each other were an argument where I once again shut you out. But now I think about what Claudia told me last night, how you acted to protect Jeremy when you didn't know who these Dragon Guards were. About what Constance told me, how you stood between him and that monster instantly. I think about how many times you've tried to ask me and how determined you always were. How you've never shown anger toward me, no matter how many times I turned my back and walked away to end any discussion of you leaving." She paused, then reached out and gripped his hands. "Is this really what you want to do?"

He nodded. "You know it is."

She sighed, then smiled. "Can I ask why? I know at this point it's something I should know, but..." She laughed softly. "This is the first time we've ever actually... talked about it."

He held up his book and opened it to the first story. "You said you read this while we were missing?" he asked. She nodded. "In this first story," Daniel continued, "the Dragon Guard was the daughter of a miner." He flipped to the next story, and then the next. "The second story is about the son of a king, the third about an orphan. Do you know what they all have in common?"

She thought for a moment before shrugging. "What?"

"It didn't matter who they were or who they *used* to be. They all wanted to do something worthwhile... and they did. They did incredible things by saving lives and even entire cities. They were heroes to so many people."

She took the book from him. "Daniel," she said, "life isn't like that. Not everyone can be a hero just because they want to be. Look at us. We barely make enough marks to get by. Life doesn't just let these kinds of things happen. It resists and tries to beat you down. You won't get the treatment the people in your book got. Very few people respect the

Dragon Guard and fewer think they're even needed anymore. I won't lie that until last night, I didn't think they were worth anything either."

"It doesn't matter what other people think," he said. "I won't let it get in my way because I know the truth. They're still out there doing good, and I want to be a part of that."

His mother sighed again. "You are just as stubborn as your father." She smiled at him. "Okay, I understand. But just so you know," she said, leaning in and hugging him, "you're already a hero to me and Jeremy."

"Thanks, Mom."

She let him go and ran a hand over the cover of the book. "You better go tell them they're going to have company on their journey."

Daniel felt his heart swell. The sense of a heavy weight holding him down began to lighten. With a grin, he nodded at his mother, and after another quick embrace started down the street toward the inn where the Dragon Guards were staying. This didn't feel real. His mother said Claudia had spoken to her last night. If not for Claudia, he doubted the conversation would have gone as well as it did. He would never be able to repay her for this. He was finally going to Vigil. As the thought crossed his mind it dawned on him, something so simple and obvious but at the same time terrifying: He was leaving. He knew he would come back to Sapella one day, but that wouldn't be for a long time. He looked at the homes and shops on the main street. He would be gone a couple of years at the least. But he wasn't going to back down now, not after everything that had happened.

He approached the simple, two-story inn with a sign above the double doors reading *The Hearty Hearth*. The moment he opened the doors, he was bombarded by a dozen conversations and the overpowering smell of alcohol and cooking meats. The interior was filled with people sitting at tables and workers running to and from the kitchen carrying food and drink. The middle of the room had a large fire pit set into the floor. Four stone pillars supported the chimney above it and several cushioned chairs surrounded it. Daniel looked around the room until he spotted Kenneth towering over the crowd even while sitting at a table at the back corner of the room. The much-smaller Mila sat beside him, her hood up.

When Kenneth saw Daniel, he waved at him vigorously and shouted across the room, "Hello, lad, it's good to see you!"

Daniel strode over and sat next to him. "Hello, Kenneth." He looked at Mila, who hung her head low. "Hello, Mila."

Kenneth nudged her with his elbow. "Don't bother with this one," he said. "She's not really a morning person."

Daniel smiled. "She's probably hungover." Mila turned her head enough for Daniel to see a glare beneath the hood.

Kenneth laughed loud enough to turn several heads. "Nonsense!" he roared. "Mila's never drank more than a sip of wine for as long as I've known her. It makes her rather boring at parties, to be honest." He smiled and nudged her again before turning back to Daniel. "So how are you, lad? Sleep well after our little adventure?"

"Yeah, I guess." Daniel took a breath. "I just wanted to say thank you for saving us yesterday. I never really got a chance to say it before."

"No thanks are needed. As a warden of the Dragon Guard, it is my obligation!"

"Warden?" Daniel said. "That's one of the sects, isn't it? Like a scholar?"

"Exactly like that!" Kenneth stroked his beard. "Tell me, lad, how much do you actually know about the Dragon Guard?"

In spite of how much Daniel wanted to be a Dragon Guard, he realized didn't know much about them save for the very basics. "Not a lot, honestly," he said. "Most of what I know I heard from other people or read in the storybook I've had since I was a kid."

"I see," Kenneth said. "Well, don't take what most people say about us to heart. I was much like you when I first left for Vigil. All I knew was that they slayed dragons in the old days."

"Are dragons still around?"

Kenneth raised an eyebrow. "An excellent question. What do you think?"

"Well, not anymore. I don't think so, anyway. Someone would have seen one by now if they were, right?"

Kenneth nodded. "More than likely, I suppose. Very dangerous and infamous creatures, so perhaps it's not so bad they aren't a common sight anymore."

A voice spoke from behind him. "Good morning, everyone."

Kenneth clapped his hands together. "Claudia! Will you be joining us for our morning meal?"

"Of course," she said. Claudia sat next to Daniel and smiled at him. "Morning, Daniel. So, did you happen to speak to your mother this morning?"

"Thank you," he said, "for whatever it was you said to her. I don't think I'll ever be able to repay you."

"You don't need to repay me for anything. I just helped her see things in another light." She waved a waitress over and ordered a mug of cider before turning back to Daniel. "So what were you all discussing before I interrupted?"

Kenneth answered before Daniel could. "The lad was just telling us how excited he was to be joining us! Isn't that right?"

Daniel grinned. "When do we leave?"

Kenneth roared with laughter and slapped Daniel on the back so hard he couldn't breathe for several seconds. "Wonderful!" he said. "We were planning on leaving around noon. It will be a joy to have a fresh face among us."

Daniel's jaw dropped. "You're leaving today? I don't know if I'm ready to leave today."

Kenneth laughed again. "Well, you best get ready lad," he said. "My suggestion for you is to go say your goodbyes and to gather your things. Don't worry about provisions, we'll take care of those. Just bring the necessities, clothes and the like."

Daniel wasn't sure what to say or do. Suddenly he felt panicked, that he had to get out of the room. "Okay," he stammered, "I guess I'll see you later today?"

Kenneth waved him on. "Go on now, make the most of your morning here, you won't have another for quite a while!"

Mila elbowed Kenneth hard in the side, making him wince. He looked at her with a confused expression as Daniel stood.

Claudia squeezed Daniel's arm reassuringly before he rushed out the door.

CHAPTER FOUR

6th of Horace, 26th year of the Fourth Age.

DANIEL STOOD OUTSIDE the inn and felt so overwhelmed he thought he would fall over. Not knowing what else to do, he started walking aimlessly. He was in a daze. He felt as if he'd walked only a few feet before he found himself at the fountain. He sat cross-legged on its rim, facing the dragon statue that sprayed water into the air.

One of the reasons the Dragon Guard had lost so much respect was because so few people believed dragons were real. Even if they had been real, they weren't around anymore. And if there weren't any dragons, what was the point in a group of dragon slayers? The idea he would be considered something useless suddenly seemed to matter a lot more than it had less than an hour ago.

He felt a tap on his shoulder. It was Evelyn Nilia. "Well, hello there, Mr. Summers," she said.

Her eyes were slightly sunken in and her hair was disheveled. "Hello, Ms. Nilia," he said. "Are you all right?"

She sat next to him. "I'm fine," she said. "Just a little tired, I suppose. I had a surprise visit and a long night with an old friend. I'm glad you made it out of that forest all right." She nudged him and smiled. "Must have been pretty exciting, seeing some real Dragon Guards in action!"

He smiled weakly. "Yeah, I guess you could say that."

She crossed her arms. "Young man, I've known you since you were six. I can tell when something is bothering you. What's wrong?"

He was quiet for a minute. "I'm a little overwhelmed, I guess."

"Overwhelmed? By what?"

"I'm finally able to go; they said I could travel with them, but they also said we're leaving today."

She bit her lip and nodded. "But isn't this what you wanted?"

"It is," he said. "But I just thought I would...have more time, I guess? I just didn't think it would happen so fast."

"You've had nearly a whole year," Evelyn Nilia said. "Even more, if you count the couple years leading up to this. That's anything but fast. Any more time and it will be too late."

"I guess," he said. "I'm just worried about what my mom is going to say. She agreed to let me go but, I don't think she thought I would be leaving so soon."

"I'm sure she will understand. Sometimes the best things happen faster than you would ever think and without warning. All you can do is just keep going and hope it turns out for the best. Besides, the Dragon Guard needs more good men and women like you."

He ran his hand through his hair. "Do you think I'm doing the right thing by becoming a Dragon Guard and leaving like this?"

She smiled slightly and shook her head. "That is a stupid question, Mr. Summers."

He smiled. "Do you think she'll be okay after I leave?"

"That is also a stupid question. She will be just fine."

Daniel knew she was right, but in the back of his mind he worried for his mother. He knew he would see her again, but at the same time it felt as if this would be his last day with her. He also knew this was just his nerves getting the better of him. But he wasn't sure he could shake them off. Then his mind drifted to Connie. He had been trying to avoid thinking about the fact he would be leaving her just as he was his mother and brother. But now that thought was at the forefront. He would miss her humor, and her smile. Everything about her.

He wanted to talk about something other than the fact he was leaving, even for only a few moments. "So, uh, I gave Connie her necklace."

Thankfully, Ms. Nilia took the hint. "Oh, that's wonderful! What did she say?"

"She said it was perfect." He stared at the water in the fountain. "Thank you again, really. Not just for the necklace, but for everything."

"Anytime, Daniel."

She left him at the fountain. He sat there a while longer before deciding he had wasted enough time and started to make his way home. Kenneth had said they would leave around noon. It was still early. The sun was low, so he had some time. He knew that his mother wouldn't like the idea of him leaving so soon. He didn't either. But as Ms. Nilia had said, she would be fine. Even if it took a couple of days, she would pull through, just like he would.

When he reached the front door, he gently pushed it open and found his mother by the fireplace, her journal and a pen in her hands. She'd been writing in it for as long as he could remember. She had dozens of them already filled and stored in her room. She always said they were for him and Jeremy to read one day.

"Back already?" his mother said. When she saw the look on his face, she set the journal aside and stood. "What's wrong now?"

He felt as if he was about to stop breathing. "I talked to Kenneth and the others. They told me we're leaving today. At noon."

Her mouth was agape. She simply stared at him for several long moments. "Well," she said, "I guess you better get ready." She turned and walked to his room.

He was dumbstruck. That was the last thing he had expected her to say. He followed her to his bedroom and stood in the doorway, watching her as she silently knelt down, opened the dresser at the end of his brother's bed and started stuffing clothes into a pack.

"Mom, are you okay?"

"Of course I am."

"You're packing Jeremy's clothes."

She stopped. When she spoke, her voice trembled. "So I am."

"Mom, I know we both thought I would have more time before I left."

She sighed. "A day," she said. "That's how long it took for me to feel like I'd lost both of my boys and then get them back. Now I feel like I'm losing one of them again. I just thought I'd have a day or two so I could, I don't know, process all this."

"I'm sorry, Mom," he said. "Maybe I should stay a couple of days? I'm sure I can make it to Vigil fine on my own. It would give us some time."

"No, no, you can't do that. If you're going to go I'd rather it be with them so I know you're safe. You can't wait just for me. The sooner you're at Vigil the better I'll feel."

He looked at her for a second before kneeling down and pulling her in for a tight hug. "Thank you," he whispered. He moved away and glanced at Jeremy's clothes. "Where's Jeremy? I should talk to him before I go."

His mother wiped at her eyes. "Mr. Creek asked for his help to finish moving out," she said. "He won't be back until this evening." She started crying openly. "It's going to break his heart that you won't be able to say goodbye."

He leaned in and pulled her into another embrace. "Mine too."

She squeezed him so hard he struggled for breath. "I'm going to miss you."

"I'll miss you too, Mom."

When she finally released him, she stood and composed herself. "You should pack," she said. "I have to get ready to go to the bakery."

She left the room. Daniel sat on the floor for a while before he grabbed the bag. He put Jeremy's things back in the dresser and started packing his own. He felt as if he was about to break down. Every piece of clothing he put in the pack felt heavier than the one before it. He dropped a tunic onto the floor. When he picked it up, he noticed how violently his hands shook. He felt sick. It had been one thing when

44

he had wanted to go, but now that he was *going* it was another thing entirely. It wasn't a dream anymore. It wasn't something he could hope for and fantasize about.

The moment his mother had agreed to let him go, right after Kenneth told him they would be leaving today, he felt different about the whole thing. Now, looking at his hand shake, he knew it wasn't just nerves. He was scared. No, he was terrified. He didn't know why, he had no reason to be. This was what he'd always wanted. So why did his heart feel like it was about to jump out of his chest? He moved off the floor and sat on his bed. His heartbeat was like thunder in his ears. He stood and without really realizing where he was going, walked out the door. His mother called after him, but he couldn't make out her words as he walked down the crooked steps and down the street.

This was ridiculous. He had no idea where he was going or why. He felt angry at himself for feeling like this, which only seemed to make it worse. Before he knew it, he was standing on the old wooden bridge over the river. He sat with his feet hanging over the water, watching in silence as the river flowed beneath him.

"Hey, Daniel."

Without looking, he knew who it was. Connie walked over and sat on the bridge next to him. She placed his book and pack between them on the wood and looked at the water below them.

She sounded unsure about how to start the conversation. "Went to your place to talk," she said. "Your mom told me what happened. So… are you okay?"

He didn't reply.

"So, uh, you're leaving today, huh? That's pretty sudden."

He kept his eyes on the river. "Yeah, it is."

"It's a good thing though, right?" She nudged him with her elbow. "Just means there's no chance to back out now."

He sighed and rubbed his temples.

"Okay, sorry, bad joke," she said while picking at the old wood and tossing a sliver into the water. They watched it float under them. "So what's wrong?"

"I guess I'm scared." He felt dumb for saying it. He shook his head and cupped his face in his hands. "I know it's stupid and I shouldn't be. This is what I've wanted to do for so long. But now that it's actually happening, I can't get over this awful feeling in the pit of my stomach." He stood and started pacing. "I mean, this isn't how people act when something like this happens for them. It's literally a dream coming true and all I want to do is crawl in a hole and hide until the opportunity passes."

Connie stood and gripped Daniel by the shoulders, making him stop. "Daniel, nearly everyone feels like this when this kind of thing happens."

He looked at her, confused.

"Daniel, what you're doing is terrifying! In my opinion, something would be wrong with you if you weren't scared, or if there wasn't a horrible sinking feeling and overwhelming urge to just hide away. Almost everyone gets scared that the dream is better than the reality. Most people would rather have the guaranteed feeling of failure or disappointment than the unknown and the fear it won't turn out like you hope."

Daniel turned his head away to avoid her gaze. "I just…I don't know if I can actually bring myself to go."

"Were you scared at the waterfall when you had to protect Jeremy?"

He looked at her again. "Of course I was."

"But you did it anyway. You stood between him and that monster without any hesitation. You did that in spite of the fear and you'll do this too. If it turns out to not be what you thought, then you'll do more than just make due, you'll make it better." She let go of his shoulders and leaned down to pick up his book and bag. "Sometimes we just have to get out of our own way and let life be terrifying."

He nodded and took the book and bag. "Thank you, Connie."

"Of course." She hugged him. "The Dragon Guards are at my house, trying to work out a deal for some horses from my father."

He smiled slightly. "They're going to get robbed."

She nodded and grinned. "Yeah, they probably will."

He sighed deeply as he looked at the plain, black leather cover of the book. "I'm going to miss you."

"I'll miss you too," she said. "Now, don't you have somewhere you have to be?"

He smiled at her. "If I said no, would you still make me leave?"

She smiled back. "Better get going."

"What if I said maybe?"

She glared at him and gave him a slight nudge. "Get out of here already."

Daniel grinned and nodded before starting off toward her home. He didn't have to look back to know she was crying.

"That man robbed us."

Claudia smiled as Kenneth brought the subject up for the fifth time. "He robbed *you*," she said.

Kenneth scoffed and avoided eye contact. "Even a man in Luden wouldn't charge me seventy gold marks for three saddled horses. It's absurd!"

"His daughter warned you."

"We're broke!"

She smiled again. "*You're* broke."

Kenneth mumbled to himself as they rode down the forest road away from Sapella's Crossing. Daniel frequently looked behind him as they went. He wasn't sure why. Sapella's Crossing had disappeared from sight long ago and the further away they got, the heavier the weight on his chest felt. He glanced at each of his new companions. Kenneth and Mila rode in front on a black and a grey mare, respectively. Claudia was next to Daniel on a white mare, with Daniel atop a dark bay gelding. It was Connie's horse, relatively young at five years. It had been given to her by her father, who had been rather upset to hear she was giving it to Daniel for his trip. He had glared up until the moment they were out of sight.

Daniel turned to look at Claudia. "So," he asked, "we're going straight to Vigil?"

"Unless something comes up, yes. We're passing through Grey Gate first, followed by a night in Silvum. Then it's a straight shot to Vigil."

"What's Vigil like?" Daniel said. "It's a city, isn't it?"

"Not an official one according to the council," Claudia answered.

"How many Dragon Guards are there?"

"Not as many as we would like. Many of us don't actually stay within the city for the better part of the year. Most are out on assignments like we were a few days ago, until the Autumn's End Festival."

The conversation helped ease the feeling of dread in Daniel's gut. He was grateful Claudia was so cheerful with her answers. It was beginning to rub off on him.

Kenneth laughed. "You're an inquisitive lad, aren't you?" he said.

Mila spoke quietly from beneath her hood. "It's a good trait."

Daniel shrugged before resuming his questioning: "So why won't the council make Vigil an official city?"

Claudia pursed her lips, clearly annoyed at the answer she had to give: "To put it simply, they don't like Dragon Guards."

"That's it? They don't like you?"

"I said I was putting it simply." She sighed and looked thoughtful. "The brunt of the blame goes to Grey Gate's and Dawnstone's councilmen. They...strongly 'dislike' Dragon Guards and have enough gold to sway the other members to agree."

"Why do they dislike Dragon Guards so much?"

She grinned at him. "We have our suspicions, though nothing concrete yet."

Daniel was unsure what she meant or how to respond, so the conversation ended there. They had been riding for hours. Most of the time had been spent in silence, while the rest was filled with casual conversation. Just after midday, Mila had started teaching Daniel about the various plants they passed. Now the sun was dipping low and the world around them dimmed. Mila rode ahead of them to look for a place to set up their camp for the night. She returned a few minutes later to lead them into the trees, where they found a small clearing surrounded by undergrowth, with an open view to the night sky above them.

Kenneth dismounted and handed his reins to Mila. "Why don't you and Daniel get the horses unsaddled?" he said. "Claudia and I will get a fire started."

Mila and Daniel led the horses to the edge of the clearing. Mila pulled out four long stakes with rings at their tops and drove them into the ground before tying the horses' reins to loops so they could begin removing their saddles.

"You'll be fine."

Mila's voice startled him. He turned to look at her as she slipped one of the saddles off. "What do you mean?" he asked.

She set the saddle down, then straightened and faced him. "I can tell you're scared," she said. "Don't be. You'll be fine. I can already tell you're a quick learner."

He tilted his head to one side. "What makes you say that?"

"Part of being a ranger involves being able to read people, being able to tell what they're made of and who they are. You'll make a good Dragon Guard."

He nodded awkwardly, suddenly feeling embarrassed. Silence followed her statement and after a few moments he felt the need to break it. "When did you join? Were you younger than me?"

"Ten years ago. I was seventeen. I left for Vigil against my family's wishes and arrived far later than I planned too. Showed up during the Autumn's End Festival. They were having new recruits swear their oath at the keep when I showed up banging on the city gate in the dead of night and nearly frozen. A warden named Obadiah was on watch and helped me into the gatehouse before I died in the snow. He kept me by the fire while he spoke with the captains and commander about delaying the ceremony a little while longer, until I could stand and speak. I was swearing my oath with the others shortly after."

"They delayed the ceremony for you? Why would he do that? Did he ever say?"

"It was thanks to Obadiah. He had just finished his training and was very well regarded by them all. He convinced them I was worth it. I suppose he saw something in me he thought was worth the effort." She gave out a short laugh. "That, and I technically did make it to Vigil in time, just not in the usual manner. But I owe Obadiah my life. I would have died in the cold without him..." she sighed quietly, "I truly cannot imagine my life without him at this point."

The two of them finished unsaddling and tending the horses before making their way over to the newly built fire. Daniel took a seat on the cool grass next to Claudia while Mila sat on the far side with Kenneth as he dug through his pack and withdrew several hunks of dried meat and a loaf of bread. He broke the bread into portions and passed it and the meat around the fire.

Claudia nudged Daniel as they ate. "Daniel, you have a book about Dragon Guards, yes? Could I see it?" He nodded and retrieved it from his saddlebag as she continued. "I'm so happy you brought it. It's not often a book about Dragon Guards pops up that paints us in a positive light."

Daniel handed it to her. Claudia pried it open and began reading. She hadn't even passed the first page before she furrowed her brow.

He looked at her, curious. "What's wrong?"

She closed the book and examined the cover, then the spine where the tittle was written, before opening the book again and repeating the cycle after glancing at several more pages further in. "Where, did you say this book came from?" she asked thoughtfully.

"My father gave it to me, not long before he left."

She hummed thoughtfully. "Who was your father?"

Daniel shrugged. "He worked for Mr. May, he broke horses. Why, what's wrong with the book?"

She tapped the cover. "This book is from the Vigil library... well, it is several books actually. Multiple different journal entries copied down."

She clearly didn't notice the confusion on his face. "What?" he said. "Are you sure?"

Claudia shook her head in astonishment. "I've read these very pages dozens of times, though they were never all within the same cover. There seems to be at least seven different journals copied down in here, though not in their entirety."

"Wait, journals? Isn't it just a storybook?"

"No," she said. "This is a history book, a series of journals from rangers and scholars from the late Second and Third Age." She handed it back to him. "Do not lose this. I'll need to make a copy when we get to Vigil. We'll have to find out exactly which entries were copied from where."

Mila looked at her curiously. "Is that wise to let him keep it? The things written in that book are incredibly valuable."

Claudia shrugged. "I see no harm in letting him keep it. It was a gift from his father, regardless of where it came from, and he's already read it several times. As I said, I'll make a copy when we get to Vigil."

Daniel stared at the book in his hands in a state of utter bewilderment.

Kenneth clapped his hands together before standing. "Well then!" he said. "I think that's enough chatting. We best get some sleep as we have a lot of riding ahead of us. I'll take first watch and ensure the fire keeps going."

Kenneth unhooked a bedroll from one of the saddles and tossed it more at Daniel than to him. Daniel sat for a few moments longer, staring at the book in his lap, before putting it down and laying out his bedding. He didn't lie down right away. Instead, he opened *Hidden Efforts: A Recount of History* and began reading it in the firelight with a new perspective on the events told within.

CHAPTER FIVE

13th of Horace, 26th year of the Fourth Age.

GRIFFON HART WALKED down the wide and dark side streets of Forge. All around her she heard hammers striking steel and the sounds of bellows stoking dozens of fires, both providing a tune to the medley of curses thrown around by the local smiths when a hammer didn't strike quite like they hoped or when their leather gloves didn't protect from the heat. She hated the sounds. They were constant in this city, a never-ending drone that numbed her mind and caused her to tune out the world around her. Even in the night they were always present.

She was making her way down the long, winding street as quickly as she could, a purchase order clutched tightly in her hand. She glanced at the numbers again and felt an overwhelming sense of unease. Six crates of raw iron, three gold and fifty silver marks. Her father wasn't going to be happy about the price, but she had gotten it as low as she could, even going so far as purchasing the materials from the Whitley mine. They had by far the cheapest prices. Admittedly, the Whitleys sold below-average purity of metal, but Griffon had no choice. She had to take what they could afford.

Compared to most of the Forgemasters in the city, her father was small time, having only five workers beneath him, including one of her brothers. They didn't have nearly the manpower to take on larger orders and had to make do with the work none of the others bothered with. More often than not, the small jobs didn't pay well enough to support them properly. They hadn't received a decent contract in well over two years, which meant they hadn't been paid well in over two years. It was starting to show in both their appearance and their general health. They needed something soon or she wasn't sure they would last much longer.

Griffon sighed as she finally reached their small home set at the south-western corner against the city walls. To one side and connected to their home was the smith itself. The wall adjacent to the narrow street was open to the air, allowing the smoke and heat to escape. The other walls were covered in shoddy racks meant for various tools. Her father was attempting to make do with the bare minimum after he had to sell what little tools they'd had. Looking into the smith only made her more worried about their situation. She headed past the open wall and stepped through the front door into their home.

She was greeted by the familiar, dull-grey walls of cracked stone and the rotting wood floor. The interior was freezing and would stay that way as long as they remained without work.

Griffon's older brothers, Mathis and Richard, were seated beneath the grimy sitting-room window, playing a card game. They gave her a brief glance as she entered. Mathis was the oldest at eighteen and had short, dirty-blond hair, as well as a wide and muscular build thanks to his hours working metal with their father. Richard was a year older than Griffon at seventeen. He had light, sandy-colored hair that hung down nearly to his shoulders. He was much like Griffon in his build, nearly six feet tall and thin, making him look almost frail. Across the room, her father Timothy had his head down and was thumbing through their logbook studying the record of all recent sales and purchases. His white, thinning hair hung down over his brow, nearly covering his eyes.

When he saw Griffon, he picked up a quill from an inkwell and spoke in a gruff, tired voice: "How much was it?"

Griffon sighed and braced for his upset. "Three gold and fifty silver marks. They wouldn't go any lower."

He scoffed and looked at her with the same sky-blue eyes that all four of them shared. "Three gold? Where did you go for it?" He frowned, flipped to the last page of the ledger, and jotted the number down.

"Whitley," she said. "They were they only ones we could afford."

He scowled. "Chances are you just bought us six crates of stone."

She tried to smile to ease his irritation. "I did the best I could."

"Should have sent Mathis." He shook his head before looking to her brother. "Go fire up the forge, boy. Once those crates get here we have work to do."

Mathis nodded and jumped up to head out the door. He roughly jostled Griffon, knocking her aside as he shouldered passed. She bit her tongue and glared at the back of his head as he disappeared.

Her father stood and started for the door as well. "There's an auction starting up at noon, at the northern base. There's seven contracts available." He turned and glared at her before stepping through the door. "Get one."

Griffon sighed. She hated the auctions. Everyone always looked at her like they looked at her mother. "Why can't Richard go?"

Her father glared at her and brushed his hair from his forehead before answering. "Because he has no spine for bidding. At least the other forgemasters might pity you. It's the only thing you're any good for anymore."

She felt her face heat and her jaw clench. "Yes, sir."

Griffon turned away from her father and walked across the house to the bedroom she shared with her brothers. She shut the door, knelt beside her bed, and placed her fingers between the cracks of two floorboards. She firmly gripped one and lifted. The board gave way, revealing a small, holey, patchwork coin pouch.

She dug into her pockets, withdrew a handful of silver, and smiled. The real reason she had gone to the Whitley mine was that the owner was the only one in Forge who seemed to treat her decently and supported her desire to get out of the city. He had given her a faulty receipt;

the price had been three gold marks flat, while the fifty silver went into her stash. She was halfway to being able to buy passage on one of the trade ships. She planned on making her way down the coast to a fresh start once spring arrived.

Feeling slightly more hopeful than she had moments earlier, Griffon placed the coins in the bag and dropped it back into the hole before covering it up and heading out the door. She heard her father call after her, but she was out and onto the street quick enough to avoid him and whatever he wanted. She walked toward the cliffs and mines in the rear of the city. By taking a few shortcuts through the alleyways, she made it to the base of the north wall in roughly a half hour. She scanned the small buildings set at the bottom of the towering cliff wall before turning her eyes upwards.

Forge was located in a quarry that spanned an entire mountainside. The north, west, and east walls were sheer cliff faces rising several hundred feet into the air, forming a natural defense. The mountain, known as the Iron Rise, was abundant in minerals and jewels, iron being the most prominent. It was the reason for the founding of the city. Because of the easy access to the metal, smiths from all across Edaren flocked here to practice their trade. Now Forge was the primary source of armaments for every city watch and town militia in Edaren, as well as for most standard metal work.

The cliffs surrounding Forge were dotted with entryways to various tunnels, all owned by different foremen. Next to each of them were rather unsafe-looking ramp ways and pulleys attached to wooden platforms that ferried workers up and the metals they retrieved down. Due to the cliffs, the city was constantly washed in shadows, save for a small amount of time just before and after midday. The gloom of shadows, the dull stone, and the constant drone of noise combined to give the whole city an oppressive tone.

Griffon peeled her eyes away from the towering rock walls and looked toward the building that served as the auction house. Dozens of people waited outside for the doors to open and the bidding to begin. She made her way over and stood off to one side of the crowd, though that didn't stop the stares from those gathered. The silence that always hung in the air before an auction was broken as a voice called for everyone taking part to make their way in. She waited for most of the crowd to enter before she followed behind.

Even though she entered last, several people still looked at Griffon over their shoulders. She tried her best to ignore them and disappear into the corner of the room while she waited for the auction to start. She didn't have to wait long. Several men and women dressed in finely crafted, embroidered clothes that stood out among the normally drab colors of Forge made their way onto a wooden stage at the front of the room. One of the men carried a large book up to the podium at the center and placed it on top before opening it and addressing the room.

"Thank you all for coming," the man said. "We have seven contracts up for bid today. We will start with the lowest pay offer and work our way to the highest." He scanned the book again before speaking. "We'll start with Ms. Dryer from the township of Luden."

Griffon immediately tuned out the rest of the sentence. Contracts from Luden were never worth the time or the effort. More often than not, they would be canceled halfway through the deadline or the forge-master would never get paid at all. Forgemasters in Forge made their money through contracts with merchants and traders from other cities. What the forges were paid was decided by auction. Forgemasters or their representatives bid on projects. With each bid, the pay they would receive for the job went down. For the forgemasters, this made for a fine balance between the employees one had to pay versus the time the contract would take in order to make a decent profit. Too often, small forges like those run by Griffon's family were forced to the sidelines.

The contract from Luden sold quickly, as only one man bid on it. The next contract was from Dawnstone, but it also was unenticing, as the pay was too low for the workload. It went unsold. As the contract holder made his way offstage with a distraught look on his face, the third contract was announced. The holder for this one stepped up next to the auctioneer; he was a tall, frail-looking man with sunken cheeks and deep set eyes. His skin and hair were the color of dirty snow and he looked over the room with an expression of annoyance.

"Now, Mr. Dale is requesting two hundred sets of iron manacles," the auctioneer said. "Four links of one-inch iron rings in length. The contract must be fulfilled in the timespan of one year or a penalty will be assessed in the form of a 50 percent pay cut. A completed set of manacles shall be provided for reference upon purchase of the contract. The price begins at two gold and fifty silver marks per set, totaling five hundred gold marks."

Two hundred manacles in a year, Griffon thought. A single one would take no longer than a day, maybe two factoring in unseen delays. The time given was absurd and the price more so. It sounded like a city contract, most likely for the Dalisia Royal Army. City contracts always paid well, but still, offering so much for seemingly so little? This was obviously in anticipation of the price drop during the bidding phase, but even so it was far over what was necessary. Griffon was so caught up thinking about what their family could do with the money that she didn't realize the bidding had already begun.

The first few bidders tried to keep the price as high as possible, so the bids dropped only by small intervals of copper and silver marks. Griffon had to get this contract. This amount of money could sustain her family for well over a year while at the same time letting them finally start to get out of the hole they had been in for so long. They could buy better tools and get more workers, which could lead to better contracts. This could start a chain of events that would save her family. She gave the other bidders time to drop the price to one gold and ninety silver marks before she joined in.

"One eighty!" She dropped her bid by a full ten silver to scare her competitors away.

It did just that. Several irritated bidders cast angry glances in her direction as the price began dropping in larger intervals of silver. They all knew this was a valuable contract, easy to fill and highly profitable if the forge was the right size. For Griffon's family, it was still profitable even at fifty silver marks. She could go lower than anyone else and most of them knew it.

"One seventy!"

The bid came from across the room at the opposite corner. She recognized the bidder as Mathew Fox. He was virtually a king in Forge.

He owned several forges and could use any one of them to fulfill a contract. Each was a different size with varying amounts of employees so he would never risk losing a profit on a smaller contract and could essentially monopolize the whole system. Now that he was in the running, her hopes of winning dropped. She decided to try anyway. She had to.

"One sixty nine!" She dropped her bid one mark below his each time he raised his hand.

After several more drops, the rest of the room stopped bidding. Most of the Forge operations were too large and carried too much overhead to settle for such a low price. Now that it was just between her and Fox, they glared at one another from across the room as the price dropped to one gold and fifty-two silver marks. But now they slowed their pace. The price drops had gone back to copper, Griffon still dropping hers only one below his. She hoped to simply annoy him and wear him down. Then Fox averted his gaze toward her and stared straight ahead. He seemed to forget her presence and lifted one hand to exaggeratedly scratch at the stubble on his upper lip. Griffon's eyes widened. She felt a twinge of fear as she realized what was about to happen.

She felt a heavy hand firmly grip her shoulder and a sharp point dig into her lower back. It was an enforcer, someone paid to bully and threaten the competition into backing down. She felt the thin knife dig into her back with a slight increase in pressure. This wasn't the first time she had been threatened. She knew the routine by now. Say nothing and wait for current contract bidding to finish. She realized she had been too aggressive. If she had slowed it down then maybe he would have let her have the contract. But she had pushed too hard and he had chosen to push back to save his pride.

She mentally kicked herself as she heard the auctioneer declare the contract sold to Fox for one gold and fifty one silver marks. The auctioneer started reading the next contract and Griffon was surprised when the blade at her back lingered. Her anger rose to a breaking point. Fox was shutting her out for the rest of the auction. She knew her father would be furious with her. For a moment she considered bidding and risking the knife but knew it would be slightly less painful to let her father throw a rage. Her frustration boiled as the next contract for the Crescent Wings mercenary company went with no bids for several long and frustrating moments. Eventually it was declared void and the man was dismissed until the next scheduled auction. It had been for a decent amount, and the perfect contract for her family, but it had still been far too small for any of the other smiths, including Fox, to waste their time on. Coming home with a terrible contract would have been far better than returning to face her father emptyhanded. Her face flushed red and her hands balled into fists. This was absurd, being forced to stay silent like this. She hated being unable to fight back, she hated being helpless, hated *losing*.

The last contracts were sold and the auction ended. The moment the auctioneer dismissed the crowd, the knife was removed from her back. She turned to get a look at the enforcer but he had already melted into the crowd. She was fuming as she roughly pushed her way through everyone to start her walk home. Halfway back, she stopped and turned into an alleyway. She leaned against the wall and looked at the sky between the two buildings. With a sigh she slid down the wall, sat on the cold, hard-packed dirt, and watched the dull-grey clouds drift by until she felt a drop of rain land on her chin. Her father was going to be furious. They currently had no income. Griffon had just lost their only chance at any for a long while.

She hated this feeling of dread. She knew what was going to happen to her when she returned home but knew there was no way to prevent it. On one hand she was actually thankful it was her rather than Richard. They were similar in build but her brother was far more sensitive than she was. Not that it made it any better. She sighed again and moved away from the wall and out onto the street to start her slow walk through the city. The rain began to lightly fall, further dampening her mood.

Griffon sighed. "I guess it's best to get it over with quickly," she mumbled, "then leave and give him time to cool off."

She slowly walked toward home, her head hung low. As she entered the craftsman district, her eyes caught motion to her right through a long alley. She snapped her head up and recognized Mathew Fox. He was speaking to someone hidden from her view. To her surprise, Fox looked frightened. She was too far away to make out the words he was saying and her curiosity got the better of her. She quickly ducked into the alley and made her way forward, keeping to the shadows. As she got closer the conversation became clear.

Griffon crouched next to the wall and listened to Fox speak with a tone dripping with fear and tinged with anger: "I was under the impression that this was a city contract. If you're an independent looking for this many manacles you are clearly looking to operate out of Edaren authority, which means that you can find them somewhere else."

The hidden man's tone was smooth yet intimidating. "What you know doesn't change anything," he said. "The contract was never stated to be given by any city. That was entirely your own assumption. In addition to you being bound by city law to complete the contract, I can *make* you fulfill it. Though I'd rather you do so willingly. It would be far less taxing."

"I'm not making anything for you," Fox said. "I don't know what these are for but if they aren't for the Royal Army or a city watch then I will have no part in this!"

She heard the man sigh. "I see," he said. "As much as I'd love for us to get what we need another way, the manpower required is not something I have at the moment. So let's just see if we can change your mind."

Griffon moved closer to get a better view of the hidden man, but was too focused on their conversation to pay attention to her own footing. Her foot caught on a brick that had fallen from the nearby building. She stumbled forward and grunted as her elbow scraped against the wall. Faster than she had thought possible, she felt several pairs of hands grip her arms and shoulders. She didn't have time to react as they covered her mouth and lifted her up to drag her forward through the alley and shove her to her knees. One of them roughly grabbed her by the hair and forced her gaze forward.

She locked eyes with the figure in front of her. Dale. She glanced around and saw that in addition to the three men gripping Griffon, two other men and three women behind him carried swords at their hips. Dale had his hands clasped in front of him and looked at her, his head tilted to one side.

"Who is she?" He was speaking to Fox again.

"Uh, she was bidding against me at the auction."

Dale sighed. "*Who* is she?"

He stuttered. "I-I think her name is, uh, Hart."

With another sigh and a roll of his eyes, he motioned for the men holding Griffon to let go of her mouth. "Who are you?" he asked.

She tried to come up with another name but her mind was blank. Unable to lie, she simply told the truth. "Griffon."

"Griffon... *what?*" he spoke the last word through gritted teeth.

"Hart. I'm Griffon Hart."

"All right then, Ms. Hart, what were you doing in the alley?"

She had no idea how to answer.

After a moment of silence Dale lightly nodded. "I see. Well, Ms. Hart, my name is Cardin Dale, and you should know that I don't appreciate liars and spies." He motioned to the men holding her and they drug her backwards through a doorway.

She knew there was no point in struggling but she did anyway. She pulled against their hands but didn't have the physical strength or leverage to break their grip. She wasn't even sure they noticed her struggle. They took her down a short hall and into a large open room with a vaulted ceiling and support beams spanning between the walls. She recognized the smell and the heat of lit forges before she could see anything. Several lit forges with open stone chimneys lined the walls, while a few others sat cold and unlit. She assumed it was one of the larger buildings Fox owned.

She continued to struggle as the two men dragged her through the room toward another door at the far end. All she managed was to increase her panic as they held firm. As they neared the door, one of the men loosened his grip and reached behind his back. A moment later his legs collapsed under him and he fell to the floor. Both Griffon and the other man looked at him in confusion that lasted only a second before Griffon spotted the black feather fletched arrow protruding from between his shoulder blades. The second man released her arm and reached for the sword at his belt but was stopped short as another arrow flew through the air and into his throat. He made no sound and fell to the floor in a heap.

Griffon was stunned. She stared at the arrow protruding from the man's neck for several heartbeats. His blood oozed around the shaft and ran down his neck, pooling on the stone floor. It took every bit of effort she could muster to pull her gaze away from the arrow in the man's neck. She scanned the room. When she couldn't see anyone, she rose cautiously to her feet. She realized it didn't matter where the arrows came from as they clearly hadn't been aiming for her. She decided to try to get out of the room as quickly as possible. She walked the rest of the way to the door behind her and turned the handle. It opened into an empty storage room with no windows or visible exits.

She pulled it closed without entering and made her way back to the only other door in the building. She knew it was unlikely that Dale and Fox had left, but there was no other way out. At the very least she had to see if it was safe. Before she made it halfway across the room, however, the door swung open and Dale stepped through, followed by Fox and six others. When they saw her standing alone next to two dead men, the six drew their swords. Fox seemed to stare in awe at Griffon. Dale simply seemed annoyed.

Dale looked at each of the bodies before speaking. "All right, Ms. Hart, what are you? Couldn't be a warden, you don't have the steel in your eyes. Scholars tend to keep their hands clean of this sort of thing. A ranger, then?" He glared at her as a look of confusion crossed her features. He motioned to the six. "It's not her. One of you on the door, the rest of you spread out and search the room. That ranger from Navia probably followed us here."

They did as they were told. Five of them formed a line across the room with Dale in the middle. The line started slowly moving forward while their heads swiveled back and forth, scanning the room. Fox stood near the door looking dumbstruck next to the single guard. As the line of armed men and women made their way toward Griffon, she started to back away, not that it mattered. They seemed to be ignoring her completely.

Not knowing what to do, Griffon started to scan the room as well, trying to pick out a hidden figure from the shadows. Her eyes settled on a patch of black that seemed out of place. A hooded figure jumped from the support beams onto the top of a cold forge without making a sound. She watched with fascination as the figure stepped off of the forge and onto the floor. The door was just in front of the ranger. The guard was watching the line of his companions as they searched, completely unaware of the person behind him.

The ranger looked to be a man, though his loose-fitting clothing and hood made it hard to be sure. He carried a bow in one hand and made his way to Fox. With a quick swing, the ranger struck him in the back of the head with the bow, sending Fox to the ground. The moment the wood of the bow connected, the men and women around Dale turned at the noise. The ranger drew an arrow from the quiver hanging at his belt. He nocked the arrow and fired in a single smooth motion, striking one of the women in the center of her chest. The man that had been guarding the door was slow to react. The ranger brought his hand up, open palmed, into the man's nose, sending his head reeling back. The ranger quickly smashed him in the throat with the bow, sending the thug to the floor.

As the man fell, the remaining men and women under Dale's command charged. With another quick motion, the ranger downed another with a second arrow. The ranger tossed the bow aside and unclipped a small hand axe from his belt as the other three closed in. The ranger blocked an overhead strike from one of the approaching men. Using the axe head, he twisted his opponent's sword down and to the side and brought his other hand around up into his gut. When the man doubled over, the ranger lifted his knee to strike the man in the face, sending him into unconsciousness.

One of the women swung at the ranger, but he was too quick. The ranger spun out of the way of the downward swing and planted the axe firmly into the woman's gut. He left it there as she fell back. The ranger dropped to the ground and swept out the legs of the last fighter, knocking her to the ground. The woman's head hit the cold stone with a sickening thud. Now Dale charged at Griffon and grabbed her around the neck. He stood behind her with a dagger pressed against the side of her neck and a hand gripping her hair. The ranger retrieved his axe from the fallen attacker before slowly making his way toward Dale.

The ranger stopped roughly ten feet away when Dale shouted, "Get back, ranger! Come any closer and her blood is on your hands!"

The ranger froze and stared at them without a word. The ranger's armor was dotted with spots of blood. His face was hidden in the shadows of the black hood.

"Drop all your weapons and back away!" Dale shouted.

The ranger did as instructed, dropping the axe and unclipping the quiver from his belt. It fell to the ground and spilled arrows onto the floor.

"I said all of your weapons," Dale barked. "Don't take me for a fool! I know how your kind likes to hide things."

Slowly, the ranger reached behind his back to let two small pouches drop. Several knives and thin, needle-like darts rolled onto the floor. The ranger also reached up under the heavy black scarf and removed another short, wide blade, letting it too fall to the ground with a *clang* that signaled the sheer weight of it. When the echo receded, the newly unarmed ranger backed away from the small arsenal on the floor and spread his hands wide to signal he had no more weapons. Griffon had no idea what was going on, but since the hooded man had saved her from the two men before and dealt with the others, she figured the ranger was on her side.

Dale tightened his grip on Griffon. "Good," he said. "Now tell me: How did you find me?"

The ranger shrugged. "You Disciple lackeys tend to have an odor. Not hard to track." The ranger was indeed a man, though his voice was softer than Griffon had expected.

"Cut the act." Griffon felt the dagger press harder into her skin. "Now tell me."

The ranger took a small step forward. "Why don't you tell me something instead? What do you need the manacles for? What have you been up to lately? If you need that many, it's got to be something pretty big."

They continued to bicker back and forth. Griffon tuned their words out as an idea formed in her mind. She glanced at the ranger, giving him what she hoped was an almost imperceptible nod. She could tell he noticed by the fact the he balled his hands into fists. Griffon likewise balled her right hand. Then, with every ounce of her strength, she hammered her fist back hard between Dale's legs.

His grip on her released immediately. The knife moved far enough away from her throat to allow her to move down and sideways, out of his reach and out of the way of the ranger. At the same moment, the ranger lifted an arm and flexed his fist downward while keeping the arm straight out. There was a barely audible click, followed by silence. After a moment, Dale lifted a hand to his throat and stared at the ranger with wide eyes. He slowly sank to the floor, still gripping his neck.

Griffon looked at Dale as he lay still on the floor, his eyes blank and staring straight ahead as what little color had been in his skin drained away. The veins on his neck turned a sickly green that worked its way up to his face. The ranger retrieved the weapons from the floor before walking over to the corpse. Reaching down, the ranger lifted Dale's hand away and pulled out a long, needle-thin dart from the center of the dead man's throat. He wiped the blood off on Dale's shirt and placed it in the appropriate belt pouch before turning to face Griffon.

"Are you hurt?" he asked. She said nothing and simply looked at him. "Is that a no?"

She stammered out her response. "Oh, uh, no, I'm fine. Who are you?"

"That doesn't matter. Who are you?"

"Griffon Hart."

"Well, Griffon, I thank you for the little bit of assistance you were able to provide in dealing with Mr. Dale. But now you need to leave."

She felt rooted in place. She glanced at the door and saw Fox lying next to it. "Will he be all right?"

The ranger followed her gaze and shrugged. "He's fine," he said, "though he'll have a rather severe headache in a few hours." He looked at her again. Even with his eyes hidden, she felt the stare. "You will too if you don't leave now."

She was clearly over the line and managed to force her legs to move. She stepped past him. When she was several steps away, she quickened her pace and jogged out the door, slamming headfirst into a full-fledged rainstorm. She broke into a run.

CHAPTER SIX

14ᵗʰ of Horace, 26ᵗʰ year of the Fourth Age.

GRIFFON SAT ON her bed with her back tucked into the corner of her room. She ran her hand over the still-tender bruises along her neck and cheek. Her father hadn't been happy that she'd lost the contract and had dived into a bottle, followed by the familiar routine of teaching his daughter what it was like to disappoint him. Now she hid away in her room with Richard while her father sat at the table in the main room with no sign of stopping what he had started the day before. She'd lost count of how many bottles he'd gone through in such a short time. She hated having to live like this, having to hide because she wasn't strong enough to fight back. What had happened in the alley with Fox and Dale was no different.

She still had no idea what that had been about and hadn't seen the Dragon Guard since. An investigation to look into the incident had been started by the city watch earlier that morning. As far as she knew, there hadn't been any developments, but they were looking for the man or woman that had killed Dale and the others. They hadn't tried to contact her for questioning. It seemed Fox refused to speak for most of the night, or so the rumors were saying.

Griffon was thankful to not be involved anymore but still wondered why the Dragon Guard had killed Dale. It had clearly been a planned attack on the ranger's part, an assassination. But did the members of the Dragon Guard really do such things? She had heard rumors around the city about things like this but had never given them much thought.

Griffon was startled by a light knock on the window. Richard looked at her curiously as they both stood and went to the window. She looked through but saw no one in the alley. She knew she wasn't just hearing things, so she pushed the window open to peer out. She looked both ways and down the narrow alley behind their house and still saw no one.

"You should start looking up more often. Could save you time."

The voice made Griffon jump back and nearly fall to the floor as she tripped over her own feet, but Richard reached out and caught her arm to pull her back up. She composed herself as quickly as she could before she and her brother leaned out and craned their necks to look up at the hooded Dragon Guard sitting atop the roof with one leg dangling over the side, swinging back and forth. He held a knife in one hand and was slowly peeling the skin off an apple.

"What are you doing here?" she said more out of shock than curiosity.

"Griff, who is this?" Richard asked.

"If I'm being perfectly honest," the ranger answered Griffon, "ignoring my better judgement." He tossed aside a chunk of apple skin.

She shook her head in confusion. "What are you talking about?"

"Long story short," he said, "one of Mr. Fox's employees showed up at the forge before I could finish…dealing with the others. So the bodies were found and now Mr. Fox has finally decided to speak. He is claiming that you are responsible for the deaths." He cut a slice from the apple and popped it into his mouth.

Her mouth dropped open and her eyes went wide. "He blames me?" she said. "How? Why would he think it was me?"

Richard retreated back into the room. "Griff, what's going on?" he asked. "Did you have something to do with what happened?"

The ranger ignored Richard and answered Griffon: "The last thing he remembers was you standing over two bodies."

"But you *shot* them! There were arrows! Besides, why would I kill them?"

He cut another slice as he spoke. "Your motive would be Mr. Fox getting the contract and you letting your anger get the best of you. Your method, regardless of how ridiculous it is… seems to be irrelevant since you are the only suspect."

She hated to admit it but, aside from the method, it made sense. Fox had won the contract out from under her and doing so supposedly made her angry enough to assault Fox and kill Dale and the men and women that tried to protect him. It was ridiculous, but they would take Fox's word over common sense since he had so much influence with the city and its councilmen.

She shook her head. "So if he blames me, why haven't guards come to arrest me?"

"Oh, they're about to, and that would be the reason I'm here. They're on their way."

She was going to be arrested. She wasn't sure what to do, so she scolded him: "Why didn't you say that first?"

He raised his hands in defense. "To be fair, you kept asking questions," he said. "But now I'd say you have only a minute or so."

"What am I supposed to do?"

"I suggest you either hide or run."

"Can't you help? Tell them it wasn't me?"

He sighed and scratched at his chin. "As much as I would like to, doing so would compromise my own task, and I'm afraid if I don't see it through then many more people will be in a much worse situation than you. As it is, I shouldn't even be here."

"Griffon, what is going on?" Richard exclaimed. "Who is he?" He gripped her shoulder and turned her to face him.

She sighed and started pacing. "It's hard to explain," she said, "but yesterday, Mathew Fox and some man named Dale tried to kill me. The guy out there saved me but...now the guards think I killed them all."

While she couldn't see him, the ranger continued to add to the conversation: "That really wasn't all that hard to explain was it?"

Griffon's father called her name from the main room. Richard looked at her briefly before he ran to the door and bolted it closed.

She went back to the window, but when she looked up she found the Dragon Guard was gone and only a few strips of apple skin were left on the ground of the alley in his place. Furious, she walked away from the window and started pacing once more. Her father called her name again, followed by several footsteps making their way to her door.

She was panicking now. "What am I going to do?" she said. "I can't go to prison, but they'll never believe me when I tell them what happened."

The handle of the door turned. Her father tried to push it open but was stopped by the iron bolt. "Griffon!" he shouted. "Get out here right now!"

Richard looked from her to the door and back again. Then he dropped to his knees, pulled up the board that hid Griffon's stash, and handed her the pouch. "Go," he said. "I don't understand exactly what happened but that doesn't matter. Just get out of here while you can."

Her father started banging against the door furiously as several voices on the other side conferred with one another. This couldn't really be happening, could it?

She held the pouch in both hands and looked at her brother. "What about you?" she said. "He'll be worse than ever."

"I'll be fine. He can't do much worse than he's done before."

She heard shuffling outside her door. The banging grew fiercer. A gruff voice she didn't recognize called to her: "We know you're in there Ms. Hart. Get out here!"

With no other choice, Griffon climbed through the window and lowered herself to the ground outside. She paused to look at her brother as he gave her a small and timid smile. She turned and started running before she could change her mind or lose her courage. The moment after her gaze left Richard and the room, she heard the wood of the door crack as the bolt broke free. She glanced behind her and saw a city watchman peer out the window and catch sight of her as she bolted through the back alley. She raced through a right turn, aiming for the main part of the city and away from the wall her home sat against. She lost her bearings twice in her rush, but with a quick look at the towering cliffs, she managed.

Griffon had no idea what her plan was, but she knew to at least keep off of the main streets as much as possible until she could figure it out. After several minutes she finally ceased her frantic run and slumped down against a wall that was well out of sight of any main roadway or window. She placed her head in her hands and tried to think, but all that came to mind was how utterly helpless she felt. She had been threatened out of a contract, kidnapped, and nearly killed. Beaten by her father. Now she was wanted by the city watch for several murders she didn't commit and she had no way to prove it wasn't her. All in one day.

She sat there for a long time, waiting for something to happen, anything to give her a sign of what she was supposed to do now. She didn't have enough marks to pay for transport on a ship. Even if she did, the only way to the docks was through the one and only gate in the city, and they would never let her through. The longer she sat, the more hopeless she felt. Crime wasn't a common issue in Forge. When it did happen, the city guards were relentless in ensuring the perpetrators were caught. As if waiting for that very thought, several voices accompanied by the sound of chainmail and armored footsteps drifted her way from around the corner.

She stood and quickly started off through the alley. Frustrated with her lack of options, she sprinted down the long, narrow path as fast as she could. She made it only a few feet before another group of guards rounded the corner ahead of her. They spotted her immediately and started after her. She skidded to a stop and turned around before ducking into another branch off the byway. She ran as fast as she could, though she had no idea where she was going. She just wanted to get away, to have time to think. But once again she had to slide to a stop as she was met with a dead-end wall. She turned to run back the way she'd come, but had nowhere to go when the guards pursuing her blocked the way.

There were four of them. The closest took a step toward her. "You're only making this worse, Ms. Hart," he said. "Come with us and we'll make sure you're treated well enough."

Well enough. The words echoed in her head and hit her like a fist to the gut. They didn't care about what she had to say at this point. She had known from the beginning that her side of the story wouldn't matter. After hearing her pursuer's words, she knew that they only intended to take her to a cell. She looked at the walls around her—too high to climb, and no doors or windows to escape through. She had nowhere to go. She had always thought she knew the city well enough to find her way even in the dark, but clearly she had overestimated herself.

"Ms. Hart," the man said, "don't do anything stupid." The guard in the lead took another step toward her. She continued to step back until she felt the wall against her shoulder blades.

They all slowly moved toward her. When the one in the lead was close enough, he lunged forward and gripped her by the wrist. Two more flanked her and grabbed her arms and shoulders. She struggled and kicked out at them fruitlessly. She simply wasn't strong enough to win this fight and she knew it, but she wasn't going to be dragged into some dark cell in the mountain for a crime she didn't commit without a fight, no matter how pointless it was. The guards kept an iron grip on her arms as they dragged her down the alleyway toward the main road, and then, just as in the smithy the day before. Something strange happened to her captors.

The guard in the lead stopped walking and lifted a hand to his neck. Then his knees buckled and he fell to the ground. The guard next to him crouched to look him over while the other two tightened their grip on Griffon. But the second guard proceeded to mimic the first's actions and slumped over his fallen ally. The guards holding Griffon's arms released her and looked around fearfully, their hands resting on their sword hilts, though they still blocked Griffon from escaping down the alley by standing in front of her.

She didn't try to push past them. Instead, she followed suit and looked up and down the alley. She caught movement out of the corner of her eye from high up. Standing on the roof of one of the buildings lining the alley wall was the Dragon Guard. When the guards had their backs to him he lowered himself to the ground with barely a sound and darted toward them.

He closed the gap in an instant. His hand axe seemed to appear out of thin air. He flipped it around and struck the first guard across the back of his leg with the blunt end, making him kneel down involuntarily. The ranger then brought his other hand around and with an open palm, struck the first guard square in the face, sending him onto his back.

The second guard was slow to react. The Dragon Guard was already on him before he had turned to face him. The ranger hooked his arm around the guard's neck and stood behind him, squeezing. The guard struggled for breath. In his panic, he ignored the sword in his hand. In moments he went still. The hooded man lowered him to the ground as the guard's sword clanged against the ground. Griffon stared in shock. She had no words for what had just happened. The Dragon Guard stood and placed the axe back in his belt before kneeling down and placing an ear against the guards face, listening for his breathing. With a satisfied nod he stood and began walking away from her. When he was a ways down the alley, he turned and paused.

"Well, come on," he called in an annoyed tone. Without waiting for a reply, he started walking again.

Without any other option, she started after him. He led her back to the main street and down another alleyway to a back road. He took turns onto streets and alleys in a seemingly random manner, though he clearly knew where he was going. At least, she hoped he did.

They hadn't seen anyone for several minutes, so she worked up the courage to speak: "You didn't kill them, did you?"

"They'll be fine," he answered. "Just a little bruised and groggy...well, the one will have a rather crooked nose."

"I thought you said you couldn't help me. What changed your mind?"

"My conscience."

She smiled in spite of the circumstances. "Where are we going?"

"I'm getting you out of the city."

"How are you going to do that?"

"Let me worry about that. Just keep up."

He led her through the twists and turns of the city's side paths until the sky started to grow dark. Finally, they came to a stop at a shabby home set against the place where the wall and the eastern cliff face met. A single lantern, barely hanging on its hinges, lit the one window just to the side of the wooden door. When the ranger pushed it open, its rusted hinges groaned in protest. They stepped inside the small, two-room building and were hit by the heavy smell of mildew and dead rodents.

"Wait here," he said. The hooded man stepped through a small doorway blocked by a cloth hanging over the frame.

Griffon heard a few clicks and the sound of wood scraping against stone before he pulled the cloth aside and motioned for her to follow. When she stepped through, he stood near a hole in the floor. The section that had been in its place leaned against the wall on a set of large rusted hinges.

"This leads out?" she asked as she stepped nearer to peer into the hole. A ladder led down into darkness.

"It does. After you, Ms. Hart." He motioned for her to step down.

As much as she didn't want to, she started the slow climb down. After the first few rungs it grew darker and she had to move slower to ensure that her footing was secure. It went further down than she had thought. After a few dozen feet, she finally felt solid ground beneath her. She looked up and saw the ranger was starting his own climb down the ladder with the lantern in hand. After the first few rungs, he reached up and pulled the section of floor back into place. She heard a few soft clicks echo in the tunnel. He quickly reached the bottom and started down the tunnel without a word to her.

She caught up to and walked side by side with him. "How long has this tunnel been here?" she asked quietly.

"Years. It's an old Dragon Guard passage so we can get in and out without being seen."

Griffon was quiet for a moment before asking the question that had been bothering her since the event with Dale. "Do all Dragon Guards..."

"Kill people in smithies? Only if we have to, and not usually in a smithy. But we do ensure it's for the good of everyone when we do."

She furrowed her brow. "How is killing Dale good for everyone?"

He didn't answer.

They walked in silence for nearly half an hour. The tunnel was mostly a straight shot with only a few small turns. One of those ended at another ladder. The Dragon Guard climbed first and quickly reached the top. Griffon couldn't see what he was doing but after he disappeared from sight, she figured he expected her to follow, so she started climbing as well.

When she reached the top, she was met by another, much shorter tunnel with the entrance blocked by tall weeds and shrubbery. It narrowed to the point that she had to shimmy through it sideways. She pushed her way through the foliage on the other side and stumbled into a short cave that led into the evening air. Griffon took in her surroundings. She was in the thin and sparse tree line just east of Forge. She could see the city wall just past the trees a short distance away.

"I'm sure you can find your own way from here," the ranger said with a sigh.

Griffon took a deep breath. Even though she was out of the city, she still didn't know what to do. She supposed her best bet was to head for the harbor and try to buy passage to Navia or Dalisia. It was far too late into autumn for her to walk anywhere without supplies. Even if she had them, the closest city was Dalisia, and that was nearly a month away by foot.

He leaned in to examine her face in the dark. "Will you be all right on your own from here?"

She nodded. "Yeah. I'll be fine. Thank you for helping me."

He sighed again. "It was my fault this happened to you," he said. "Dale never would have made it to the city if I had done my job properly. So trust me, no thanks are needed."

He turned, pushed aside the foliage, and headed back into the tunnel, disappearing from sight. She watched as the lantern light was cut off abruptly, along with the sound of stone grinding against stone. Curious, she stepped back into the cave and was astonished to find no visible entrance to the narrow crack in the back wall from which they'd emerged. She stood there for a moment admiring the seamless entrance she couldn't actually see. Finally, she left and headed toward the harbor. She stuck to the sparse tree line to ensure she was out of sight of the wall, though she couldn't imagine it would matter with the sun nearly gone.

After several minutes of walking, Griffon stepped onto the wooden boards of the harbor. She paused to glance around and get her bearings. The area itself was barren of people, though there were plenty of ships moored at the docks. With winter fast approaching, the captains of every vessel were trying to get in one last haul before the freezing cold and snow set in. She only hoped this would help her convince one of them to take her aboard for a far lower price than was normally required. Seeing as how she was short by about half of what she would need, her hopes weren't high. But she resolved to try, regardless. She didn't really have another option.

Griffon spotted an inn at the far side of the harbor and figured that was the best place to start. She made her way over and stepped inside. It was nearly empty, save for a few tables of haggard-looking men and an equally haggard bartender behind the counter adjacent to the door. She stepped up to the grimy and sticky surface and waited for the bartender to make his way over.

"Not really the best place for a young lady like you to be at this hour," the bartender said. "Need a place to stay?" He seemed genuinely concerned for her as he glanced back at the men dotting the room.

She shook her head. "No," she said, "I don't. I need to pay for passage on one of the ships docked here. Do you know who I could talk to?"

The bartender raised an eyebrow. "Well," he said, "there are three captains leaving tomorrow. I know two of 'em wouldn't mind taking you aboard if you can pull your weight and pay the fee. The third, well, he would take you if don't mind paying with something other than marks."

It took her several seconds for his meaning to sink in. When it did, her face flushed a deep red. "Where can I find the other two?"

"Captain Colton is at that far table over there, on his way to Navia. Captain Andrews is by the hearth, bound for Dawnstone."

She thanked the bartender and made her way to the fireplace to speak with Andrews, as he was the closest. The captain and his men were laughing amongst themselves. When she approached, one of them tapped a man with a large brown beard and balding head on the arm.

This man craned his head to look at Griffon. The laughter stopped as all eyes turned to her.

The balding man who she assumed was Andrews examined her up and down before speaking: "What can we do for you this evening, miss?"

Trying to appear more confident then she felt, she extended her hand to him. He gripped it tightly. "My name is Griffon Hart. I need to secure some last-minute transport."

"Where exactly are you heading?" the captain asked. He stroked his beard.

"Dawnstone." She figured it best to choose where he was heading to minimize inconvenience for him. If she changed her mind she could always step off the ship at another port if and when they stop.

He nodded. "I see... have you ever sailed before?"

"No sir."

He sighed and drummed his fingers on the table. "How much do you have for passage? My usual rate is two gold marks, three if you can't contribute properly."

She handed him the coin pouch. "One gold, fifty-seven silver, and eighty-three copper marks, on my last count."

Several of the men at the table openly laughed at her and were quickly silenced by a stern look from the captain. He gingerly took the bag from her and handed the pouch to the man to his left, who poured the coins onto the table and began counting quickly.

"Why," the captain said, "should I allow a young woman on my ship with no sailing experience for half the usual passage fee?" He didn't sound upset. It was closer to curious.

"I have no real answer for you," Griffon said. "All I know is that I need to be somewhere other than here."

He looked at her for a long while. When his crewman finished counting the coins, he placed them back in the pouch and handed them to the captain. "My count," the crewman said, "is one and fifty-seven plus eighty-three copper exactly, sir."

The captain nodded and tossed the pouch back to Griffon. "Sorry, miss," he said. "Unless you can pull your own weight on my ship or pay the proper amount, I'm afraid you'll have to find another way."

She sighed and nodded. "Thank you for your time.

She turned to walk away as he spoke again: "Good luck to you, miss."

With slumped shoulders, she made her way to the other end of the room to speak with Captain Colton and hopefully have better results. Unfortunately, she was met with the same. With a feeling of hopelessness, she stepped back to the bar and sat on one of the stools, her head in her arms as she tried to figure out what to do next. Surely there were guards patrolling the harbor that had been told about her and given her description. She couldn't stay here long. It already seemed a miracle she hadn't been spotted already.

Maybe I can get some supplies from the sailors...enough to get to Dalisia, at least.

There were farms between Forge and Dalisia. Surely one or two farmers would help her; let her stay for a night as she traveled. Griffon was startled out of her thoughts by a light tap on her arm. She lifted her head to see the bartender hand her a small mug.

"I can't afford this," she said, eyeing the drink in front of her and suddenly realizing her thirst.

He smiled. "You aren't paying for it."

"Who is?"

He smiled wider. "I am. You look like you could use something to lift your spirits."

She gripped the mug and felt the heat radiate through her hands. "What is it?"

"Warm cider. Don't worry; it won't mess with your head like the hard stuff."

She lifted the mug to her lips and took a long draw. It warmed her whole body and sent chills down her spine. She thanked him and he nodded politely before stepping away. Griffon sat there for a long time, enjoying her drink and still having no idea what she was going to do. She couldn't pay for a ship. The more she thought, the less sure she was that she could even get supplies. Even if she did, winter was nearly here, so walking anywhere wouldn't end well. Edaren winters were harsh and travel was never recommended this close to autumn's end if you weren't seasoned in survival. She placed her head in her hands and tried not to scream out of pure frustration.

"I hear you need a ship." A tall lanky man with long matted black hair spoke as he sat next to her.

"Leave her alone, Dent," the bartender called form the other end of the counter, more annoyance in his tone than anything resembling a warning.

"Mind your own business," the new arrival said. "I just want to help the young lady."

Griffon knew nothing about this man aside from what the bartender had said, but just looking at him turned her stomach. She knew she wanted nothing to do with him. "Thanks," she said, "but I'll find another way."

He leaned over the counter to look at her face. "Aw, don't be like that. I can help you if you just," he looked her up and down and tapped his fingers on the counter, "help me."

"Help yourself." She stood and started to leave, but Dent grabbed her arm.

"I'd rather *you* do the honors," he said. He yanked her closer. She heard several men at the table behind her laugh.

She gripped the mug of cider on the counter and brought it around hard, striking Dent across the face to send him reeling back. He released her arm momentarily. Griffon bolted for the door but one of the men from Dent's table stepped in front of her, blocking her path.

Dent recovered and stepped up behind her to grab her by the shoulders. "I normally don't like fighters," he said, alcohol on his breath as he whispered in her ear, "but I think I'll make an exception."

"Let the young lady go, Dent."

Dent turned around, still holding her. Captain Andrews was calmly walking over to them, along with his six crew members.

"Back off, Andrews," Dent said. "This isn't your problem."

Andrews looked at Dent, and then glanced at the now-empty mug lying on the floor. "My men and I were having a rather nice evening before we set out tomorrow," he said, "and all this commotion interrupted that. So now I consider it my problem."

Griffon took a sidelong glance at Captain Colt across the room. Colt and his crew looked at Dent with tense stares and appeared ready to spring out of their seats at a moment's notice. Several of the men fingered the hilts of daggers and knives at their belts.

Dent suddenly shoved Griffon away "Fine," he grunted angrily, "her face isn't as fresh as I prefer anyway, already been marked with a nice badge."

Griffon stumbled forward and ran a hand over her previously bruised cheek as Dent stormed out the door, trailed by his men. Andrews leaned over the counter and whispered to the bartender, who nodded briefly before disappearing into the kitchen. Andrews sat on a stool and motioned for Griffon to do the same, which she did quickly. He held out his hand without a word and after a moment, Griffon realized why. She placed the coin pouch in his palm.

He stuffed it into one of his pockets as he spoke: "You will work whenever able, whether it is cleaning, cooking, or heavy lifting. If you do not know how you will be taught. You will sleep in the cargo hold, you will not disturb any of my crew when they are at work lest you rather be dropped off on shore, and you will not complain. Not a single word." He raised an eyebrow. "Understood?"

She stretched out her hand and he took it. "I understand," she said. "Thank you."

"You'll sleep aboard the ship tonight, one of my men will provide you a blanket and escort you aboard *The Royal Jewel*."

Griffon considered something for only a moment before speaking. "Sir, uh…Captain Andrews, I've changed my mind. I don't want to go to Dawnstone."

He narrowed his eyes, clearly annoyed. "Then where *do* you want to go?"

She was tired of having to be rescued. Tired of not being able to fight back and protect herself from people like Dent, like Fox and Dale, like her *father*. She was going to change that. She was going to make it so she never needed help again.

"I want to go to Vigil."

CHAPTER SEVEN

15th of Horace, 26th year of the Fourth Age.

ARON CROSS HAD never been happier to lay on a thin, old, and unstable straw bed with a leaky, shoddy roof over his head in his life. He had left Dalisia fifteen days earlier. Half that time had been spent on the ground under the stars by a fire, something he wasn't used to but didn't hate. He had never been this far away from home for this long. The farthest he'd ever gone was Wayside, and that had been only for the duration of the six-day trip down The Draw and back. But here he was, sitting on the edge of an old rickety bed in a cross castle between Wayside and Grey Gate, his journey still stretched out before him. He was headed for Vigil, which meant he still had over another month of traveling.

He yawned, stood, and stretched before walking across the rough stone flooring to the small, round window set into the far wall. The sun was just starting to rise and was sending gold rays through the dirt-encrusted glass. He gazed at the small courtyard of the old war fort. It was built directly over a three-way fork in the road, with wide, arching doorways over each fork, their gates long removed. Between the doors to Wayside and Sapella's Crossing was a stable that was badly in need of repairs. Across from it, next to the door to Grey Gate, was the inn that Aaron was in now. Behind the inn was a stone tower just on the outside of the wall, with a bridge across the gap connecting them. A narrow and cracked staircase led up to the tower from the side of the inn.

The courtyard itself was just a large dirt patch with a few tufts of dead grass dotting it. Several chunks of the wall that had broken away over the years and been left to become part of the ground as weeds and grass slowly grew over and through them. It was a mess, but he was grateful for it nonetheless.

Aaron smiled as he crossed the room to the dresser near the door. He dressed and headed out into the narrow hall and down the creaking steps into the cramped and poorly lit lounge area.

Several tables and chairs sat uncomfortably close to one another, a small candle on each tabletop. Half the candles were unlit, giving the room a darker tone then it should have had, defeating the purpose of the room. He stepped around tables and made his way to the door and outside into the cold. Aaron crossed his arms and took a deep breath, watching the air fog in front of him. Edaren was cold year round. Winters were often deadly for the poorer citizens with their lack of proper clothing and lack of proper heat in their meager homes. Aaron hated the cold. He wished he had been able to leave sooner.

It hadn't been easy deciding to leave Dalisia, even after waiting as long as he had. His father had tried everything he could to keep him home, but thankfully Aaron's two sisters and his brother were supportive of his ambition to become a Dragon Guard like his grandfather. They risked their father's anger, aiding Aaron by helping him steal away on his "father's" horse—the same horse his father had taken from him to ensure he "did as he was told." Aaron's brothers and sisters also helped him gather the supplies he needed for the trip, such as a bedroll and dried meat so he wouldn't starve on his way. The profession of Dragon Guard wasn't exactly encouraged in Edaren. Rumors swirled surrounding the order and its lack of intervention during the War of Sovereignty. But Aaron had always taken his grandfather's word and love of the order over anyone else's opinions.

Aaron walked across the courtyard to the stables to check on his horse, Bella, a white mare that was probably too old for a trek this far but was the only one he had been able to afford. He had purchased her a year before, when he'd first started planning his journey. Aaron stepped through the stable door that hung by a single hinge and was greeted by the owner of the inn, a tall, round man with a short brown beard and balding head.

Roland, the inn owner, was brushing Bella. "Morning Mr. Cross," he said with a wide smile. "I trust you slept well?"

Aaron returned the smile and nodded. "Better than I have for quite a while."

"Happy to hear it! You know, when my family purchased the deed to this land, my great grandmother was worried it would be nothing more than a money pit. She thought it would never turn a profit and sustain our family. But my great grandfather proved her wrong and turned it into the best cross castle inn this side of Quiver Lake!"

Aaron said nothing and simply smiled and nodded as the man rambled. He had told Aaron this story the previous day when he first arrived, and again last night while he dined before bed. Roland was clearly proud of what his family had turned this old war outpost into since it was decommissioned in some long-forgotten war and left in the hands of the Royal Army. The army had left it unused for years before auctioning it off for next to nothing. Aaron half-listened for when the man might want him to reply and instead focused his thoughts on when he would leave.

It would have to be soon. He wanted to reach the base of The Spines in two days at the least. After that he would have to keep an eye out for all sorts of things as he rode along the path at their base. Everything from valgrets to highwaymen roamed those mountains. Aaron's thoughts were interrupted when he heard Roland's wife shouting at him from the wall above them. He caught only the last couple words—she wanted her husband to greet the new arrivals at the gate. Roland excused himself and stepped out of the stables in a huff, muttering some rather unkind things about his wife.

Aaron watched him go before turning to his horse and gently patting her on the flank. He lingered for only a moment, as his curiosity got the best of him and he stepped back outside. When he emerged, he found Roland speaking with a young woman and a young girl, likely the woman's daughter by the way the girl clutched the woman's leg and hid her face in her dress. Neither had a horse, though the mother carried a pack with two bedrolls strapped to the top. Both looked exhausted and in need of a bath. Aaron wondered what brought them here on their own as Roland led them into the inn while the mother showered him with thanks.

With a smile, Aaron decided to return to the stable and finish tending to Bella. He finished brushing her and cleaned her hooves, which wasn't really necessary at the moment but he chose to busy himself with the chore anyway. In addition, he gave the horse a small amount of grain that Roland kept on hand. He stepped back into the daylight and couldn't help indulging in his habit of cracking his knuckles one at a time. It always made his mother wince, but it was a practice he'd gotten from his grandfather and had never been able to break.

Aaron enjoyed the warmth of the sun for only a moment before he heard Roland's wife shouting at her husband again. Most likely she shouted from the tower they used as a makeshift home and storeroom. Aaron turned toward the archway just as four riders crossed the threshold into the courtyard. One was a plainly dressed boy that looked sixteen, only a year younger than Aaron. The other three, however, made his breath catch in his throat. They were Dragon Guards, all three of them. Two were women. One of the women had the armor of a scholar, while the other wore the clothing of a ranger. Their companion wore the heavy studded leather of a warden.

Aaron had never seen a ranger before, but his grandfather had been a scholar and still had the armor in a chest at his home. His grandfather would still have been at Vigil, but he had been injured and lost his sight during his time there and had decided it would be best to return to his family in Dalisia. Seeing a trio of Dragon Guards just over a dozen feet away, Aaron wasn't sure how to react. He had never spoken to a Dragon Guard other than his grandfather before. He had seen one occasionally in the streets of Dalisia but only in passing glances. He wasn't sure what to say to them or for that matter if he should say anything. Then again, he supposed it wouldn't hurt to at least speak with them.

He was about to make his way over when the ranger and the boy took the reins of the four horses and started for the stables behind Aaron. He quickly stepped in and held the gate open to allow them easy access. They moved past him. The ranger cast a nearly blank expression his way while the boy gave a light smile and a nod of thanks. They led the four horses to the nearest stalls and tied them to the available hooks to begin tending to them. While they did so, Aaron suddenly felt awkward. He slowly stepped over to the ranger, smiled, and asked, "Would you like some help?"

She barely seemed to notice him.

He decided to try something else. "So, what are Dragon Guards doing way out here?"

Suddenly he felt he had made the wrong choice of topics. The ranger tensed and turned her head just enough to look at him out of the corner of an eye, partially obscured by her hood. "Does it matter?" she said.

Aaron took an involuntary step back. "Uh, no," he said. "I was just wondering. I've never met another Dragon Guard aside from my grandfather."

She narrowed her eyes at him. "Your grandfather was a Dragon Guard?" she asked.

"Yeah. He was a scholar."

After several moments of her looking him over, she motioned with her head toward the third stall in the line just on the other side of the boy. "You can start on Ebon if you want to help."

Aaron smiled and stepped around her and the boy to get to the stall that housed Ebon, a jet-black mare. He was a stranger, so he removed her saddle slowly so as not to frighten her, though she seemed calm enough and wholly unconcerned by the unknown hands.

"I'm Aaron, by the way," he said to the boy, hoping he might be a bit warmer than the ranger.

Thankfully, he was. The boy smiled and extended a hand over the chest-high wall between them. "I'm Daniel," he said. He pointed a thumb at the ranger: "And that's Mila."

The ranger said nothing and continued with her task.

Aaron noted her lack of interest and figured it would be best to speak with Daniel for the time being. At least he seemed happy to talk.

"I didn't really expect to run into any Dragon Guards so far from a city. Are you traveling with them?" Aaron asked.

Daniel nodded. "Have been for about a week."

"Where are you going, if you don't mind my asking?"

Daniel glanced at Mila as if asking permission to answer. When she shrugged her indifference, he turned back to Aaron. "We're on our way to Vigil."

Aaron felt his heart leap. He was more than willing to make the trip on his own if he had to. But the possibility of having company of any kind was ideal.

He was silent for several moments without realizing how much time had passed and was snapped back to the present by Mila. "If you're going to ask, then ask," she said. "Don't stare like an idiot."

He was caught off guard by her statement and wasn't really sure if she was addressing him or Daniel until he noticed they were both looking at him.

Aaron stuttered slightly in spite of himself: "Uh, ask what?"

Judging by the motion of her head, the ranger appeared to roll her eyes. "You're going to Vigil and you would like to travel with us."

He wasn't sure how to respond until he noticed Daniel had a slight smile on his face as he spoke. "She does that," Daniel said. "Don't worry, you'll get used to it."

With that they finished grooming and feeding the horses in what Aaron felt was an incredibly awkward silence. By the time they were done he was still slightly confused by the way he had been "invited" to join them. He wasn't sure if he *had* been invited. He hoped so and was excited about the idea of not traveling alone anymore. He had never been on his own back in Dalisia, so when he'd started this adventure it had been a rather depressing first few days. He had gotten used to being alone but he certainly didn't like it. Something as simple as being able to cross the courtyard and step into the inn with Daniel and Mila was a welcome change. A smile spread across his face.

The moment they were inside, Aaron saw the other two members of the troupe sitting at a table in the corner of the room. They strode over. It was the first time Aaron was able to get a look at the other two. The man was a giant. The woman looked like a child in comparison, though she seemed to hold herself with a rather intimidating level of confidence.

The woman smiled and spoke in a friendly though cautious tone: "Who's your new friend?"

"This is Aaron," Daniel said, "and Aaron, this is Claudia and Kenneth."

Aaron smiled timidly as Daniel took a seat and Aaron chose the one next to him, which placed his back to the wall. The moment he was seated he felt Mila staring daggers at him.

"Move." She didn't say the word like a command, more like a warning.

He was slightly taken aback. "Excuse me?"

"Move. Sit somewhere else."

Confused and embarrassed without knowing why, he stood and took the only other seat at the table, across from her. After they were all situated, Kenneth nudged him. "Don't take it personally," he said. "She outright refuses to have her back to a room."

Claudia cocked her head to one side. "So, Aaron," she said, "what brings you to this...lovely cross castle?"

"I'm actually going the same place you are. I'm on my way to Vigil."

She raised an eyebrow. "Really? Well, we'd be more than happy to have you along if you'd like some company on the road."

He smiled. "I would appreciate that very much. Traveling alone gets, well, lonely."

Kenneth sat between Aaron and Daniel and extended an arm around each to pull them in. "Wonderful! The more the merrier! We'll be a regular caravan in no time!"

"Fantastic," Mila said. "Maybe in Grey Gate we'll pick up a tunnel rat."

Claudia glared at her before speaking. "So, Aaron, where do you hail from?"

Aaron spoke through a light laugh as Kenneth still gripped him tightly. "Dalisia. My family owns a small shop on the riverfront."

Kenneth sighed happily and released the two. "I do love Dalisia," he said. "Nothing is more relaxing than sitting and watching the ferries travel down The Draw."

Claudia took a sip from the mug she held in front of her. "What made you want to join the Dragon Guard," she said. "Not something most people even consider nowadays when they have the option. Especially from someone as far out as Dalisia."

"My grandfather," Aaron answered. "He was a scholar."

Her face softened as she obviously mistook his meaning, "Oh, I'm sorry."

"Oh, no, he's still alive," Aaron said. "He lives with my family now. He lost his vision during his time at Vigil and decided to move back to Dalisia to be with his family. He didn't think he would be much help at Vigil without his sight."

Kenneth nodded exaggeratedly. "Understandable. It would be a hard life at Vigil without one's vision."

Claudia nodded in agreement before asking, "When did he leave the order?"

Aaron thought back to when he was a boy. "Must have been about ten years ago, or near enough."

"Ten years..." Claudia paused a moment, as if remembering. "Is his name Nathaniel Cross?"

Aaron felt his heart leap into his throat and for a moment he had a hard time speaking. "Y-yes, it is."

She narrowed her eyes. At the same time, a slight smile crossed her face. "I do believe I've met him. He was a wonderful man. I do hope he's doing well back at home with your family at the uh, shop, did you say? On the river?"

Aaron felt his face turn red. It didn't seem Claudia was going to press the matter further, so he decided to change the subject as quickly as he could. "So, uh," he said, "where are you all coming from?"

Claudia thankfully let the conversation change course. "Sapella's Crossing," she said.

"What were you doing there?"

"Saving me, mostly," Daniel said.

"Saving you?" Claudia said with a laugh. "Well, there was a bit more to it than that."

His curiosity piqued, Aaron pressed for more. "What happened?"

Kenneth clapped his hands together dramatically and leaned forward. "I do hope you like a good story."

CHAPTER EIGHT

22nd of Horace, 26th year of the Fourth Age.

ARON SAT HUNCHED over in his saddle as he and the rest of his group made their way down a road that had turned south and now ran parallel to The Spines. It had been a week since he had joined with the Dragon Guards and during that time he'd become rather good friends with Daniel. He had learned much about what had happened to Daniel leading up to their meeting at the cross castle and had been astounded at his good fortune. Now they were nearing the city of Grey Gate. Knowing what little he did about the city, Aaron wasn't looking forward to their visit. But at the moment, his thoughts were focused on the story Kenneth had been telling for the majority of the day.

"That's not true," Claudia said as she shook her head slowly.

Kenneth glared at her. "How do you know? You weren't there! You were still on the bank down river trying to pry your sword from that tree."

"But I was there." Mila kept her eyes ahead as she spoke.

Kenneth mumbled to himself as they continued down the ragged dirt road.

Aaron leaned forward in his saddle to look at Mila, who rode beside him. "So what did happen then?" he asked.

She shrugged. "Kenneth had his back to the cliff wall with it bearing down on him. It started moving faster towards him and tried to ram him with its horns. Kenneth leaped out of the way and was about to start running."

"I was not running! I was simply repositioning myself!" Kenneth protested.

"After that," Mila continued, "the inadana was stunned for a moment, the cliff was unstable already and that hit was just enough to shake loose a rockslide. Buried it beneath the stones and barely avoided doing the same to Kenneth. He was nowhere near it when it actually died."

"I'm telling you I knew the stones were unstable," Kenneth said. "It was all part of my plan!"

Claudia rolled her eyes. "What a grand plan it was."

Kenneth began mumbling to himself again.

Aaron smiled. "So how far past the Bulwark were you?"

Claudia looked up. "Not far," she said. "You could still see the mountains from where we were."

"How far outside of Edaren have you gone?" Daniel posed the question to Claudia.

She paused as if running through their list of assignments. "Furthest Ken and I have been was there, actually. Mila has been as far as Krida across the south sea."

Mila nodded. "Not many venture into Wolves Wood," she said. "Though I'd take it over the savage wilds of Krida any day."

"How far does the forest stretch?" Daniel asked.

"We never saw the edge."

"You said you had a guide. How did he know the area so well?"

"He makes his home in the forest," Mila said simply.

Aaron raised an eyebrow. "He lives in Wolves Wood? Isn't it haunted?"

Claudia laughed lightly. "By Verhova, no," she said. "But it can be very dangerous if you aren't prepared."

Kenneth sighed. "I'd rather be back at that river then stepping even a single foot inside Grey Gate."

Daniel looked at the three of them curiously. "If you hate this place so much," he said, "why are we even here? Couldn't we have gone around?"

Claudia shook her head. "No, I'm sorry to say. The Spines is almost impassable and stretches from one coast to the other. Far too jagged and steep in most areas for horses or even people and the passes that are safe for travel are too far away. It would take us weeks to get across the mountains. Grey Gate is the only direct route through."

Aaron looked ahead to the road that ran along the mountainside. Grey Gate was located in a pass just ahead of them, though it was still hidden from view. Kenneth had assured him they would arrive within the hour. Aaron had an idea of what the city would look like from stories he'd been told by his grandfather. It was built inside the mountain itself, a series of long tunnels in a grid pattern, stretching deep into the mountains on either side of the canyon which likewise was lined with buildings.

Briefly, he took his gaze away from the road and scanned the mountain range that housed the city. The peaks were steep and quickly disappeared from sight as they stretched into the clouds. According to Mila, the valgret they had encountered at the falls in Sapella's Crossing had come from these mountains. The Dragon Guard had heard rumors of a pack roaming the west side of The Spines that had been attacking travelers on the road and killing the livestock of farmers. At first they'd thought nothing of it, believing the few rumors and reports were isolated incidents and the gossip was simply getting out of hand. But once the reports became more frequent and the details of each tale more consistent, the Dragon Guard had sent Claudia and the others to investigate.

Mila was able to track the valgrets from their most recent sighting to a grove high up on the west side of the peaks. Once they were found, the three Dragon Guards began to wipe out the pack to ensure they caused no more harm. But several of the creatures escaped their initial encounter. With their territory taken from them, they fled. The trio pursued the remnants of the pack and had been following them for just over a month, picking off the stragglers when they could.

Kenneth stopped ahead of them at the entrance to the wide pass. He shouted, snapping Aaron's attention back to the present: "We've finally arrived!"

Aaron and Daniel spurred their horses faster and met Kenneth at the entrance to the canyon. The mouth of the pass was well over fifty feet wide. Its walls were sheer cliff faces rising nearly out of sight before turning into steep inclines. The pass itself narrowed as it went until it came to a dark, grey stone wall. It took the group another few minutes of riding to reach it. The bricks there were four feet tall and wide, with the wall stretching forty feet high. A tower twice as tall was built partway into the cliff walls at each end, with wide open ledges near their peaks for archers or siege equipment.

In the middle of the wall was a gate covered with thick iron studs and bands. The section of wall around it was thicker and taller by several feet. Aaron recognized it as a gatehouse. It was where the inner workings of the gate were stored, as well as an area for guards to rest and relax, or in times of battle, to prepare and recover. Beyond the gate was a true sight. Carved into the cliff walls were narrow pathways, windows, and door-ways that hinted at countless rooms hidden beneath the stone, as well as the vague shape of buildings and homes made of the cliff walls. It all seemed so foreign to Aaron compared to the standard city structures he was used to in Dalisia.

Standing atop the wall were two guards dressed in dull chainmail, a tabard embroidered with the crest of Grey Gate on each of their chests. Three coins, two silver and one gold on top, formed a triangle set before a plainly designed gate.

Claudia and Mila soon caught up. As they all approached, one of the guards raised a hand. "State your names and intentions!" he shouted, his voice echoing off the cliffs.

Kenneth raised his hand and removed his heavy leather gauntlet, revealing a steel band veined with orange around his wrist. "Kenneth

Patch, warden of the Dragon Guard," he said. "We seek rest for a night before moving on to Vigil."

The guards leaned toward each other and conversed for a moment before disappearing from view for several minutes. Aaron looked to Kenneth, who kept his gaze on the wall ahead of them with a look he hadn't seen before. The Dragon Guard was tense, nervous. There was a loud grinding sound, followed by the gate slowly swinging open toward them, revealing a grey stone slab that still blocked the way. As soon as the first gate settled in place, Kenneth spurred his horse forward and they all followed closely behind him. Without a word spoken between them, Claudia and Mila put themselves on either side of Daniel and Aaron so the two of them were between the three Dragon Guards.

As they neared the stone slab, another loud grinding sounded followed. The stone sank slowly into the ground. Once it settled and the grinding stopped, they crossed through into the short tunnel of the gatehouse. Aaron glanced up and saw several guards peering down at them through slats and grates set into the bricks above them. He knew enough about cities to know those were the last line of defense should the gate be breached, a place for defenders to pour oil or rain down arrows. Aaron was thankful they were welcome visitors when he thought of what it would be like to try and weave through during a siege. Once the quintet was through, they were greeted by another guard that walked with perfect posture and his chin slightly raised allowing him look down his nose at those around him.

Upon seeing him, Aaron heard Mila mumble under her breath: "Damn."

The guard's shoulders and hands were armored by plate that was edged with gold inlay. His face bore a scar that ran from one ear down to his throat on the other side. He also wore the most self-assured smile Aaron had ever seen.

"Greetings, Dragon Guards," the man said. "What brings you to Grey Gate on this cold autumn evening?"

Mila's replay carried no small amount of disdain: "Hello, Flint...I see that you're still in good health."

He narrowed his eyes and his smile faded slightly. "Yes, I'm rather stubborn when it comes to my health," he said. "It takes a lot to put me down. So tell me, what can we do for you?"

Claudia replied before Mila could. "We're just passing through. Need a place to rest."

He nodded and motioned to their hands. "Of course," he said. "As you know, my job requires me to ask you to show me your bands."

Claudia, Mila, and Kenneth lifted their hands and removed their gloves to show him the steel bands around their wrists.

The guard never even glanced at their wrists. He kept his eyes firmly on Daniel and Aaron. "What about them?"

"They are trainees for the order," Claudia said.

"Are they Dragon Guards as well?" Flint grinned.

Claudia's tone had a bite of annoyance to it. "As I said, they are trainees."

"Have they gone through your ceremony or whatever it is you people like to call it? They wear no bands as far as I can tell."

Claudia narrowed her eyes. "They will receive their bands when their training is complete. Is that all, captain?"

The guard looked them over one more time before motioning for a young man in ragged clothing. "He'll take your horses to get them fed, watered, and brushed," the guard said. He pointed down the street behind him as they dismounted. "The closest inn is on Service Level. Take the seventh underpass on the right, and then go straight until you reach the stairs. The inn is down the right passage at the top."

Claudia handed the boy her reins, as did the others. He took their horses to one side of the gate where the stables sat snugly against the wall.

Just before they started walking, Mila brushed past Flint and motioned to his face. "Nice scar, *captain*."

He smirked. "Thank you. Makes me look rather dashing, doesn't it?"

"Not the word I'd use."

Before Mila could say more, Claudia gripped her by the shoulders and the group started walking at a brisk pace. Aaron glanced back to see the stone slab slowly rise and close the gate behind them while Flint continued to stare them down. When it settled in place, Aaron had a sinking feeling in his stomach. He suddenly wanted to leave the city as soon as possible.

"Well, that wasn't what I expected," Daniel whispered.

Mila elbowed him hard enough to make him stumble. "No talking," she said.

Aaron looked around him. From here, it certainly didn't feel like a city. The pass itself narrowed at its middle before widening back out toward the other gate a great distance away, making him feel trapped in a chute like an animal. He couldn't imagine what it was like inside the tunnels. For that matter, he wondered how expansive they had to be to claim this as a city. The walls of the pass were lined with tunnels set several dozen feet apart, with decorative archways that led into the mountains. He attempted to count them but gave up when he passed twenty on each side.

Now that they were within the pass itself, the pathways and carved homes on the cliff wall seemed less inviting. Just above head level were several stonework bridges that spanned the width of the pass to the other side, allowing citizens to cross from one wall to the other. In spite of all this, it still seemed far too small to be called a city.

They made their way past the first six tunnels and turned into the seventh. As soon as they stepped inside, Aaron felt claustrophobic. The tunnel was lit with hanging braziers that cast only a small amount of light and gave brief pockets of warmth. The walls were bare and rough, made of cracked stone with wooden support beams every few feet that were equally cracked and rough. Doors and small windows lit with candles were set in the walls at awkward intervals. Some were left open. Aaron peered inside as they passed to find that most were what he assumed were homes, though each was made up of only a single room. Some had nothing in them except for a candle on the floor. They passed several people in the tunnel. All of them looked tired and somber as they shuffled along. Some were simply slumped against the wall, their heads between their knees.

The farther they went, the worse it got. Doors now either hung awkwardly on their hinges or were absent entirely. There was also a growing smell of mildew and rot, among other things. They finally came upon the stairs the guard had mentioned and started up, the only sounds being the echo of their footsteps and the occasional cough or moan of discomfort behind them. The Service Level was such a drastic change from what they'd seen moments before that Aaron wondered if they were in the same place.

The walls and ceiling here were covered with light red clay. Ornate braziers hung from the ceiling in place of the plain and shoddy ones hanging below. The braziers were also placed much more frequently, giving the tunnel a far warmer color and feel. The tunnel itself was wider than the previous and every door was accompanied by a sign hanging either above or next to it indicating the purpose of the establishment inside. There were people everywhere moving between the doors or simply standing and happily conversing with one another.

Aaron whistled. "Well," he said, "now it feels like a city."

The tunnel stretched as far as he could see, with branch-offs that people poured out of and into, just like the streets of Dalisia. It took his breath away simply thinking about the time it must have taken to carve it all out of the rock.

Claudia nodded at the crowds. "Service Level," she said. "Everything from a barber to a mercenary can be found here. It's where most of the residents spend their days."

Aaron read the signs around them as they walked past. There really was everything here, from scribes and butchers to things less…dignified, to say the least. They turned to the right. Just a short way down the street was an open double door with a sign reading *Prospector's Rest*. They stepped through and Aaron scanned the main room of the inn. The walls were the same red clay, with paintings hung haphazardly here and there, all of which were crooked. A fireplace sat at the far side of the room and every seat was filled with patrons. Waiters and waitresses ran frantically around the great room with trays of food and mugs. People laughed and shouted over one another. Being underground, the noise was amplified. Aaron already felt his head beginning to pound.

They approached the bar. Kenneth gingerly pushed aside a man who had fallen asleep with his head on the counter and an empty mug in his hand. The bartender was a tall and portly man who seemed to struggle to lean over the counter and get close enough to speak with Kenneth. After a few words, Kenneth handed him a handful of silver and bronze marks. The bartender nodded and motioned to a young girl with blonde hair. He pointed toward a door near the fireplace and raised five fingers. She nodded and motioned for the group to follow her through the maze of tables and customers. They followed her through the door into a hall with doorways on both sides.

The girl led them to the end and pointed to the doors on either side of her. "These two are yours, three beds on the right, two on the left. If you need anything else you know where to find us." She smiled and fished out two keys from her pocket, she checked the small wooden tags hanging from them, nodded and passed them to Kenneth before heading back to the main room.

They all entered the room on the right and closed the door behind them. The room was barely able to fit the three beds it had, none of which looked large enough for Kenneth. Aside from the beds, the only other furnishing was a small table with an oil lantern and a short dresser missing one of its three drawers.

Aaron sat on one of the small beds. "Well," he said, "This is cozy, isn't it?"

"Morning can't come soon enough," scoffed Kenneth.

Claudia ran her fingers over the band hidden beneath her glove. "I want us at that gate and ready to leave at first light, no later."

Mila tapped her foot. "We need to set a watch on the doors tonight," she said.

Daniel looked at her curiously. "What for?"

"Let's just say Flint is…less than trustworthy. He's with some people that do not take kindly to Dragon Guards."

Kenneth nodded and opened the door back into the hall. "Well, since we're here, it'll be nice to have a proper meal. A drink wouldn't hurt either. Does anyone care to join me?"

"I'll join you in a moment." Claudia said.

Kenneth looked to Aaron and Daniel with a raised eyebrow. "Well, lads?" he said. "Hungry?"

Daniel shook his head. "No thanks."

Mila brushed past them and into the hall. "I'm going to take a walk."

Claudia gripped Mila by the arm and looked her in the eye. "Don't do anything foolish," she said. "Let him be. He'll be dealt with eventually."

Mila nodded, and then continued out the door. Aaron watched her go with a raised eyebrow as Kenneth followed and shut the door behind him, leaving Claudia with Aaron and Daniel.

"They don't like opening those gates, do they?" Aaron said the moment the latch of the door clicked shut.

"They didn't seem to like the two of us," Daniel said. He sat on the bed across from Aaron. It creaked under his weight.

Claudia shrugged. "The people here tend to not like anyone."

"Why are people here so untrusting?" Daniel asked.

She started removing her armor as she spoke. "Well, it was a border gate before the war between Edaren and Prect. After Dalisia conquered Dawnstone, it became a place for refugees of the war to wait for their homes to be rebuilt. But that never happened, so they started mining the mountain for ore and gems to make the marks needed to buy back their lives. It just kept growing from there until it became Grey Gate."

"Is the whole city like Service Level?" Daniel shifted on the bed causing it to groan again.

"More or less. The levels get nicer the higher up you go."

"How many are there?"

"There are four on each side of the pass. First is Slum Level and we're on Service now. Above us is Market Level, then last is the city's storage centers."

"What about the other side?" Daniel asked. "Is it the same?"

"First is the slum, same as this side. Above that is Common Level, followed by Noble and then Military Level at the top. The outside of each, which you could see from the pass, is mostly housing for the rich. They think they own the right to fresh air." Claudia sighed and turned to the door. "Well, I need a drink...or several."

Daniel watched her close the door behind. "Well," he said, "they don't seem very happy to be here either."

Aaron shrugged. "Grey Gate has never been very welcoming. So I don't really blame them."

Daniel shook his head. "No kidding. That guard sounded almost angry they opened the gate for us."

"He probably was. They normally charge a toll to open the gates but they can't force Dragon Guards to pay."

Daniel tilted his head to one side. "Really? Why not?"

"It's part of Edaren law. Cities aren't allowed to deny passage to any member of the Dragon Guard unless they've committed a crime of some sort. It's a really old law that the council doesn't actually want around anymore. They've been trying to get it abolished, but for that to happen it needs a unanimous vote in the council. Forge's councilman manages to keep it around."

"Why would Forge side with the Dragon Guard on that?" Daniel asked.

"Vigil buys a lot of ore from the mines. He wants to keep it that way, so he stays on the commander's good side by keeping the law in place."

Daniel raised an eyebrow at the explanation. "You sure know a lot about Edaren law."

Aaron felt his cheeks burn and avoided eye contact. "Uh, comes with living in Dalisia, I guess."

CHAPTER NINE

23ᵗʰ of Horace, 26ᵗʰ year of the Fourth Age.

DANIEL LAY ON the stiff bed, tossing and turning for nearly an hour. His sense of time told him it was well after dark, but having no visual reference was disorienting. The fact that Kenneth snored endlessly didn't help either. They hadn't even been in Grey Gate for a full day and he already disliked the city. While the upper levels were visually appealing, it all had a sense of confinement, like no one here really had a choice whether or not they stayed. Slum Level was the worst. He dreaded having to walk through it again to leave. Everyone on that level seemed broken, like they had lost their will to live and were simply waiting for death. He hoped maybe a walk would help him sleep so he stood, dressed, and went into the main room of the inn.

The first thing Daniel noticed when he exited the hallway was the music. A young man played a lighthearted tune on a flute, accompanied by a rapid fiddle played by a young woman who looked at her partner with doe-eyed admiration as they played. Several of the patrons tapped their feet and clapped along with the tune, while a few were up and dancing in front of the hearth. Daniel watched them from the door for a moment, mesmerized by the sounds, before he noticed Mila sitting at the far corner of the bar, a wall at her back and side. For a moment he considered leaving her alone, but she had already noticed him and gestured slightly with her head to the seat next to her. He could tell she was already a bit drunk. Feeling awkward, he crossed the room to take the seat beside her.

"What are you up for?" she said, resting her head in her hand and staring at him.

"Couldn't sleep." He eyed her nearly empty mug, which sparked a question. "Why don't Kenneth and Claudia know that you drink? Seems a little odd to hide it from them, doesn't it?"

She chuckled. "Because I'm a ranger," she said. "Secrets are in my nature." She motioned to the bartender to bring her another drink. "And because the things I'm trying to forget were done in secret. Seemed rather fitting when I took up the habit."

"What are you talking about?"

She wagged a finger in his face and laughed. "Now if I told you that, it would be breaking the rules." She closed her eyes and bobbed her head along to the music before stopping suddenly and looking at the empty mug in front of her. "You know…in spite of everything I've done, and what I probably will do, I wouldn't change any of it. If I were to die tomorrow it would be with no regrets."

"Kind of contradicting the whole drinking-to-forget part, aren't you?"

She nodded. "I absolutely am, but those things I did are what made me, *me*. If I hadn't done them, then I would be someone else, and that other person might not have helped you at the river. That other person might not drink like a horse," the bartender placed another mug in front of Mila. She took a long draw before continuing. "and if that person didn't drink, what fun would they be?" She laid her head in her hand again and stared at him. "What about you? Who are you?"

The question, oddly enough, gave him pause. He wasn't sure how to answer it. "I don't know yet."

She laughed. "*Yet* he says! Now that is a good answer!" She took another drink before slamming it back on the counter. "You know, there is something about you I like. I can't put my finger on it, but I like it."

He shrugged awkwardly under her gaze and she smiled before draining her mug again and turning around on the stool to stand and start for the hall leading to their rooms.

She stopped and waved for him to follow. "We better get some sleep, I have a feeling tomorrow is going to be an interesting day."

"Thank you for your cooperation," the guard captain said. He signaled to the men atop the wall to begin lowering the stone gate.

The man in line ahead of Daniel sneered at the captain. "You're all a bunch of thieves!" he said as he peered down from atop his wagon.

The captain looked up from his papers and raised his hand. The gate, midway down, stopped moving. "I do believe the price has just changed," the captain said. "What unfortunate timing for you." He nodded toward the back of the wagon.

Two guards that had been on the sidelines ran forward to remove another wooden crate and a linen sack from the back and carried them into a door set in the wall. The trader stared in furious disbelief as more of his livelihood was stolen from him. He struggled to speak for a moment before half spitting his words at the captain. "I'm going report you to the Council. What you're doing cannot be legal!"

"You do that. Tell them Watch Captain Flint says hello."

The trader continued to fume but wisely kept his mouth shut to avoid any further loss. Flint signaled for the gate again. Once it was down, the trader snapped the reins in his hands, causing the horses towing the last of his goods to trot through. When he was well on his way, Flint waved Claudia and the others to ride over with their horses and stand by him.

"Greetings, Dragon Guards and," he looked at Aaron and Daniel for a moment, "*company*. I trust your horses are in good health?"

Claudia spoke as she rode past the captain without breaking stride. "They are, and if that's all then we will be on our way."

"Of course." He raised his hand and the stone gate was slowly raised just enough to block their path. "But those boys still have to pay for the toll."

Claudia abruptly pulled her horse around to face him. "Are you denying passage to a member of the Dragon Guard?"

"Not at all. I am after all not only a strict follower of the law but I have the privilege to enforce it." He looked up from his papers and pointed at Daniel and Aaron. "They aren't Dragon Guards, therefore they still have to pay."

"They are our recruits. Denying them is the same as denying one of us," Claudia said. She dismounted and stood toe to toe with Flint.

"They wear no bands around their wrists nor do they wear the black or the armor of your order," Flint said. "Therefore there is no indication they are anything but regular citizens on their way through our fair city, who by coincidence seemed to have arrived and are leaving at the same time as you. The lovely man you saw a few moments ago arrived yesterday and left just before you. Should I assume he too is a member of your order and allow him free passage simply due to the coincidence of time?"

Claudia was fuming. She looked ready to kill Flint until Mila placed a hand on her shoulder.

"How many marks is the toll?" Claudia hissed.

He seemed to consider for a moment. "Let's keep it reasonable, say...ten gold marks. Each."

Kenneth spoke up from the back. "You can't be serious."

"I've never enjoyed jokes."

Mila cut in. "We'll trade a horse. A good horse can fetch you fifteen in Dalisia easily."

"This isn't Dalisia," Flint said. "I'm afraid there's not much of a market for horses here. Confined spaces and all that."

Mila's face went dark. She took a slow step toward the captain. "Do you really want to do this, Flint? Keep me in this city for longer then you really have to?"

He stared her down and lifted a finger to tap at the scar casually. He spoke so quietly to her that Daniel almost missed what he said: "I hope your aim has improved."

Claudia pulled Mila back by the shoulder and then remounted her horse, spurring it toward the other gate. "Fine, we'll take Gamblers Pass."

As the rest of them headed for the other gate, Flint called out, "That's a wonderful plan, but those two still have to pay for us to open the gate. Until then I'm afraid they aren't going anywhere. The three of you, however, can leave anytime you want."

Kenneth slammed the door to their small room and started pacing, his face dark red. He looked ready to go on a rampage. Claudia seemed equally furious, while Mila simply stood in the corner, tapping her chin thoughtfully.

"So what do we do now?" Daniel said, looking to each of them in turn.

"Maybe you guys should go without us and come back with the payment?" Aaron said. He sat on his bed and cracked his knuckles absentmindedly.

"It's a two-week journey to Vigil from here," Claudia said, "and we'd have to make it there and back. By then you might not be here anymore."

"What do you mean?" Aaron asked.

"We have only so many marks at the moment," Claudia said. "The inn would kick you onto the street once you ran out and you'd be forced down to Slum Level. The people down there aren't the most...friendly sort."

Mila mumbled in the corner, "Flint wouldn't let them last more than a day, regardless."

Aaron tapped his foot nervously. "Could we climb over the wall?"

Claudia shook her head. "Too high," she said. "We wouldn't make it halfway before a guard spotted us."

"Maybe there's a sympathetic guard that would let us through?" Aaron said. He was grasping at straws at this point. Even Daniel knew that.

"Sympathy doesn't exist among the guards here," Claudia replied. "Chances are they all get cuts from the marks and the goods they steal.

They won't want to risk losing that. Not to mention that most of them fear Flint or are deathly loyal to him. Neither of which is exclusive."

"There has to be a way out of here and someone who knows what it is," Mila said.

Claudia sighed. "If we're going to find it we better do it soon. We have only enough silver for another two days at the inn. After that we'll be in the slums."

Mila took off her scarf and threw it onto one of the beds. "I'll take Daniel to Market Level and see what we can find out from the vendors."

Claudia nodded and pursed her lips. "Good idea," she said. "Kenneth can take Aaron around Service Level. Maybe the bartenders and inn-keepers will have a lead. I'll walk the residential levels. We'll meet back here at dark. See what we've learned, if anything." She made her way to the door. "Remember, keep this quiet. If the city watch find out Aaron and Daniel are trying to leave without paying, they could end up in prison or worse."

Claudia, Kenneth, and Aaron left the inn while Mila took a few moments to remove her armor. When that was done, she led Daniel to a set of stairs a short distance away from the inn that led up to Market Level. When they crested the top of the stairs, Daniel looked across a sea of people that filled the wide passage. Market Level was far more crowded than both Service and Slum Level combined. The walls were the same color clay, but every few feet an alcove was cut out in the stone for a stall and small room behind it, presumably for storage.

Daniel nearly shouted to be heard over the noise of the crowd: "So why did you want me to come with you?"

Mila leaned toward him: "Think of it as a learning experience. Just stay close and don't talk to anyone unless I say."

She started forward at a casual walk, stopping at several stalls and looking over the items before moving on to the next. She passed a woman selling embroidered shawls and tunics and without breaking stride grabbed a long, brown and black shawl from the lowest shelf while the merchant's back was turned.

Daniel furrowed his brow as she placed it around her shoulders. "Is there a reason you stole that?" he whispered.

"I'll give it back when we're done here."

"Okay…but why do you need it?"

"Everyone knows what Dragon Guards wear, be it our leather or our black, and most people won't talk to a Dragon Guard about anything. Therefore I need to not *look* like a Dragon Guard." As she spoke, she wrapped a thin, forest-green cloth around her waist to cover the rest of her black. Daniel hadn't even seen her take it. When she noticed the look he was giving her, she shrugged. "What? I'll give this back too."

Mila continued walking from stall to stall, never stopping for more than a few moments. She never spoke to the vendors or other customers, though a few times he noticed she lingered in one place longer than another. Other times she passed a stall entirely and moved on to the next. Mila continued this for nearly an hour. After trying and failing to understand her plan, he decided it was time to ask.

"What exactly are we doing?" He walked at her side as they left another stall and made their way to the next.

"We're listening," she answered. "Try it. Focus on the conversations around you. You'll be surprised what you hear."

Daniel nodded and followed her advice. He went to the stall opposite her and started mindlessly looking over the wares. As he pretended to be interested in various animal hides sewn into blankets, running a hand over the furs, he listened to the people around him. Though he tried to focus, there were too many voices at once and he couldn't make out any of it. Frustrated, he decided to pick out a single voice and focus on it while attempting to tune out the rest.

An older man's voice was far louder than those around him so he focused as best he could. He was speaking to a vendor at the next stall over. In spite of the fact that Daniel was able to tell his voice apart from everyone else, he was only able to pick out a couple of words in the chaos. None of them were anything particularly useful from what he could tell. The voice started to grow quieter, so Daniel guessed he was walking away from him. Exasperated, Daniel stopped listening altogether and instead looked for Mila. She leaned against a wall a short distance away, watching him with a raised brow and a thin smile.

When he made his way over, she leaned in. "Well?" she asked. "What have you heard?"

He shrugged. "I didn't hear anything useful. There are just too many voices all at once. How am I supposed to pick anything out from all of it?"

"It helps to listen for key words instead of the entire conversation. After some practice, you'll be able to pick out words even in the loudest markets and inns. Then, when you hear one of them, you focus on that voice only. For instance, I heard someone say Dragon Guard. So I listened to them more closely and they went on to talk about you and Aaron by saying 'those boys at the gate.' Shortly after, they said, 'I wonder if they'll go see Barden.' Which was followed by some laughter before the conversation changed topics."

"So what does that mean?" Daniel asked.

"It means we find out who Barden is."

"How exactly do we do that?"

"Like this." Mila walked to the closest stall and leaned on the table.

The merchant, an elderly man with a short beard, stepped up with a smile on his face. "See anything you like, miss?"

Mila didn't hesitate to get to the point: "Do you know a man named Barden?"

The merchant rolled his eyes and crossed his arms. "Oh, by Verhova," he said, "what do you want with that drunkard?"

Mila too crossed her arms, feigning impatience. "He owes me a lot of marks. Where can I find him?"

The man sighed. "Guess I shouldn't be surprised. If he's not at the Prospector's Rest getting drunk or enjoying himself at Talia's Temptations, you can probably find him in his poor excuse of a business at the northern corner of market."

Without another word to the man, Mila walked back to Daniel. They continued on their way without a glance back.

He raised an eyebrow. "To be honest," he said, "I didn't expect you to simply ask about him."

"Oh, and why not?"

He shrugged. "Well, after the whole disguise thing and the listening to others conversations, key words and all, I figured you would of had a grander plan."

"You work with what you have," Mila said. "The merchant gave me the knowledge that he's a well-known drunk. Also judging by his reaction to the name, I guessed he was usually in trouble of some kind. Gambling tends to go well with alcohol, so it was an easy jump that he would owe me money."

"Okay. So what's next?"

"We find out why his name was mentioned along with yours."

She led him to a stall where an elderly woman was selling herbal remedies and incense. The woman's wide smile revealed several missing teeth. Mila browsed the various vials of plant oils for a few minutes before picking out a vial of king's bloom extract and digging into the coin purse at her belt.

She smiled at the woman. "King's bloom is good for bleeding and infections, correct?"

The woman nodded. "A good few drops on a bandage can halt bleeding almost instantly," she said. "You can make a salve from the core of the flower as well but that's far messier."

"Perfect! How much for a vial?"

"Twenty copper." She grinned as Mila handed her the marks.

"Speaking of prices..." Mila leaned in. "Did you hear about those two boys at the gate this morning, the ones with the Dragon Guards?" She raised her eyebrows and grinned.

The woman laughed lightly. "I think everyone in Grey Gate has heard at this point. Can you believe the gall of those cowards, trying to leverage the law to get them through!"

Mila waved her hand. "It's a ridiculous law," she said. "They hardly do anything anymore. Why should they be allowed special treatment?"

"Frankly," the woman said, "the whole of Vigil should be torn down and its citizens sent to fend for themselves in the wilds like my ancestors were when they stood by as Edaren destroyed most of Prect. It's far from the worst they deserve, but it would certainly be a start."

"Do you think Barden will do anything about the whole thing?"

"Oh, please, that man is a joke. I don't think he'll be able to do anything for them even if he wants to. The guards watch him far too closely since Lisa's arrest."

Mila nodded. "Fair point, I suppose. Well, thank you for the extract." Mila smiled and walked away with Daniel in tow.

When they were a fair distance away, she tossed the vial onto another stall as they passed. She repeated this process four more times, using the information she learned from the previous conversation to further advance the next. It worked better than Daniel had thought it would. When Mila reached a point in a conversation where she could no longer add to it to glean new info, she simply moved on. After well over two hours, they'd learned quite a lot about Barden and the reasons he was mentioned.

His wife, Lisa, was arrested under the charge of smuggling travelers out of Grey Gate. Barden and four others were under suspicion of the same act, but they had been absent from the area when Lisa was arrested. With no other evidence against them save for rumor and no confession from Lisa, they managed to stay free for the time being. Since his wife's arrest, their general store was struggling due to his reputation as a suspected criminal and his clear decline into depression, which he treated with frequent trips to the local bars and, other, establishments. This in turn led to a fast-growing debt to several locals due to a gambling habit he picked up at the same bars.

Now Daniel and Mila were on the far northern side of Market Level, where the stalls had all been replaced by doors and display windows of a more standard market feel. There were fewer and fewer people the further they went. When they reached the end of the tunnel after nearly another hour, they stopped before a single door with a wooden sign hanging above it that read *Barden's Bargains*. Mila tried the handle but found it locked, so she knocked lightly and waited. When no answer came, she tried again. When the door still remained closed and there was no indication it would be opened, she frowned and pulled out a small, brown leather case that was clipped to her belt.

She opened it, revealing dozens of small metal picks, some with hooked or oddly shaped ends and others curved slightly along their length. After making her selection, Mila went to work on the lock. She quickly swapped one of the picks out for another, much shorter one and after only a minute; Daniel heard a click come from the door and a satisfied hum from Mila. She stood, pushed it open, and stepped inside. The room was small and lined with wooden shelves, most of which were empty. At the back of the room, a balding man sat in a chair with his feet resting on the counter and an empty bottle in his hand. Several more bottles were scattered on the floor around him.

Mila sighed and rubbed her temples. "Oh Verhova you can't be serious."

Daniel looked at her. "What is it?"

"I know him."

She walked over to the man, with a look of pity on her face. After a moment, she kicked the chair out from under him, sending him crashing to the floor. Barden huffed and rose rather quickly to his feet, swinging his arms out wildly and babbling nonsense at an unseen assailant.

When he noticed them, he attempted to smooth the wrinkles of his clothing and compose himself. "I, uh, yes…good evening."

Mila rolled her eyes. "It's well past noon."

He looked surprised. "So it is," he said. "Well then, I suppose you're here to buy something?"

"No. But I do want to know when you started going by Barden rather than Jeremiah."

Barden looked at her with squinted eyes for a moment before realization washed over him. "Strike me blind…Mila? What in the world are you doing here?"

"I was looking for you. Seems you've made a bit of a name for yourself around here."

"I uh…I suppose you could say that. What do you need? I shall assist you to the best of my, uh, current abilities." Barden set his chair upright and sat down with very little grace, nearly tipping over again. He picked through the bottles at his feet until he found one with liquid still inside and lifted it to his lips.

Mila reached over, took the bottle from him, and set it on the floor. "Jeremiah. What are you doing here? Why'd you leave Vigil?"

He frowned and watched her with a dead stare. "You know why."

"You only ever did what you had to."

"That doesn't mean I liked any of it."

She sighed and nodded. "All right. So why Grey Gate?"

"It's an easy place to hide," he said. "You know that. They knew my name but not my face. Easiest solution was a new name, and so here I am."

She looked at him for a long moment and nodded slowly. "So, you got married?"

He nodded and bit his lip. "I did. Lisa...she was everything to me."

"She got arrested. You were both smuggling people out of Grey Gate along with a few others from the city."

Barden leaned over, grabbed the bottle from the floor, and looked at the little bit of liquid left inside. "Quit stating facts we both know and get to the point. What do you want, Mila?"

"Three of us are escorting two young men to Vigil and we can't pay the funds for their passage." She paused, apparently to read his reaction. "So we need you to get them out. That's what you do now, right?"

Barden looked Daniel up and down before he shook his head. "Sorry," he said. "I can't do that. Even if I could, the way out isn't safe anymore."

Mila rolled her eyes and crossed her arms. "Jeremiah, you know—"

"Barden. I don't know anyone by the name 'Jeremiah'."

She nodded. "Barden. You know we can handle ourselves. Just show us the way."

"I have no doubt that you and I assume Claudia and whoever else is with you can handle yourselves," he said. Barden pointed at Daniel. "His safety is what I would worry about."

"You let me worry about him," Mila said. "Tell me about the way out."

He smiled and swirled the drink around. "You've always been so damned stubborn."

She grinned. "You're one to talk."

He nodded to Daniel. "Who's he to you?"

Mila shrugged dismissively. "Someone worth the effort. You know what that's like."

He stared at them for a long moment before speaking to Daniel. "Well...aren't you a lucky kid." He turned back to Mila and sighed. "When the people that were stuck here after the war started mining to earn the money they needed to buy their lives back, some of the mineshafts they dug out intersected with caves. I used some of these caves to smuggle people out of the city."

"So why'd you stop?" Mila said.

"The caves mostly collapsed during the eruption of Dragons Maw, one of the few that didn't, recently become a satlis den. The very one you're now seeking to use."

Mila exhaled heavily. "Of course it is. How long ago did the satlis move in?"

He glared at her. "Happened about two years ago."

Mila tapped her chin for several long, tense moments before speaking: "Can you take us there?"

"No. I am not going in there"

"You don't have to. Just show us where it is."

Barden looked at the floor before shaking his head: "I can't do that."

Mila narrowed her eyes. Daniel could tell she was trying to come up with another approach. "Why?" she asked, "Why do you do this?"

"What? Drink?" Barden said. "It's not for the flavor, I'll tell you that much. But I think you already know that."

"No, why did you help people like Daniel and Aaron get out of the city? Where did it start? You left the Dragon Guard. Why not go somewhere quieter, live in peace?"

He lifted the bottle to his lips but stopped short of drinking it. He looked at the ale swirling around the bottom before sighing and lowering it to the ground. "Five years ago," he said. "The Dragon Guard was recruiting again, so Grey Gate always had a couple of young men and women passing through. There was this one girl, couldn't have been more than fourteen." He bit his lip and shook his head. "The captain then wasn't what Flint was, but he still charged twice as much. The girl, like most, didn't have enough marks. She was here for weeks trying to earn the money, doing whatever she could…but the year was nearly over, so she'd finally had enough of it. Stole a rope and tried to climb over the east wall."

"What happened to her?" Daniel asked in a whisper.

"They have archers in those towers during the night. At the very least, it was quick." Barden placed his face in his hands briefly before lifting his eyes to look at Mila again. "She reminded me of my sister when I was younger." A smile crossed his face that quickly faded. "It wasn't the first time it happened and it won't be the last. My wife and I decided to do what we could for whoever we could. Didn't matter who they were or why they needed out. All that mattered was that they were trapped here by a corrupt system."

"What about the satlis?" Mila said. "How did you find out they took the place as a den?"

"Two years ago. It'd been several weeks since the last run, so we had no idea they were there. I led a man and his son to their deaths. Those Shade damned cats nearly killed me too. I closed off the passage and haven't gone back since. The others in our operation left the city for good, but Lisa wanted to try one last time to see if the cats had gone nearly a month later. Told her it was stupid, they don't move on like that, but I couldn't stop her. Guards caught her and those she was leading just before they went into the tunnels. They're in prison now but, probably saved their lives."

Daniel was afraid to ask his next question but he felt he needed to know: "What happened to Lisa?"

"Guards will tell you she's in prison too. I know better than that with Flint in charge."

Mila leaned in and placed a hand on his shoulder. "I understand your hesitation so I'm not asking you to lead us through. Just show us the entrance and we'll take care of the rest. I won't make you go down there again."

He shook his head once more. "I refuse to be the cause of more death."

"No one is going to die. I will not let that happen."

He stared at the floor for a long while. "I need to think on this," he finally said.

Mila leaned back and nodded. "I understand. We're staying at Prospector's Rest. If you decide to help us, you can find us there."

CHAPTER TEN

24th of Horace, 26th year of the Fourth Age.

THEY PASSED NO one as they went through the slums. Every door was closed. The group of six was deep in the south side slums, trying to keep their pace quick as they wound through dozens of main passages and offshoots of narrower tunnels. The further into the mountain they went, the fewer doors and braziers were set into the walls, until the tunnel was as it had been long ago, just a mineshaft. After so many turns, Daniel lost track of which way they were heading. If they were separated he didn't think he'd ever find his way out. Finally, Barden led them down one last tunnel which brought them to a wall with a single, iron-banded door in its center.

Barden had come to the group that morning at the inn and told them he would lead them to the tunnels. But he would go no further than that. Now he stood before the sturdy door and fumbled in a bag at his side before pulling out a set of keys. He cycled through them before finding the one he wanted and sliding it into the oddly pristine padlock.

When the lock didn't release, his eyes widened in surprise before he tried another key. Daniel thumbed the pommel of the iron short sword that now hung at his waist as he watched Barden work.

Kenneth and Mila had gone into Market Level just after Barden's visit that morning to procure the items they would need for their now-extended journey. Since they lacked funds, at Claudia's suggestion they'd sold their horses. They hadn't been able to get even half of what they were actually worth and walked away with a total of ten gold marks for all five of them. Kenneth, needless to say, had been furious, but they weren't going to simply leave them in the stables for the city guard to have for free—if not out of respect for the horses, then out of spite for Flint and the guards. Aaron hadn't liked having to leave Bella behind, but had agreed it was necessary in the end. Daniel was equally upset about leaving Connie's horse. It had almost felt like having to leave home again. He never thought he'd be brought to the verge of tears over a horse.

The morning purchases included a short sword each for Daniel and Aaron. The swords were, in Kenneth's words, "of a quality befitting a child's toy." But after a treatment with Kenneth's whetstone, they were plenty sharp and would do well enough for the time being. They purchased, in addition to the swords and their fresh supply of food, a fire-starting kit for Daniel. Torches for each of them were strapped to the undersides of their packs, as well as two decorative glass vials that they'd filled with oil they "commandeered" from an unlit brazier in the slums not two hours earlier.

Daniel's mind quit wandering when he heard Claudia whisper to Barden in the dark. In spite of her attempt to stay quiet, her voice echoed in the empty tunnel: "What's wrong?"

Barden fumbled with his keys. "I don't know, it won't open... my key isn't working."

A familiar voice called from behind them: "It appears someone managed to get a key for the old one, so we had to change the lock. Safety concerns and all that."

They whirled around to see Flint flanked by ten guards, their swords drawn, walking toward them and blocking the path back to the city.

Flint stopped a dozen feet away. "Barden," he said, "I'm so disappointed. I had my suspicions, of course, but I had hoped I was wrong. I rather like you. Shame you happen to be a part of...*this* lot." He sighed and motioned for the guards behind him to move forward. "By the law of the land of Edaren and the authority given to me by the Representative of Grey Gate, the Third Seat of the King's Council, I place you all under arrest under charges of smuggling."

Claudia stepped in front of Daniel and Aaron, her sword drawn. Behind him, Daniel heard the strain of wood as Mila drew an arrow and took aim. The guards paused and glanced at one another, concern clear on their faces due to the quick and aggressive motions made against them.

Mila spoke quietly to Daniel and Aaron: "Get behind me."

Without a word, Daniel did as he was told. Aaron quickly followed suit, placing them directly behind Mila, with Barden still at the door fumbling with the keys, hoping the impossible would happen and one of them would work on the new lock.

Flint raised an eyebrow. "Then, am I to understand you will be resisting arrest? Oh, how fun."

Daniel glanced behind him at Kenneth, who was slowly moving toward the door.

Barden threw down the keys and rushed forward to stand in front of Claudia. "Enough of this, Flint," he said. "I take full responsibility. Leave them out of this."

Flint shook his head. "Regardless of your personal feelings of guilt," he said, "I'm afraid you're all responsible at this point." He waved for the guards to advance.

The first guard approached. When he was close enough, Claudia darted around and past Barden, slamming her open palm up into his nose, breaking it and causing blood to flow down his face as he cried out in pain. The second guard was startled by Claudia's speed. She took advantage by lunging forward again. This time she swept out her foot and knocked his legs out from under him, causing the guard to fall to the ground under the weight of his chainmail. A third guard recovered quickly enough to swing wide at Claudia's midsection, but he was far slower. Claudia raised her sword in defense, letting the blades collide and hold firm against one another.

Daniel heard Mila release the bowstring with a resounding *twang*. The third guard cried out in pain as an arrow punctured his thigh in the gap between his chainmail and leggings. He cried out as he fell to the ground and clutched at the wooden shaft in his leg. Behind them, Daniel heard Kenneth grunt several times. When he looked back, he saw the huge warden bashing the door with his shield. The wood was cracked and the old and weak iron was bending inward. After several more strikes, the wood connected to the latch shattered. The door flew open in a shower of dust and splinters.

Kenneth stood to the side and called out: "Let's go!"

Daniel and Aaron ran through the doorway, followed by Barden and Mila. Claudia kicked back another guard before turning to follow, allowing Kenneth to bring up the rear, his shield raised as he backed down the narrow tunnel and formed a living wall between the two groups.

Flint shouted angrily as he ripped the arrow out of the fallen guard's leg: "Get up and go after them!"

The guards attempted to follow but the passage was only wide enough for them to move single file. When the group of guards came close enough, Kenneth lashed out with his shield, shoving them back and causing them to fall atop one another. After the lead guards regained their footing, Kenneth slammed his shield into them again, sending them to the top of the tangled mass of bodies before he turned and ran down the narrow passage after the rest of his companions.

They'd had no time to light a torch so they ran as fast as they could manage in the darkness. Thankfully, it was a straight tunnel with little variation in the floor and walls. After several minutes their pace slowed gradually until they came to a complete stop. The old mines were quiet save for the sound of their heavy breathing. Daniel heard someone shuffling through a pack, followed by the flashes of spark stone. A torch flared to life, momentarily blinding him.

Barden lifted another torch to the flame to light it before he passed it to Claudia. "Hopefully they won't follow us this far," Barden said. He motioned further down the mine. "Stay close. If you go down the wrong branch, you'll be lucky to ever see daylight again."

With that, they started into the darkness, Barden leading the way. Kenneth and Claudia brought up the rear with the rest of them in the middle. The walls of the mine were rough and the wooden supports looked rotten and brittle. They passed several branch-offs which led to nothing but more darkness, as well as a few cave-ins that blocked the way further into the mountain. Daniel couldn't imagine what it would be like to be lost down here without any light or sense of direction. Who knew what else could lurk in these tunnels, waiting for something to stumble into it? If satlis had found their way in, something else must have at one time or another.

Daniel placed a hand on the hilt of his new sword. He wasn't sure why, but it felt reassuring to have it beneath his palm, to know it was still there and ready in case anything happened. Kenneth had taught him and Aaron the basics before they set out to meet with Barden that morning, so it was all still fresh in his mind—the way to grip and stand, and how to properly jab or swing. Kenneth had also told them the ways a satlis was likely to attack and how best to avoid them altogether should they end up in a fight with the creatures.

Daniel had asked Claudia about them after he and Mila had returned to the inn. They were some of the most dangerous animals that roamed the mountains of Edaren. They tended to stay within their burrows during the day and ventured out to hunt the night hours. They killed their prey with potent venom from their fangs and maimed anything they couldn't kill with their spike covered tails.

Daniel kept running over it all as they marched on through the darkness, taking only three turns during the next hour in spite of the dozens of passages they passed. As they went, he examined the walls of the mines and could see marks and divots in the stone where ores and jewels had no doubt been mined away years earlier.

"Barden," Claudia said, "I've been curious about how you came to know this route in the first place." Daniel heard him hum softly as he thought. "Was a map sold to me by one of the older families of the city about a year after I left the Dragon Guard," Barden answered. "He said he could trace his family line back to the nobles of Shale. The whole system of tunnels was mapped at one time and this map showed most of it."

Daniel furrowed his brow. "Why would he sell a family heirloom like that?"

"Well, he smelt a lot like black blood."

Daniel knew the term. Black blood was a highly addictive drug. The only reason Daniel had heard of it was that at one point it'd had a presence in Sapella's Crossing. A dealer had tried to set up a den for it but had simply vanished shortly after arriving. The residents of the town became aware of the drug's presence only when an addict was forced to go without it for several days and lost his mind. The dealer's body was found later in an abandoned home, along with the bodies of several others who had been a part of his operation. All of them, it seemed, died of natural causes. Though no one actually believed that, but there had been no other explanation.

From what Daniel had heard, black blood was rampant in Luden. Thinking about the power of the drug always made him uneasy, so he pushed it out of his mind. Instead, he focused on their slow and cautious walk. They continued on for another hour until they came to a shabby wooden wall with a narrow door. It had so many chains and locks that Daniel was worried it would be impossible to open. Barden began unlocking and removing the multitude of chains, setting them gently on the floor to avoid making any unnecessary noise.

It took Barden several minutes to remove them all. When he was done, he stepped to one side. "The cave is a straight shot with only one fork," he said. "Take the *right* passage if you want to get out safely and quickly. The left has an abrupt edge followed by a steep incline, shortly after that there is another steep climb on the way out. It also eventually leads outside, but it's a much longer route so I don't recommend it."

Aaron spoke, concern evident in his tone: "What are you going to do? You can't go back now. They'll do worse than just arrest you."

Barden shrugged. "It was bound to happen eventually. Who knows," he said with a weak smile, "maybe I'll share a cell with my wife." Daniel felt a twinge in his heart at Barden's words.

Kenneth ushered Daniel and Aaron through the door and placed a hand on Barden's shoulder as he passed. "May Verhova protect you," he said. "When we get to Vigil I'll see if there's anything we can do for you and your wife."

Barden seemed surprised at the gesture. He mumbled a thanks under his breath as Kenneth stepped through the narrow opening.

Mila was about to step past but Barden grabbed her by the arm. "You make sure they make it through," he said.

She nodded and lifted his hand from her shoulder. "They'll be fine," she said. "I give you my word, Jeremiah; I'll make sure of it."

With that, she and the others stepped through and Barden shut the door behind them. Claudia used her torch to light each of the others' until they all carried their own source of light. Then, with a deep sigh from Claudia, they started off into the cave, the sounds of chains and locks being put into place behind them. The walls here were smoother than in the mines. Hundreds of stalactites hung from the ceiling. A few longer ones nearly reached the floor, so they had to step around them. All was silent save for their breathing and footfalls, and the always-distant dripping of water. It was obvious why no one spoke. While satlis tended to settle in one area, it was also possible they had been driven out by any number of other predators.

Their hope for an empty cave was quickly dissolved. The ground was littered with bones of varying sizes. Not long after they came across the first corpse, a half-eaten deer. Quickly they started seeing the remains of more animals. Some were simply bones with shreds of muscle and tendon hanging from them, while others were recent kills. Most of the latter sat rotting as a testament to the creature's tendency to hunt for sport rather than sustenance. The smell was astoundingly awful. A mixture of rot and excrement filled Daniel's nose before they had even stepped fully into the carnage, and as they walked it only grew worse.

Daniel stepped carefully over bones and around carcasses as he leaned under and moved around more stone spikes. He couldn't see any satlis, but they had to be near. Any sound would surely draw them in. Now that the danger was fully apparent, they moved more slowly than ever, which to Daniel was agony. With every step, he felt that his heart would stop out of fear that an unseen bone would snap under his weight and bring the whole den upon them.

Slowly, a new scent started to overwhelm the others. Daniel immediately recognized it from home: elk. He knew it from a herd that passed by Sapella's Crossing every year. It was musky, like sweat, and was overpowering everything else. Shortly after the smell registered, the corpse appeared, illuminated by their torches. The body was fresh. Blood still pooled around it and only a few sections of its body were missing. As Daniel passed, he noticed a bright yellow liquid oozing from puncture wounds on the animal's neck, barely visible in the dim torchlight but distinct enough against the brown fur that it was hard to miss.

The silence in the tunnel was broken by several soft, scratching sounds. At once, everyone stopped and looked around frantically. Daniel was afraid to breathe for fear he might make noise or miss hearing something important. Another few scratches echoed in the long tunnel. This time, Daniel saw the source. Ten feet ahead of them on the right wall, barely noticeable in the dim light, was a narrow alcove just off the ground. Hanging from it and curled along the ground like a coil of rope was a long, quilled tail.

The scratches echoed again. Daniel saw the tail shift slightly as a leg of the hidden animal kicked out of the alcove, its claws scraping across the stone. It reminded Daniel of the movement of a dreaming dog. He glanced at the others. The only one who hadn't seemed to notice was Kenneth. He was the closest to it, just four feet away, and still advancing. In another moment he would be virtually standing on the tail of the animal. Claudia, the closest to Kenneth, waved her arms frantically, trying unsuccessfully to silently get his attention.

With no other choice, she hissed, "Kenneth!" In the silence of the cave it was deafening.

Kenneth turned. Claudia pointed to the coiled tail just in front of him. He glanced down and his eyes widened. He looked back up at Claudia, who glared at him for a moment before quietly motioning for all of them to continue forward. She directed them to walk in single file at the center of the cave.

Now they moved with even greater caution. Daniel carefully placed each step and kept his breathing as low and steady as he could. His heart beat so fast and loud in his ears that he was surprised the animals couldn't hear it. As they went, the walls revealed more and more alcoves. Not all housed a satlis, but the deeper they went, the more the creatures appeared. There were dozens of alcoves along each wall. Most had one, if not two, satlis sleeping within.

The cave narrowed drastically, bringing the band of interlopers uncomfortably close to a satlis as it slept, giving Daniel a chance to get a good look at the beast. It was five feet long and very lean, with clearly defined muscles. Its body was covered in small, thin quills that at first glance looked like fur. On closer inspection, Daniel saw that the quills were solid and came to a needle-thin point. The highest concentration of quills rested along the animal's spine. The face was clearly feline, with two fangs at the front of its mouth that curled over its lips and stopped just above the lower jawbone. The most defining feature of the creature was its tail. It was at least three times the length of its body. The mass of quills at the end looked like it belonged at the end of a mace. After his extensive look, Daniel kept his eyes cast down at his feet. He feared that if he looked at it any longer, it would wake and pounce on him. The fear was unfounded, he knew that. But fear didn't always conform to logic.

Then, up ahead, Daniel saw something he never would have expected. Four of the creatures were just outside an alcove at ground level. They were kittens, small enough to hold easily in one's arms. Unlike their adult counterparts, their tails were the same length as their body, lacking the mass at the end. In addition, it was clear that their fangs were not as pronounced.

The four kittens seemed to be playing while their parent slept in the alcove next to them. They rolled and bit each other and seemed to take no notice of the five intruders in their home. The kittens played just at the edge of the torchlight, darting in and out of view. Daniel and the others stopped and glanced at one another. Several long moments passed before anyone made a move. Then Mila stepped around Kenneth and slowly started to cross to the left wall. She motioned for the rest to follow. They hugged the left wall, trying to stay as far from the kittens as possible while also avoiding the alcoves next to them.

After only a few steps, however, one of the kittens stopped playing and stared at them. It made no movement aside from a few quick flicks of its tail. After several moments, the other three noticed their sibling's gaze and followed suit. They all stared with sickly green eyes that shimmered from the light of the flames. Mila and the group took another few steps forward. The kittens reacted by stepping backwards hurriedly while keeping their gaze focused on Mila. Daniel feared what would happen if they stepped forward again, but he knew they had no choice. They couldn't go back.

Mila lifted her left boot to take another step. The moment her foot touched the ground, the kittens ran to their sleeping parent and cried out with high-pitched mewls. The satlis sleeping in the alcove reacted to the sounds immediately. It lifted its head, ears twitching rapidly and locked eyes on the five intruders.

Everyone froze for what seemed an eternity. The satlis's eyes darted between the five of them. Slowly, its face turned from concern for its kittens crying out for help to anger at the intruders that had walked into its den.

Just as it was about to cry out and alert the rest of the den, Mila shouted: "Run!"

The satlis roared furiously. All around them, the cavern was filled with the sounds of creatures awakening and answering the roar with mirrored calls. The five of them ran as fast as they could. Daniel risked a glance behind, only to see that every one of the animals they'd passed was now in the tunnel, most of them charging after Daniel and the rest, fangs bared and snarling viciously. When he turned forward again, he was greeted by the sight of Kenneth slamming one of the beasts aside with his shield as it leapt at him. The animal was sent through the air and into a stalactite as the rest of the group ran past.

Mila reached into her quiver, turned on her heel, and in the same motion drew back her bow. How she was able to pick out her target and fire so quickly was beyond Daniel. Yet an instant after she released the string and let the arrow fly, he heard one of the satlis's cry out.

Mila finished continued turning on her heel until she was facing forward again and called out: "Claudia! We need a wall!"

Without replying, Claudia reached into the pack that always hung from her shoulder. As far as Daniel could recall, he had never seen her open it before. Now she reached inside and removed a red orb that easily fit in her palm. It appeared to be made of clay, similar to the tunnel walls within Grey Gate, with a short wick on one end. Claudia gripped the orb tightly and ran the wick across a section of her belt that held a piece of spark stone. The wick caught and started to rapidly burn away. She dropped the orb onto the ground as they ran. After a couple of moments, a loud *thud* echoed in the cave, followed by a brilliant flash of light that faded before an orange firelight persisted.

In spite of their circumstances, Aaron skidded to a stop and stared at the bonfire behind them. "What was that?" he asked.

Daniel too had paused at the spectacle. The cave was quickly filling with smoke while the walls, floor, and ceiling were coated in flames. Beyond the flames, Daniel could see the outline of a horde of satlis dashing back and forth by the burning wall, trying to find a way past it to their prey.

Claudia spoke through ragged breaths. "It was an ingera, it's a scholar weapon."

Aaron sounded stunned: "I thought scholars were supposed to be diplomats."

Claudia turned and started off again. "People have forgotten a lot about what we are and aren't. Let's go, the fire will only last for so long."

The exchange lasted no more than ten seconds, but already the fire had started to dissipate. Smoke now choked the tunnel in a thick veil. Shortly after the group resumed their mad dash, they found where the tunnel split. The pass to the right had only a slight rise while to the left was a near-straight drop down a rocky slope like a cliff edge parallel to them.

Daniel hadn't seen any more alcoves along the walls, but now something new blocked their path. Walking slowly toward them were five satlis, twice the size of the ones behind the wall of fire. Daniel didn't even have to ask to know they were females. The smallest of them at the back carried a rabbit in its mouth while another, the largest at the front of the group, effortlessly carried a young fawn by the neck. This satlis was tall enough that the legs of the deer didn't even touch the ground. The five animals paused in their tracks at the sight of the humans running down the length of the tunnel. Daniel felt his breath catch in his chest and quickly drew his sword.

The beasts dropped their kills and bared their long fangs. Even in the low light of the torches, Daniel could see a sickly yellow liquid drip from the tips. The beasts charged at them with a low roar. Their first target was Kenneth at the front. The largest satlis was the fastest and the first to leap through the air at the warden. Kenneth raised his shield in front of him. The animal slammed into it. Kenneth used his shield like a catapult to toss the animal down the cliff slope into darkness. It howled in fury as it vanished over the edge before it was abruptly cut short. He had no time to reposition himself to meet the next attacker. Instead, Mila intervened.

She drew back her bow and planted an arrow in the animal's breast as it rose to swipe at Kenneth with its front claws. It reeled back but was otherwise unharmed by the shot. The other three satlis charged past Kenneth and went for the rest of them. One dashed past Claudia. As it passed, it swept its tail out to the side at her knees. But Claudia had clearly dealt with these beasts before. She swiped her blade in an upward arc to cut off the animal's tail as it came for her legs, sending half of the tail harmlessly to the side. The satlis skidded to a stop and screeched at the sudden pain before turning, enraged, to strike at Claudia. The scholar had already turned and was now charging at the animal. While it screeched at her, Claudia drove her blade into its mouth and up through its head, killing it instantly.

At the same time, Kenneth swatted aside another satlis with his broadsword while blocking its tail with his shield as the satlis tried to arc it around behind him like a whip. Daniel heard Aaron yelp. He turned to see Mila grab Aaron by the collar and yank him out of range of one of the beasts as it tried to flank them. Aaron fell to the ground in a heap but was soon back on his feet. Daniel turned his gaze ahead again. When he did, he was greeted by teeth.

The smallest of the animals had reached Daniel. It suddenly seemed as if this was the longest moment of his life. All he could see were rows of teeth with bits of flesh and fur stuck between them and sickly yellow saliva dropping from their points. He didn't know what to do or how to stop what was about to happen. But it didn't matter. The next thing he felt was a pair of hands on his shoulders as he was shoved aside towards the cliff edge. He managed to turn his head and see Mila standing in his place. The satlis opened its maw wide and forced her to the ground beneath it. Everything seemed to move in slow motion. Mila and the animal were on the ground while Kenneth was sprinting toward them, his sword raised. Daniel saw Claudia out of the corner of his eye as she stood behind them, screaming something he couldn't hear. Aaron stretched for Daniel but was clearly beyond his reach.

Then he crested the cliff edge and they were lost to his sight. He saw a wall of stone rise up in their place as he fell. Then there was nothing but a sharp pain in his back and head, followed by blackness.

CHAPTER ELEVEN

25th of Horace, 26th year of the Fourth Age.

GRIFFON SAT WITH her back against the railing of *The Royal Jewel* as the sun finally reached its peak in the sky. The soft rays bathed her in a rich glow, driving away the late autumn chill. She had been at sea for ten days and had been working off her debt to Captain Andrews nearly every moment of it by cleaning the deck, polishing every scrap of metal no matter how useless it seemed to be, helping the cook, and cleaning up after every meal. In spite of her life in Forge, she had never been this sore nor had this many blisters. But she couldn't have been happier.

Griffon felt lighter and more at ease then she ever had in the city. She knew it was partly because she had set a goal for herself and every day she was drawing closer to it—closer to finally having control over her own life. It made her feel that she was finally moving forward. Soon others would see her as something more than the daughter of an abusive drunk and a whore.

Her attention was caught by the sound of heavy footsteps. She turned to see Captain Andrews approaching with a smile across his face. He stopped beside her and placed his hands on the railing to look out over the sea. "Ms. Hart," he said, "I thought I should let you know that we'll be arriving at Navia within the hour."

She jumped up and stretched her arms out behind her, causing her shoulders to pop as she spoke. "How long will we be in the city?"

"Hopefully we'll depart tomorrow evening after we restock some supplies and drop off some of our cargo."

"How long will we be at sea after we leave Navia?"

He stroked his beard. "About a week and a half, give or take a couple of days, depending on if the wind stays favorable." He turned to walk back to his cabin at the rear of the ship.

"Thank you again, captain."

Without stopping or looking back, he replied, "You've thanked me every day, Ms. Hart, it is no longer necessary."

She watched him go before leaning on the railing. She disagreed with that statement. To her it would be necessary every day until they arrived. With a content sigh, she turned to the front of the ship to look at the mountains in the distance. Navia was just on the other side of them. As she watched the peaks grow ever closer, she glanced at the figurehead adorning the bow of the ship. It was an elegant woman in a flowing dress, holding a round ruby in front of her with both hands.

The Royal Jewel itself. Andrews had said they'd caught at least a dozen people trying to steal it from the figurehead in the dead of night. He had never done anything about it and simply laughed as they tried to pry it free. It would never budge from its position. Even if it did, he said, it was worthless. Nothing more than colored glass. She smiled at the thought of someone perched on the figurehead's arms attempting to wrestle the ruby free.

She turned to look back at the shoreline. They weren't far from it. The waters along the southern coast dropped off quickly and were void of reefs or rocks, allowing the ship to stay well within sight of land. The Spines extended into the ocean, forming a wall of steep slopes and cliff faces that had been the main sight for the better part of two days. Griffon watched the terrain drift by them and fell into what was almost a trance, where time seemed to pass in an instant. Before she knew it they were rounding the edge of the mountains and Navia was finally in full view.

The city buildings were all made from a light grey stone quarried from the mountain range, along with redwood taken from Highwood Forest just beyond the walls. The city ran partway up the mountain. A shining, large mansion sat on the slopes above the city looking over it all. Griffon didn't have to live in Navia to know it was likely the home of the councilman and his aides. She looked to the harbor, which was crowded with people and ships of all sizes at nearly every available dock. She could see everything from a trade vessel like the one she rode on to a Royal Army patrol ship.

The Royal Jewel approached the city and settled at a dock as far from the other ships as possible due to Andrews's preference. Several crewmen leaped onto the dock to tie the ship off to the available moorings. When that was done, they laid down the gang plank and immediately began unloading the portion of their shipment bound for local clients. Griffon walked down the ramp and set foot on the solid, unswaying wood of the dock, feeling instant relief. It was nice not to feel the constant motion of the sea beneath her feet, but also odd after so many days rocking endlessly back and forth.

A man with a large, leather-bound book approached the ship with a stern look on his face. Griffon assumed he was the harbor master, which meant he would be looking for Captain Andrews. She stopped him by placing a hand on his shoulder as he passed. "Excuse me," she said. "Do you know where I could find an inn, preferably something cheap?"

He glanced at her hand and slowly lifted it off his shoulder with a look of annoyance. "What you want is The Barge, north gate."

"Thank you."

Griffon started into the city at a slow walk, taking in the sights. Thankfully, Captain Andrews hadn't taken all of her money as he'd originally planned. He chose to leave her ten silver marks to pay for a place to stay, as well as food when they docked in Navia so she could stay well out of the way while they worked and prepared for the next leg of their trip. She was grateful for it. It was one of the many reasons she thanked him so often. She sidestepped dozens of sailors and workers who never even glanced her way as they busied themselves. She passed hundreds of crates and bags of various goods lining the edge of the harbor, which featured linens, leathers, and even minerals from Forge. Stepping off the wooden planks and onto the stone streets, she couldn't help but marvel at the bright and cheerful tone of everything and the sheer number of people walking the city.

If she ever had to pick between here and Forge, then Navia was the clear winner. Everyone wore brightly colored and embroidered clothes. In comparison, Griffon stood out like a sore thumb in her ragged grey and brown. The further into the city she went, the more people seemed to happily acknowledge her. She received smiles and welcoming nods. All of it made her uncomfortable after living in Forge, where the most likely attention one received was someone barking to get out of their way.

Griffon arrived at the north gate in a little over an hour. She would have arrived much sooner, but she couldn't help taking her time. Everything in Navia was such a drastic change in comparison to the darkness and bitterness of Forge. It was jarring in a welcoming way and she wanted to savor it for as long as possible. She scanned the buildings around her and read the signs that hung from them until she located one in the shape of the inn's name sake hanging above a door inscribed with the words The Barge. She smiled and started for the inn, but paused in her tracks when she heard someone shouting from atop the gate. She stopped to listen.

The first voice spoke with urgency: "Get the manway open!"

Another unseen voice spoke from the same area: "Quickly, one of them is injured!"

She cocked her head and tried to catch the rest of what was being said, but it was drowned out by the chatter of city residents as they too paused to see what was transpiring. She turned away from the inn and made her way to the gate as the smaller door set in the gate itself was unlocked and swung open by a guard. Moments later, a woman in leather armor and black clothing ran through the opening, followed by a younger man with short black hair wearing a more traditional outfit and a panicked look on his face. They were followed by a much larger man in heavy leather plating who burst through with another woman dressed similarly in his arms. Her face was pale and her armor was caked with blood.

Griffon recognized them immediately. Dragon Guards, three of them! She tried to make her way through the still-gathering crowd to get a better look, but was pushed back when the larger man forced his way through and past her, trailed by the younger boy. Both were led by a city guard. Griffon noticed that the other female Dragon Guard had stayed behind and was speaking to one of the city guards with hurried words and frantic motions. The guard nodded quickly and ran after the others at a full sprint.

The female Dragon Guard sighed and leaned against the wall, her head in her hands. Now that her companions had left, the crowd started to disperse, allowing Griffon room to approach her. The woman didn't acknowledge Griffon right away. Griffon stood by her with her hands clasped behind her back. After a few moments, the woman finally lifted her head and wiped at her eyes.

"Can I help you?" she said.

"You're a Dragon Guard, right?" The moment the words left Griffon's mouth, she realized how stupid the question was.

"What do you want?"

"Just to talk to you, I'm actually—"

The woman cut her off before she could finish. "Look, any other time I'd be happy to speak with you, but right now there's a lot going on and I just need to think for a moment."

Griffon was about to reply, but before she had the chance a city guard appeared and pushed past her. "Captain Theo has asked to speak with you," the guard said.

The Dragon Guard groaned and rubbed her temples. "Of course he has. Where is he?"

"He is heading for the clinic to meet with your companions."

The woman nodded and moved away from the wall. "Take me to them."

The guard led her away, leaving Griffon to stand alone, more curious about the situation than before. The woman held in the man's arms had looked nearly dead. This woman had said a lot was going on, so whatever had happened was clearly more than a single injured comrade. As much as Griffon wanted to know the story, she realized there was no point in trying at the moment. She would leave the matter alone for now. It was time to purchase her room at the inn and get something to eat.

CHAPTER TWELVE

25th of Horace, 26th year of the Fourth Age.

ARON PACED THE small room as he, Kenneth, and the captain of the city watch waited for Claudia to arrive. As much as he worried for Mila and her wound, he feared more for Daniel. He was still down in the cavern with the satlis. Barden had said that both passages would eventually lead out, but Daniel could be hurt or a satlis could have followed him down the slope. The unknown of it all was what worried him the most.

"Shade curse you boy, would you quit pacing!" the captain said with a glare. Aaron sheepishly took a seat next to Kenneth.

Claudia entered the room and stepped up to the captain, anger etched across her face. "What do you want?" she said.

He raised his chin and looked down his nose at her. "I was informed you asked one of my men to organize a search party. I'm afraid I must deny your request."

A look of sheer disbelief replaced the anger. "What?"

"I won't spare my men to go off on some foolish errand. If you have a missing Dragon Guard, I'm sure you three can handle it without the help of the city watch."

"He's not a Dragon Guard, he's a *boy* trapped in a cave. He could be hurt. We need to find the second entrance to get him out before it's too late."

The expression on the captain's face softened for only a moment. "If that is the same cave in which your companion received her injury, then I stand my ground with even more conviction. None of my men will be leaving these walls. Boy or not, I don't trust your order enough to risk their lives."

Kenneth got up slowly and stood in front of the man. In spite of the captain's stature, Kenneth dwarfed him. "Are you telling me you are going to leave him to die?" he asked. Kenneth's tone was oddly calm, which seemed to set the captain even more off balance.

In spite of this, the captain lifted his chin again. Aaron could tell he was trying to be tough, but there was a hint of fear in his tone. "If he is down there with those things, then that boy is already dead."

The moment the man spoke the word "dead," Kenneth slammed his fist into the captain's face, sending him flying off his feet and into the wooden wall behind him, which shuddered and sent plumes of dust from the gaps of the boards into the air. The captain slumped to the ground. Aaron saw cracks in the wood where his back had struck. The captain held his hand to his nose, which poured blood between his fingers. Without a word, Kenneth walked to the door. With a single kick it flew open hard enough to crack and splinter the wood around the latch. A moment after he walked out, several guards rushed in. Upon seeing the captain on the floor, they rushed to his aid.

Claudia crossed her arms and looked down at the captain. "You're lucky he only punched you."

Aaron walked out of the room and outside. He scanned the street until he caught sight of Kenneth heading back toward the north gate. Aaron ran to catch up to him. When he did, Kenneth didn't even turn to look at him as they walked.

"Kenneth!" Aaron said. "Where are you going?" Aaron stepped in front of him, but Kenneth moved around him without speaking and continued down the street. Frustrated, Aaron started shouting at him, "Kenneth, what are you doing?"

"I won't let him die down there," Kenneth replied without breaking stride.

"So what's your plan? The way we came out is blocked!"

Aaron knew there was another entrance, but they had no idea where it was. The one they had exited was now blocked by a cave-in. They hadn't planned on blocking their way back into the cavern, but when they'd emerged it was still well before sunrise. Instead of retreating into their caves, the satlis would have pursued them into the forest. Out in the open, they would have had no chance against the creatures. So Claudia had used an ingera as a last resort—two, in fact. She'd lit them and tossed them up the slope over the mouth of the cavern as they exited. A loud blast had followed, and then a wave of force Aaron had never experienced knocked the breath out of him. When he'd looked back, the cave had been blocked by rubble from a rockslide caused by the curious orbs.

Kenneth gritted his teeth and set his jaw firmly: "I'm going to find the other entrance and bring him out."

"How? You have no idea where it is!"

They reached the north gate. Kenneth shoved aside the guard by the manway. "Then I'll find it." He threw the door open and walked out without looking back.

Aaron stared for a moment in disbelief. Kenneth was acting irrationally. It was nearly impossible to find one particular cave in a mountain range that was dotted with them. Without knowing what else to do, Aaron turned around and started back. Hopefully Claudia would go and talk some sense into Kenneth. He would just have to hurry before he got too far from the city. He rushed past confused bystanders and nearly fell more than once before he found Claudia as she was leaving the clinic. Her face was beet red and her hands balled into fists.

"Claudia!" Aaron said. "Kenneth went out the gate. He said he's going after Daniel."

She brushed past him. "So am I."

Aaron stood still, dumbfounded. Everyone was brushing him off and ignoring what actually made sense. The chances of finding the entrance were so slim that without a detailed map of the mountains or a guide who knew the area, they had no way of knowing where to look. It didn't help that Kenneth and Claudia were outright ignoring him, something he was entirely unused to.

He followed her. Like Kenneth, she never turned to look at him as he spoke. "You want to find one cave in a range of mountains stretching from one coast to the other," he said. "How are the three of us supposed to do that? It could come out near the peaks for all we know."

"Two of us. You're staying here."

For a moment he struggled to speak. "I-I'm what?"

Now Claudia stopped to face him. "Aaron, it was one thing to take you through the den because we didn't have a choice. But now we do. You will stay here and wait. We'll be gone for no more than two days regardless of what we find." She turned and began walking again.

"But I can help! He's my friend. You have to let me come!" Only now did the words actually hit him. Daniel was his friend, his only one. Despite the many other things afforded to him, Aaron had never had the luxury of friends.

They reached the gates. Claudia placed her hands on his shoulders. "Aaron, I'm sorry, but no. Kenneth and I will move faster on our own and we'll be out there after dark in satlis hunting grounds. It's not safe for you." She reached into a pouch at her belt and withdrew five silver marks. "Here," she said. "Take this. There's an inn right here by the gate. Rent a room and wait."

Aaron tried desperately to come up with an excuse as to why he had to go with them. "What about the guards?" he asked. "Kenneth just assaulted the watch captain. They won't be happy with us. Is it smart to just leave me here?"

"I smoothed it over with him as best I could. If you just stay at the inn they'll leave you alone."

The guard opened the manway for Claudia. She left just as Kenneth had, leaving Aaron to throw up his arms in frustration as he watched her go. At this point there was nothing for him to do but wait for them to return. He looked around until he located the inn and strode over, his head low and his mind racing. Without breaking stride, he pushed the front door open. The inn's main room was smaller than he had expected, with only a few people sitting at the bar enjoying a drink and another couple across the room next to a hearth set in the wall. Walking slowly, his eyes looking at the floor, Aaron approached the bar and waited for the tender to finish serving a young girl her drink.

"What can I do for you, young man?" The bartender spoke with a gruff, gravelly tone.

"I just need a room for a couple of days," Aaron said. He handed him the marks, which the bartender quickly took and counted.

When he was done, he nodded. "I'll go get you a key." He disappeared into the back room, leaving Aaron to stare at the bar top as he waited.

After a few long moments, the girl across the bar leaned toward him. "You look like you need a drink," she said.

Aaron glanced at her as she slid him a full mug, presumably hers.

The bartender returned and handed Aaron a small rusty, key. "Second on the left. Stairs are through that door." He motioned to the back of the room.

Aaron thanked him and ordered a bowl of stew. Now that there was a moment to sit still he suddenly realized he hadn't eaten in well over twelve hours. The man again disappeared into the back. The girl across from him got up and moved to the seat next to Aaron. She leaned forward and smiled.

"I'm Griffon," she said. "You're the guy that came in with those Dragon Guards, right? What's your name?"

"Aaron."

"So what happened to the one with the blonde hair? She looked pretty bad when you all showed up."

Aaron didn't answer. He just sat with his head in his hands.

Griffon bit her lip. "So...where are your Dragon Guard friends?"

He turned to look at her. "Look, Griffon, I'm kind of having a bad day. One of my friends might die, another might already be dead, and

I'm stuck here by myself for about two days until the other two get back. So I'd really like to be left alone right now."

They were quiet for a while. She swirled her drink before taking a sip. The bartender returned and placed a bowl in front of Aaron before leaving to attend to some new arrivals.

Aaron lifted his spoon as Griffon spoke again: "So what happened to all of you?"

He dropped his spoon into the bowl, causing several drops of the thick brown broth to splash out and spread as they landed on the smooth bar top. He rubbed his temples. "You don't give up, do you?" he said.

"It's kind of a new thing for me. So what happened?"

"Do you want the long version?"

She shrugged. "Seems like we both have the time."

CHAPTER THIRTEEN

25th of Horace, 26th year of the Fourth Age.

ASHARP, THROBBING, NEARLY unbearable pain was all Daniel could feel. There was nothing but a constant pulse that originated in his right ribcage and spread outward, in a beat matching the rhythm of his heart. Daniel tried to sit up and was greeted with shooting pain so intense that it threatened to make him black out. In spite of the overwhelming discomfort, he managed to sit up and gently place a hand on his side. Fresh waves of pain made him wince and lay down again. He slowed his breathing and kept it shallow, which helped somewhat.

He strained his eyes to see anything around him, but he was in total darkness. He didn't feel his pack on his shoulders, so he started to grope the cold ground, hoping it had landed nearby. After nearly a minute of finding only rock, he started to panic. What if it had fallen off of him during his tumble and was stuck along the slope? What if there was another drop near him that he couldn't see? Daniel's mind raced with countless scenarios that only intensified his fear. Finally, he felt his fingers brush over a thick leather shoulder strap. He uttered an audible sigh of relief that made his side flare with fresh pain.

Daniel pulled the pack to him. His stomach sank when he found no torch strapped to the bottom. With another sigh, he resumed his blind search. It had to have landed near the pack. He ran his hands over the dirt and across stones for only a few moments until he gripped the smooth wood. He relaxed slightly and placed it across his knees as he started to rummage through the pack. He was surprised and thankful that the glass vial of oil had remained intact. He quickly uncorked it and poured some onto the rope wrapped around the end of the torch, trying his best not to waste a drop. Using a quarter of the vial, he then resealed it and pulled his fire-starting kit from the pack. It was a rough steel file, along with a square of spark stone with a small handle attached to one side. He gripped the handle in one hand and started to drag the file across the stone, sending sparks down to the soaked rope and bursts of light that illuminated the dark cave in quick, blinding flashes.

After several attempts, a flame flickered to life. Daniel held the torch aloft for several moments as the flame grew and his eyes adjusted. When he was able to see properly, he stood and scanned his surroundings. His sword lay just at the edge of the light. He quickly retrieved it and placed it back in the sheath. The simple weight of it reassured him, causing him to breathe a sigh of relief. He looked at the slope he had tumbled down. It was far too steep for him to climb in his condition. Even if he could, he wasn't sure he would want to. The sun had surely risen at this point, so the satlis that hadn't been in the cave before would be now.

Instead, Daniel chose to make his way down the tunnel. Barden had told them this path would lead out eventually. He just hoped it wasn't too far. He kept one hand on the wall as he walked, making sure to check behind him periodically, though he had no idea what he would do if he found something following him. It just made him feel more in control of the situation. For a long while, he walked with only the sounds of his light breathing and footfalls to accompany him in the hollow tunnel. When he came to a steep upward slope, he paused to examine it.

It wasn't nearly as steep as the one he had fallen down but all the same it made his side hurt simply thinking about climbing it. He chose to sit for a moment and mentally prepare himself for the task. He took his pack off and dug through it until he found his meager supply of dried meats and bread. He pulled apart the small loaf and was disappointed to find it was stale. He devoured it all the same. As Daniel ate, his mind wandered to Mila and the others. He hoped they'd made it out all right.

The trio had surely encountered worse out in the wilds before, and Aaron was capable enough, more than Daniel at the very least. He still worried about Mila. The last thing he remembered was her pushing him aside and the satlis tackling her to the ground. If anything happened to her on his account, he wasn't sure if he could forgive himself for not being more aware of what was happening around him, for not being able to help.

Determined to make it out of the cavern and see what had become of his friends, Daniel placed his remaining food back into the pack and threw it across his shoulders before turning to the rock wall in his path. He began the slow and painful climb, taking extra time to ensure his hand and footholds were sturdy before putting his full weight on them. The last thing he wanted was to fall down another rocky slope. It was a miracle he hadn't been killed the first time. Twice he nearly did fall, once when his handhold gave way and again when his foot slipped on a damp stone. The climb itself strained his side, causing him to wince with every movement. Finally, after what seemed like hours but was probably closer to thirty minutes, he made it to the top and rolled onto his back.

Daniel took a short respite to regain his breath before he got to his feet and started down the path again. After only a few steps, he stopped short. Behind him, he heard several light scratches, followed by what he guessed were pebbles falling down the slope. He whirled around and looked down the drop, extending the torch over the edge. The firelight illuminated far enough for him to see about halfway down, but no further. He saw nothing save for the skid marks where he'd nearly fallen near the top. He stayed a moment longer to listen but all was quiet.

Now more cautious than before, he turned and continued down the tunnel, glancing back after every few steps. He focused on listening for a break in the otherwise rhythmic sounds he made as he went. After another several minutes he heard something again, not scratching but the sound of a stone rolling across the ground. He held the torch out behind him and scanned the darkness. His breath caught in his throat.

Daniel's gaze locked onto a set of sickly green eyes staring back at him from the shadows, just beyond the light of the torch. The satlis never moved and never blinked as he slowly backed away. With his free arm, in agonizing slowness, he drew his sword while trying to keep his fear in check. The eyes were at the very edge of the torchlight, reflecting the flickering flames. It gave them an eerie yellow glow that flickered back to their natural green. The satlis continued to stare at him. When he had backed far enough away that the torch no longer illuminated its eyes, it remained in the shadows.

Then everything happened at once. Daniel lost his footing and stumbled backwards. He didn't fall, but for a moment he had to take his eyes off where the satlis had been. When he looked back, it was charging at him with incredible speed. It was one of the smaller ones, about five feet long which meant it was a male. Though no less deadly. He regained his footing quickly and readied himself just as Kenneth had shown him—sword held out in front of him, the tip pointed skyward and slightly forward, his feet shoulder-width apart. He held the torch behind him and tried to keep his muscles loose and "springy," as Kenneth had said many times during their short training session.

The satlis was on him quickly. It lunged with its mouth spread wide. Dull yellow saliva dripped from its fangs. Daniel thrust his sword forward, jabbing at the exposed belly as it soared through the air toward him. But both it and he were off balance. The tip of the blade went wide. Instead, he cut along its lower side and wounded it. It collided with him and they both were thrown to the ground.

The wind was knocked out of Daniel. The satlis lifted its head and was about to bite down on his neck. He barely reacted in time, striking out with the torch and hitting it in the side of the head, causing it to reel back.

The satlis clawed at its freshly burned eye as Daniel rose and sprinted down the tunnel as fast as he could. His side screamed in protest and he struggled to breathe. Each step jostled his ribs and sent fresh flares of pain through his body, but he kept running. The cave began to slowly grow brighter. In the distance, Daniel saw daylight. He was almost out. He suddenly felt lighter. The pain began to dull. He quickened his pace.

To his left, Daniel saw a blur of motion. He skidded to a stop as the satlis darted past him.

It took him a moment to register what the pain in his legs was. As it had passed, the satlis had whipped out its tail. Quills had dug into his left calf, ripping his trousers and tearing gashes in his flesh. Thankfully, the tail had only grazed him, but it was enough to make him stumble and drop to one knee.

The satlis whirled around and blocked the way forward. The side of its face was charred. It snarled viciously as it took a cautious step forward. Daniel noticed it seemed to favor its left side and limped with every step. Its breathing was also heavy and ragged. It was injured. Then Daniel remembered the satlis Kenneth had thrown down the slope.

Daniel saw the creature's muscles tense. He readied himself to parry another lunge. Instead, however, it abruptly turned and struck out with its tail. Daniel dropped low as the tail went high over his head. He backpedaled as quickly as he could, trying to get out of its reach. But he was too close to move far enough in time. The tail swept out again, lower this time, causing the quills to rip into his right hand as he lifted it instinctively to try to stop the strike. The blow left gashes across the back of his hand and ripped the sword from his grip, sending it skipping across the ground.

Daniel managed to keep himself from screaming by biting his tongue. He clutched his hand to his chest in an attempt to slow the flow of gushing blood. Now that he was disarmed, the limping satlis advanced toward him. It seemed to understand that Daniel was vulnerable without the sword, so now was the time to charge in for the kill. Yet it took slow and cautious steps as it eyed Daniel's left hand. Then Daniel realized— fire—he still held the torch! A rough idea formed in his head. He held the torch in front of him like a sword. At the same time, he slid his pack off his right arm and set it on the ground. He dug through the contents until he felt the glass vial.

Daniel never took his eyes off the creature. It stared at him with a new sense of caution now that fire directly blocked the path to its prey. Daniel pulled out the vial, held it as best he could in his injured hand, and waited for the creature to come closer. He knew he would only have one chance at his idea. He wasn't even sure that it would work. He was likely to hurt himself more than the satlis, but at this point he had no other ideas or options. It was this or death.

The stalemate lasted only a moment longer before the satlis leaped at him.

Daniel raised the torch in front of him. He was again knocked to the ground, with the satlis on top of him. Holding the torch above him against the animal's neck, he pushed as hard he could to keep its snapping jaw and claws at bay. At the same time, he pushed against the beast's chest with his legs. In spite of his efforts and the animal's injuries, its strength and longer reach allowed it to run its claws along his shoulders and chest, tearing his tunic and skin.

With his injured right hand, Daniel raised the vial and smashed it with all his strength against the side of the satlis's head. The moment he connected, glass shattered and oil drenched its face, along with Daniel's hand and forearm. The glass cut into both of them. The satlis reeled back and screeched as it clawed at its own face in an attempt to dig the shards out. The satlis managed only to push the glass fragments deeper in its blind confusion and pain. During its frantic reaction, Daniel scrambled to his feet, his screaming ribs protesting. With pulses of pain and blackness at the edges of his vision, he watched the animal for a moment, waiting for the chance he needed.

When he saw it, he swung the torch wide, striking the satlis in the face and setting the oil that coated its face aflame in a quick and brilliant flash that engulfed its entire head. The creature panicked and reared back onto its hind legs as it furiously attacked an unseen foe. Daniel backpedaled to avoid its wild flailing and frantically searched the ground until he found and retrieved his sword. Turning back to the animal, he watched as it continued to panic and inhale flames, each outcry of pain leading only to more. It lashed out with its claws at the empty air. When it pulled them back in, readying to lash out again, Daniel lunged forward. He sank his sword into its chest halfway up the length of the blade.

The satlis bellowed again and struck out a final time with the last of its strength. It fell, catching Daniel across the chest with a claw swipe before hitting the ground. It writhed for several moments before finally going still. The smell of burning flesh hung thick in the air. Daniel sank to his knees and pressed his injured hand to his chest. As his adrenaline receded, the pain began to fully register. If every breath and movement had been pain before, it was pure agony now.

He rose and tried to remove his sword from the satlis's chest. With what little strength he had left, it took him nearly a minute to pull it free from the animal. When he finally did, it came quickly and made him stumble and nearly fall to the ground again. The sudden jolt of motion caused pain so intense in his injured leg and ribs that he nearly passed out. He took a moment to gather himself before he slowly turned and picked up his pack. He was so weak that he simply dragged it along behind him as he hobbled to the mouth of the cave.

The danger was gone, but Daniel found himself still gripping his sword firmly in his hands. He finally stepped into the light, not bothering to sheathe or drop it. The sun was setting. Though the sudden brightness was blinding, he welcomed not being able to see because of the light instead of its absence. He was higher on the mountainside than he hoped he would be. He began a slow and painful climb down the rough hillside. He stumbled and slid, barely registering what he was doing. Before he realized it, he had reached the bottom and was leaning against a tree to catch his breath. He put a hand to his chest through his shredded and wet tunic. It came away red. In his haze he had one thought: Stop the bleeding.

He walked through the forest in a stupor and fell to his knees. He got up. Stumbled. Got up again. Each time he fell, it became more of a struggle to rise. The fourth time he fell he couldn't bring himself to rise again. He simply knelt upon the ground. Daniel felt like he was floating. Everything was spinning and he struggled to breathe. He tried once more to rise, placing a hand on the ground to steady himself, but his hand buckled under his weight and he fell on his side. Even with blurred vision and only half a right mind, he spotted one thing that seemed out of place in the forest. It was a golden crown, sitting in the grass beneath a tree.

In a moment of clarity he realized that couldn't be right. He had to be hallucinating. His mind and vision cleared slightly, allowing him to see a dozen other splashes of gold around the first. Suddenly he knew what they were. A distant and seemingly useless memory crept to the forefront of his mind. Mila and an old woman. They were speaking about flower extracts and salves made from their cores. *"A salve to stop the bleeding."*

Daniel had a surge of strength and managed to crawl to the patch of king's bloom. He ripped several of the plants from the ground and stripped away the petals, leaving only the white pollen core. He looked around. When he spotted a flat stone, he set the petals on top in a pile and lay the flat of his sword across them to crush and mash them down as best he could. He cut his hand across the blade and mixed in his blood, taking no notice of the pain. When the combination had become a thick lumpy paste, he caked his wounds with the crude salve. The moment his wounds were covered, the bleeding stopped. Daniel managed to breathe a sigh of relief as a comforting, cool tingling spread outward from the wounds. He closed his eyes and collapsed onto the damp grass under the darkening sky.

CHAPTER FOURTEEN

26ᵗʰ of Horace, 26ᵗʰ year of the Fourth Age.

AARON TAPPED HIS foot anxiously as he leaned against the wall of The Barge. Kenneth and Claudia had left to try to find the second entrance to the satlis den and, hopefully, Daniel along with it. That had been late the previous afternoon. Now it was approaching a second nightfall. Aaron didn't like the idea of his friends being out there for another night. Rather than sit inside, he chose to wait outside with his eyes on the manway of the north gate. He crossed his arms to ward off the autumn breeze and sighed. He'd been here for several hours and didn't plan on moving until Claudia and Kenneth walked through that gate with Daniel in tow.

"You're still here, huh?"

Aaron turned to see Griffon step out of the inn holding two mugs with slight wisps of steam rising from each. She handed him one. He smiled and asked, "What is it?"

She leaned against the wall next to him and sipped her drink: "Cider."

He looked at the drink and shrugged. He took a swig, felt the warmth radiate throughout his body, and was pleasantly surprised by the flavor. He'd never had cider before. Now he saw why his mother favored the drink so much.

Griffon was quiet and watched the manway with him for a moment. "So," she said, "are you going to stand here all night?"

He answered without turning to look at her: "If that's how long it takes."

"You could still come with me, you know. Captain Andrews is kind of a pushover. I'm sure he'd let you aboard for the last leg of the journey. You could certainly help more than I do."

"I'm not going to just leave them behind."

"What if they don't find him?"

"They will."

She sighed. "Okay, what if they do find him?"

It took him a moment to realize the meaning of her words. "He'll be fine."

"I hope so," she said. "I really do." She downed the rest of her cider and moved away from the wall. "Well, for what it's worth, I guess I'll be seeing you at Vigil pretty soon."

He smiled. "I look forward to it."

She smiled back before turning to walk into the city and toward the harbor. He really did look forward to their next meeting. She seemed rough at first glance, but she seemed far more caring than she wanted to let on. He really was thankful she had stuck around until the very last moment for him. When she was out of sight, he turned back to the manway and sighed.

He couldn't stand this. He hated not knowing. Even if it turned out badly, it would still be better than the waiting. In addition to that, Mila's condition was worsening by the hour. He had gone to see her briefly that morning. Her skin had been nearly devoid of color. The local medics were using the salve that Claudia had provided before her departure, but even it seemed to have no lasting effect. He shook his head and tried to shake the fear off. He couldn't think about that now. He sighed again before drinking the rest of his cider and placing the mug on the ground.

Another hour passed before the guards atop the wall signaled for the manway to be opened. Aaron moved away from the wall and made his way to the door at a full sprint. It swung open and the guards stepped aside to allow Claudia through. She grabbed the closest guard by the shoulders and spoke to him in hurried words. When she finished, he nodded and ran down the street.

Aaron skidded to a stop next to her. "Claudia!" he said. "What happened? Did you find him? Is he okay?"

She smiled and placed a hand on his shoulder. "He's fine. A little banged up, but okay for the most part."

Then Kenneth entered through the manway, cradling an unconscious Daniel in his arms. Aaron hadn't expected his friend to be unscathed, but he didn't think he would be this bad. Daniel's tunic was shredded and bloody, exposing his chest and shoulders, which were coated with a dull, yellow paste. His hands and calf were crudely bandaged with cloth torn from Kenneth's sleeve, with more of the paste seeping through. Daniel's skin was pale and dotted with dark purple bruises. His right ribs looked almost black.

Aaron's voice was a whisper: "What happened?"

The three of them hurried toward the apothecary's shop as Kenneth recounted what they'd discovered. They'd found Daniel in the forest near the base of the mountains just as night fell. He had managed to prepare some king's bloom to treat his injuries and stop the bleeding before he'd collapsed next to the flowers. While Claudia treated his wounds properly, Kenneth had followed Daniel's rather obvious trail up the mountain a short ways and into the cave. Had there not been a trail leading to it, he doubted they'd have ever found it. It was above the tree line, the opening small and hidden behind an outcropping of rock. Unless someone was right on top of it, one would never know it was there.

Not far inside the cave, Kenneth had found the corpse of a satlis. Its face was burned beyond recognition. It had been stabbed through the heart and had a large gash across its ribs. Not far away, Daniel's still-burning torch lay on the ground, indicating the encounter had been recent. Once his wounds had been properly treated, they'd started back for Navia. But with night upon them, they'd chosen to set camp in a clearing where they could properly guard Daniel and keep watch in the satlis hunting grounds during the long night.

When they arrived at the apothecary's shop, one of the medics that had been treating Mila was waiting for them. He moved to take Daniel, but Kenneth scowled at him, making the man shrink away. Instead, the medic led them to a room on the far side of the building with a single bed and a water basin with several towels and various medical supplies set at its side atop a table. Kenneth laid Daniel on the bed and Claudia immediately began inspecting his body, looking for visible wounds and any that she might have missed in the woods. Kenneth excused himself to check on Mila.

When Claudia had finished, she wet a cloth from the basin and cleaned her hands. "Well, I don't seem to have missed anything," she said. "He has two broken ribs, but other than that it's all surface injuries, bruises, gashes, and the like. It's a good thing he sealed that chest wound or he might have bled out before we found him."

Aaron breathed a sigh of relief. "So, he'll be fine then?"

"Eventually, yes. Though he will have quite a few new scars."

"How long will it be until we can leave for Vigil?"

Claudia's expression changed. She avoided Aaron's eyes as she spoke. "It's going to...be a while."

He had been afraid of this. "How long, exactly?"

She sighed and continued to avoid his gaze. "About six weeks until Daniel can leave. His ribs need time to heal. Until then, we can't let him ride or walk that far."

Aaron rubbed his temples. "Then two more after that for the actual trip."

She turned to look him in the eyes. "I'm so sorry, Aaron. He won't make it before winter."

Aaron leaned back in his chair. He'd had a feeling that would be the case after seeing the injuries Daniel had sustained. He hadn't known Daniel long, but that didn't matter. Aaron ached for his friend. He knew that this was something Daniel had wanted more than anything.

Aaron brought his hands to his face and closed his eyes. "We were so close."

Claudia pursed her lips. "You can still make it, Aaron," she said. "I'll stay here and treat him and Mila while Kenneth goes with you the rest of the way to Vigil."

Aaron shook his head. "No. I'm not going without him."

Claudia shook her head. "Aaron, be reasonable. I know a lot has happened these last few days, but you can't pass on this. It's your only chance."

"It's his too. He'll be too old the next time you recruit. We both will! He's been waiting for so long, I can't just leave him here while I go on. It isn't fair or right."

"Aaron. Regardless of the way life was for you in Dalisia, this isn't something you can *make* happen, no matter how much you want to. If he can't make it before next year then that's just how it has to be. As much as I agree that this isn't right, we can't move Daniel that far by foot. Even if we did have a horse, the ride would hurt him just as much if not more."

Aaron ran his hands over his face and through his hair in frustration. He knew he couldn't get his way like he did in Dalisia, though even back home he'd try his best not to abuse his family's status. But no matter what happened or how he did it, he didn't want to leave Daniel behind. Yet he saw no way to move him safely.

Then he remembered something so obvious he felt like a fool for not thinking of it before. Griffon! She was traveling by sea to Vigil. She'd said the ship was leaving that evening if everything worked as the captain planned. If he hurried to the harbor, they might still be there.

"What about by sea," Aaron asked. "Would he be able to travel by ship?" Aaron felt his heart swell with hope.

Claudia pondered it for a moment before shrugging. "He'd be fine as long as the sea was fairly calm. But we don't have the gold to pay for passage on a ship."

Without stopping to explain himself, Aaron turned and started out the door. He heard Claudia call out to him, but he kept going. He had no time to make her understand his plans if he had any hope of catching the ship before it departed. That is, if it hadn't already. He exited through the main door and ran at a full sprint through the crowded streets toward the harbor. His heart beat double time as he prayed they were still there. He pushed through groups of people to reach the harbor, where he jumped down the short set of stairs onto wooden docks. He looked from ship to ship and realized he had no idea what Griffon's ship looked like or even what the name was.

The one thing he did have was the name of the captain. He looked for the harbormaster and spotted the man jotting something in his logbook while speaking to another man who looked upset. Aaron ran up to the harbormaster, grabbed him by the shoulders, and turned him around.

The man looked almost terrified as Aaron spoke quickly and a little louder than he had intended: "Which ship belongs to Captain Andrews? Is he still here?"

It took the man a moment to register what Aaron was asking, but when he did he scanned through his records until he found the page he was looking for. "Andrews captains *The Royal Jewel* at dock twenty-five." He pointed toward the opposite end of the harbor.

Aaron thanked him and ran in that direction, counting the dock numbers as he went. Thankfully, when he reached twenty-five, he found the ship was still there. He took a moment to catch his breath. The ship in front of him was like any other trade vessel, built for storage rather than speed. It was wide and long, with about a dozen crewmen loading various crates and barrels into the hold via a pulley crane connected to the main mast. He looked down the length of the dock that ran along-side the ship and saw Griffon sitting at the end, her feet over the water, looking at the ocean beyond.

Aaron stopped just short of her. When he spoke, she was clearly star-tled at his presence: "I need your help."

"What happened?" she asked, her smile quickly fading.

He gave her a brief explanation of what had happened and their inability to take Daniel the rest of the way by land. She listened quietly and nodded occasionally.

He sighed and extended his hands in front of him, palms up. "So I need to talk to the captain," he said, "to try to convince him to take not just me but Daniel and the others as well."

"I don't know, Aaron," she said. "I mean, you have no idea what had to happen for him to let me on board without having to pay full price. One more person I don't think would be hard to swing, but five? For no extra pay? I don't think he'll go for it."

He shrugged. "I've got to try."

She shook her head and sighed. "I'll go get him. I can't promise he'll even come down here though."

Griffon went up the ramp to the deck. Aaron waited patiently for her return while he watched the crewmen work in a flawless rhythm from years of experience. After several long and agonizing minutes, Griffon made her way back down, followed by a man who looked irritated to even be entertaining the idea of speaking to Aaron.

"Well, boy, give me the story, and it better be a good one," the captain said, already sounding like he was exhausted by the whole thing.

Aaron gave him a brief overview of what had happened. He skimmed over the unimportant details to get his point across quickly. When he was finished, he took another quick breath. "So," he said, "that's everything."

Andrews didn't say anything at first. He simply stood there with his arms crossed and stared at Aaron with stern and weathered eyes. "I have no qualms about taking on more passengers," he finally said. "Gives me and the crew a few extra marks to make it through winter. But unless I'm actually paid those marks, I'll have to deny you. I've already done my charity by taking the girl on board."

He turned away, but Aaron dashed forward and stood between the captain and his ship. "I can pay you, just not up front."

Andrews seemed on the verge of outright laughter. "Good try kid, but I'm no fool."

"Do you have paper?"

"What?"

"Paper, and wax for a seal."

The captain narrowed his eyes. "Why?"

With a heavy sigh, Aaron reached down to his belt. He took a moment to reconsider what he was about to do. He had wanted to make it to Vigil without having to resort to this, to prove he didn't need his father's approval. But this wasn't for him. He truly felt that this was worth the price of his father being able to lord it over him. For that reason alone, he handed a thin leather pouch to Andrews, no larger than the palm of his hand.

The captain held the pouch gingerly in his hand, clearly skeptical. "This is?"

"Just open it."

Andrews sighed, unsnapped the pouch, and dumped its contents into his hand. A single gold ring. On its own it was rather unremarkable, plainly designed though well-made.

What made Andrews raise an eyebrow was the sigil etched into it. "Where did you get this?" he asked in a whisper.

Aaron sighed. "My father."

Andrews lifted the ring and inspected the sigil, a six-pointed star with an X behind it.

"If this isn't real, you know you'll be arrested," Andrews said. "As will I, if I choose to entertain this."

"It's real," Aaron replied. "I just need to write the payment order, sign it, and seal it. Then you can give it to my father when you return to Dalisia. He'll make sure you get paid."

"If he doesn't?"

"He will, and if not... Well, you know where to find us."

CHAPTER FIFTEEN

28ᵗʰ of Horace, 26ᵗʰ year of the Fourth Age.

DANIEL FELT TERRIBLE. He forced his eyes open with more effort than he ever thought it would take. The first thing he saw was a wooden ceiling lined with support struts. He heard the sound of rolling waves and the creaking of wood, as well as dozens of footsteps above him. He was lying in a rope hammock next to a wall and covered by a heavy wool blanket that did little to ward off the cold. He turned his head to see a dozen or so identical hammocks lining the room, along with several unlit oil lanterns attached to the beams the hammocks hung from.

He felt himself roll slightly to one side and then slowly to the other before going back again. He was on a ship at sea, that much at least was clear. He had no idea how he'd gotten here. The last thing he remembered was a satlis attacking him in the caves as he tried to make his way out, and then nothing. He tried to speak into the poorly lit space but managed only a strained croak followed by a fit of coughing so painful it made his vision blur. He gripped his side involuntarily, which only caused the pain to flare more the moment he touched it. After a few moments, the coughing subsided and his vision cleared.

"Should have guessed you were the one making all that noise. About time you woke up."

Daniel craned his neck and saw a blonde girl about his age standing on a set of steep stairs.

"Where am I?" His voice was so hoarse and strained that he worried she wouldn't understand him.

"You're on *The Royal Jewel*, a trading ship bound for Dawnstone, with a short stop at Vigil." She strode over and leaned against the pole at his feet.

A ship headed for Vigil. The gap in his memory worried him. "How did I get here?"

"I don't know all the details, but your friend Aaron managed to get you all on board."

"Aaron…how?"

"I'm not really sure. He didn't seem to want to talk about the details."

Daniel was curious how out of all of them, Aaron had managed this. But it would have to wait. "How long was I out?"

"Two days since we left Navia. But you were out before that."

He laid his arm across his eyes and sighed. He supposed it could have been worse. At least he was still alive. Though he didn't quite feel like it. His head and side throbbed insistently and his hand was bandaged and numb up to his elbow, while his calf felt as if there were a vice around it.

His voice was gravely and hoarse when he tried to speak again. The girl took notice and handed him a water skin from her belt. He took it and happily drank half of it, reveling in the cool and soothing feeling in his throat.

He spoke again as he handed it back to her: "What exactly happened to me?"

She shrugged. "I don't have the whole story. You'd have to ask one of the Dragon Guards. They found you out in the woods."

He was told to wait while she went above deck to get someone who could properly explain. She was gone for only a minute before Claudia quietly came down the steps. She dragged over a nearby stool and gingerly took a seat near his feet.

"I'm glad you're all right, Daniel," she said. She fussed with her hands while she spoke. "How are you feeling?"

"My side hurts pretty badly. So do a lot of things. Otherwise I guess I'm okay."

"Well, that's not going to end anytime soon. You have two broken ribs, so be careful with everything you do. You also have some pretty deep gashes along your chest and shoulders, and I have to ask you to refrain from using your hand until it heals."

"So how did I get here?" Daniel asked. "The last thing I remember was a satlis attacking me, and then it just sort of goes black."

Claudia nodded, then briefly recounted how they'd found him and about the satlis corpse. She told him how Aaron had met Griffon and how he had come up with the plan to transport them all by ship, though she avoided explaining exactly how Aaron had managed to convince the captain to allow them aboard. Daniel pressed to find out more, but after a few attempts he let the matter drop.

He smiled and touched the fresh bandages that were wrapped around his chest and shoulders. "So I treated my own wounds? Being with Mila in Grey Gate was more of a learning experience than I thought it was. Never would have known what king's bloom did without following her around."

Claudia didn't reply. Instead, she looked down at her feet.

Daniel noticed her change in demeanor. "Claudia, what's wrong?"

"I'm sorry, Daniel," she said, her voice cracking.

"What happened?"

She looked up. There were tears in her eyes now. "The satlis...the bite is too close to her heart. I can't stop it. All I've done till now is slow down the venom."

He stared at her for several long moments. "Until now? So you mean..."

Claudia wiped at her eyes. "I don't think she's going to make it to Vigil."

"How long?" he croaked out the words as he felt a lump rise in his throat.

"You should go see her."

Daniel was in shock. He couldn't breathe. It was as if the air in his lungs had been snatched away.

After he stayed silent for a long while, Claudia stood and placed a hand on his shoulder. "The captain allowed us to treat her in his quarters," she said. "Come on, we'll go together."

Claudia helped him rise. The next minute was a daze. Before he knew it, he felt salt spray on his face and had to shield his eyes against the sun. Crewmen were everywhere on the deck and in the rigging above. It was a torrent of noise, with words being thrown around that Daniel had no way of knowing the meaning of. He'd never been at sea before and wished he had more of a chance to actually enjoy the experience, but right now that seemed unimportant.

He crossed his arms to ward off the cold air, which was only made cooler by the constant spray of water and rush of the wind. His legs felt heavy as Claudia gently pulled him toward the rear of the ship. They stopped before a rather plain but large door set between two sets of stairs leading up to the ship's helm.

Claudia gently nudged him toward the door. "She should be awake," she said. "If you need me, I'll be right here by the door."

Daniel nodded, gripped the simple handle, and swung the door open. The captain's quarters, oddly enough, were rather sparse. A desk sat against one wall with a shabby chair next to it. The walls were bare save for a map of Edaren. The floor had a small tattered and torn rug. At the far end of the room, beneath a small, square window, was a large, cushioned bed. Mila lay there, propped up by several oversized pillows. Her eyes were closed. Her chest rose and fell in a gentle rhythm. Daniel took a few steps forward before trying to speak.

"Hi, Mila." His voice cracked when he said her name. The sinking feeling in his gut grew worse.

She opened her eyes and lifted her head to look at him. Her eyes took his breath away. They were almost completely red. "Hey," she said in a weak voice. "Glad you're okay."

He nodded. "Thanks to you."

She smiled briefly and laid her head back onto the pillows. "It's my job."

He felt his heart twinge and struggled to speak. He felt like he was choking. "Not to die."

She opened her eyes again and was quiet for a few moments before waving him over. He sat on the edge of the bed and waited for her to speak.

She leaned forward slowly, wincing as she did so, and gripped his hand. "I know what you're doing."

He just stared at her and shook his head. "What?"

"This is not your fault."

He shook his head and bit his lip. She was wrong. It *was* his fault. If only he'd paid attention and not simply stood there, left himself out in the open and vulnerable to the satlis attack. She wouldn't have had to take his place. She did what she did because he was foolish.

She gripped his hand harder. "Stop. I know what you're thinking. You did not make me do this. I made a choice to step in front of you, and I'm okay with it."

He balled his hands into fists and shook his head. "I wasn't worth it!"

"Daniel," she said, leaning forward further and gripping his chin, forcing him to look at her, "living is not a thing to be ashamed of. Never feel guilty because you didn't die. If you don't think you're worth it, change that. Be worth it. If you really think I made the wrong choice, then make it the right one. But I want you to know this is one of the few choices in my life I don't regret."

Daniel couldn't see through the tears welling in his eyes. He lifted his arm to wipe them away. He hated this. No one should die for him. He would never be worth it.

They were quiet for what seemed like ages before Mila sighed and spoke with a tone far too chipper for the circumstances. "Did I ever tell you about the time I was in general training and I almost set Vigil's library on fire?"

He lifted his head and stared at her. "What are you talking about?"

"It was my first year, and we were in the middle of a history lesson. The lesson had to be moved to the evening after a break-in to the vault in the keep. Everything was chaotic for a while after that. But because of that, the lesson was conducted by candlelight in the library. I was not the most graceful person when I was younger," she said with a short laugh. "I was sitting by myself at the far end of the table, and when I had lit the candle in my lantern I forgot to close the lantern door on it."

Daniel shook his head. "Mila, I don't—"

"Let me finish. I forgot about the door and when I moved the book in front of me, and I accidentally pushed the lantern off the table. No one seemed to notice. When I bent down to pick it up, I saw I'd set the carpet on fire. I was panicking and didn't want anyone to find out, so I did my best to put it out as quietly as I could. In my haste I thought to just put the book over it to snuff out the flames, but I covered them with the book *open*. Needless to say, the pages caught fire. I shut the book to snuff them out and gathered my thoughts enough to do what I should have the first time and slammed the book down on top of the flames, leather cover down. Everyone in the room heard and turned to look at me and all I could manage to do was shrug."

In spite of himself, Daniel felt a smile creep across his face. He gave in to her attempt at lifting his spirits. "Then what?" he asked.

She smiled and laughed her rare laugh. "When the lesson was over, we had to turn the books in to the library keeper. He saw the marks on the edge of the pages and asked what happened. I just told him that was how I got it and sprinted out of the library. But he figured it out obviously and started shouting after me just as I got out the door. I had to run laps around the keep every night for a week straight."

Daniel grinned. Then he looked down at his hands, which were shaking. A long silence followed that hung in the air between them like a heavy fog.

Finally he croaked out his words. "I don't...I don't want to be the reason you died."

With his eyes still on his hands, he saw hers reach over and steady them. "You're not."

He sighed and gripped her hand. He would do his best to enjoy this time with her. No matter how hard it was. "Was the library carpet the only thing you set on fire?"

She grinned and leaned back into the pillows. For the next several hours, Mila told story after story. Of the first time she had field training and caused the senior Dragon Guard to break an ankle. About the day she was assigned to the rangers and how she was so nervous she missed the first training session. About the day she got married, to who, and how much of a shock it was to everyone. Daniel was equally surprised to learn this fact about her. She told him of her husband, Obadiah and how their life together. Learning so much about her life managed only to break his heart more. But he wore a smile for her. He knew these stories were as much for him as they were for her. She told them to ease his guilt, and to ease her own fear of what was coming. She told stories until the moment she was no longer breathing.

CHAPTER SIXTEEN

11ᵗʰ of Sanya, 26ᵗʰ year of the Fourth Age

ELEVEN UNEVENTFUL AND gloomy days passed aboard *The Royal Jewel*. For most of them, Daniel simply laid in the hammock below deck, with Aaron and Griffon keeping him company. But today he was on the main deck at the bow of the ship, eagerly waiting for the city to come into full view. They had woken early that morning and watched the sun rise and climb higher into the cloudless sky as they made their way further down the coastline. Now it was before them. At first they saw nothing but a hazy outline in the distance, slowly coming into focus. Once it was a clear picture, Daniel's breath caught in his throat.

The city of Vigil sat on the edge of a cliff that rose out of the water. The wall around the city was made of light grey stone, with watchtowers set at regular intervals along its length. It was flat along the cliff edge before shifting into a half circle around the rest of the city. Several buildings towered over the wall, but none compared to the keep at the core of the city. It was set on a hill rising above everything else, with a squared wall around it barely visible above the neighboring buildings. The keep also had a tower in its center that rose nearly to the clouds. It was wide at its base and thinned out in the middle before expanding into a crown-like design that had the tower passing through it to end with a flat top.

At the water was a small flat area that sat nestled between two cliff faces with a wide path that wound its way up a steep ramp that seemed to be carved out of the stone itself at its rear that split off in two directions, one ran along the edge of the cliff towards a pair of watchtowers and the other continued winding upwards to the city itself. In the clearing at the water itself there were a few buildings dotting the area with docks built along the water's edge with only a couple of ships sitting idle at them.

A few sailors walked the length of the docks or worked to unload their cargo with the pulley cranes on their ships and Daniel watched with fascination as *The Royal Jewel* made its way to one of the docks beneath the cliff. When the ship was alongside it, the crew swung into the practiced routine of tying off the ship and laying the gangplank over the gap. When his ship was secure, Captain Andrews ordered the crew to begin unloading their own cargo, then ushered his five passengers onto the dock.

"While I very much enjoyed having you aboard my ship, I'm afraid I have work to do," Andrews said. He looked at Claudia. "I have to set out tomorrow if I'm to return home on schedule. I trust you will…uh…retrieve you're…"

Claudia sighed quietly. "Rest assured captain, I will make arrangements."

He nodded and started to turn away, but paused. "I am sorry for your loss," he said.

"So am I."

Claudia led the others down and past the rest of the docks. They sidestepped crates and workers, and then moved between and past several warehouses. On the other side of the warehouses, they stepped off the raised wood of the harbor and onto the hard-packed dirt road. They made their way up the long road, taking in the sights below them as they rose higher up the cliff. When they reached the gatehouse, Daniel was already exhausted from the walk, his calf and ribs throbbing in protest. He tried his best to ignore it as they stepped into the shadow cast by the gate.

It was far larger and more imposing than the one at Grey Gate. The gate itself was made up of light red wood covered in thick iron bands with a raised portcullis just in front of it. Two guards manned the gate, one dressed in simple chainmail and the other in Dragon Guard warden plate. The gate had a manway set into it on the right side that was left partway open.

Kenneth waved to the warden and jogged ahead, pulling him into an embrace. "Obadiah my friend," he said, "it is good to see you again. It has been far too long!"

Daniel's heart jumped into his throat and he stared dumbfounded at the man, Mila's husband. The man wasn't as old as he had expected from the first story told to him on the road so long ago. He looked to be in his early thirties. He was bald, clean-shaven and stood as tall as Kenneth, though was not nearly as wide. Slung across his back was a great sword wrapped in a black oil cloth. The hilt sat well above his head, while the tip of the blade nearly scraped the ground.

Obadiah broke their embrace before he spoke. "It is good to see you alive and well, Kenneth," he said. He turned to Claudia and nodded politely, "and you as well, Ms. Wells."

She smiled and gave him a light hug. "It is wonderful to see you again, Obadiah," she said.

Obadiah turned to the rest of the group and examined them one at a time. "New recruits, I assume?"

Claudia stood behind the three and placed a hand on each of their shoulders as she told their names in turn.

Obadiah motioned for the other guard to open the manway. "I don't wish to delay you any longer," he said. "Commander Hall should be in his office."

Claudia led them through while Obadiah grabbed Kenneth by the arm and leaned in close, speaking in hushed tones. Daniel didn't hear what was said between them, but he had a pretty good guess when Obadiah's expression changed and he fell back against the wall, his hand covering his face. He chose not to think about it and tried to focus on taking in his surroundings as they emerged from of the gatehouse.

To Daniel's surprise, they weren't actually in the city yet. What he couldn't tell from the ship or down in the harbor was that were in fact two walls. They now found themselves in a large swath of open grassland between the outer and inner walls, which seemed identical. Both were made of the same stone, with bricks that were roughly four feet tall and wide, bringing the height of both walls to nearly forty feet. Spanning the gap between the two were narrow stone bridges with thick support pillars. The space between the walls seemed to mirror their height at forty feet.

Curious, Daniel was about to speak, but Griffon asked the question before he could: "Why are there two walls?"

Claudia smiled and glanced over her shoulder. "This is a defensive area called a 'killing field.' Vigil is the only city in Edaren that has one."

Daniel saw Aaron nod slowly as he looked out over the tall grass between the walls. "Attackers break down one wall," Aaron said, "and have to walk through a field of traps before having to break down another. Shale had one as well. It's why they remained unconquered until the end of the war."

Daniel glanced to the side and thought he caught several glints of metal through the blades of grass, but before he could lean in for a closer look, they were already across the field and at the second gate. Unlike the first, it had no manway and hung slightly ajar to allow passage. As at the previous gate, guards stood on each side of this gate, though neither were Dragon Guards. They both gave slight nods and friendly smiles as the group passed through the gap. When they were through the gate, Daniel felt a surge of relief.

He was finally here. He had made it. The city was nothing like he'd imagined. It was far bigger and more populated than he anticipated. The streets were made of the same grey stone as the walls. Along their length were light posts at regular intervals; hanging side by side from each were three narrow banners. One was colored red with a sword standing on its tip, the second was yellow with an open book, and the third was green with an open eye. All three were placed within a stylized kite shield.

Daniel was curious: "What do the banners represent?"

Claudia glanced at them before removing her glove and showing him the band around her wrist. He'd never gotten a close look at it before. Now he saw it was engraved with the same symbol as the yellow banner.

Claudia slipped her glove back on as she spoke. "Vigil has no crest, unlike other cities, so we tend to use the symbols for the Dragon Guard sects. Red is for the wardens, yellow are scholars, and the green is the rangers."

Aaron raised an eyebrow. "The citizens are okay with that?" he asked. "Most people don't really want to be associated with Dragon Guards anymore."

Claudia smiled sidelong at him as they walked. "Most of the people here know better. They live with us on a daily basis. They don't give in to the rumors that plague the other cities and are happy to fly our banners."

"Most people?"

She shrugged. "There are always a few."

The buildings lining the wide street all seemed to be shops of some sort, with display windows taking up the majority of the walls that faced the street. Along the road were hundreds of people heading in every direction. It was overwhelmingly crowded. It took the five of them just under an hour to reach the wall of the keep. When they did, they were greeted by two more wardens who quickly ushered them inside with short greetings to Claudia and polite smiles to the trio following closely behind her.

The other side of the keep was wide open, with a stone-bricked path leading to the main door. The rest of the area was grass that stretched from one wall to the other and, from what Daniel could tell, all the way around the keep itself. Directly ahead of them was a set of wide stairs that narrowed as it climbed toward double doors that Daniel would have called a gate if they weren't such a marvel. They were intricately carved, displaying a battle at the base of the doors that slowly gave way to a line of clouds, and above them, a trio of intimidating-looking dragons.

The dragon at the center was the largest, with a squared jaw and a sword displayed at the center of its chest. The one to the right had a set of long, curved horns and an open book on its chest. The final dragon on the left was the smallest and most slender of the three, with an open eye at the center of its breast. It was hard to miss the fact that the three shared the marks of the sects. As curious as Daniel was about the shared symbols, he figured now was not the time to ask.

The keep itself seemed smaller up close but no less impressive in spite of it. It was dotted with windows higher up, while the first floor seemed to have none. From what Daniel could tell, there appeared to be five floors in all. For the most part the exterior was rather plain aside from a few decorative pillars going up its length to the roof, which sloped steeply until it met the base of the tower that was at its center.

Daniel craned his head to look up the length of the tower. When he glanced at the others, he saw Griffon doing the same with wide eyes and Aaron standing with his mouth agape. Claudia let them marvel for only a moment before ushering them up the stairs. She gripped an iron ring to pull open one door, allowing them inside.

The first room was wide and long, with a set of stairs at the back and doors lining the walls. Between each door was a glass display case. Daniel looked closer as Claudia led them to the stairs. Most seemed to be old weapons and armor. There was a large war hammer with a shattered head and a broken handle, as well as what looked like a longbow that had been snapped in half. They didn't look like anything terribly important, but to have them on display in the main hall of the keep, they clearly had some significance. He didn't have time to see what else was displayed before they started up the stairs, which quickly turned into a spiral with a landing at every floor. When they reached the sixth landing, Daniel knew they were now in the tower itself.

"So, where are we going exactly?" Daniel asked as they passed the seventh.

Claudia responded over her shoulder. "To see Commander Hall. He needs to approve of your entry into the Dragon Guard. Just a short interview with Captain North and then he'll take you to where you'll be staying."

"When do we start training?" Griffon asked with a slight grin.

"On the first of Eren," Claudia said. "The current trainees will have their band ceremony, then you'll start your training."

"Current trainees?" Daniel thought for only a moment before it clicked and he continued, "Training takes five years?"

She nodded and urged them down a short hall connected to the tenth landing, which quickly ended at a plain, dark, wood door. She reached up and gripped the iron ring to knock twice. Moments later, the door opened and a woman in warden plate with long, white hair and vibrant viridian eyes looked to each of them in turn before letting them pass and shutting the door behind them.

They found themselves in a circular room. The walls were lined with the same type of glass cases they'd seen earlier, though these were filled with what Daniel could only imagine to be trophies. He saw several large teeth and scales, as well as various weapons with serrated blades and jagged edges and a few pieces of ornate, steel-plate armor, dented and warped by some long-finished battle. At the back of the room was a tall, stained-glass window depicting a red, a green, and a yellow dragon standing side by side. Below that was a wide wooden desk with several open scrolls and stacks of books atop it.

At the center of the room was a squared table with a map of Edaren spread out on top of it. The map had several figurines placed on various cities and landmarks, with others placed in the wilderness. Standing around the map table were three individuals, all of them were dressed in Dragon Guard leather.

At the head of the table was a warden with short, blond hair and dark, forest-green eyes. On his right was a ranger, his black hair tied into a tail and face covered in stubble. The ranger looked the three of them up and down with grey eyes. To the left of the table was a scholar with short, black hair and a neatly trimmed beard. He never took his ocean-colored eyes off the map.

The warden at the head of the table addressed them: "Scholar Wells, I'm glad to see you've returned safely. To what do we owe this visit?"

Claudia crossed her arms over her chest, bringing her wrists together with a clank. "Commander Hall, I apologize for the intrusion. I did not realize you were in the midst of a meeting."

He waved his hand. "We're not," he said, "just getting a quick update on our operations. Nothing terribly important at the moment. What can we do for you?"

"Approval for these three." She uncrossed her arms and stepped aside, gesturing to the trio.

Hall smiled widely and waved the three of them forward. They stepped up nervously and waited as the woman who had opened the door for them retrieved a set of papers and spread them out on the table before she picked up a nearby quill from an inkwell.

She placed the tip on the paper before speaking: "Names?"

They spoke their names in turn and she jotted them down on separate papers. She then asked for their ages and where they were from. When she finished recording the information, she made her signature at the bottom of the pages before passing them to the other captains who likewise signed them, finishing with the ranger who then tucked them under his arm.

"Perfect," Hall said. "Now Captain North will just ask you some questions and then he'll show you where you'll be staying." Hall paused and looked at Claudia. "While they do that, I would like a report on that pack you were sent to find."

"Of course, commander," Claudia said.

The ranger motioned for Daniel, Aaron, and Griffon to follow. He led them quickly back down the hall and stairs to the floor below. Directly off the stair landing was a small room with several chairs inside and a second door at the far end.

North pointed to Daniel and Griffon. "You two wait here. Mr. Cross, come with me."

Aaron and North went into the second doorway and left the two of them alone. Griffon fell into one of the chairs set against the wall with a sigh. Daniel did the same. He briefly scanned the room as they waited. Aside from the chairs lining the walls and the two doors, it was empty. As they waited, he felt and heard his heart beating twice as fast as normal. He knew that there was nothing wrong at the moment, yet in spite of that he felt nervous, even terrified. He tried to control his breathing to calm himself.

"What do you think they're talking about in there?" Griffon asked, her voice startling Daniel in the quiet.

"I have no idea. I don't know what they would possibly need to ask us."

Griffon apparently had nothing to say in response. The silence resumed with a new sense of awkwardness.

Daniel felt the need to keep the conversation going. "So...why do you want to be a Dragon Guard?"

Griffon replied with a light shrug. "Honestly, I never wanted to be."

"So why are you here now?"

"It's a long story, but I guess..." She bit her lip. "I guess it just came down to me being tired of not being able to protect myself. Something happened back home and a Dragon Guard helped me through it. After seeing what he did, he kind of inspired me to come here and learn to how to fight back. So I wouldn't ever need to be helped again."

In spite of their time at sea together, he hadn't really had the chance to speak with Griffon about anything like this. He was curious about the circumstances of her departure. "What happened?"

"I'd rather not get into it. Let's just say I had to leave home and he helped me get on my way." She turned to him and smiled. "What about you, why are you here?"

He felt her unease and decided to go with the subject change. "It's what I've wanted to do for as long as I can remember."

"That's it?"

"What do you mean?"

She laughed lightly. "I mean you just wanted to be one so you're here? There's nothing else?"

He smiled as he thought about how he would explain it. "Do you like to read?"

The question seemed to confuse her. "What?"

"Read, stories about adventures and things like that."

She looked up at the ceiling. "I never learned to read, but I do remember a poem that my brother used to tell me about a lone wolf wanting to be human. Does that count?"

"Close enough." He pulled his pack off his back and set it on the floor.

The one thing he would never part with was inside. He pulled the book out and set it on his lap. "I love reading. My father taught me when I was really young before he left." He sighed and smiled at the memory. "I've always read books where there's a hero that comes along and protects people just for the sake of protecting them, even if the hero doesn't get anything in return."

"So you want to be a hero like that?"

"Yeah, I do."

"Sort of childish, isn't it?" Griffon said. "Seems like you'd be better off playing with wood swords and pretending to save the day."

"I don't think so. If there were never any heroes in the world, then it wouldn't be what it is now. I think everyone *can* be a hero to at least one person in some way. The problem is that most people don't try." He paused to consider his next words. "You said that a Dragon Guard helped you leave Forge. He went out of his way to help you even though he didn't get anything out of it. So wouldn't you consider him a hero?"

Her response was quiet and thoughtful. "I suppose so."

"Ever since I first met Claudia, Kenneth, and Mila...they've been heroes to me. If it wasn't for them, I'd be dead on the bank of the Arrow. I never would have made it here. They didn't have to go out of their way like that. They could have just kept walking. They took the time to try."

Griffon seemed to consider his words. Before she could respond, the door across the room opened and Aaron stepped out.

He sat down in the chair next to Daniel with a heavy sigh. "He said to send you in next."

Daniel stood and looked at him curiously. "What did he ask?"

"Nothing, really. It was...weird. Felt more like a casual conversation. Just a lot about home, family, friends, and things like that."

Daniel, more confused than he had been a moment ago, went to the door and pushed it open. It was empty save for a table and two chairs on either side of it. North sat on one end with a paper placed before him and a quill in his hand. Daniel took the seat across from him and waited for North to speak first.

"Hello, Mr. Summers. As you know, I'm Captain North. I lead the ranger sect of the Dragon Guard. Have you ever met a ranger?"

"Just one. Her name was Mila."

"Right, Ms. Den. How could I forget? Mr. Cross told me what happened. Her death is a great loss for the Dragon Guard. She will be missed." There was a short pause before he continued. "Do you have any family, parents, brothers, or sisters?"

"My mother and one brother."

"What are their names?"

"Lilly and Jeremy."

He nodded and wrote on the paper again. "No father?"

"He left when I was young. I don't remember much about him."

He nodded again and made several more notes., Daniel was more confused than anything at this point. The questions didn't seem relevant to becoming a Dragon Guard in any way.

"Grandparents?"

"I never knew them. They lived in Dalisia but my mother moved to Sapella when she married my father."

"Do you have any religious beliefs?"

"Uh, no, I don't."

North narrowed his eyes. "You hesitated."

"I just...never really thought about it before."

North jotted down another line on the paper as he asked his next question. "How much do you know about the history of Edaren?"

Daniel had to think for a moment. "Not much, I guess. I learned a lot from Claudia on the way here, but aside from that there weren't many chances for history lessons in Sapella."

The interview continued for several minutes. The questions seemed to be mostly about Daniel's past and the people in Sapella—names and relationships, interesting landmarks in the area, or what happened there recently. Daniel wanted to come right out and ask what any of this had to do with being a Dragon Guard, but he felt that he wouldn't get an answer.

North finally folded the paper he'd been writing on and sealed it with wax, using a stamp with the ranger symbol as he spoke. "Well, thank you Mr. Summers, that will be all. You may send in Ms. Hart." Both curious and confused, Daniel left the room to sit next to Aaron before sending

Griffon in. Her interview passed quickly. When it was over, North had them follow him back to the stairs. They started down toward the ground floor and the main entry room, but then North turned into one of the side doors. After leading them through a maze of halls, North took the new recruits through another door that led to the back courtyard of the keep.

At the moment, the area was empty, but it was clearly one of the main areas for exercises and training. There were rings carved into the ground and tall stakes with protruding arms sticking out. Further down was a row of squares covered in burlap and filled with straw that Daniel guessed were archery targets. Opposite them and tucked into the corner on the east side of the wall was a long, plain-looking stone building with only a few windows and two doors adjacent to each other. When Daniel turned to look down the length of the courtyard, he saw another building across the way that mirrored the first building.

North led them to the structure on the east side and pushed open the door closest to the keep wall. Inside was row after row of straw beds with single-door wardrobes between them. Dotting the room were several boys and girls engrossed in conversations of their own. Only the two closest to the door seemed to take notice of the captain.

A boy with shaggy gold hair and brown eyes stood and greeted them: "Good afternoon, Captain North."

"Mr. Thorn, wonderful timing," North said. He gestured at Daniel, Aaron, and Griffon behind him. "These are our newest arrivals. Can I trust you to show them around and explain the rules?"

"Of course sir, leave it to me." Thorn smiled wide at Daniel and the others as North turned on his heel and left through the still-open door.

The boy extended his hand. Aaron was the first to shake it. "My name's Zachery," the boy said. He gestured to the boy behind him, who looked exactly like him except while Zachery had blond hair, his was jet black. "This is my younger brother, Alan."

Daniel shook Zachery's hand, next followed by Griffon. When they were all acquainted, Zachery motioned for them to sit on the bed across from him.

"So here are the basics," Zachery said. "Floors three and up in the keep are off limits. First floor has the kitchen and dining area, but other than that it's mostly storage. Second floor has a library and the rest is personal quarters for the Dragon Guard and the few full-time workers, like the kitchen staff." He bit his lip. "There was something else..."

Alan answered him without looking up from a box he held in his hand: "The curfew."

Zachery snapped his fingers. "Right! You can walk around the city as long as you're back before sundown. You can't leave here before sunrise."

Griffon tilted her head to one side. "That's it?"

Zachery shrugged. "That I can remember, anyway. Oh, and girls sleep next door."

Daniel looked around the long room. There was only one other door, at the far end where the corner of the keep wall would be. Small, unlit lanterns hung from the wall above each bed just below narrow shelves set halfway up the wall.

Daniel turned back to Zachery. "So, how many people are here?" he asked. "Recruits, I mean."

"I think there's fifteen going through training now," Zachery said, "and twenty-two waiting to start, counting you three." He looked over at the other recruits in the room. "The only guy here I've really talked to is Robert." He pointed to a boy with short, coal-black hair and jade eyes.

Alan spoke again without looking away from the puzzle: "He's a jerk."

Zachery elbowed him hard enough to make him fall sideways. "Other than Robert, there's Lace and Robin next door. They showed up with him, I think. They're all from Silvum. Oh, there's also Clara. She's nice but you can barely get a word out of her, always has her head in a book."

"How long have you been here?" Aaron asked. "Where did you come from?"

"Alan and I have been here about two weeks, came down from Dawnstone. How about you guys?"

"I'm from Dalisia," Aaron said. "Daniel is from Sapella's Crossing and Griffon came from Forge."

Zachery whistled softly. "Wow, long way off. Hard journey?"

Daniel and Aaron both smiled at one another before Daniel answered: "You have no idea."

"What happened?"

"Have you ever been to Grey Gate?"

Daniel started recounting what had transpired to the best of his memory. From the moment they reached the gate and the welcome they were given to the venture into Market Level to find Barden. He skimmed over most of the details. When the story reached the point where they ventured into the den, Aaron took the reins. Daniel actually paid close attention once Aaron reached the point where Daniel had been knocked down the slope. He'd been told what happened in snippets when they were at sea, but not in this amount of detail. He hadn't wanted to hear it at the time.

"After Daniel fell into the darkness" Aaron said, "Kenneth reached Mila, grabbed the satlis by the tail, and pulled it away from her before driving his sword through it. Then he picked her up and threw her over his shoulder and we started running. Claudia fended off any of the smaller males that passed the fire she left behind. It didn't take us long to reach the exit but by that time the whole horde was on us. Claudia had to collapse the exit with one of those orb things she carries around," Aaron took a deep breath after he finished continuing his tale.

He then told about how he met Griffon, and as before refused to answer when Daniel cut in and asked how exactly he'd secured their place on the ship. At this point it was Daniel's turn to tell his side of the tale. When he was finished Zachery's jaw hung open.

"That's incredible! You really killed one yourself?" Zachery asked Daniel.

Daniel shrugged and blushed slightly. "Barely, and it was injured. Kenneth thinks it was one he'd thrown down the slope."

"That's still really impressive!" Zachery said. "Biggest thing I've ever killed was a rat at the orphanage."

"Got it!" Alan exclaimed suddenly. He held up the box triumphantly.

Zachery took it from him and examined the different sides of the cube as Daniel leaned in to see what exactly it was. It was a puzzle box. Daniel had never had one himself but he had seen them before. It was a simple metal and wooden box with a single lid. It had eleven small movable tiles on the lid that were nearly an inch thick with a space for a twelfth tile that remained empty. The goal was to line the tiles up in the correct order that allowed a long pin to slide through them like a key, allowing the box to be opened. Most often they were filled with sweets or a toy as a reward for the child that solved it.

There were smaller tiles that usually came with it that were meant to make the game more challenging by adding more variation to the tiles.

"I'll make it a little harder this time," Zachery said. He shuffled the slats back and forth, twisting the cube in a random manner until the three pictures were a jumbled, unidentifiable mess. He handed it back to his brother, who started to carefully slide the square slats around. Daniel watched him for a moment as he considered the movement of each piece.

Aaron leaned forward, his elbows on his knees. "You said you were in an orphanage?" he asked.

Zachery replied as he watched his brother go about solving the box: "Yeah, our parents died when Alan was only a year old. The rest of our family lived in Volignis when Dragons Maw blew, so we didn't have anyone left to go to."

"I'm, uh...I'm sorry to hear that," Aaron said.

Zachery laughed briefly. "Not as sorry as we were. That place was horrible. It smelled terrible and the food was awful. Actually, the food was probably the reason for the smell, now that I think about it."

Griffon leaned toward Alan to examine the puzzle. "So, what made you come here?"

"They kick you out when you turn eighteen," Zachery said, "so I'd only be there another two months, and I wasn't going to leave Alan there by himself for another five years while I was here training. So he came with me since he just turned thirteen. Besides, this seemed like a better alternative to the Dawnstone city watch. They've never really been the nicest people."

"You made this one too hard," Alan said. He furrowed his brow as he continued to fiddle with the cube.

"Just keep working on it," Zachary said. "You'll figure it out. You always do."

CHAPTER SEVENTEEN

30ᵗʰ of Sanya, 26ᵗʰ year of the Fourth Age.

DANIEL WALKED QUIETLY down the halls of Vigil with his fingers laced behind his head. The keep was a hive of activity as the majority of the Dragon Guard was currently present at Vigil for the Autumn's End Festival. Claudia had said the only members of the Dragon Guard absent from the festivities tonight would be those out on permanent assignments. Aside from them, everyone was ready to celebrate not only the New Year but the new wave of recruits joining the Order. Daniel sighed as he took another turn down a hall heading for the kitchen. He was trying his best not to think too much about the days to come.

It had been two and a half weeks since he arrived at Vigil with Aaron and the others, and over that time he'd familiarized himself with the layout of the first two floors of the keep. He'd also spent a considerable amount of time in the city itself. He had learned there were three gates that led into the city, one each at the north, west, and east walls. Each of these opened onto a wide road heading straight through the city to the keep. The keep itself had only the one gate on the north wall. Several times, Daniel had nearly been caught past curfew on the wrong side of the gate with Zachery and Alan.

But for the moment, he would be staying within the keep walls. He was heading for the courtyard on the west side of the keep, as he'd been doing almost every day for the last week and a half. The fastest way to do that would be through the chaotic kitchen and out one of the small side doors. He walked through open doors into the dining hall and stepped past large, dark, wooden tables set in long lines that faced a stage at the far end of the room. The room was lit with hanging chandeliers, each holding dozens of lit candles. In addition, braziers built into the walls surrounded the room.

Daniel was actually quite excited about the celebration—mostly because of the food. Jonathan, the Vigil chef, was truly a master of his craft. Daniel's mouth was already watering at the thought of the upcoming meal. He stepped through a curtained-off doorway leading to the kitchen. The moment he was inside, he encountered a wall of noise and waves of aromas that battered his senses in a wonderful way. Jonathan had his staff working overtime for the band ceremony that would take place in a little less than an hour. It was where the current novices would receive the bands they would wear around their wrists for a lifetime, the mark of a true and full-fledged Dragon Guard.

Daniel started through the kitchen, sidestepping cooks and taking extra care not to knock anything off of the countless tables or stumble and fall against one of the boiling hot, brick ovens that lined the outer wall. The ceiling of the kitchen was twice as high as the rest of the first floor. Near the top were rows of windows letting in enough natural light to fill the whole room.

"Daniel!"

He scanned the faces to his right for a few moments until he saw Zachery standing next to a table of covered trays, waving frantically at him. Daniel made his way over to him as quickly as he dared in the chaos.

"Hey, what are you doing in here?" Daniel said while glancing from tray to tray. He couldn't tell what was in them but the smell was intoxicating.

Zachery grinned. "Jonathan's been teaching me to cook and asked for my help with some of the simpler stuff."

Daniel leaned away from the table, feigning fear. "Well," he said, "if you're cooking, then I might not want to eat tonight after all."

Zachery faked a hurt expression. "I'm not that bad."

"So what's in these?" Daniel asked as he switched to a smile and pointed to a tray.

Zachery removed one of the lids, letting the steam inside pour out. "Meat pies. Made them myself...mostly."

"What do you mean, mostly?"

Ignoring the question, Zachery put the lid back on and turned back to face Daniel. "So where are you going, anyway?"

"The west wall," Daniel said. "Just for a little while."

Zachery pursed his lips and nodded. "Well, hurry back. There'll be people pouring into the hall any minute now."

Daniel nodded before turning and walking to the narrow door in the kitchen's corner that led outside. When he pushed it open, he had to cross his arms to ward off the cold air before stepping into knee-high, powdery snow and shuffling his way to the west wall. The evening sun was laid out before him. He soon reached an ornate iron fence that was only a little taller than he was. He pushed open the old, rusted gate and walked past the stone markers in the ground, some decorative and elegant, others simple and plain. A short way into the graveyard, he stopped before a simple marker of white stone with *Mila Den* carved at its peak.

Since her funeral shortly after they'd arrived, Daniel had come here as often as he could. He would stand and talk to her about nothing in particular, things that happened that day or what he was looking forward to. He wasn't sure why he did it. He didn't know if she could hear him somehow from wherever she was, but Claudia had told him Mila had been as close to a Vigilant of Verhova as a Dragon Guard could be, so maybe she could.

"Hey Mila, tonight's the night," he said. "I uh, I guess this will be the last time I talk to you before I'm an official recruit." He shifted his weight from one foot to the other. "Pretty nervous, I guess. I know I shouldn't be. At least that's what everyone tells me. You told me that once too…wish I would listen and stop freaking myself out so much."

Daniel felt a little ridiculous standing here talking to what was essentially a rock. Yet he felt obligated to at least make the effort. She had traded her life for his. She had done something incredible for him and he had to repay her somehow. This was the only way he could think of.

He sighed and looked down at his feet. "I still wonder what would have happened if you hadn't been there with Claudia, my brother, and me at the river. I don't think the three of us would have lasted until Kenneth got there without you…and then down in the den." He bit his lip and felt his eyes welling despite his best efforts. "You should be here instead of me."

He looked up at the sky. The evening light painted it dark orange. Streaks of purple cut across it in waves as the snow was fell in large, puffy flakes.

A voice spoke behind him: "They say Verhova lets those who've passed paint the sky for the living."

Daniel turned to see Obadiah walking toward the grave. He wore his warden armor but lacked his great sword. He followed the tracks Daniel had cut in the snow before stopping next to him and looking down at the stone before them.

Obadiah smiled briefly and crossed his arms. "I like to think she paints the sky every time I visit."

Daniel looked at the colors overhead again. "She's a great artist."

"She was many things, but an artist was certainly not one of them. Although purple was her favorite color," he said with a slight chuckle.

Daniel looked back at the grave. He suddenly felt awkward. He knew Obadiah came here more often than Daniel did, but this was the first time they'd been here together. Daniel hadn't really even spoken to Obadiah before. He always felt guilty whenever he saw him.

The silence was agony, so Daniel felt he needed to say something" "So, uh…how long were you together?"

"Eight years, I think? Or near enough it doesn't matter. She was so quiet at first, but when I really got to know her she was hard to keep up with."

"How so?"

"Believe it or not, she was quite the drinker, though she didn't let many in on that little secret. She was slow to trust people, but if she ever revealed that about herself, it usually meant she liked you. She frequented a bar on the north side of the city in her off time. Could drink anybody under the table, and she always got a bit chatty after she had a few. Silvum Shade Ale was her drink of choice."

Daniel grinned. "I believe it."

"I remember when there was a span of a few months during the last wave of trainees. The ranger instructor had been injured during an exercise and Mila was chosen to fill in until he recovered. She was so stressed that she made the mistake of going out drinking one night. The next day she was supposed to give six trainees a lesson." Obadiah started to laugh as he spoke again. "She was so hungover; she had them sit quietly in the dark and told them it was stealth training."

Daniel grinned at the thought. "How well did that go over?"

Obadiah laughed again. "In all honesty, I think they may be the best group of rangers we've had in a long while."

They stood in the quiet evening air for a while longer. The tension Daniel had felt was gone. He had been worried Obadiah would blame him for what happened. He was grateful he didn't, though that didn't change Daniel's own thoughts on the matter. He knew if he had just been faster, if he had been more aware, then he and Mila's husband wouldn't be standing here now, staring at a marker bearing her name.

The snow stopped falling before Obadiah placed a hand on Daniel's shoulder and ushered him toward the keep. "Suppose it's time for us to get in there," he said.

Daniel sighed as they made their way through the partially filled-in tracks back to the kitchen. They stepped inside and quickly made their way through the chaos and past the curtain into the dining hall. The room was filled with hundreds of conversations going at once as nearly every Dragon Guard was in attendance. It was a sea of black, though there were of also citizens from Vigil among the crowd, including members of the city watch and close friends of individual Dragon Guards.

The light and cheerful tone of the conversations made Daniel smile the instant he stepped inside.

At the center of the room was the towering form of Kenneth dancing with the much shorter Claudia. They were both laughing as he clumsily struggled to keep in step with the fast-paced music. Daniel looked from table to table, searching for a familiar face to sit next to. He was thankful when he spotted Zachery and Clara at a table near the stage. He could see that Alan, Robert, and Lace were also present. He hurried across the room and happily took a seat next to Clara and Zachery.

Clara's red hair was so dark it was almost black. It hung down in front, nearly covering amber eyes that darted across the pages of the book spread out on the table in front of her. Lace Woods had auburn hair and steel-grey eyes. Both features matched her sister, Robin, who at the moment was absent from the group. Though that's how it always seemed to be. Lace was timid yet friendly, while Robin was stern and rarely said a word to anyone. Robert, meanwhile, had curly, coal-black hair and chocolate brown eyes. The fact he sat furthest from Daniel was a bonus. Robert was stubborn and arrogant. He seemed to thrive on conflict and arguments.

Zachery nudged Daniel hard with his elbow as he sat. "About time you got here!"

"Has the commander given them their bands yet?" Daniel asked.

"Not yet, but he was just over at their table, so I think they're starting."

No sooner had Zachery finished speaking than Commander Hall stepped onto the stage, followed by his captains: warden Samantha Coe, ranger Logan North, and scholar Martin Hawk. Each was fully adorned in armor and carried a wooden case under one arm as he or she went to stand to one side of the commander, who was at the center of the stage. When they were all in position, the room began to quiet.

"Tonight," Hall said, "we are proud and honored to present a wave of trained and eager Dragon Guards their bands."

The fifteen current trainees made their way onto the stage and lined up next to Hall, opposite the captains. They wore black and were also adorned with scarves.

When they were in place, Hall continued: "Tonight we send another wave of youth into the world bearing our mark, the mark of a true Dragon Guard. It is our badge of honor. It also represents our burden, placed around our wrists to remind us of what we fight to prevent: a life in chains."

Hall motioned to Coe, who stepped forward and opened her case. She presented the first seven in line with a band engraved with the symbol of the wardens. Each of them slid the band onto their wrists. Many of them simply stared at it for a long moment when it was in place.

They were snapped back to attention when Captain Coe began speaking: "We as wardens are the representatives of Belladux, the Right Hand. Wear this symbol to show that you will stand against the tides of darkness in defense of the innocent, and as judges of the corrupt."

Cheers rose from those gathered in the room and were quickly silenced when Hall raised his hands. He nodded toward Hawk, who quickly stepped forward and gave the next five in line their bands.

"We as scholars are the representatives of Lestice, the Voice of Creation," Hawk said. "This symbol represents our task to preserve and discover knowledge for the protection of mankind, and to use it for the destruction of those that would shadow the world in ignorance."

Again a cheer rose from the crowd that was silenced just as quickly when North stepped forward.

"We as rangers are the representatives of Ocudai, the Seer," North said. "This symbol shows that there is no place the darkness can hide from us. It shows that we will go and do what is necessary to end the fight before it begins."

Hall turned to face the room as the cheers faded. "We are the representatives of Verhova," he said. "We stand against an ever-present danger to our world. But we will never stand alone."

The newly banded Dragon Guards saluted their captains and commander in unison, accompanied by a roaring wave of applause that seemed to only grow louder. In spite of Daniel's apprehension over having to take the stage next, he found himself clapping and cheering along. Before he knew it, the room was signaled to be quiet again. Hall ushered the new Dragon Guards off the stage along with their respective captains, then motioned for the members of Daniel's table to begin making their way up the stairs on the side of the stage.

Hall spoke as they lined up beside him: "While we are now fifteen stronger, we still pale in comparison to our old glory. But tonight we welcome another wave to bring us that much closer to what we were."

He turned and nodded at them. They had practiced this dozens of times before. To misspeak now would not only be embarrassing but in the eyes of many older Dragon Guards, a bad omen. So they all spoke together, letting their voices blend in perfect harmony as they swore their oath.

> From now until my hour
> I will not waver
> I will not fall
> I will not cower
>
> With the strength of my arm
> With the speed of my feet
> I shall guard the weak
> As long as my heart beats
>
> I am a safeguard
> I am the sword
> I am the shield
> I am a Dragon Guard

The moment the last word was spoken, the room erupted in cheers that threatened to deafen Daniel. In spite of the auditory pain, he couldn't help but smile at the sheer joy he felt in the room. Commander Hall let the celebration go on a few moments longer before lifting his hands to quiet the crowd.

He clasped his hands together. "Tomorrow is when their journey truly beings," he said. "To train the new wave, we need capable instructors"—he sighed and smiled—"and after many, many long discussions with my captains, I have selected the three that will take up the responsibility of making these young men and women the finest trainees we've seen yet.

For our future wardens, we have selected Obadiah Den. For the rangers we have chosen Austin Pine. And finally, Claudia Wells will train our scholars." Each of the new instructors stood and saluted as their names were called, accompanied by the applause of those gathered.

"Now," the commander said, "let us celebrate with our new and future brothers and sisters!"

The hall erupted into cheers once more as Daniel and the others made their way off the stage and back to their table. They all walked with wide smiles and chatted excitedly amongst themselves. It was a dream come true. Daniel looked at the faces of his friends and could feel his own mirroring theirs. Yet his heart felt heavy. While he was excited about the opportunity he had now, he was also afraid. He didn't know why. He wanted the feeling to go away, just for tonight at least, so he could enjoy the fact he'd made it even this far. But Connie's words from the day he left echoed in his head, she had told him that things like this were supposed to be terrifying. That this feeling just let him know he was going the right way. Tomorrow would be the first true day for them as future Dragon Guards, the start of five long years of training.

Daniel couldn't remember the last time he had woken this early. He rubbed the sleep from his eyes and tried his best not to collapse where he stood. The sun hadn't even risen and yet here they stood, in line in the library, waiting for their instructors to arrive. They had been awakened by one of the Dragon Guards who had just received his band and told to dress quickly in the black attire they'd been provided. Then they had been led here to wait. It had been several minutes and none of them had spoken a word to each other. Daniel glanced around and noted where his friends stood. Aaron was directly at his side in the middle, while Griffon stood at the right end of the line with Zachery, Alan, and Clara.

It took another five minutes of waiting before the door in front of them opened and Claudia entered. She was quickly followed by Obadiah and Austin. This was the first time Daniel had gotten a close look at the ranger instructor. His hair was ash black and cut short, while his face was dotted with patchwork stubble. His chestnut brown eyes were sharp.

Austin scanned each recruit in turn, his gaze lingering on Griffon for a moment as a smirk crossed his features before quickly disappearing.

The instructors also stood in a line and faced the recruits. Claudia was the first to speak: "Good morning, my name is Claudia Wells. I will be your general education instructor."

Austin bowed slightly and smiled. "I'm Austin Pine. I'll teach you everything you need to know about the wilderness of Edaren and the beasts within it."

"I am Obadiah Den," the big man said. He crossed his arms and didn't seem at all pleased to be there. "I'll be teaching you combat."

Claudia looked at each recruit in turn. "If anyone has any questions about their upcoming training," she said, "ask now."

A dozen hands shot up before Claudia could finish her sentence, but Robin chose to simply voice her question first: "What did you mean by general education?"

"History for the most part," Claudia said, "as well as reading and writing if any of you should need it."

Clara spoke second: "When will we get placed in one of the sects?"

"After a year, we'll split you up and train you separately for whichever sect we deem you fit best, in addition to finishing your basics."

Clara tilted her head. "We don't get a say in which sect we'll belong to?"

"No."

When the next three questions were about placement within the sects and training time, Claudia sighed. "To make it simple, your training will be broken down like this," she said, counting off on her fingers. "First is general training, which will cover basic skills every Dragon Guard needs. That will take one year. Next is the start of your specialized training, where you learn the specific skills you will need in your sect, as well as some field tests with senior members. That will take three years. After that, it's full field training, where you will be sent on missions with your fellow trainees and one senior member. That will be your last year."

"Your schedules," Austin added with a cheerful chirp in his tone, "will be set in stone, with six days of training and one day off for the week. With a few exceptions, of course, once we get into the fun stuff."

Claudia nodded. "Right, anything else?" she said. "This will be your last chance to ask."

When they all remained quiet, Obadiah sighed and motioned for them to follow. "Suppose we'll start with some morning exercises," he said.

Obadiah took them outside and had them perform everything from pushups to jumping jacks in an area of the courtyard that had been cleared of snow. Daniel's lungs were soon burning. Since breathing had already been difficult enough with his still-sore ribs, he felt as if they were broken all over again. By the time Obadiah led them back inside, everyone was miserable, their faces painted bright red and stinging when they were greeted by the warmer interior of the keep. The only exceptions were Robin and Lace, who seemed to be only slightly winded. It was clear they were used to this type of activity, while the rest of them were clearly out of their element.

Even the short climb up the stairs to the library was a strain. All Daniel wanted to do was sit down and never move another muscle again. After they were finally inside the library, he was overjoyed when Claudia motioned for them all to sit at a table in a corner of the room.

She looked at them with a mischievous grin. "Enjoy your morning?" she asked. She was clearly amused by their irritated glares as she continued walking around the table. "Today we'll start going over the history of Edaren. We'll quite literally start from the beginning and give a brief over-view of what we know. When I've finished, we will go into more detail. If you have any questions, feel free to speak up. Discussion is always helpful during these lessons. Understood?"

When everyone had nodded their assent, Claudia pulled three books off a nearby shelf, each progressively smaller than the one before it. She dropped them onto the table, making a loud thud and a cloud of dust.

She pointed to each of the books in turn. "This relates the complete history of the Third Age, this most of the Second Age, and finally this one contains bits and pieces of the First. The Dragon Guard has been around since mid–First Age and has done its best to keep a consistent set of records since. Though the records are not complete, sadly."

"Why not?" Aaron asked. "If you've been around for so long, what happened to them?"

"The Dragon Guard used to be spread around the world. Thousands upon thousands of members. But the Order was nearly destroyed during a great battle fought on the shores of Edaren. Those of us that remained were among the lowest ranking and knew only so much. Even with our pooled knowledge, memory is a fickle thing, and parchment equally so. Over time there have been fires, thefts, and things simply getting misplaced. Keeping knowledge for so long is a daunting task and it's inevitable that parts get lost." She paused for a few moments before continuing. "Have any of you ever heard of a High Dragon?"

Clara raised her hand. "They were the first dragons. The Order of Verhova says that the day they return to Edaren signals the coming of Shade."

Claudia frowned at the mention of the church. "Ah yes, the Order. They claim all dragons are spawns of Shade, but that couldn't be further from the truth."

"What do you mean?" Clara said.

"High Dragons were the first dragons, but they were never spawns of Shade. They were the first four, to be exact. They were created by Verhova as guides to mankind. Each High Dragon had a specific job to do."

Zachery raised his eyebrows. "You're saying dragons...are good?"

"Not all of them. The High Dragons were sent to our world to help teach us, to show us how to best use our gift of free will. The first born was Lestice, the Voice of Creation. Second was Ocudai the Seer. Third was Belladux the Right Hand, and finally came Cadent the Left Hand."

A girl Daniel recognized as Jane spoke up. He had met her only briefly. Now she brushed a lock of cherry-blonde hair out of her eyes. "The Divine Order," she said, "teaches that all dragons are creatures of evil made by Shade to torment mankind and enslave them before the arrival of the High Dragons and, in turn, Shade. Are you saying what they teach isn't true?"

"Most of what they teach is close," Claudia said, "but not exact. But in the end, you can believe what you want. Just know that our history is one of the primary reasons we do what we do and why our enemies do what they do. After your training is complete, I have no doubts you will be fully committed to our cause."

Robin sat straighter in her seat as she spoke: "You said, 'why our enemies do what they do.' Who are they?"

"During the First Age, Cadent rebelled against the other High Dragons and Verhova."

Alan leaned in, looking enthralled. "Why would he do that?"

"Pride. Verhova had the adoration and love of the people he created and Cadent was jealous of this. His influence spread to those around him and he quickly gained a following. When confronted by the other High Dragons, he refused to see reason and started a war. His worshipers became his army. They spread out across the world, slaughtering anyone and anything that didn't adhere to them."

"Why didn't the other High Dragons stop him?" Alan asked.

"They tried. But they couldn't be everywhere at once to deal with both him and his army. Realizing this, they formed their own."

Aaron smiled. "The Dragon Guard."

Claudia nodded. "The Dragon Guard was formed from those that still followed Verhova and the teachings of the remaining three High Dragons. They paved the way for the sect structure we still use."

Griffon seemed skeptical. "How long was the war?" she asked.

"According to our records, around three thousand years."

"A war lasted three thousand years?" Griffon said.

Claudia nodded. "Time does not ravage a High Dragon. Three thousand years is to them but a blink of an eye."

"So they're immortal?"

"As far as we know. Yes." Clara raised her hand. "Clara, just speak. There's no need to raise your hand."

Clara put her hand down quickly. "So your enemies are the ones that followed Cadent?"

Claudia opened one of the books and flipped through the pages before sliding the book to the middle of the table. The page showed an imprint of a left hand. Only the very edges of the palm were marked, the fingers being thin and ending in a point. Surrounding it in a circle was a series of strange-looking runes. "This is the symbol of who we fight," Claudia said, "a cult known as the Disciples of the Left Hand, more commonly called Disciples among our order. They've been around as long as we have but have stayed out of the eyes of the greater world."

Daniel's conversation with Alphonse so long ago came to mind. He'd said the Dragon Guard "ranted and raved" about cults. It was also true that there were cults around Edaren, though they seemed to have very little influence and were few and far between. Daniel felt the history lesson was a lot to absorb in one sitting. Claudia and the others here were far from crazy. The trust he'd learned to put in them during their time together on the road made it seem likely that her words were true, even if they were hard to swallow.

Jane tapped her chin. "So what happened to Cadent?" she asked.

"The battle that took place here on the shores of Edaren ended with him and Belladux clashing. We know that Cadent ultimately lost. What we don't know is where he is now. High Dragons cannot die and we know that Belladux did not see fit to tell our predecessors where he was going when he took Cadent."

"So they're still alive?" Robin asked quickly. "How come we've never seen anything relating to them?"

"As far as we know, yes, they are alive," Claudia said. "Though we've had no contact with any of them. What we do know is that over the course of not only our history, but the history of other nations, they *have* appeared—admittedly under different names and interpretations."

Clara perked up at the mention of other nations. "Like what?"

Daniel too leaned in closer to ensure he heard this. He knew of the other nations in the world, though he didn't know much. He knew that Edaren was isolationist and slow to develop their relations to the others. But he also knew that the Council in Dalisia frequently had talks with the nation of Kunkuni, which acted as Edaren's introduction to the rest of the world. In addition he knew that Edaren had very brief and hostile first contact with the nation of Krida across the southern ocean.

"From our short history with Krida," Claudia said, "we know that they depict dragons on their religious figureheads. Beyond that we aren't sure.

The islands of Kunkuni have a similar story of four siblings that created the world alongside their parents. All are pictured as dragons. While our knowledge of the nations beyond these two is very limited, the things we've seen point to the High Dragon and Verhova relationship being a reoccurring theme across the world."

Jane seemed entirely unconvinced. "So you're telling us that an ancient cult worshiped a High Dragon from the beginning of time. That no one has seen or heard of this High Dragon in thousands of years, and that this is what the Dragon Guard has been fighting all this time? Isn't this just another case of a 'reoccurring theme' being taken too far?"

Claudia simply shrugged. "Sounds outlandish, doesn't it?"

"Sounds like you're all crazier than I thought," Jane said.

"Okay, even if that's not true, what about the regular dragons?" Griffon asked.

Claudia smiled at Griffon before answering. "All we know is that dragons were much like mankind, beings given free will. During the war, it seems most followed Cadent, thinking they were greater than mankind and clearly worthy of ruling over men. Those that survived the war and were loyal to Cadent were most likely the ones that spawned the legends and negative stories you hear now."

"But there were good ones?" someone asked.

"There were, though they were few."

"Are any still alive?" Daniel asked.

"There may be."

CHAPTER EIGHTEEN

5th of Landring, 27th year of the Fourth Age.

DANIEL WATCHED AS Aaron swung hard to Griffon's left. She lifted her shield before the blow reached her. When it connected, she countered by pushing back, sending Aaron's sword back into its initial arc. Aaron used the new momentum and pivoted on one foot, bringing the sword full circle into a backhanded swing aimed at Griffon's legs. She quickly jumped back and they resumed their standoff. They circled each other in one of the dirt rings cut into the lush green grass. Sweat covered their faces. Their padding was crossed with lines of dust where the wooden blades had connected.

One-on-one matches had been a large part of their training over the last two weeks. During that time it had become clear that Griffon and Aaron were two of the best fighters. Their match so far had lasted the longest and been, in Daniel's opinion at least, the most interesting to watch. It was certainly a far cry longer than Daniel's had been. He had been matched against Lace. While she wasn't nearly as skilled as these two, she was still leagues better than he was. In the end, he had held his own longer than he'd thought he would, but he was still unaccustomed to the weight of the shield and was unable to keep his balance when swinging or blocking.

In the five months of their training, the differences in the skill set of each of them had become more and more apparent. Aaron, Griffon, and Robin had surpassed everyone at combat with Obadiah. Clara, Robert, and Alan excelled in Claudia's lessons, while Lace was a natural in the wilderness with Austin. Zachery seemed like a jack of all trades. Daniel, however, seemed to have no discernable trait that stood out from the rest. He was average with a sword and struggled with history. He did well enough when it came to wildlife and survival techniques. This had more to do with his upbringing in Sapella and the woods around it than the training. At this point in their journey to become full-fledged Dragon Guards, he had thought he would at least start to shine in one area or another like everyone else had.

"Step in!" Obadiah shouted the order and broke Daniel's train of thought.

The two combatants moved into the next ring without breaking their stride around the edges. The matches took place in a ring roughly twenty feet in diameter, with three smaller rings within. Every time Obadiah felt a match was dragging on, he ordered the combatants to step into the next ring to shrink the arena and force the fighters to clash. Aaron and Griffon continued their standoff until Aaron had his back to the morning sun. The moment Griffon had to squint against the light, he charged forward. He swung for her midsection, but she anticipated the blow and leaped back out of his reach just in time.

They began trading blows. Neither seemed to gain the upper hand, as each swing or jab was met with shield or sword to block it. That was until Griffon found one of the narrow divots in the otherwise even terrain of the arena. She stumbled sideways. In her effort to correct herself, she lowered her shield, allowing Aaron to jab at her exposed ribs and effectively end the match with what would be a killing blow in a real battle.

When Griffon stood again, she threw down her sword and gritted her teeth while Aaron gently placed his weapon on the nearby racks. Obadiah stepped up to Griffon as she angrily unstrapped her shield. He glared at her. Her face flushed. She quickly picked up her sword and returned it to the racks as her face gradually changed to darker shades of red. This wasn't out of the ordinary for Griffon. When she failed at something, she tended to lash out. In spite of this, she was one of the friendliest people Daniel had met among the recruits.

Obadiah turned to the rest of them. "That marks the final match and a good start to the morning," he said. "You've all improved greatly over the last several months. Now, instead of your usual lessons in the library, head over to the north gate. Austin and Claudia should have finished their preparations and will be waiting for you there."

The twenty-two of them turned without question and headed for the north gate. As they walked, the buzz of nearly a dozen conversations filled the air. They shuffled around until everyone was in their preferred groups.

"What do you think we'll be doing?" Daniel asked the question to no one in particular.

Clara groaned. "It better not be another race. My legs still hurt from the last one."

Zachery shrugged. "I don't know," he said, "I thought the race was kind of fun."

"You didn't come in last."

They had been put through various different "games," as Austin liked to call them, from an obstacle course to a free-for-all arena fight and everything in between. At this point, they could be doing anything. They made it to the keep gate and were ushered out by the guards with a polite nod. Once on the road, they headed straight for the north gate. With the roads clear, they made good time, allowing them to arrive in a little under half an hour. They found Claudia waiting for them next to the gate. She was talking with one of the two city guards assigned to the gate. When Daniel first arrived in Vigil, he had been confused about how the city was protected, be it by Dragon Guards or a city guard. He'd discovered that the job had been split down the middle, the Dragon Guard working alongside a collection of volunteer civilians who were undertrained for the most part, though the wardens did what they could to fix that.

When Claudia saw Daniel and the others approach, she bid the guards farewell and without a word to the trainees led them through the gate and down the narrow road through the killing field.

Once they were across the field and through the outer gate, Claudia took them off the main road and over the short hills into Highwood Forest. It was where their games were usually held. The forest was almost entirely towering cedar trees and covered most of the eastern side of Edaren. After only idle chatter between the trainees and not a word from Claudia during their walk, they were glad to finally meet Austin just inside the edge of the forest. He was leaning against a tree sitting at the bottom of a small hill, waiting patiently for them to arrive. Claudia and Austin conversed briefly as Daniel and the others formed their usual line.

Then she faced them and smiled.

"What we're going to be doing is something the Dragon Guard has done for the last several generations," she said. "It will test your team-work, your survival skills, and your ability to form a strategy."

Austin also smiled and clapped his hands together, "This game is a favorite of mine. We'll lead some of you to a small pond and the rest to a clearing. At each one of these there is a small fort, one for each team." He paused and let Claudia take over again.

"You will be divided right down the middle into teams of eleven," she said. "Your goals for this exercise—"

Austin cut her off: "Game."

"What?"

"You said exercise. Come on, at least make it *sound* enjoyable."

Claudia glared at him for a moment before continuing. "This exercise revolves around teamwork and proper strategic planning. You have three available paths to victory. The first: You may take the opposing team's flag, bring it back to your own fort, and fly it alongside your own. If your flag is not also present then you do not win. Second, you may eliminate each member of the other team through standard sparring rules. If you are hit in any area that would be considered vital, you are eliminated.

Finally, you may also resort to capturing members of the opposing team and securing them with the rope that will be provided at your own fort. Whether a 'fatal' blow, a captured opponent, or a combination of both. Each member of the other team must be taken out."

Griffon crossed her arms. "Doesn't that just make this an extravagant arena match?" she said. "Fighting and eliminating the other team is the easiest and fastest way to win."

Austin grinned and rubbed his hands together. "Now there lays one of the more interesting rules," he said. "Each of you is allowed to eliminate only one person."

Claudia nodded. "For example: If Griffon were to fight with and then eliminate Clara in combat, Clara would be removed from the exercise. But from that point on, Griffon would no longer be allowed to eliminate anyone else. Although she may still participate in combat, any 'fatal' blow she struck from that point would be invalid."

Daniel realized there was more strategy to this than he originally thought. In Claudia's example, if Clara had not already eliminated someone on Griffon's team before Griffon eliminated her, the rest of Clara's team would mathematically be locked out of winning the exercise by the elimination option. They would have to resort to either capturing the flag or the other members of Griffon's team.

Another question came to mind. He wasn't looking forward to the answer but felt he needed to ask regardless. "How long is this supposed to last?"

"Until one team wins," Austin answered.

"So we could be out here for days?"

Austin chuckled. "When I did this, it lasted two and a half weeks."

"What do we get if we win?" Griffon asked.

Claudia and Austin glanced at each other with an uneasy look.

Austin sighed. "You get to stay."

An air of confusion settled over the recruits.

As always, Clara was the first to voice her concern. "I'm afraid I don't understand...we get to stay where?"

Claudia took a deep breath before addressing the recruits in front of her. "The winners get to stay at Vigil. The losers…will be removed from the ranks of the Dragon Guards and sent home with an escort."

At once, the entire line of recruits erupted in a voice of opposition. Daniel's head was swimming. They were going to send the losing team home. None of the recruits were happy to hear this. Austin attempted to quiet them before they were all hushed by a loud, shrill whistle from Claudia.

The scholar placed her hands on her hips and sighed. "I know," she said. "It doesn't seem fair to you right now. But life isn't fair. These are the stakes. You win or you go home, there is no other option. This is a high pressure situation and you have to show us you can succeed in spite of that pressure. You want to be here? Prove you deserve it." They were all quiet for a long moment. Claudia appeared to wait until she was sure they understood her before continuing. "Each fort has bedrolls, as well as racks of various sparring weapons and some gear. What you use depends on your personal preferences. You have the entire forest as your battleground."

"What do we do if we're eliminated?" Jane asked with considerable bite in her tone. "Do we just wait until the game is over?"

"If you are eliminated, we expect you to return to Vigil as soon as possible, where we will begin preparations to take you home should your team lose the overall exercise."

"So how do we decide the teams?" Jane asked. Daniel could almost taste the bitterness in her tone.

"You don't. Austin and I will."

Austin was quick to make his first choice. "Griffon, stand with me."

Claudia, without missing a beat, made the next pick. "Jane."

They called out names so quickly that they must have discussed who would go where beforehand. When was all said and done, the ones Daniel knew on Claudia's team were Aaron, Alan, and Jane. Daniel was on Austin's side with Griffon, Zachery, Clara, Lace, Robert, and Robin.

Austin addressed the group around him: "Claudia's group will be team one and we'll be team two. Now we'll show you to your temporary home."

After a last look at their new opponents, the eleven members of Claudia's team followed her into the forest. Daniel turned and started after Austin. As he went, he couldn't help glancing at the towering trees above them. They walked a narrow path that cut through thick under-growth. Beyond the path the forest was so dense that he wasn't able to tell where the clearing actually was until they broke through the tree line and into the open.

The fort was right in the middle of the clearing. It was larger than Daniel had expected and resembled a log home, with two floors and a flat roof with a short railing. In the middle of the roof was a tall pole with a blue flag flying at its peak. Iron rungs were attached along the length of the pole, allowing a climber to either place a flag or remove one. The wall closest to them had a tall, wide opening that had probably once included a door.

Austin led them through the waist-high grass and stopped at the opening. "Welcome to your new home," he said. "The game starts tomorrow at first light."

Clara looked at the tree line. "Which way is the other team?"

Austin shrugged and said, "You know, it's the strangest thing. I seem to have forgotten."

Clara glared at him and crossed her arms. "You forgot."

"Odd, isn't it? Oh well, I suppose you'll just have to take a look around." He started off into the forest and back toward Vigil.

They all watched him go. When he disappeared, none of them really knew what do. It was the first time they had been left on their own for something like this. Without any real instructions they felt more than a little lost—especially with what was at stake. It seemed surreal to know that at any moment in the next several days they could lose and be on their way home.

Daniel eyed the fort. "I guess," he said, "we should get our gear."

No one objected, so the eleven of them stepped through the doorway. The first floor was for the most part empty. A coil of rope hung from a hook on a pillar in the back corner of the room. A set of racks was attached to the wall opposite the doorway, with various weapons and padded armor pieces hanging from them. Next to these were several woven baskets and linen bags. Finally, a ladder was set in the center of the back wall, leading to the second floor.

Zachery pulled down a wooden longsword from one of the racks. He tested its weight before placing it back on the rack and trying another. He repeated this two more times before finding one with a size and heft he was comfortable with. Griffon followed suit, seeming to choose the longest and heaviest sword she could find. Daniel let the rest of his team pick through the gear before taking one of the remaining few. He knew the one he wanted would be left on the rack. Out of all twenty-two trainees, only a few favored the short sword. The handle on this one was short enough that he could comfortably place the pommel under his thumb. Satisfied with the grip and feel of the leather-wrapped hilt, he pushed the blade through his belt and adjusted its positioning so the blade sat comfortably below his back.

They had been taught how to use a variety of weapons during their training and all of them had found ones they favored. Aaron usually chose a broadsword. It featured a wide, heavy blade, commonly used with a shield with a hilt meant for a single hand. Zachery leaned toward a longsword, similar to the broadsword but thinner and longer, with a hilt long enough for two hands if preferred. Griffon was the only one to use a great sword, longer and wider than both a broadsword or a longsword. Its hilt was half again larger than necessary, letting one move hands up and down the hilt for greater leverage.

Daniel, Clara, and Alan, however, favored the short sword—Clara and Alan due to its size, while Daniel preferred it due to the reverse grip, a style that Obadiah had said Daniel was a natural for. Holding the blade with the tip pointing to the ground and his thumb on the pommel, it provided new angles of attack that were unconventional and unexpected. It was best employed by a fighter who preferred to take the defensive rather than offensive. The strategy was to wait for an opponent to attack and use the blade to block along one's forearm or to get in close to hamper an opponent's swing.

Daniel glanced at the remaining pieces of armor and took what was left. A set of vambraces to cover his forearms, a pair gloves as well as a lightweight, padded chest plate. When he had finished, he turned around to see that most of the other members of his team had either gone outside or up. He decided to see what the second floor held, so he headed for the ladder at the back of the room. He found the second floor was lined with cots with bedrolls laid out on top of them. A path between the cots led to a second ladder that Daniel assumed ended on the roof.

It was a convenient setup. If the other team wanted to go through the fort to get to the flag, they would have to fight through an entire room of their opponents. Daniel imagined that the other fort had a similar setup. He climbed the ladder and found the roof was clear save for the pole set in its center and supported by four thick ropes tied to each corner. Griffon and Clara were looking out over the clearing and into the forest beyond. Daniel walked to the railing to join them.

"So, how should we start?" Griffon said. She stretched her arms out behind her. Daniel heard her shoulders pop several times.

Clara winced at the sound. "Well, I noticed there's no food here," she said, "which means we have to find our own."

Daniel ran his hand through his hair. "We'll need water too."

"I saw some water skins in some of the baskets by the racks," Clara said. "There was a hunting knife too."

Griffon frowned. "So who's doing what?"

"Let's see what everyone else is willing to do, I guess," Clara said with a shrug.

Daniel could tell her mood had been dampened significantly by the nature of the exercise. Admittedly, so had his. This was new territory. The stakes required that everyone put everything they had into the fights to come. No one wanted to go home. They all wanted to be here. Some of them *needed* to be here. The idea that it could be snatched away from them was hard to grasp.

The three of them headed back to the first floor, where they gathered everyone and discussed who would go where and why. They decided to spread out in pairs in all directions so they would have better coverage of the whole area as they searched for food and water, as well as learned the lay of the land. Each pair was given water skins and a woven basket to carry whatever they might find. Griffon, Lace, and Zachery would stay at the fort to organize the inside and get a fire started outside the door.

Daniel picked up a woven basket and started to walk north, with Clara at his side. They were quickly out of the clearing and navigating the thick growth of the forest. Not far from the tree line they found an old game trail. As they walked, they kept their eyes peeled in hopes of spotting something useful.

Clara had her hands clasped behind her back as they walked. "You know," she said, "we've been friends since you arrived, but other than your trip to Vigil I don't really know anything about you."

He shrugged. "There isn't much to know."

"That can't be true. What about your family?"

"Just my mom and brother."

"No father?"

"I don't really remember much about my father," Daniel said. "He left a long time ago."

Clara seemed surprised. "Oh, I'm sorry to hear that."

"Don't be. I'm not. My brother and I turned out all right without him and my mother was able to support us just fine on her own."

"Don't you ever wonder where he went?"

"I used to. But after a while I decided that I just didn't care anymore and that it didn't matter where he went. He left. Clearly, he thought wherever he was going was more important than his family." Daniel said the last few words with more venom than he'd intended to.

Clara nodded and was quiet for a moment before adopting a lighter, cheerier tone: "What sort of work does your mother do?"

Thinking of his mother standing in the kitchen, covered in flour, brought a smile to Daniel's face. "She works in a bakery, has for most of her life."

Clara looked up at him. "You miss them, don't you?"

"Every single day." He glanced at her. "What about you? You're from Navia, right?"

"That's right. My family moved there from Grey Gate just before I was born."

"What made them move?"

"It's Grey Gate. It would have been hard for them to find a reason to stay."

"I wasn't there very long, but I see your point. What do they do?"

"My father works as a barkeeper at one of the inns. My mother"—Clara rolled her eyes—"is a very *successful* advisor to Councilman Milton. It gives her a lot of control over decisions that affect the city, which she just *loves*."

Clara clearly held no fondness for her mother's job, so he tried to change course. "What made you want to be a Dragon Guard?"

"Spite."

Her quick response surprised him. "What do you mean?"

"My mother. She thinks that I need to be a 'proper' lady so I don't embarrass our family. She controlled everything about my life, from what I wore to the people I could talk to."

"So you came here to get away from that."

"I wanted to control my own life, make my own decisions for once."

"I take it that hasn't gone over well with her?"

Clara grinned. "She was furious when I left."

"Well, for what it's worth," Daniel said, "I think you fit in perfectly here."

She smiled widely at him. "Thank you."

CHAPTER NINETEEN

6th of Landring, 27th year of the Fourth Age.

GRIFFON STOOD ON the roof of the fort looking out over the moonlit clearing. A breeze caused the shin high grass to roll like waves. She had awoken only moments earlier, but she was already fully alert and tapping her foot rapidly stay that way. She glanced over the edge of the railing and saw Zachery hunched over the fire he'd built just outside the open doorway the night before.

The previous night, after everyone had returned from their rather lucrative foraging expedition, they had all discussed and formed the basic outline of a plan. They decided to split into two groups. Five would scout the other team by making their way around the north side of the forest before looping back the long way. The remaining six would stay at the fort to guard against any attempts to take the flag. Griffon didn't expect anything to happen quite yet. It was the first day of the exercise, so chances were good the other team would do just as they were, taking it slow for the first few days to gauge how the other team would react and operate. They would all be waiting for someone to make a mistake. No one wanted to be the first person eliminated and give the other team an advantage.

Griffon stretched out her arms before turning on her heel and heading down the ladder to meet the others on the first floor. Zachery and Daniel were just outside the door preparing food for everyone while Clara warmed her hands by the fire. Griffon sighed and looked around the room. Most of the team was eagerly awaiting the morning meal. She didn't know all of their names, not well at least since she rarely spoke to most of them. But during their time at Vigil they had become her family. They were a better one than she could have ever hoped for back in Forge. She did have to admit that she missed her brothers in spite of how awful it had been back home. She only hoped that they were all right. Her father wouldn't have been in the most reasonable mood after her departure.

She worried the most for Richard. He was far too gentle to stand up to their father or brother. She just hoped that her father's rage over Griffon's departure wouldn't be directed at her brother.

It had taken some hard thinking, but Griffon had finally figured out her end goal. She didn't just want to learn how to properly defend herself. She also needed to get to the point where she'd never have to rely on people again, where she would never be stuck with someone like her father because she had no choice. And she wanted to be able to protect Richard. She'd already decided that when she finished her training, she would approach Commander Hall about the prospect of moving her brother here. Maybe there would be a place for him at the keep to work as a chef or cleaner—anything to save him from his current life. She wasn't going to abandon him.

Daniel and Zachery stepped away from the fire and into the fort with two heaping bowls of grilled mushrooms. The room soon filled with a wonderful, earthy aroma that for a moment banished Griffon's worries about her brother. Daniel and Zachery passed food out to everyone gathered. They all ate quickly and happily in the quiet of the early morning.

After nearly a minute of silence, Zachery spoke: "Think we can win?"

Griffon sighed. "We have to."

As usual, Daniel attempted to lighten the somber tone. "If not for ourselves, at least for Austin," he said. "He probably put a wager on our team."

The group shared a halfhearted laugh before everything drifted back into silence. *Austin.* Griffon bit her lip as she thought back to Forge. He hadn't told her so, but she was certain he was the ranger who rescued her. She'd recognized his voice the moment she heard him speak in the library several months earlier. The fact that his gaze had lingered on her several times since only reinforced her suspicions. She wasn't sure if she should bring the subject up with him. If she was wrong and the reason she'd left Forge came to light, it could cause serious problems, even threaten her opportunity to become a Dragon Guard. She hadn't been completely honest with Captain North at the time of her interview, though she had a feeling he knew she was lying to him. At the moment, the only people who knew she was wanted in Forge for murder were the people of Forge and the ranger, Austin. None of that was important at the moment, so she pushed it to the back of her mind.

The sun slowly started to illuminate the world outside, letting light spill through the doorway, indicating that it was time for everything to start. Griffon grabbed her wooden training sword from the floor beside her as several others did the same. She took one of the drawstrings from a linen sack and tied a slipknot at the hilt of her sword, and again around the blade, to form a makeshift strap that allowed her to carry the sack across her back. Several of the others with larger weapons, such as Robin, followed suit. The rest of them let their weapons hang at their belts. Griffon stepped outside with the other four who were going to be on the scouting run: Daniel, Zachery, Lace, and Robin.

Griffon crossed her arms and frowned. "I still don't see why I'm going with you for this."

"You're one of the best fighters on our team," Daniel said. "You're there in case we get spotted."

It made sense to her. Daniel was far from one the best fighters of their group. He was fast and smart, but she had yet to see him win in a one-on-one fight with anyone. Though he wasn't the best fighter to be sure, he hardly gave himself enough credit. If he just had more confidence in himself, he would excel. Zachery was a better fighter, but not by much. She had no idea how the Woods girls faired in a fight. She had never paid much attention to anyone outside of their group, though she vaguely remembered Robin being quite capable.

Curious, she looked at what they chose to carry as weapons: Lace carried two daggers looped through her belt while Robin had a longsword hanging from her back. She wasn't surprised to see Daniel and Zachery with their usual short sword and longsword, respectively. Griffon pulled the strap on her shoulder tighter. She was still disappointed with the weight of the weapon. It was far too light compared to what she preferred, but it was still the heaviest option.

Zachery examined the tree line in front of them. "So," he said, "are we ready for this?"

Griffon turned on her heel and started walking. "Probably not," she said, "but that's part of the fun, isn't it?"

Daniel shrugged and started after her. "You have an interesting take on fun, given the circumstances."

The rest followed them silently into the trees. They walked as quickly as they could through the thick bush to get as far as they could as fast as possible. They were heading straight north. Given the fact that the forest came to an abrupt end not too far to the south, this was the most likely direction the other team would be. It would keep their fort at roughly the same distance from Vigil while being far enough away from them to keep the exercise interesting.

They ended up following a creek that Lace and Robin had found the night before, giving them a good reference point so they wouldn't get lost in the thick forest. They made good time. When the sun was directly overhead, they spotted it. It was only a corner of the fort roof, but it was enough to make them stop in their tracks and drop to the ground. Without a word, they doubled back and looped around to the west so they could come out on the far side of the fort. They stopped with the fort nearly a hundred feet away on the other side of a thick line of trees. Griffon and the others gathered in the thick undergrowth to stay out of sight of prying eyes.

Zachery's voice was barely heard in the quiet of the forest. "Robin and I will lag behind and watch your backs. The three of you can move up and get a better look."

Griffon frowned. She wasn't the quietest of them but rather than make a fuss of it all she bit her lip and said nothing as everyone else nodded their consent. Without a word, she followed Daniel and Lace through the foliage. They moved agonizingly slow, making sure every movement would not cause a noticeable disturbance in the forestry around them. They carefully chose the placement of each foot and hand on solid ground so as not to stumble. Crouching like this was uncomfortable and awkward. She hated every moment of it. She was only supposed to be here in case something went wrong, yet here she was crawling beneath the brush to do something Zachery should have been doing. Griffon paused and looked toward her companions, who had disappeared. She assumed they had branched off to each side of her to see the fort at different angles. It took her several minutes to reach a point where she could clearly see the fort across the pond.

It was structurally identical to theirs. This one, however, sat with the entrance facing the water. The forest also grew directly next to the fort. She looked to the roof of the fort and saw four people sitting at each corner. She recognized Alan on the side closest to her right away, but the others' faces were hidden from her view. She saw no one else in or around the fort. That meant there were either more inside or they were out scouting like Griffon and her team. She decided they were most likely scouting. It would be pointless to be on the lower floors at the moment, seeing as how the four at the top of the ladder would be more than enough to hold off any number of attackers since they'd have to climb the ladder to the roof in single file.

Griffon continued examining the area but saw nothing that stood out as useful or out of the ordinary. She was about to start making her way back when she felt a tap on her shoulder. She jumped, but a firm hand on her back kept her from moving too much. She turned and saw Lace motioning to head back. Griffon nodded. They both slowly crawled back to where they'd left Zachery and Robin. Daniel was already kneeling down next to them and speaking in whispers.

"The others must be going to our fort, unless they're patrolling the area." Daniel said, again running his hand through his hair, something he seemed to do whenever he was thinking particularly hard.

Lace shook her head. "I don't think they would be patrolling. That's too much risk of getting ambushed with how thick the forest is."

"Did you see anything useful?" Daniel asked Griffon.

She shook her head. "I wasn't able to look very long, couldn't get close as quickly as you two."

He nodded and looked up at the sun through the trees. "We'd better start heading back. We can talk about everything when the whole team is around."

They started back the way they'd come and returned just over two hours later. Everyone gathered on the roof and Daniel began the brief overview of what they'd seen.

"Their fort is identical to ours, from what we can tell. The doorway faces the pond and the area around it is pretty thick."

Griffon looked to Clara. "Did you see any of them around while we were gone?"

She laughed and the others around them smiled. "Only one. I don't think he was the best choice of scout since he stumbled through the brush and into the clearing, looked terrified as he crawled back into the trees."

Griffon nodded. "There were four of them on their roof keeping watch, so I figured the others were probably doing exactly what we were."

"So, any ideas on how we want to do this?" Zachery asked. "We have three choices, after all."

Everyone was quiet as they considered the options. Griffon preferred combat elimination. Capture seemed like too much of a hassle, whether it was the flag or the other team. She also simply preferred to fight if she had the choice.

"I think it's too soon to get set on one strategy," Lace said.

Clara raised a hand. "I disagree," she said. "If we get caught in a fight, we need to know if we should go ahead and use up our one elimination or try to hold off and capture. We should decide now."

Daniel cleared his throat. "Let's try to avoid elimination if we can," he said. "Knocking one of them out just locks us out of another option. If we try to capture and end up taking someone out by accident, or if they take one of us out, we can even the playing field by just eliminating the person we captured."

Clara nodded. "Well," she said, "let's decide who will be doing what for the foreseeable future."

"I'll take guard duty," Griffon said with no hesitation. "It beats skulking around the forest."

The others quickly called out what roles they wanted to fill. After several minutes, it was decided that Zachery and Griffon would take the first night watch and rotate out periodically with the rest of the team. In the meantime, Daniel, Lace, Robert, and Robin would keep an eye on the enemy fort from a safe distance. The rest would rotate guard duty during the day, as well as gather water when they started to run low. It was far from a perfect setup, but it seemed that it would work for the time being, at least until they had a solid plan for how they were going to win and learned how the other team would operate.

Griffon was far from a tactician, but even she knew that all this would likely be decided by who would get that first elimination, unless both parties eliminated one another at the same time. An elimination would essentially lock both teams into two of the three options. The team that lost a member without using its one kill would be locked into the captures, while the team that made the elimination would have to either finish off the rest of the team or take the flag. The first encounter would determine the entire nature of the game, and in the heat of the moment even the most solid plan could go out the window.

Griffon sat on the roof, a hunting knife in hand. She was absent-mindedly digging into the wooden roof beside her with the tip of her blade as she continually swept her eyes over the dark tree line. Four uneventful days had passed. She had expected something to happen by now. Based on what Daniel and the others had said, the other team was doing exactly what they'd been doing. Everyone was waiting for someone else to make the first move. No one wanted to leave Vigil. This was the one chance they all had to be a Dragon Guard. Everyone had sacrificed something to be here. They all had their reasons, and none of them wanted to take the chance of going home.

Yet Griffon was growing tired of waiting. Since the day she'd left Forge, or even the day she'd arrived at Vigil, she hadn't gone more than twenty-four hours without doing *something*. She was starting to feel pent up and irritated at everything. She'd even thrown her plate at Zachery the night before after he had made a joke at her expense for the third time that day. The others had started giving her a wide berth after that. She looked at the small hole she had dug into the wood before sighing and placing the knife at her belt. She looked behind her at Zachery, who was slightly hunched over.

She rolled her eyes and grabbed one of the small pebbles that she had started to bring up during night watches. With a little more force than was needed, she threw it at the back of his head, making him jump as he was snapped awake. He turned to glare at her. She scolded him with her eyes before turning back around to continue her watch. She kept scanning the forest, making random choices on where she placed her eyes so she never developed a pattern that could be exploited by anyone trying to sneak closer. One of those choices landed her gaze on a low-hanging tree branch that swayed from side to side. She almost chalked it up to the wind. Then she realized that at the moment the air was perfectly still.

She focused on the spot for only a moment before continuing to scan the immediate area around it, periodically bringing her eyes back to the same spot. She never saw anything else out of the ordinary, but all the same it was close to sunrise and the others would be waking soon, so she saw no reason to wake anyone over it. It might have been nothing at all as at this point the branch had stilled itself once again. She continued the watch until the sun slowly started to peek over the horizon. She heard the others below start to wake.

Zachery stood up behind her. "Now that they're up," he said "I'm going to get some sleep."

Griffon didn't reply as he descended the ladder into the fort. She sat there for a while longer, listening to the chatter of the rest of her team below. She glanced over the edge and saw Lace and Daniel start off toward the tree line. She didn't think they were going scouting just yet so she wondered what exactly they were doing. She didn't wonder long. A minute later, they returned with Lace holding two rather large rabbits by the ears.

Moments later, Griffon heard someone climb the ladder behind her and turned to see Clara making her way up to sit with her.

Clara nudged her with her shoulder. "Sleep well?"

"Funny." Griffon looked over the edge and saw Daniel start the process of cleaning the catch. "Where did the rabbits come from?"

Clara also peered over the edge. "Lace set some snares when they were out scouting yesterday." She nudged her again. "Are you okay?"

"I'm fine."

"You've just seemed … agitated, I guess."

"I'm tired of waiting. I want to *do* something."

Griffon looked over the edge again and watched Daniel. He passed the knife and rabbit to another team member. Then he and the other three scouts headed toward the forest. They never saw anything different when they were out. It was the same report each day: four people atop the fort and the rest were never seen.

Griffon sighed and picked at loose slivers of wood. "I just hate sitting here doing nothing."

"Well. I like it," Clara said. "Gives me time to think."

"I'd rather stay out of my own head. Thanks, though."

"Ah," Clara said. "So that's it."

"What?"

"That's why you like the training and the fighting. It's a distraction, right?"

Griffon said nothing and stared at Clara, a look of irritation on her face.

Clara didn't seem to notice and continued speaking. "I was the same way for a long time. It's why I read so many books. It was a way of distracting myself, a way to stay out of my own thoughts when I didn't want to deal with everything and everyone else."

"What about now? You still have your head in a book whenever you get the chance."

"Yeah, but now I do it just for fun."

Griffon chuckled in spite of herself. After another moment, she and Clara headed down to join the others as they waited for the rabbits to be prepared. Clara was right. Griffon didn't like to be alone with her thoughts for too long. They always drifted to her brother, which made her feel guilty that she was even here. That she'd left him behind.

Just before they reached the ladder, something in the trees caught Griffon's eye. The movement was so slight that she almost missed it. The bushes just on the edge of the tree line where she'd noticed the branch sway now rustled unnaturally. Something wasn't right.

Griffon reached for the string at her shoulder to release her weapon. Clara noticed her intense gaze and followed it. She had only just landed her eyes on the same spot when all at once, six people burst from the trees and charged toward the fort.

"We're under attack!" Griffon shouted down to the others as she raced to the ladder.

Clara followed as Griffon jumped down the hole to the second floor and again down to the first; she was at the doorway before the other team had made it even halfway across the clearing. She lifted the wooden blade with both hands, while around her the others readied themselves. It was six versus seven. They had the advantage in numbers for the moment but that could change in an instant.

Griffon turned and saw Clara just heading down the ladder. "Clara," she said, "get on the second floor in case any get past us."

Clara nodded and climbed back up without objection. Griffon knew Clara was the weakest fighter in their group and Griffon didn't want to risk her being eliminated. Now, with her safe, it was an even fight. But the question remained, what was the plan was for this attack? Was it to eliminate some of their members from the game or try to take the flag?

She had no more time to ponder their strategy. The group ahead of them was close enough to clash and the first came for Griffon.

She didn't recognize the boy but it didn't matter. She raised her sword and blocked the first blow, letting it slide along its length to the ground. She was about to bring it up into his chest but hesitated as her instincts yelled for her to do it but her brain told her not to in favor of the single elimination rule. She was only allowed one. If she used it now and needed it later, she would be in trouble. But at the same time she had no real way to capture him in the midst of a fight. If she didn't do either one, it would be an endless fight until they were both exhausted.

She thought far too long on the dilemma. The boy recovered and brought his sword around hard at her midsection. She barely avoided the strike by jumping back into the doorway. That wasn't a blow she had been expected to block or even dodge. It had been too fast and had too much power behind it. They were trying to take them out.

Griffon grinned. That made things easier for her. She swung for the boy's legs. Her speed caught him off guard and knocked him off his feet and to the ground. She was about to bring her sword down across his chest when something caught her attention out of the corner of her eye. She turned quickly and saw Jane duck around the corner of the fort to head inside. She was going for the flag while they were distracted with the rest of her team. She glanced back to the fight in front of her. Her team was slowly pushing the attackers away from the door. From what she could see, they hadn't lost anyone yet.

Griffon didn't know Jane well but she knew she was a more skilled fighter than Clara. She decided that her team would be able to handle this without her in spite of the number disadvantage. Griffon turned and ran inside. Jane was already up the ladder. Griffon heard her and Clara clashing above. She leaped onto the ladder and quickly climbed its length. When she reached the top, she saw that Jane had Clara pinned against the second ladder with their wooden blades locked together. Just as Griffon finished climbing Jane shoved Clara hard into the wall, causing her to slam the back of her head into the hard wood with a solid *thud* stunning her.

Without thinking, Griffon charged at Jane and swung at her back. But Jane must have heard her coming. She ducked low. Before Griffon had time to adjust her swing, Jane rolled past her. Griffon skidded to a stop and stopped her sword before she struck Clara in the head. She turned just as Jane swung her longsword at her back. With her own sword pointed down, Griffon blocked the blow, letting it slide down her blade before pushing forward with her shoulder to try to throw Jane backwards.

The maneuver only half worked. Jane stumbled back a step before regaining her footing, allowing her to drop down and sweep her leg, knocking Griffon to the ground. Jane quickly leapt onto Griffon, pointed her sword down, and tried to jab her in the chest. But Griffon managed to use the large hilt of her own sword to knock it away. Jane lifted hers again and tried to slash downward. Griffon again brought her sword up across her chest just in time to prevent a killing blow. Jane put the full weight of her body, along with her arm strength, into her attack. Griffon was able to hold her back, but wouldn't be able to for much longer. From her position beneath Jane, she couldn't get the leverage to knock her off or strike back.

But Griffon refused to lose. She was determined to win this battle on her own strength. Her mind raced as she tried to figure out a way to gain the upper hand. Nothing came to her. Then Clara, with a back-handed swing of her sword, struck Jane square in the face. It had clearly been much harder than Clara had intended, judging by her concerned reaction. Jane's head lurched back and she slumped to the ground beside Griffon. The moment Jane's weight was off, Griffon jumped to her feet and stood ready in case she rose again.

"Are you okay?" Clara said.

"I'm fine." Griffon shoved her aside and headed for the ladder back down.

"What's wrong? We got her, didn't we?"

Griffon shouted without turning to face Clara: "I didn't need you help!"

"What are you talking about?" Clara sounded hurt.

"I don't need saving," Griffon said. "I could have handled her on my own. Just stay up here and out of the way." Without another word or a look back, she headed down the ladder.

When Griffon reached the bottom, she saw that the fight had mostly ended. The other attackers had chosen to retreat. Now that they had managed to take Jane out of the game, they had the advantage. With a sigh, Griffon leaned against the wall and mentally scolded herself as she watched the rest of her team gather themselves after the chaos.

She had lost. Again. She had sworn to herself she wouldn't ever need to be saved again, that she would learn to protect herself from anyone. It hadn't been a true fight, but it infuriated her all the same. To try to take her mind off it, she went about helping the rest of her team double check the surrounding area and regroup inside. It took them an hour until they were comfortable enough to relax. During the perimeter check, Griffon talked with Zachery and learned he had taken out the boy Griffon had knocked down after she went up the stairs. Now they had a two-person advantage, what she guessed was the primary reason the other team backed out of the conflict.

It had been an eventful morning in a rather short amount of time. The sun hadn't even reached its peak. When it finally did, Daniel and Lace came bursting through the trees at a sprint, skidding to a stop in front of the fort and doubling over for breath. Zachery ran over and helped Daniel stand up straight, while Lace sat on the ground and tried to catch her breath. Griffon offered a hand to Lace, who after a moment of hesitation reached up and let Griffon help her to her feet.

Daniel spoke through heavy breaths: "Robin and Robert got captured."

Several voices spoke at once, the loudest asking, "How?"

"We were getting ready to head back," Daniel said, "when we heard shouting on the other side of the pond. We looped around to see what was going on and before we knew it, we were right on top of them. They grabbed Robin and Robert before we could react. We had to run before they got us too."

Zachery sighed. "Well, there goes the advantage."

Daniel and Lace spent the next several minutes recounting the experience in detail. When they were done, they all decided it was too risky for the time being to go back and watch the other team's activity. They would stay on the defensive until they decided exactly how to proceed. For the rest of the day, no one felt safe venturing outside the clearing. They all stayed within the fort or just outside of it. They placed Jane on one of their cots. When she finally woke a few hours later, she wasn't at all pleased.

Griffon and Clara stood on one side of the fort by a pillar while Jane was on the other side, with Daniel between them.

Jane glared daggers at Clara as she held a hand to her nose. "You're lucky you had a bodyguard, princess!"

Clara took a step forward. "I didn't need one," she said. "You're crooked nose says that much."

Griffon knew that she had a hot temper. She also knew how to spot someone else that had one. From the moment she'd met Jane, she known they were very similar. Jane had a vindictive side, however, and held grudges. Griffon enjoyed taking advantage of that and egging Jane on.

"It could be me with just one hand," Griffon said to Jane, "and you'd still lose."

Jane tried to get up, but Daniel placed both hands on her shoulders. "Jane...that's enough. Go back to Vigil."

She glared at him for a moment before shoving him away, standing up, and storming out the door.

After several long moments, Zachery spoke up from the doorway. "So, how should we go about this?"

Clara was the first to answer. "Well, we can't win by elimination anymore."

"Why not?"

"Math. I used my elimination on Jane and you on Corey, and with two of us captured they can't use theirs."

"So we have to go for the flag?"

Griffon tapped her foot. "To do that we have to get inside," she said, "and we saw how well that worked with Jane. One person on the second floor can hold anyone off long enough until help arrives."

Daniel rubbed his temples. "Even if we had our whole team," he said, "it wouldn't make much of a difference. Since they're now at risk of losing by elimination, they'll probably stay on the defensive, which means they'll most likely post more guards."

"So what do we do?" Lace asked. "Their team has the better fighters."

Clara shook her head. "Whatever we come up with," she said, "let's just stay in pairs and close to the fort for the time being. We'll come up with something."

CHAPTER TWENTY

8th of Landring, 27th year of the Fourth Age.

SNOW LAYERED THE freezing tundra in a thick blanket that prevented any green from peeking through the pristine, white landscape. In the center of it all was the towering fortress of Drachron, a citadel of ice, iron, and stone. With jagged and barbaric-looking towers rising at uneven intervals along its roof and walls, it was an intimidating sight even to the most seasoned soldier. It was here that Marceline found herself, trudging through the ankle-high snow that covered the courtyard. All around her were the men and women of Krida, dressed in thick furs and leather to ward off the biting cold.

Savages. The single word filled her mind as she watched them go about their business.

The Kridens were tall and hulking people, their bodies thick with muscle and hair. This was her fourth visit to Krida over the last several months. During her trips between the frozen nation and the city of

Dalisia in Edaren, she'd actually grown quite fond of the cold. It had become a familiar and welcome aspect of her life.

"Matriarch."

Marceline turned toward the deep and gruff voice behind her. Gotef, a man considered tall even by Kriden standards, strode up and stopped a few steps away. His hair was woven into dozens upon dozens of braids, with countless colors intermixed with his own dark-brown locks. All of it hung over his shoulders and down to his lower back.

He quickly dropped to both knees in the snow and placed his left hand over his heart in a fist. "Matriarch Marceline, Patriarch Liater requests you in Dragon Walk."

She was actually quite surprised. Gotef had improved at speaking Edaren since she last saw him.

"Very well. Come," she said as she strode by. He fell into step behind her without a word.

Every Kriden she passed stepped aside, allowing her passage while simultaneously raising a fist to his or her heart. Each one annoyed her. As useful as they were, she couldn't stand them or their traditions. Constant war and infighting made them physically strong but mentally weak. It had lasted hundreds of years before the intervention of Liater, Marceline, and the other Fingers. Now they were of a single purpose, given to them by the Disciples. Her thoughts drifted to Liater. The man was far too clever for Marceline. He was a threat to her position, though she was also, admittedly, a threat to his.

At the main entrance to Drachron, the two men who stood watch quickly moved to the oversized door and pushed it open with heavy grunts. After Marceline and Gotef stepped through, the watchmen repeated the feat of moving the massive gate and pulled it closed.

The first level of Drachron was empty. Its ceiling towered nearly fifty feet above the floor, which was nearly double that distance from wall to wall. Marceline's heavy boots echoed across the hollow room as Gotef's quieter cloth and leather footwear kept rhythm with hers. At the far end of the room was the Goddess Gate. It was a floor-to-ceiling barrier of solid stone and steel nearly fifty feet wide. It was built into an ancient cavern that led deep into the ground, where the Kridens believed their goddess, Mutderach, slept until her foretold awakening.

The name Mutderach translated roughly to "mother of life." She was one of the four great deities that the culture of Krida revolved around. They believed she was the creator of everything in the world and that she had fought a terrible war with her mate, Gesmerad. The battle was believed to be a draw. As punishment to the Kriden people for following her and not him, Gesmerad cursed the world of her followers to eternal winter. Marceline briefly grinned to herself as she recalled the stories she'd been told during their initial encounters. It was amazing to her how their cultural beliefs were so close to reality, yet skewed just enough so that Marceline and the others were able to easily twist them and convince the Kridens to follow them without question.

They reached the far end of the room, where a circular table was placed before the door. Around it were five chairs. One was occupied by Liater, a short, frail-looking man with not a hair on his head and a pair of eyes that were nearly solid white. He wore a simple black robe adorned with fur around the neck. The collar hung low enough to expose the rune that was carved into his neck, an intimidating scar from many years ago. Marceline took the chair across from him. Gotef took the seat between them, facing the door.

Marceline smirked before speaking: "Patriarch, here less than a day and already you call for my presence. I'm flattered."

He ran a finger over the rune, ignoring her jest. "Another patrol has returned with reports of tracks outside the castle."

She frowned. "How close were they?"

"The base of the wall."

"So they are growing bolder…this is troublesome. Have they seen you or any other Disciples?"

Liater shook his head slowly. "No. I've ordered them all to remain within the halls of Drachron until we've dealt with the problem."

"What of the Kinder of Mutderach?" The term was ridiculous, but with Gotef seated with them, she had to be sure to use Kriden terminology lest he grow suspicious of their motivations.

Liater glanced at the Goddess Gate. "They remain below for now," he said. "They understand their presence must be kept secret at all costs. Even Geiod will not jeopardize our plan with his insatiable curiosity."

Marceline leaned back in the high-backed chair and clicked her long nails on the table. It was nearly a minute before she spoke again. "Do you think they suspect anything?"

"No. But I have sent out a group of hunters to track them down. I'd like to remove them before they find anything to give them reason to suspect."

"How long ago?"

He considered for a moment. "Nearly an hour."

She raised an eyebrow in annoyance. "You waited an hour to inform me of this?"

"As you said, you've been here less than a day, and with all due respect, this is *my* fortress. I don't have to inform you of anything."

She narrowed her eyes. Her gaze flicked to the rune on his neck. It would be an easy enough feat. A simple knife stroke and his contract would be broken. She would hold both Krida and Edaren, at least temporarily. While the thought was intriguing and she felt her hand twitch in anticipation, she pushed the thoughts aside. For now, she would focus on cooperation rather than rivalry.

She smiled and said, "True enough."

Liater was about to speak again but was cut off by the sound of the entry gate being opened. A single Kriden woman stepped through the entrance and sprinted the length of the Dragon Walk. She wore a plain fur tunic and leggings. The skin on her exposed arms was adorned in ritual brands depicting wildlife such as wolves and bears, marking her role as a hunter.

She came to a stop just behind Gotef and knelt, placing her left hand over her heart. Without waiting to be addressed, she spoke rapidly in Kridic. Marceline didn't speak a word of the language, so she simply waited for the woman to finish so Gotef could translate.

When the woman finished, Gotef nodded and turned to the two of them. "Six zerstoger caught. Taken to courtyard with chains."

Liater smiled. "Wonderful," he said. "Take them to a cell below. I'll deal with them shortly."

Marceline raised a brow. "Would it not be better to deal with them now? What if they escape?"

"Matriarch," Liater said with a glare. "Nothing has ever escaped the prisons of Drachron."

She smiled. "There was a time when the sun had never risen before, and a time when water never fell from the sky. There is a first for everything, Liater."

He was visibly irritated at the use of his name in the presence of the Kridens. "Then if you would like to deal with our guests yourself, you have my full support, *Matriarch*."

She stood and replied with a clear layer of venom in her tone: "Of course, *Patriarch*."

The hunter stood and led Marceline and Gotef out the gate and to the far side of the courtyard. Already there was a crowd of Kridens gathered in a wide circle. They were shouting and screaming slurs in Kridic. Zerstoger, the Mate Fallen. It was a name given to everyone that did not follow the teachings of Mutderach or her offspring. As Marceline came closer, several in the crowd saw her and moved aside to allow her a clear path to the center.

Six Dragon Guard rangers knelt on the hard packed dirt, their hands bound behind their backs with chains. They looked up at her with stern expressions that told her nothing she wanted to know. Good. It was simply no fun if they gave everything to her. She smiled at them, which seemed to unnerve the youngest of them, a girl with ruby red hair on the far left.

The one at the far right spoke. He sounded calm despite the circumstances: "You're not a Kriden."

She turned to face him. He was the eldest, judging by the prominent wrinkles and worry lines etched across his face.

She stood directly in front of him. "Very intuitive, ranger," she said. "I see they chose your sect well."

He narrowed his eyes. "Who are you?"

Then she felt something familiar. A second hand rested on hers, mirroring her movements. With it came a sense of cold—not a natural cold, but something that chilled her blood, her soul. The moment she felt it, she took the opportunity before it changed its mind and knelt down, placing a finger against the man's forehead, letting her nail dig into his skin.

"You already know."

The moment she finished speaking, the cold ran though her hand and down her finger before disappearing. When it was gone, the ranger's brown eyes rolled into the back of his head. He fell sideways into the snow with a *thud,* where he lay twitching for a moment before going still.

All around her ,the Kridens dropped to their knees and placed their hands over their hearts while they bowed their heads and mumbled in Kridic. The rangers looked at her with wild eyes as realization swept over them.

They knew who she was. Now she swept her gaze over them again, looking for something she could use, something she could manipulate. In two of the five she saw rage—too volatile. In another she saw sadness—too weak. The next was regret, which was fickle. But in the last she saw what she wanted: fear. Fear was easy. Fear was strong. She stepped over to the girl with ruby hair. Her eyes were wide with terror. She was visibly shaking. With a single act, Marceline had broken her.

"Gotef." Marceline lifted a hand and gestured for him to approach. She pointed to the five rangers. "Send them to Schahellen."

Gotef drew a thick and heavy bladed knife from his belt and strode up to one of the men that had showed her rage. With one hand, he gripped the man's hair and lifted his head, exposing his neck. With the other hand, he cut the man's throat, letting blood flow freely into the white below. Marceline never took her eyes off the ruby-haired girl. She watched the fear grew stronger. The frightened girl began breathing more rapidly as she watched her comrade bleed out into the snow. Gotef stepped up the next in the line, the man who had shown Marceline sadness when his leader had died. Again, he was left to bleed into the snow. Marceline knelt in front of the ruby-haired girl and gripped her chin, forcing her to turn her head and look at her.

Their eyes locked. Marceline reveled in the unbridled fear she saw within. Not fear of Gotef or of the Kridens, but of Marceline. When another of her comrades was sent to Schahellen, the Kriden afterlife, the girl began to openly cry. Her eyes never left Marceline's, even as she heard her allies die beside her.

Gotef let the last of the other rangers fall to the ground. When the sound of the final body hitting the snow made the girl flinch, Marceline spoke: "Who are you?"

The girl didn't reply. Instead, she peeled her gaze away and started to sob.

"Look. At. Me." Marceline gripped the girl's face tighter and forced her gaze back. "Who are you?"

The girl's voice cracked: "Angela."

"Angela, what if I told you—" Marceline was cut off by a scream as a Kriden was thrown from the fortress walls.

Marceline turned to see another five rangers standing atop the wall, their bows drawn and aimed right for her. Within an instant they released the strings and let the arrows fly. But she felt it again. The unnatural cold radiated from her. The arrows were swatted out of the air without her lifting a finger. They fell into the snow and all around her. The Kridens started praying again, marveling at the feats they thought their goddess did for her, the matriarch of their religion

Marceline shouted at Gotef: "Take them!"

He shouted orders in Kridic. Every Kriden gathered ran for the towers set along the wall to overtake the rangers. Even those that were unarmed showed no hesitation in following the orders given. The rangers ran along the length of the wall, making for the corner furthest from the fortress. They stopped briefly, apparently to discuss something. Then two took aim at her again while the rest turned and fired on the Kridens swarming out of the towers. Marceline smiled. They knew what she was. They had to take the chance to kill her, even if it cost them their lives. They knew they wouldn't get another opportunity like this.

She smiled wider as she saw the arrows fly from the strings again. She lifted her hand and attempted to summon the cold as before. But it wouldn't come to her. Marceline scowled and tried to force it out, but without a response she was simply a target. One of the arrows planted itself in her thigh. The other went wide to the left. She grunted and fell to one knee. With gritted teeth, she gripped the wound and cursed.

Fickle abomination, she thought. *Never here when I actually call for you.*

She gripped the arrow and broke the shaft before pulling it out the back side of her thigh, causing pain to shoot through her leg. Looking up, she saw the rangers disappear over the wall. She didn't know how they had climbed the stone walls, but they had been smart enough to ensure they had a way down again. Then she caught slight movement out of the corner of her eye. A sixth ranger was attempting to pick the lock on Angela's chains. The five on the wall had been a diversion for this one to rescue their only living ally. She locked eyes with the ranger and felt it again, the fickle cold urging her to act.

Marceline lifted her hand and forced the cold out through her palm, sending it in a wave to crash into the man's head as he crouched just over Angela's shoulder. The wave struck him and sent him flying back as his neck was snapped. Angela screamed. Marceline took a deep breath as she stood, the pain from her thigh surging along her body, but she ignored it and strode over to the girl. Angela looked at her with a fresh surge of fear in her eyes.

Marceline knelt and gripped her chin again. "Angela," she said. "What if I told you that you never had to be afraid again?"

The look on her face turned from fear to confusion, then back to fear as she tried to understand the question. Marceline reached behind her back and drew a short and slender knife. She brought the tip to rest on the girl's forehead and looked into her eyes again.

Marceline lifted the girl's chin with a single finger. "At this very moment," she said, "what do you want more than anything in this world?"

Angela spoke through her tears: "I don't want to die."

"What will you give?"

"Anything! Please just let me live!"

Marceline felt something new: warmth. A warmth that grew to a blistering heat, resting on the back of her hand, gripping her tighter than anything she'd felt in a long time. She was accepted. She directed the warmth into the tip of the blade and let it guide her hand as she slowly carved a rune into Angela's forehead.

CHAPTER TWENTY-ONE

10th of Landring, 27th year of the Fourth Age

GRIFFON HAD HER back to the fort, her knife in one hand and a small hunk of wood in the other. The last two days had been uneventful. Out of sheer boredom, she had decided to try her hand at wood carving. After a dozen or so cuts along her hands and fingers, she came to the conclusion that she was awful at it, but pressed on regardless. The constant motion of cutting away small pieces helped calm her and gave her something to focus on besides hitting someone or dwelling on her family in Forge.

Movement flickered in the corner of her right eye. She turned to see Daniel making his way over. He spoke before he stopped walking: "I have an idea."

She sighed. "Is it a good one?"

He paused before answering: "Probably not."

After he didn't continue, she raised an eyebrow. "Are you going to tell me what it is?"

Again he took a moment to consider his answer. "Well, you're a big part of it, so I kind of have to."

"I'm not going to like it, am I?"

"You're going to hate it. Come on."

He led her through the fort and to the roof where Clara, Lace, and Zachery were already waiting patiently. Griffon took her place in the group while Daniel stood in front of them and pointed toward the forest. "So, here's what I've got," he said. "They have to win by capture now and they already have two of our members. We need to win by elimination. Or we can try to go for their flag."

Griffon rolled her eyes. "We know that. What's your point?"

"My point is," Daniel continued, "why not try for both at once? We rescue our two teammates while at the same time trying for the flag, taking out whoever we can as we do it."

"I don't follow."

"We break out Robin and Robert while at the same time trying to get the flag."

Zachery frowned. "To do that," he said, "we need to get inside and they aren't just going to let us walk in."

"What if they take us in?"

Griffon didn't quite follow. "Why would they let us in?"

"They capture one of us."

"You want to give them more of an advantage?"

Daniel pointed to the knife at Griffon's belt. "They have to tie us with rope," he said, "and we have a hunting knife. So we hide the knife on someone. Let that person get captured and in the middle of the night he cuts the bonds while most of the other team is sleeping. Then we suddenly have three people inside the fort with none of the others are aware of it."

Clara smiled and shrugged. "It's simple," she said, "but more often than not, simple works the best."

Lace nodded and asked, "Who do we let get captured?"

Daniel scuffed his foot along the rough wood of the roof. "Well, if I had to pick, I would want Griffon inside. She's the best fighter on our team, so if something went wrong, hopefully she could at least use her elimination."

Griffon wasn't thrilled at the idea. "So you want me to lose a fight and get captured…on purpose?"

"It's only one fight," Daniel said, "and in turn, you would further our chance of not going home after all this."

Griffon realized Daniel knew how much she hated losing. She had displayed as much during previous exercises. He was taking advantage of that. But he was also right. They had to win or they wouldn't be here much longer.

"You're right," she said. "I do hate this plan."

Clara placed a hand on her shoulder. "Come on, Griffon, this could be what we need to win."

Griffon considered the idea. No matter how much she tried to change her mind she still hated the idea. But in the end, she relented. "What would I do when I'm inside?" she asked. "Even if I get them free, we could only take out three people."

Daniel turned to Lace. "How far can you jump?"

She wrinkled her forehead. "Excuse me?"

"Behind their fort is a tall tree with a few large branches coming pretty close to their roof."

"Right, I remember seeing it."

"You're pretty small," Daniel said. "I think most of those branches could easily support your weight. If Griffon and the others cause a commotion inside while I and a few others do the same outside, hopefully the lookouts will go down to help or at least look away from the flag. Then you can jump from the tree to the roof, grab the flag, and make your way back before they even know it's missing."

"Suddenly it's less simple," Clara said with a groan.

Lace raised an eyebrow. "What if they see me in the tree?"

Daniel shrugged. "How often do you look up?"

Griffon knew what he meant but it took a moment to register for Lace. "Up?"

"The branch I'm thinking of looked about eight feet above the roof

241

and six feet away," Daniel said. "What are the odds they're going to look above them while on watch?"

Griffon sighed and crossed her arms. "So let me get this straight," she said. "You want me to lose a fight and get captured on purpose, use a knife that they hopefully don't notice, cut my ropes, then distract them long enough for Lace to jump out of a tree so she can grab the flag and run away?"

"Yeah," Daniel said, "that's pretty much it."

Griffon stared at him. "Did you eat a bad mushroom?"

Zachery laughed lightly. "Oh, come on," he said, "it's not that bad of an idea. It could work."

Griffon threw her hands up in defeat. Even if she wasn't the one sent to get captured, they would still go through with the idea, so she might as well give in. Having her inside *was* their best chance. "Fine," she said. "When?"

"The sooner the better," Daniel said. "I was thinking tonight, Griffon and I could head over there to 'scout,' let them see us, and then while we have them occupied trying to grab Griffon, Lace will climb the tree and wait for Griffon to be taken inside and cause a distraction. While that's happening, I'll go back for Zachery and a couple others and we can sit outside across the pond. When it all starts we can rush over and help with the distraction."

Griffon sighed deeply. She wasn't looking forward to any of this.

"This plan is stupid."

Daniel chuckled at Griffon's comment. "You agreed to do it."

"It's still stupid," she huffed.

Griffon lay on her stomach next to Daniel beneath a broken tree trunk with trails of moss hanging from its sides like curtains to hide them from view. She fidgeted with the knife tied tightly around her forearm by a pull knot as they waited. They'd been here for just over two hours. Lace was waiting for them to start a commotion to give her a chance to scale the tree just behind their fort. Likewise, they were waiting for the chance to get noticed by someone without making it painfully obvious that they wanted to be noticed. This was drastically more difficult than Griffon had thought it would be. After the first hour, she was ready to simply jump up and shout at them to come and grab her to get it over with.

"You ready for this?" Daniel nudged her with his shoulder.

"No. But it's not like waiting any longer is going to help."

They crawled back to the other side of the log and started to head in the direction of their own fort. They stayed close to the edge of the pond but out of sight for the moment. They had already decided on the spot where they would stage their sighting. It was an area with a gap between the trees, large enough for them to be seen if they stood in just the right area but with enough cover so that it would make sense for them to be passing through it on their way back. In the area was an exposed root, perfect for her to "trip" on. She hated to admit that having her trip and curse loudly enough for the others to hear was something that was entirely plausible.

When they reached the spot, Daniel made his way to the other side of the gap and nodded at her. She frowned one last time and glared at him before sighing and taking several steps forward. She had asked if this part of the plan was entirely necessary. Everyone save for her had said for the sake of fooling the other team, it was. At this point, she was sure they just wanted to make her look like a fool. She "tripped" and hit the ground harder than she had anticipated. Even though she'd planned to shout out, she did so simply on reaction alone, surprising herself.

From the ground, she glanced at the fort through the gap and saw the lookout facing in their direction and pointing toward them. Daniel rushed to her side to help her up. They started through the forest with Griffon faking a limp, allowing the others an easier chance to catch up. When they heard several people crashing through the underbrush, Daniel looked at her and grinned.

She nodded, sighed, and pushed him away while pulling her wooden blade free. "Go!" she shouted. "I'm just slowing you down!"

Without a word, he gave her a reassuring smile before disappearing into the forest. She turned around just as three people broke through the trees and into view. It was Aaron, flanked by two other boys. *Shade curse it, why him?* She screamed at herself in her head when she saw Aaron. It was the first time she'd seen him since the game had started. She'd been trying to forget the fact that they were on separate teams. Seeing him also brought up the image of Alan's face in her head. No matter who won this exercise, no one was going to be happy with the results.

Aaron quickly glanced down at her leg as she obviously favored her right over the left. He motioned for the other two to flank her while he stayed at her front.

"Come on, Griffon," he said. "You're hurt, so it's just easier if you come with us."

She shrugged. "Yeah," she said, "but when do I make things easy?"

To her he looked almost sad for a moment. "Fair enough."

She struck out for the boy on her right, who ducked low and barely avoided being hit in the shoulder. The boy to her left lunged forward to grab her, but she gripped the long handle of her blade with her second hand and pivoted on her "good" foot to bring it around and stab at his midsection. He had to skid to a stop and turn his whole body to avoid the tip and nearly fell into her as he did so. As she finished the motion, Aaron jumped in and gripped her left arm before she could reposition herself. Since it was the side she was faking the sprain on, when he tugged on her arm, instead of putting weight on her foot she simply let herself fall into him. He quickly looped his arms underneath hers, then laced his fingers behind her head to hold her still.

Aaron backed up to a tree to stabilize himself under her weight while she struggled for a moment before sighing and ceasing her efforts. They took a rope hanging from Aaron's belt and started to tie her wrists. The moment they started, she worried they might notice the knife and ruin the whole plan. They had tied it around her forearm with a simple slip knot so hopefully once inside it would be easy enough to get to it and begin cutting themselves free. But given the fact it had to be within reach once she was inside, it was not a well-hidden item. But it was the best they could do. Several times, as they looped the rope, she thought they paused and she had a moment of panic. But when they stood and started to walk her back to the fort, her heart calmed and she inwardly celebrated. It was working so far. If everything else went as she hoped, they would be headed back to Vigil tomorrow.

When they brought her inside, she found the interior was as they had assumed, identical to their own fort. In the far corner, Robin and Robert were tied to one of the support pillars, their hands behind their backs. Robert perked up at the sight of her, while Robin simply glanced at her before rolling her eyes and leaning her head back against the pole before closing them.

Aaron led Griffon over and tied her to one of the rings at ground level, placing her back to Robin, before standing and looking at her with a concerned look. "Is your ankle okay?" he asked.

She smiled in spite of herself. "Fine," she said. "I'll just have to stay off of it for a few days."

"Well," he said with a short laugh, "that won't be too hard."

She struggled not to give him a sarcastic reply that would give away her intentions. Instead, she smiled at him as he turned and went up the ladder to the second floor, leaving the two boys that had been with him to watch their prisoners from the doorway. Out of every one of the trainees at Vigil, she thought Aaron would be the hardest for her to see go. It was true that she liked Daniel a lot in spite of his overall quiet nature, and Clara was one she could go to for help when it came to academic knowledge. Zachery was good for a joke and Alan was far cleverer then he let on. But Aaron had a gentle and caring nature that warmed her heart when he showed how worried he was for someone.

She shook her head and tried to refocus. She looked around the room for anything useful, but other than the several baskets of food in the opposite corner there was nothing of note. She looked at the two boys in the entryway and noticed one of them had placed her sword against the wall. She would have to get that back quickly if she had any hope of being a suitable distraction after they escaped. For that matter, she would have to figure out how to arm Robin and Robert as well. With no other option at the moment, she leaned her head back against the pole and closed her eyes to wait.

Griffon slept, but only lightly, as she woke several times at the slightest sounds around them—a creak in the wood above as someone upstairs moved, a slight nudge from Robin as she adjusted to get more comfortable. After what must have been several hours, she seemed to snap fully awake and alert. She lifted her head and looked at the doorway. She recognized Alan leaning against the wall, looking out at the pond. She hadn't seen him since the day she'd spotted him on top of the fort. It made sense, as he was the youngest and one of the least-skilled fighters out of all of them. His team would keep him out of combat as long as possible.

Her sword was no longer resting against the wall. A quick scan of the room revealed that they'd placed it on the rack across from her, along with several other swords likely belonging to the rest of the team. That would certainly make things easier. More than enough time had passed that she was sure Lace would be ready and in position to snatch the flag. Hopefully, Daniel and the others were ready as well. She nudged Robin several times until she snapped awake. She started to speak, but Griffon glared at her. Robin raised an eyebrow.

Griffon leaned close and whispered, "Knife tied around my right arm, slip knot."

Robin's mouth twitched into a smile. She twisted her position to lift her hand as high as she could. Griffon had to slump down to get the angle just right which was horribly uncomfortable, but Robin was finally able to slowly lift her sleeve and grip the rope to undo the knot. Griffon felt the weight vanish. She braced for the sound of the knife falling to the ground and was thankful when instead, she felt the rope around her wrists rub along her skin as Robin started to slowly cut through her bonds.

It seemed to take forever. When Griffon finally felt the ropes around her wrists drop away, she had to resist the urge to celebrate. She quickly grabbed the knife from Robin and went about cutting her free while trying to stay in the same general position. Again, they went slowly. When Robin was free, she quickly woke Robert and placed a finger to her lips to quiet him as he lurched awake. After he was loose, Griffon caught Robin's eye and nodded toward Alan.

Robin stood without a sound and first went to the rack. She picked out a longsword before slowly making her way over to Alan. Griffon likewise went to the rack and removed her own blade before passing one to Robert. When she turned toward the door, she saw Robin do something she hadn't expected. Robin stood behind Alan and made a soft click with her tongue to get his attention. The moment he turned, she swung her sword and struck him hard across the face, sending him backwards into the wall with a crash. He quickly brought both hands to his mouth and nose. Griffon heard a muffled cry.

Griffon ran over to him and knelt to check the damage to his face. She could already hear the commotion above as the lookouts clearly heard the sound. Alan had tears openly streaming down his cheeks. With his eyes closed tightly, he gripped his nose and mouth with both hands. Sometimes it was hard to remember that he was the youngest of them all; there were very few moments like this where it was obvious. When Griffon looked at him, all she could think of was Richard, her frail and timid brother. She pulled his hand away and saw that a tooth had been broken, and more than likely his nose judging from the amount of blood that was flowing.

Griffon stood and shoved Robin back hard. No longer caring about stealth, she released her anger and shouted, "What is wrong with you?"

Robin stared at her with an annoyed look in her eyes. When she made no motion to reply, Griffon balled her hand into a fist and swung at her head, but Robin leaned backwards and smoothly avoided the swing. Now her expression changed from annoyance to amusement, which only made Griffon angrier. She heard someone coming down the ladder behind her and chose to deal with Robin later. She scowled one last time at Robin before shouldering past her and running outside. "Let's go!" she yelled.

Robin and Robert ran to the left side of the pond while Griffon veered right. The moment they were out in the open, they heard several shouts from the roof. Griffon looked back to see two of the lookouts disappear down the ladder. Several more people poured out of the doorway, with another stopping to check on Alan. Again Griffon felt her anger flare at Robin, but had to push it aside for the moment. She kept up the ruse of her sprain to entice the other team to follow her.

They were on her quickly enough. Two jumped in front of her to cut her off. She saw four more head for Robert and Robin. Aaron had come after her again and now stood in front of her, sword in hand. Without a word he swung for her "good" leg, obviously expecting her to stumble when she put weight on the sprain. Instead, she jumped over the blade, then moved forward with a wide slash that nearly caught him in the chest.

A look of surprise crossed his face. Griffon pressed her advantage, taking solid steps toward him as she swung with both hands. She never stopped her advance, forcing him to backpedal. Their swords locked when he blocked a low slash at his side, but it lasted for only a moment before he dropped under her blade and out of the lock, letting the weight she'd been pushing into him throw her off balance. As Griffon fell forward, he rose again and tried to get her in another grapple to hold her in place. In front of her, the second boy tried to occupy her by swinging at her shoulder. Rather than block and get grabbed from behind, she dove under the boy's swing and rose behind him, swinging her sword as she did so to strike him in the ribs.

The blow sent him to the side a few steps and out of her way. She didn't see what he did after that and instead focused on Aaron, who quickly closed the gap between them. He swung for her shoulder. She ducked the blade and heard it whiz over her, but he had anticipated the reaction. In the same motion, he brought his leg around and hit her in the chest, sending her to the ground. The blow knocked the wind out of her. At the moment, she couldn't see herself winning this fight. She'd never been able to beat Aaron before. If things kept going the way they were now, she wouldn't this time either.

She managed to rise to one knee as Aaron gripped her wrist and twisted her arm behind her back to hold her in place. "Give up," he said, "and drop your sword."

She looked over her shoulder and smiled against the strain. "You'll have to break my arm first," she said. "Sorry, but I'm not going home."

"You know I'm not going to do that, but you can't win this fight, Griffon."

"Then we're going be here a while, aren't we?"

Just as he was about to reply, a short wooden blade was placed gently on the side of Aaron's neck. "I'm sorry, Aaron."

They both looked at the wielder, making Aaron sigh as he stood. Daniel was behind him, a short sword in his hand. Aaron let go of Griffon's wrist. She quickly clutched it to her chest and massaged it to get the feeling back.

Aaron sighed helplessly. "I should've been watching my back better, I guess. Good luck to both of you, no matter who wins in the end."

Daniel glanced at the fort behind them. "I'm sorry, Aaron," he said. "I wish we'd been on the same side."

With a confused expression on his face, Aaron followed Daniel's gaze. When he saw the empty flagpole, his jaw hung open. "How..." he said, then started over. "When did you manage to do that?"

Griffon also looked at the empty pole atop the fort. They'd won. But the victory was incredibly bitter to Griffon. While it had been their goal, this wasn't something she was going to savor. The remainder of the night was spent spreading out around the forest to make sure everyone was informed that the game was now over and they were no longer fighting with one another. When everyone had been told, they all made their way to the fort in the clearing for their final night since no one favored walking back to Vigil in the dark.

Plenty of congratulations were thrown at Griffon for pulling off the rescue and at Daniel for coming up with the plan, though the majority of praise was piled on Lace. She had been the most distant from the rest of them until now, aside from Robin. Upon receiving so much attention, she found herself smiling and seemed to be genuinely enjoying her time in the spotlight. But after several minutes, it seemed to end. She receded back into an antisocial mindset after stern and angry looks from both Robin and Robert as they pulled her back into their fold. Griffon couldn't understand how Lace managed to be around them. Robin seemed like an abusive person, while Robert with his superiority complex was a drain to talk to.

Aside from the praise, there was equal parts of disdain toward Robin for what she had done to Alan, which quickly spread through the group like wildfire. His nose was, by way of a minor miracle, unbroken, so he would be fine aside from a chipped front tooth and a severe distrust of

Robin for the foreseeable future. The remainder of the night, however, was tainted by a downer tone that was oppressive enough to dampen most conversation. None of them were happy with the outcome. Those that had won were burdened with the knowledge that they had just sent half of their comrades home. Those that lost were being sent home, forced to abandon their aspirations. All of them were losing friends. This weight sent most of them to sleep outright the moment they lay their heads down.

Griffon, however, was unable to follow suit. She rose from her bedding and climbed down the ladder to the first floor, where she gingerly stepped over and around everyone who slept. She made her way outside and around the corner of the fort to lean against the wall. She looked up at the stars for a moment, then drew her knife from her belt and pulled a small wooden figure out of her pocket. It was supposed to be a warden holding a great axe above his head, but at the moment it looked like a fat man holding an oblong log.

She started to chip away pieces from where the axe head was meant to be as her thoughts wandered. After several minutes and a few blood beads on the tips of her fingers, she was thoroughly frustrated. She sighed, put the knife back in the sheath at her belt, and tossed the figure to the ground.

She couldn't focus at the moment. She kept thinking back to her fight with Aaron, which made her angry, which made her think about how she was going to be losing him, which made her angrier. That took her thoughts to how she had lost to Jane, and in turn to how she had treated Clara, which she still had not apologized for. The combination made her feel not just angry, but also ashamed. Her thoughts were a whirlwind, all of them negative.

"What is this supposed to be?"

Griffon turned to see Daniel holding the carving she had tossed away.

"It's nothing," she said. "Just something to pass the time." She walked over and tried to take it from him.

He leaned away from her and tried to get a better look at it in the dark. "Oh, come on," he said. "What is it?"

She crossed her arms and shrugged as she felt her face start to burn. "Just a warden, I guess."

He nodded. "Oh, yeah I can see that. Kind of. Have you ever done wood carving before?"

"No. It's just something I wanted to try."

"You're pretty good at it. You'll have to show it to me when it's done."

Griffon snatched it from him and stuck it back in her pocket. She leaned against the wall while Daniel did the same. They didn't say anything and just watched the stars above them for a long while.

"So what's wrong?" Daniel asked, turning to face her.

She shook her head. "Nothing's wrong."

"Liar."

She sighed. "You should know what's wrong."

"Yeah, I guess I do. Winning is kind of bitter, isn't it?"

"To put it lightly."

He ran a hand through his hair before speaking again. "Well, I'm pretty sure I can tell something else is wrong. So what is it?"

"Nothing important."

"I doubt that if it's bothering you this much." When she didn't reply, he stepped in front of her, an eyebrow raised. "So? What is it?"

She hesitated for a moment. "I guess...I'm just angry at myself. I'm angry that I needed help with Aaron, and with Jane."

"You're mad that you needed help?"

She sighed. "Look, I came here because I wanted to be able to protect myself instead of always having to rely on others to save me when I'm in trouble. I was tired of needing help to fight back because I'm too weak to do it by myself."

He was quiet at first, as if waiting for Griffon to say more. When she didn't, he shrugged. "That's it?"

"What do you mean, 'That's it'?"

"You're mad because your friends helped you when you were in trouble?"

She felt her cheeks flush. "When you say it like that, it sounds stupid."

He laughed. "Well to be honest, it kind of is. Everyone needs help every now and again. Even if they don't want to admit or ask for it, and you're only getting stronger so you won't always need it. You're one of the best fighters out of twenty-two people. *Twenty-two*! I wish I was even half as talented as you. So what if you don't win every fight? I mean, you were fighting two against one, and not only did you hold your own, you took one of them out. You're anything but weak."

Griffon slid down the wall and sat down in the cool damp grass. "After living in Forge and being bullied by the bigger players for contracts, and just the way people looked at me because of who my parents were...I just wanted to be able to stand on my own, against anything."

"I understand that," Daniel said. He sat down next to her. "But letting others help you isn't being weak. If anything, it makes you stronger. It means you don't let your pride get in the way. In the end you still won, just not on your own."

She thought on it for a moment. She supposed in the end all that should matter was that each fight was won. Even if she hadn't done so on her own. Her side had come out on top, though in this particular situation she wasn't sure that was a good thing. The more she thought about it, the more she was sure that was enough. Even if she couldn't do it by herself, she could make sure the side she was on won. That would be as much her victory as everyone else's.

"Thanks, Daniel."

He grinned at her. "Don't thank me. Just help me get better with a sword."

She smiled and gently shoved him. "I think that's a lost cause at this point."

The next morning was equally depressing for them. They all rose slowly as the exertion from the last several days was finally catching up to them. Just as they were ready to start their trek back to Vigil, they looked out over the clearing to the tree line. Austin and Claudia were making their way over, along with Obadiah. The trainees watched them approach. When they reached the doorway, they gathered around the three instructors and waited to hear what they had to say.

Claudia was the first to address them. "You all performed wonderfully.

You all did well adapting to the other team, as well as forming excellent strategies."

Daniel looked at Austin with an annoyed expression. "You were watching us, weren't you?" he said.

Austin shrugged. "Not me personally. But there were a couple of rangers that had some free time."

Obadiah crossed his arms and grunted. "Can we get this over with?"

Claudia nodded. "Right," she said. We have some news for all of you. At the start of this exercise, you were told that the winners would be allowed to stay and that the team that lost would be escorted home. We're here to inform—"

Austin spread his arms out wide and shouted, "We lied!"

Claudia glared at him as the trainees stared in confusion. None of them thought they'd heard correctly.

Aaron was the one to voice their thoughts: "What do you mean, exactly?"

Claudia gave Austin a dirty look for another few moments, then turned back to the trainees. "We told you that one team would go home and one would stay," she said. "This was because we had to give you proper motivation."

Obadiah pointed at Zachery. "You never give a battle in the training yard your all," he said," unless you think you're about to lose."

Austin pointed at Daniel. "You tend to avoid conflict altogether if you can help it. You rarely take the initiative."

Claudia then motioned to Robin. "You prefer to act independently during team exercises."

They all were still thoroughly confused. Alan raised a timid hand. "So... none of us are going home?"

Obadiah made a sweeping motion to all of them. "None of you had ever given a task your best effort," he said. "To offset this, we gave you the highest stakes we could. This battle obviously could not be a matter of life and death, so we decided that this was the closest we could get."

Austin nodded. "Battles in the real world are life and death," he said. "There is rarely if ever a middle ground. All of you sacrificed much to come here, some more than others. This was essentially the same thing to you. This was life or death."

Claudia sighed. "Proper motivation."

Their words slowly dawned on the trainees. One by one, smiles started to spread throughout the group. Soon they were all overjoyed. None of them was losing anything. Griffon took a deep breath. Without thinking, she leaned over and pulled Aaron into an embrace, who quickly returned it.

CHAPTER TWENTY-TWO

7th of Anden, 27th year of the Fourth Age.

DANIEL'S TRAINING HAD been ongoing for eight months. He didn't feel that he had progressed much. Yet in spite of his opinion on his own growth, Commander Hall had decided it had been plenty long enough for them all to receive some minor experience in the field. Daniel wasn't sure that what he was doing now should count toward that. The trainees were using their day off to rotate shifts with the city guard, walking patrols and dealing with public issues along with a normally scheduled Dragon Guard. Public issues more often than not were simply an argument gone too far or a pickpocket caught in the act. It wasn't what Daniel had expected when Hall first told them they would be doing "field work," but at least it broke up the routine every week.

Today was Daniel's turn to patrol the harbor and cliff side just outside the city, which was the most uneventful area of Vigil from what he had been told. Based on personal experience so far, he was able to confirm that. But it could have been far worse. He was just grateful to be assigned with Kenneth, who he hadn't seen in several months save for passing glances and the occasional wave across one of the keep halls or the courtyard. Currently, they were discussing Daniel and Aaron's training progress as they made their way down the steep path from the city gate.

"Not a single match?" Kenneth said with clear surprise. "He's far more talented then I initially thought."

"More so than me at the very least," Daniel said. "Even when he's on the verge of losing, he keeps calm and somehow manages to turn it around every time."

Kenneth nodded. "Aaron is a strong young man and has a level head," he said. "You're skilled in your own right. Don't sell yourself short." He paused. "How is the rest of your training progressing?"

"Pretty well, I suppose. Austin says I'm a good tactician and Obadiah says he's never seen someone so adept at not being hit...though I'm not sure if that's a compliment."

Kenneth laughed loudly and smacked Daniel across the back. "See, lad?" he said. "I knew you would do just fine here!"

"Sometimes I feel like it wasn't worth the price."

"What do you mean?"

Daniel shrugged. "Barden is probably in jail right now and after what happened to Mila...I mean, it was me for them. It just doesn't seem like a fair trade."

Kenneth placed a hand on Daniel's shoulder, forcing him to look at the huge warden. "You have to stop thinking like that," he said. "They didn't trade themselves for anything. Barden did what he did for you and Aaron because he felt it was right, and Mila made her choice for her own reasons. Not because she was trading herself for you."

"Still doesn't seem fair."

"Life isn't fair, Daniel. People make choices and some of those choices end in the worst way possible. You can never think about what could have been different because that insults their memory. You must take what they gave you and make the most of it."

Daniel didn't answer as they started walking again. They continued their walk down the long path, passing no one as they went, simply taking in the stunning view of the ocean beyond and the docks below. Ships were moored at nearly every available inch and dozens of sailors worked to load or unload trade goods and travel supplies. It was only the second month of summer, so it was still the prime time for trading while the weather was good and there were few chances of a sudden storm. The sight of the ships brought back the memory of Daniel's arrival in Vigil, then further back still to his journey from Sapella's Crossing and meeting with Aaron. That, in turn, brought up thoughts of home.

He smiled and wondered how his mother would react to him patrolling the city with Kenneth under the Dragon Guard name. Or how his brother would react, for that matter. Jeremy always thought the world of his older brother. Daniel knew that, though he never truly appreciated it until now, when he was no longer spending every single day with him. Finally, he thought of Connie. He knew how hard it had been for her to finally see him go. How hard it had been for him *to* go. Now that he was here, though, the thought of being able to see them all again seemed incredibly far away. He felt a rising in his chest that told him he better think of something less upsetting before he broke down.

As they were about to pass a branch off of the path that led to one of the watchtowers along the cliff wall, one of the city guards caught their attention. He was standing at the base of the tower waving them over and shouting something they couldn't hear. They exchanged a glance before quickly making their way over. The guard vanished back into the tower and they quickly followed him up. When they emerged at the peak they stood on a balcony with the man pointing straight out into the ocean.

Before they even finished stepping off the stairs, the guard started speaking. "There's a ship approaching. It's flying the Dragon Guard flags. But there were no arrivals scheduled for today."

Kenneth peered into the distance. "It looks like one of our scouts," he said, "but I can't see anyone aboard. Though it is difficult to tell at this distance... it does appear to be empty. Odd."

As the ship came closer, Daniel was able to make out more details. The peak of the single mast flew the tricolored flags of the Dragon Guard. Aside from the lack of personnel, the ship looked perfectly normal.

Kenneth furrowed his brow and handed Daniel the logbook. "Check the log," he said. "What ships are out at the moment?"

Daniel took the book, struggling to keep the pages down as the wind blew against the cliff side. He scanned the names of the ships that were currently out on an assignment and the ones which were at port. The Dragon Guard had a dozen smaller scout ships like the one approaching now and two larger war ships, both of which were moored down the beach at the Dragon Guard's private docks.

"There are three," Daniel said. "One investigating a wirvus report on the northern coast, and another scouting the Krida coastline. The last is supposed to be moored at the base of The Spines near Navia, where there was some valgret activity near a farmstead."

"Which is due back the soonest?" Kenneth asked.

"The one on the northern coast, due back end of the month."

After a while of simply watching the ship come ever closer, Kenneth sighed. "Let's go, lad," he said. "We'll wait for them on the dock. Let's find out what brought them back early."

They made their way out of the tower along with the guard and all of them headed down the long steep path as quickly as they could manage. They jogged past the warehouses and workers until they stood at the edge of the docks that the ship appeared to be heading for and waited. It was closing the distance quickly. Daniel noticed something that worried him greatly. "Kenneth," he said, "they aren't slowing down."

"They aren't on a proper approach either. Coming in at an odd angle."

The scout ship was riding the wind toward the dock, moving alarmingly fast. Daniel still saw no one standing at the helm or anywhere else for that matter. Kenneth grabbed Daniel by the shoulder and they slowly started to back away, which quickly turned into a sprint down the length of the dock as the ship slammed into it with an ear-shattering *crack*, sending wood shards flying in all directions and making the planks beneath them shudder from the impact. The sound of wood scraping wood was deafening as the ship slowly came to a halt. Cracked and broken, the ship was being held afloat only by the dock at this point.

The sudden stop had broken the single mast, making it fall forward to rest over the dock. The flags slapped against the water on the other side.

Kenneth turned to the guard and spoke quickly. "Get to the keep and alert the commander."

The guard nodded and sprinted toward the road leading to the city gate while Kenneth and Daniel slowly approached the ship. Kenneth drew his sword and took his shield from his back. Daniel followed suit, drawing his own sword and letting Kenneth take the lead. They had no idea what could be on the ship, so caution was the best course of action for the time being. Embedded all along the hull were throwing axes with double-bladed heads, each intricately detailed with what looked like fire, along with a short spike at the bottom of the handle. The handles were also lined with white and brown fur. The ship was a few feet taller than the dock and had lodged at an upward angle, so Kenneth had to climb over the edge to board. When he was over, Daniel followed to see what they had both been dreading.

"By Verhova, what happened to them?" Kenneth spoke in a whisper.

The deck was covered in blood. Bodies were strewn about, each inflicted with wounds of various sizes. Most were lying on the deck in their own blood which explained why they saw no one on board. The scout ship was meant to house at most six people. Judging by the clothing, the crew had been rangers, while the other three bodies were men larger than Kenneth. They clearly didn't belong. They definitely weren't Dragon Guards, judging by their choice of clothing or lack thereof. They wore no tunic or upper body armor, so their chest and backs were exposed. Their legs were lightly armored and their trousers were covered and lined with fur. Gripped in their hands were swords and axes large enough to match their stature.

Kenneth spoke softly, as if he might disturb them: "Don't touch anything if you can manage it."

Daniel heard coughing and turned to see there was a ranger at the helm that still lived. They were hidden behind the wheel again, explaining why they couldn't see her from afar. She was starting to come to, coughing up blood as she tried to rise to her feet, but only managed to fall away from the helm and to her knees.

Kenneth ran over and placed a hand on her chest and back to gently lay her against the cabin wall. "What happened here?" he said gently. He placed a hand over a wide gash on her stomach to try to slow the bleeding.

She spoke through ragged breaths and blood: "Krida...hand..." Her breathing came in quick spurts for a few moments before she went still.

Kenneth removed his hand from the wound and stood. He looked thoughtful for a moment before turning to the cabin and heading inside. While he was gone, Daniel turned to inspect the strange men that he guessed were the attackers. Their backs were covered in identical scars. On closer inspection, he saw that the scars were part of a pattern along their whole backside. They looked almost like wings, starting at the shoulder blades and extending to their lower backs. Their hair was long and seemed to be multicolored and braided into multiple thick strands, with bones and adornments weaved into the locks.

He turned from the bodies to examine the weapons they'd carried. Some were simple clubs made of large chunks of bone from a creature he wasn't sure he would ever want to see. There were also broadaxes. Like their smaller counterparts in the hull, they were covered with intricate marks that looked like fire coming off the edges of the blades. The hafts were covered with dark leather and different-colored fur ran along their length. He felt the fur and found it heavy and coarse.

Kenneth emerged from the cabin. "There's no one else aboard."

Daniel was still inspecting the blades as he spoke. "She said Krida...did the Kridens attack them?"

Kenneth walked over and crouched down by Daniel. "They're not the friendliest folk, from what I hear. Judging by all this, I'd have to agree."

"So what are they doing here?"

"That is a good question, lad."

Kenneth instructed the city guards that were still nearby to keep civilians off the docks and for the sailors to halt their work and stay onboard their ships for the time being. It took nearly two hours for a group of rangers and scholars to arrive and board the ship. The scholars asked if anything had been touched. Kenneth told them that the only thing that had been moved was the woman who'd been at the helm. This seemed to annoy them slightly.

Kenneth took Daniel back to the road leading up to the gate and they started their slow walk back. The rangers had said the commander wanted to speak with them since they had been there first hand. By the time they made it to the keep and up the stairs to the commander's office where the council was already waiting, it had been close to an hour. Daniel felt oddly nervous. He hadn't had many chances to speak with Commander Hall, only brief words in the dining hall or as they passed one another on a rare occasion.

Kenneth was the first to enter the office, leaving Daniel to wait outside the door for several minutes before he was allowed inside. Now he stood across the table from the four leaders of the Dragon Guard. His fear started to creep back as Kenneth left the room and closed the door behind him. The sun's rays filtered through the stained glass behind Hall, painting the room in myriad colors.

"Hello, Mr. Summers," Commander Hall said. He leaned forward and rested his arms on the desk. "Tell us exactly what happened."

He did as he was asked and told them everything he could remember, even the smallest details such as the feel of the fur and the designs on the blades. When he was finished, the captains exchanged glances. Hall rubbed his chin while Captain Hawk walked around behind Daniel, motioning for him to follow before tapping on the map spread out on a table just behind Daniel.

"Are you absolutely sure she said 'Krida' and 'hand,' nothing more?" Hawk asked, sounding slightly unconvinced.

Daniel nodded and looked at where Hawk was indicating on the map. It was a shoreline across the sea from Edaren with the word *Krida* written in large, flowing letters over the landmass. The map beyond the shore was blank, meaning it was uncharted territory.

He looked back to Hawk. "I'm sure. It was 'Krida,' then 'hand.'" Before they could reply he continued. "I don't mean to pry, but why would the Kridens attack us? Claudia hasn't told us much about them yet since we're mostly focusing on Edaren history and geography at the moment. I never really heard much about them back in Sapella. But I thought they kept to themselves for the most part."

Hawk bit his lip and considered the question. "The Kridens are rather...primitive. They're a tribal community. Stature is based on skill in battle and battles are waged between tribes. Beyond that, we don't know very much. The language barrier is hard to overcome when they try to kill you every time you try to speak to them."

"So why would they be on one of our scout ships?"

Coe stood and started for the door. "I think that's enough questions," he said. "Matters like this aren't your concern. If you wish to know more about the Kridens, there are books in the library that you can consult. You are dismissed from your duties for the day. Thank you for your assistance, Mr. Summers."

With that, Daniel was ushered out the door and back down the stairs. He knew that the captains could handle whatever was wrong, but he still had a feeling that he couldn't shake. It was as if a heavy chill had settled over him, making him feel stiff. He tried to shrug it off as nothing more than the adrenaline of what had just happened wearing off. He decided that he might as well go to the library and check on the books Coe had mentioned, if for no other reason than to fulfill his curiosity.

He quickly walked down the stairs to the library and started combing through the shelves, looking for anything that might relate to the land across the sea. His frustration mounted as he searched the hundreds of books on the shelves. He had found where the proper books should have been but the spaces on the shelves were empty. He kept looking and when he still came up empty, he simply stood in the middle of a row of shelves and stared at the space. He could forget it and find something else to occupy his time, but now, with his curiosity piqued, he knew that wouldn't happen. He returned to the library entrance and saw Claudia standing over a tall stack of books, a look of concentration on her face. He strode up to her. She held up a finger as she finished reading a page in one of the books and quickly wrote a few lines down on a parchment next to her.

"I thought you had patrol duty today," she said. She set the book aside and grabbed another without looking at him.

"I was told that I was dismissed for the rest of the day after what happened."

"What happened?" A look of concern flashed over her face. He quickly explained.

"Interesting," Claudia said. "So what are you doing here?"

He gestured to the row of shelves where he'd been looking. "I was trying to find some of the books on Krida that Captain Coe mentioned, but they aren't there. I was hoping you would know where they were."

"Hmm," Claudia said. "I'm not sure but I'll check the log for you."

She walked over to a nearby desk set against the wall and opened a drawer to pull out a thick, leather-bound book. It was the log where the titles of books currently removed from the library were written, as well as the name of who had them. She scanned the pages until she finally tapped a line.

"Looks like Clara has them, along with..." she paused as she counted, which was quickly followed by a sigh, "about a dozen others."

"I should have guessed it was her," Daniel said. He smiled before heading for the door. "Thank you, Claudia."

He exited the library through the main doorway and circled around the keep to their barracks. He reached the two-door building and approached the door to the girls' boarding house. He nearly opened it without thinking but stopped short and lifted his hand to rap his knuckles on the door instead. A few seconds later, the door swung inward. Griffon stood on the other side holding a half-finished wood figure.

She looked at him curiously. "What?"

"Is Clara in there?"

"No. She's on gate duty. Why?"

"She took some books from the library a little while ago. I was wondering if I could borrow them for a bit."

Griffon looked at him for a moment before stepping to the side and letting him through the door. The long room was almost identical to the boys' side, with cots and wardrobes lining each wall, though the girls had the added benefit of dividers between their beds.

"Her bed is in the back right corner," Griffon said." She's read most of them a dozen times and hasn't taken them back yet, so help yourself."

Daniel strolled over to Clara's cot and saw that strewn around it were dozens of books. Some had bookmarks sticking out of them and some were open with the spine facing up, while others had been left open to whatever page she was on. Clara may have loved to read, but she certainly didn't take care of her books. It looked like a storm had blown through the area. Daniel sighed and searched through the mess until he found the ones he was looking for, three books titled *Kriden Culture*, *Krida and Edaren Relations*, and *The Southern Reports*. Once he had the books in hand, Griffon quickly ushered him out without a word. Back in his own room, he sat on his bed and decided to start with the one he thought would interest him the least, *Krida and Edaren Relations*.

Krida and Edaren first made contact in the 1,802nd year of the Third Age, 527 years earlier. The name for the nation came from the natives. The meaning of *Krida* was currently unknown. Like the name, not much else was translated. There were a few words here and there, but nothing of note. Aside from the obvious lack of knowledge on each other's language, it seemed Edaren and Krida started off on relatively good terms. The two nations were close to one another and trade quickly started between Edaren and some of the coastal tribes.

But for an unknown reason, trade stopped just after two years of steady contact. Any envoys sent by Dalisia from then on were killed once they set foot in tribal territory. In addition, Krida tribes that had been near the shoreline suddenly went inland, where the stronger and more savage tribes made their home. Shortly after, organized patrols started dotting the coast. Dalisia wrote the land off and decided to simply let the Kridens be for the time being and would attempt to reestablish contact later when the Kridens' assumed paranoia had calmed. Daniel didn't see anything else of note in the book so he set it aside and picked up the next.

Kriden Culture seemed to simply restate what Hawk had told him. Daniel skimmed the book before setting it down.

The book *The Northern Accounts* was far more interesting. It was a series of journal entries written by several rangers and scholars who were tasked with watching the Kridens from just after the first contact to a short time after contact was cut off. The first section was written during first meetings. After a brief scan, Daniel skipped over them until he found sections relating to when the Kridens became openly hostile.

> *2nd of Alistar, 1,807th year of the Third Age.*
>
> *Tommy and I followed a freshly uprooted tribe. Nothing seemed out of the ordinary. It seemed they were simply picking up and moving as they tend to do. I would have written it off as such, but they are heading in the same direction every other tribe has been the last few days. Something is definitely going on. We're just waiting on reports from Joseph and Conrad before we pursue.*
>
> —SADIE

Daniel flipped through several other entries. Most of them were reports on strange behavior from the tribes. Their numbers were slowly shrinking, with no obvious cause. He flipped ahead. The year 1808 was mostly bare of entries. The few that were there only chronicled how nothing seemed to be happening. However, the next year of entries were made by several different people. A section of these caught his eye.

> *4th of Oren, 1,809th year of the Third Age.*
>
> *We can't get close enough. Sadie tried two days ago and we haven't seen her since. The fortress is larger than Vigil's keep, three or maybe four times the size. It's big enough for every tribe to live in and then some. How we didn't notice this thing popping up is beyond me. Every tribe must of have been working together on this, which goes against everything we've learned about them. I have an awful feeling about this but until we can get a good look inside, there's nothing more I can do but speculate.*
>
> —TOMMY

9th of Lathic, 1,809th year of the Third Age.

Now that construction is finished there's less activity outside, so I was able to get close enough to scale a wall. I witnessed some strange ritual in the courtyard involving fire. Some of the more powerful tribe leaders were standing with their backs to a brazier while a few women used different brands on them. I couldn't make out the shapes. They spoke something after each burn. Since none of us speak Kridic, I'm going to consult Tommy's translation notes and try to figure it out. Probably won't help, but it's worth a try.

—JOSEPH

23rd of Landring, 1,810th year of the Third Age.

Joseph is dead. He tried to scale the wall again, but a patrol was out of sync with the rest and caught him halfway up. Tommy and I are returning to Vigil to report what we've learned and try to gain a better insight on it. Hopefully the rest of the scholars can put their heads together and figure this out. We might have to try to get the Edaren council to intervene, depending on what we find, but knowing them they'll write this off as Dragon Guard paranoia and push it aside like they did with Wolves Wood.

—CONRAD

The entries from the four Dragon Guards ended there and picked up with another group sent out after Conrad and Tommy's return some months later. Daniel skimmed their entries. After what had happened to the group before them, these Dragon Guards seemed far more cautious and watched from outside the walls rather than risk scaling them. Supposedly, the Kridens rarely left the fortress during that time, save for hunting and gathering large amounts of wood or stone from the nearby forest and mountain quarry. Daniel jumped ahead. It seemed that nothing changed over the course of several years.

All of this was some time ago so he wasn't sure how much of it was still relevant. It did give him a better idea about where the burn patterns he saw on their backs were from, though not what they actually meant. It also explained why they were on the scout ship. They must have caught the rangers and chased them to the boat, which was moored somewhere on the shore. With most of his curiosity sated, he decided to let the matter be and leave it in the hands of the captains. He was sure they could handle it. Whatever it was.

CHAPTER TWENTY-THREE

30th of Sanya, 27th year of the Fourth Age.

THE TWENTY-TWO TRAINEES stood in the same room they had waited in for their interview with Captain North one year ago. They had been standing here for several minutes while Obadiah, Claudia, Austin, and the leaders of the Dragon Guard conferred with one another in the room beyond. Daniel shifted his weight from one foot to the other as they waited in suspense. Today was the thirtieth of Sanya, which was the last day of the last month of the year. They were being divided into their respective sects within the Dragon Guard. Daniel was excited, but at the same time he felt as if his heart was about to give out.

He glanced up and down the row and saw that everyone was just as anxious as he was. This was the moment that would define the rest of their training and, no doubt, a large portion of the rest of their lives. After several more agonizing minutes, the door in front of them opened. They all tensed as the commander, captains, and their instructors stepped through. The captains and instructors formed a line in front of them while Commander Hall stood in the middle, an open book in his hands. He looked up and down the line of uneasy faces in front of him. They tensed under his gaze as his eyes passed over them.

"You all look terrified," he said with a smile, easing their nerves slightly before he continued. "Today is an important day for you all. You've completed your general training and are now moving into one of the three sects of the Dragon Guard. First are the wardens."

Eleven were called. Among them were Robin, Griffon, Aaron, and Zachery. They all looked thrilled with their placement. Zachery's joy was the most evident as he sported a wide, toothy grin. Second to be called were the scholars. As Daniel had expected, Clara was chosen, along with Alan and Robert, making a total of six.

Hall closed the book with a loud thud. "That means the other five of you are our rangers. Your specialized training begins tomorrow, the first of Eren. I suggest you all go out and enjoy the festival for a while. But you are required to return to the keep by sundown and await us at the front entrance. Tonight is a bit of a...special event."

They were dismissed. Once they were outside the keep, they all quickly split into their selective groups. Daniel was in a daze as they made their way down the steps to the first floor and then outside. He'd had no idea which sect he would be placed in, but being chosen as a ranger felt...off. After all he'd learned, he'd wanted to be a warden, someone that stood and fought on the front lines to protect everyone around him. Being a ranger felt almost wrong.

Zachery lifted his brother off the ground and spun with him. "Woo!" he yelled. "One year down!"

Griffon punched Zachery in the arm. "Quiet!" she said. "The whole city will hear you."

Aaron grinned. "Come on, Griffon," he said. "Let him have some fun. I can't imagine Obadiah will allow much of it starting tomorrow."

Daniel smiled at his friends. He'd been with them only a year, but it felt like a lifetime. In his mind, they fit their sects perfectly. Griffon was a talented fighter in spite of her hot temper, which could be beneficial in a fight. Aaron was calm in almost any situation and was by far the most skilled with a blade. Zachery was excellent at adapting to the flow of events. In contrast, Clara had a knack for knowledge retention when it came to history or politics. If there was ever a question that needed an answer, she would likely be the one to provide it. Lastly, Alan was becoming a highly skilled doctor.

"So what should we do?" Alan said as he bounced on the balls of his feet.

Zachery thought for a moment. "Why not go down to the market district?" he said. "There's always lots of traveling traders arriving for the festival."

"You don't have any money," Griffon remarked.

He shrugged. "Clara does."

Clara glared at Zachery. "Don't you dare volunteer me for that again," she said. "Last time we went to the market and I offered to pay, you went way overboard."

"How did I go overboard?"

"You tried to buy a dog."

"What's wrong with that?"

"Someone already owned it! Besides that, where would you have kept it?"

They continued their lighthearted "argument" as they had dozens of times before. Daniel tuned them out as he was lost in his own thoughts. After a few moments, he shrugged. "I'll pass," he said. "You guys go ahead."

Aaron looked at him with a worried expression. "Are you okay?"

"Yeah. I'm just going to take a walk. Clear my head a little."

Zachery shrugged. They all stepped through the gate and out into the city, with one last glance in Daniel's direction from Aaron. When they were gone, Daniel walked through the courtyard and over the frost-covered grass until he came to one of the corner towers. He opened the door and glanced up through the wooden supports crisscrossing the empty, vertical space. Spiral stairs wound their way up along the wall until they came to the top floor, which led out onto the wall. He started up. When he reached the top, he stepped out onto the north wall. He sighed and brushed snow away from the battlement to clear an area for him to sit and look out over the city, his feet dangling over the edge.

Snow coated every roof and street, covering everything in a thin, pure, white sheet with bits of grey stone peeking through. Smoke rose from chimneys dotted around the city and along the few streets he could see clearly. People were going about their day preparing for the festival by setting up stands, stages, and decorations. He wondered how many people knew about the Disciples of the Left Hand and about what dragons really were or what the Dragon Guards' true purpose was. What *his* purpose was.

It all felt so surreal. He was going to be a ranger in the Dragon Guard. There were still days when he woke up and didn't quite believe how his life had turned out since that autumn day in Sapella's Crossing. It had started with a peaceful walk with Connie along the edge of the Arrow before he'd headed down to the falls with her and Jeremy. Then the valgret had turned the day on its head. His rescue cemented his desire to be a Dragon Guard. He wanted to be like the ones he read about in his book. To be like Kenneth, Claudia, and Mila.

"You're likely to fall off the wall with all this ice."

He turned. Kenneth was walking toward him from the opposite tower. "What are you doing here?" Daniel asked.

"I'm on patrol duty for the evening," Kenneth said. He sat next to Daniel, though he kept his feet planted on the wall and his back to the city. "So, how are you feeling? Obadiah told me what sect they'd chosen for you."

"When did you find out?"

"Just a few moments ago. He caught me as I was entering the east tower." He looked at Daniel and frowned. "Not happy with the choice? You have a look about you that I've seen far more often than I'd like."

"Not sure. On one hand, I'm excited to have come this far. But on the other hand, I don't feel like a ranger."

Kenneth laughed lightly. "Well, you aren't a ranger yet. Still have some training to do first. But I think it's a perfect fit for you."

"I don't know," Daniel said with a sigh. "I just always imagined myself as the hero, standing out in front of everyone, ready to protect them."

"Lad, that passion is what makes you a perfect ranger."

"What do you mean?"

"I've seen it since the day we met in that forest. The way you placed yourself between me and your brother when you had no idea who I was. The way you asked any question that came to your mind during our trip. Your determination to fulfill your dream of coming here. You are a clever and insightful young man. You are the type of person who would do *anything* to protect others, no matter the cost, and for rangers that cost is often very high."

He handed Daniel a folded black cloth. Daniel held it out and let it fall open. It was a long, ragged black scarf with frayed edges.

"After what happened to get you here, I don't think there's anything else you could be."

Daniel clutched the ragged scarf in his lap for a moment. Mila's scarf.

"Thank you, Kenneth."

"Don't thank me. It was Obadiah's idea. Big softie, that one. Said he meant to give it to you but you all left so quickly."

Daniel smiled and wrapped the scarf around his neck. It wasn't as heavy as he thought it would be. In fact, it was rather light, but still quite warm, and soft as well.

Kenneth placed a hand on his shoulder. "She would want you to have it. The ragged look of it suits you quite well. Makes you look rather dashing, if I'm being honest." He grinned.

Daniel smiled back at him as Kenneth stood. With one last glance at Daniel, Kenneth turned and walked into the tower to continue his patrol. Daniel sat on the edge of the wall a while longer before deciding it was time for him to stop sulking and start celebrating his new role. He went down the tower and out the gate to head for the market district and find his friends.

Several hours later, the trainees were patiently waiting on the stairs just outside the keep entrance. It was moments from sundown, which meant it was nearly time for what Hall had simply called a "surprise" for them. They had no idea what it could possibly be, but that didn't stop them from guessing.

"Maybe they're preparing a feast for us!" Alan said while lying down on one of the steps, looking up as snow fell onto his face.

Daniel shook his head. "All you think about is food."

Zachery shrugged and said, "Hey, if its Jonathan's cooking I'm all for it."

"There's already the festival feast," Daniel said, "so I doubt that's what's happening."

They heard the main doors open. Collectively, the twenty-two of them turned to see Austin step out and stand at the top of the stairs. "Good," he said, "you're all here. Well, this will be interesting. Hope you're ready." He motioned to the door. Everyone stood and followed him in.

Inside, Claudia and Obadiah waited at the base of the stairs. When the recruits crowded around, Claudia addressed them with hint of amusement in her tone. "Now, we're taking you to meet someone. She's a bit of an... oddity. But treat her with the same respect you would treat Commander Hall."

With a new sense of curiosity, they were led up the stairs to the fourth floor, then the fifth, and then beyond. They had never been allowed this far into the tower before. They kept quiet, as if speaking was forbidden and even the slightest sound would be frowned upon. Slowly, they climbed higher in the tower, passing several doorways leading to unknown rooms with unknown contents. Even after several minutes, they had yet to reach the top. Daniel knew that if it hadn't been for all the exercise they'd been put through, he would be falling over from exhaustion. Building his endurance and muscle tone had been a slow process, but it had been a noticeable one.

When at last they reached the top of the spiral stairs, they stepped into a short hallway with a single iron door at the end. Obadiah and the other instructors walked to the door and faced all of them as they crowded into the hall.

Austin gave a knowing grin as he gripped the handle. "Don't freak out."

He turned the handle and pushed the door open, allowing himself and the other two instructors through first. From where he stood, Daniel could see only the three of them. The rest slowly trickled through the doorway. Each one of them stopped in their tracks, then stumbled forward as those behind pushed to get in. They found themselves on a large, open, stone platform. Lit braziers lined the edges, giving the area a soft and comforting glow.

But most surprising was the brilliant, silver-scaled dragon. It lay near the right edge of the tower on its belly, its forelegs crossed in front of it and its tail hanging over the side. It had a long snout and a slender body. Its wings were folded in at its sides, but even so Daniel could tell they must be double the length of its body, which was roughly forty feet from the tip of its tail to its snout. It had a set of horns that curved slightly upward at the top of its head, with another two at the back of its jawbone curling downward towards its neck.

It turned its head towards them, and Daniel could see that its eyes were much like a cat, though they were colored light lavender, barely discernable in the low light. It was beautiful in a slightly terrifying way. It seemed to look at each of them in turn without turning its head. Its eyes simply darting this way and that. In spite of what Claudia had taught them about dragons, all he could think of right now were the songs sung in taverns and things said in children's stories. That they were evil creatures bent on destroying everything mankind had built. They did nothing but destroy and cause chaos.

Claudia's voice was reassuring in the tense silence. "Don't worry, she's not going to hurt you."

"I made no such promise."

The sudden voice coming from the slender beast was alarming and made most of them shrink back. But as alarming as it was it also seemed, calming. It was clearly a feminine tone and had a hint of amusement in it. Almost like a mother or an older sister teasing their younger sibling. When it saw them all back away it laughed lightly, at least Daniel assumed it was a laugh. Even being nearly eight feet away the heat from her breath was apparent in the cool night air as it exhaled.

Austin grinned and stepped forward to stand next to the dragon. "It's wonderful to see you again," he said to the creature. "How was your nap?"

"Refreshing," the dragon answered. "I feel fifty years younger."

Hall raised a hand as if presenting the dragon to them. "This is

Argera," he said. "She is the oldest living Dragon Guard and a dear friend of mine."

None of them made a move or sound as the dragon stared at them.

Argera glanced down at Commander Hall. "Rather unenthusiastic group this time around," she said.

The more she spoke, the less concerned Daniel felt, though it wasn't by much.

Robin was the first of them to speak, though it was only a whisper: "This was the last thing I expected to see."

Argera turned to her and squinted at her curiously. "I do hope you mean that in a positive sense."

"That depends..." she answered.

Commander Hall smiled. "Argera has been part of the Dragon Guard for over two hundred years. She's one of our most vital members and she's your newest instructor."

Robert took a tentative step forward. "What's she going to teach us?"

Argera lowered her head, which with the length of her neck brought her within inches of the group, and answered, "How to kill dragons."

"Is that all you do?" Robert asked.

"No."

Obadiah spoke up for the first time: "She is also vital in the forging of our weaponry and tools."

"How so?" Robert said.

Argera laughed again. "Take a wild guess." With the last word, a short plume of fire left her lips before quickly dissipating.

Clara too had found her voice. "Dragon fire...is that what makes Dragon Guard steel so strong?"

"Partly," Argera said. "At the very least, it gives it that oh-so-lovely orange etching."

Robert continued to press for information. "Is that all?" he asked. "Just dragon fire?"

"Not exactly," Argera said. "There are other steps."

A question came to Daniel's mind. When he spoke, his voice cracked slightly: "So you're not the first dragon to be part of the Guard, then?"

"No, I'm not," Argera said. "My lineage can be traced back to Forus, who fought in the war of the First Age. Each generation since has served the Dragon Guard."

Clara tilted her head. "Commander Hall said you've been around for over two hundred years. How long do dragons live?"

Argera seemed to think on her answer for a moment. "If my brood mother was any indication, we live upwards of three hundred years."

"You don't know for sure?" Clara sounded disappointed.

"Every dragon that has been a part of the Dragon Guard has died of something other than old age. So at the moment, none of us really know."

Claudia chimed in with a hint of sorrow in her tone: "One of the many things we've simply lost to time."

"Are there other dragons in Edaren?" Robin asked.

Commander Hall raised a hand to quiet them. "I believe that is enough questions for now," he said. "You'll have plenty of time with her over the next few years. Argera has some other matters to attend to before you'll begin your training with her. Now I suggest you get some sleep before tomorrow."

Daniel stood in a long and wide room on the first floor of the keep along with the four other ranger trainees. It wasn't the first time he had been in here but it was the first time that five straw target dummies were hung from the wooden rafters above them. To his left was a table covered by a heavy cloth alongside a much smaller table with two chairs at each end. On the floor were five circles across from the targets in a line. Daniel glanced at the four trainees. Lace and Jane were to his left. On the right were two boys who he did not know well, but at the very least knew their names, Eric and Bradly.

They had all been woken at first light and told to wait here by Austin's new assistant. It only took a few minutes before the door opened. Austin walked through and stood next to the covered table alongside his assistant, Tara, a tall girl with long, black hair tied into a tail. Austin motioned for the five to join them while Tara removed the cloth from the table, revealing an array of items hidden beneath. There were short swords, knives, daggers, and axes, as well as several small pouches and devices Daniel couldn't identify at a glance. In addition, there were five sets of ranger armor.

Austin sat on the corner of the table. "This armor will protect your vital areas," he said, "while still allowing free movement. I suggest you put it on to get used to the feel."

They did as they were told. The vambraces and gloves were snug but not uncomfortable. The shin guards and chest plate were likewise form fitting. What seemed to throw Daniel off the most were the shoulder guards. They didn't restrict his movement, but their presence was off-putting. He only hoped he would get used to them quickly.

When they were finished, Austin continued. "Training from here on out will be as much a test of physical ability as it will be problem solving. I'll be presenting you with a lot of scenarios. To solve some of them, you will be using these." Austin reached for a small leather pouch and unclipped the top, revealing at least a dozen short and thin knives. "Throwing knives. Easy to hide if removed from the pouch and useful if there's a target in range and you don't have the time or space to use a bow."

He then gave them an overview of most of the weapons and tools on the table, asking them to place each on their belts when he finished explaining its use. When they had gone through every item, Austin instructed them to stand in one of the red circles on the floor.

"Now listen closely," he said. "Tara is going to come to each one of you and ask you to remove your weapons and hand them over to her."

Bradly looked and sounded annoyed: "You just gave them to us."

"Yes, I did."

Tara went to each of them in turn. They all complied by removing and handing over their weapons, which she placed back on the table.

Austin clapped his hands together. "Good. Now, see the target in front of you? Your job is to kill it."

After some hesitation, they all moved to step forward. The moment they were out of the circle, Tara spoke: "Do it without leaving your marked space."

For a moment, Daniel thought he'd misheard. He looked at the target, then at the floor between them. It had to be at least ten feet away. Without being able to approach it and with no weapons, he had no way to do this. Austin had said they would be confronted with problem scenarios, but Daniel didn't expect one just yet, or one like this. Clearly there was a trick to this. He just had to find out what it was. Austin sat at the smaller table with Tara, who pulled out a deck of cards and began dealing them out while the trainees looked on in confusion.

Jane crossed her arms in frustration. "Are you going to tell us what we're supposed to be doing?"

Austin answered without looking up. "We already did. Kill the target without leaving the circle. If you don't have the means to do so, then you weren't listening to me."

Daniel ran his hand through his hair. Clearly, Austin had given them a clue. He thought back on what little had been said, but nothing jumped out at him as odd or relevant. He started looking around the room, thinking maybe there was something he had missed.

After several minutes, Lace started tapping her foot. "How long," she said, "do we have to do this?"

Austin shrugged. "That depends on how long it takes you. Let's hope you're all as good as I think you are. Feel free to sit down, just don't leave the circle."

It was well after sunset when Austin finally let them leave for the barracks. It had been an entire day in that room with only a few breaks to eat and relieve themselves. During that whole time, they had no idea what they should be doing. Upon leaving, their weapons had been returned. Austin told them to keep them on at all times to get used to the feel of their weight before the more difficult training started. Daniel and the other boys went to their side of the barracks. When they entered, Daniel saw that everyone else had already returned and were fast asleep and snoring.

Daniel made his way to the back of the room, where his bed sat next to Aaron's. When he glanced at his friend, he saw that his upper body was bare and covered with fresh bruises. Not really feeling tired enough to sleep after his uneventful first day of training, Daniel lit a candle and picked up his old storybook from home before sitting on his bed.

Only he and Aaron were at this end of the room, so he knew the light wouldn't disturb anyone else. He placed the light on the shelf above his bed before flipping through the pages aimlessly, reading a few lines here and there, until he finally drifted into sleep.

He must have been sleeping for only a few hours before he heard a loud crash. He opened his eyes to see Aaron holding sitting on his cot and holding his foot, which was bent at an awkward angle.

"Aaron? What happened?"

"I can't see, that's what happened." Aaron spoke in an irritated whisper.

"What are you doing?" Daniel asked as he sat up straight.

Aaron glanced at the other end of the room toward what Daniel hadn't yet noticed. Daniel followed his gaze. The other warden trainees were also waking and dressing.

He turned back to Daniel before speaking. "Obadiah told us to meet him at first light." He paused and looked at Daniel. "How was the first day of ranger training?"

Daniel thought for a moment before answering. "I'm not sure yet," he said. "Still figuring out the first test."

"What?"

"Don't worry about it. You better get going."

Aaron shrugged and put on his gear before stepping out the door with the others. Daniel sat on the bed and mulled over the test until the sun started to rise. He sighed and made his way back with the others to the room they'd occupied the previous day. They entered to see Austin and Tara already inside.

"Good morning, everyone," Austin said with a wide smile. "Hope you're ready for another exciting day."

None of them said anything as they went to their circles. They all knew what was coming and were clearly dreading it as none of them had a solution to the test yet.

Austin nodded happily when they were all in place. "Good," he said. "Now, listen closely. Tara is going to ask each one of you for your weapons. Afterwards, your task is the same as yesterday. Kill the target without leaving the circle."

Something clicked in his mind. Austin had said to listen closely. This time he took that to heart. Austin said that Tara was going to *ask* for their weapons. Could he refuse her? Surely it wouldn't be that simple.

As he finished this thought, Austin scolded Jane, who had done just that. "Nice try, Ms. Powell, but that's not going to happen."

"Why not?" Jane crossed her arms.

"Because we can see them."

Jane scowled and handed Tara her weapons. So refusing wouldn't work, but Jane's encounter gave Daniel another idea. He had only a moment before Tara was in front of him, so he moved quickly while trying to keep his motions slight and inconspicuous. When she was before him and asked for his weapons, he complied. When she placed them all on the table, Austin turned to them again and gestured to the targets. When no one moved right away, he shrugged and sat at the table with Tara, who again pulled out the deck of cards and began dealing.

Daniel hesitated. He was having second thoughts about his idea. If he was wrong or in some way broke the rules, then this could end poorly for him. Then again, no rules had been stated aside from staying within the circle. Once Tara had finished dealing the cards and placed the deck between her and Austin, Daniel decided this was the only way to kill the target that made any sense to him. He slipped the throwing knife out of his sleeve and lifted his arm. He only hoped he wouldn't miss. With an overhand throw, as he'd been taught months ago, he hurled it at the target hard enough to bury half the blade in its burlap and straw chest. Everyone turned to look at the source of the sound as it hit with a solid *thump*.

After a moment, Austin stood and clapped his hands together excitedly. "Fantastic!" he said. "I was hoping one of you would figure it out before tomorrow. North said this might have been too difficult for a first test, but I had faith in all of you." Austin walked over to the target and retrieved the knife. "Now, can anyone guess the reason for this type of exercise? I'm going to guess that you can't."

No one answered right away as they all considered. Austin paced the line, looking at each of them in turn. When no one answered, he spoke again, flipping the knife as he did so. "The Dragon Guard tries to keep many secrets," he said. "The existence of dragons and Disciples, forging techniques, and alchemical recipes. But there is one thing that many members even in the Order don't know about rangers. Rangers are more than scouts, tacticians, and strategists. We're the darker part of what the Dragon Guard has to do. We're assassins."

They all stared at him in confusion. After a few moments, Austin frowned and said, "Not the reaction I was expecting."

Daniel shook his head. "Why," he said, "would the Dragon Guard need assassins?"

Austin started pacing. "I'm going to propose a scenario to you," he said. "Let's *hypothetically* say that a man in Dalisia, through bribery, blackmail, and assassinations of his own, as well simple politics, is able to find a seat on the Council. With this seat, he begins courting the daughter of the king. During this time, through strange circumstances, the *son* of the king is killed. A year later, after all possible suspicion of this man is absolved; he marries the daughter, putting him in line for the throne through marriage."

Austin continued pacing, watching their faces for any reaction. "Then," he said, "several years later, the current king, who is well into his old age, passes naturally. Placing this particular man on the throne. Now, let's say that this man is a Disciple of the Left Hand. With the throne under him, he has total control over Edaren. How does the Dragon Guard stop him?"

None of them answered right away. As far as Daniel could think, there was really nothing that could be done.

Austin kept going: "We can't petition the Council for a bloodline investigation—he's already known to be on the throne by marriage. We can't accuse him of slaying the king—he was already well past the age most men die and clearly passed due to that. We can't accuse him of killing the son to fall into succession—he married after the son's death, making the motivation for that blurry and hard to prove."

Eric raised a hand. "Couldn't the Dragon Guard gain favor among the Council and petition them to remove him from the throne?"

"On what grounds?" Austin said. "He has shown no ill intention to the land of Edaren or any particular city as of yet. To add to that, as the king he has the right to veto a Council seat and force an election of a new member by the respective city prolonging any petition submitted by at least a year. The fact of the matter is that he had total control over Edaren, and there was *almost* nothing we could do about it. We do what we have to do, not because we enjoy it but because it is necessary. If Disciples are left alone long enough, the things they will do would make you physically sick."

Daniel's thoughts drifted back to a year ago, when he and Mila were sitting in the bar in Grey Gate. She had told him she was drinking to forget the things she had done, the things she did in secret. Now he knew what she meant. He was even more unsure about how he felt about his placement in this sect. Why was he chosen to be an assassin for the Dragon Guard? He didn't think he'd have the stomach for it, or the strength to do what would be asked of him.

"This world is a darker place then you realize," Austin said. "The king that took that throne through deception set into motion the battle that razed and erased Prect from the map. Had the Dragon Guard acted upon the knowledge we had at the moment we had it, Prect would still be here and thousands upon thousands of people wouldn't have had to die. Grey Gate would not have turned into the cesspool of corruption it is now and the Disciples would have lost years of planning. As it is, we acted too late. The new king's plan was in motion and there was no stopping it."

Jane stared at him as realization spread over all their faces. "You're talking about the death of King Reynald," she said. "The king of Dalisia, he was the one that stoked the fires for the war between Edaren and Prect."

Austin nodded. "Had we acted sooner, there wouldn't have even been a spark. Rangers do what we do because if we don't, people die. It is always our last resort and even then we hesitate to use it."

Bradly shook his head. "There's no honor in assassination," he said. "It's not a fair fight. You're killing someone in cold blood."

Austin glared daggers at him. "Killing is killing and it is never the preferred method. During the time leading up to the death of Reynald, the Dragon Guard petitioned the Council for both a bloodline check and to remove him from the throne on grounds of conspiracy and countless other accusations that even at the time seemed outlandish. We were trying *everything* to see him removed from the throne."

Austin walked over to Daniel and handed the knife back. Daniel took it and found his hands were shaking. The realization that rangers were what they were was unsettling. While he understood the purpose of it, it did not make the truth easier.

"War is not fair," Austin said. "Death is not fair. Someone scheming, killing, and bribing their way onto the throne is not *fair*. What you need to learn is that there is no such thing as a fair fight. Someone is always faster or stronger. Someone has always had more experience or training. Someone is always smarter or has the better weapon. The very concept of a fair fight is ludicrous. Someone always has the advantage. I'm here to make sure that someone is *you*."

CHAPTER TWENTY-FOUR

14th of Eren, 28th year of the Fourth Age.

"KEEP THE PRESSURE on him!" Obadiah shouted.

Zachery and Griffon were on either side of Aaron. Out of the corner of his eye, Aaron caught sight of Griffon swinging her great sword at the back of his legs. He jumped back and over the swing, kicking up snow as he went and nearly slipping on the slick slush. Aaron raised his kite shield in front of him at just the right moment to block a swing from Zachery's longsword. Then he caught the blur of steel as Zachery tried to bring the parrying dagger around to hit Aaron's ribs while he was distracted with the sword. Aaron twisted his shield to direct Zachery's sword to the side, allowing him to block both weapons before stepping back and safely out of range.

They had been in warden training for two weeks and Aaron had never been more exhausted in all his life. Every day, all day long, Obadiah pitted them against each other in uneven matches. He told them that the best way to gain experience and skill was to be in the thick of combat.

They could practice forms and swings all day, but it would amount to nothing if they couldn't perform them in the heat and pressure of a fight.

It was near the end of the day's training and Aaron had been pitted against four of the other trainees. He wore his full set of warden leather plate, while his opponents were in only their black, giving them the edge in speed. While normally a fight this lopsided would last only seconds, for the purpose of practice Aaron was allowed to be hit a maximum of four times before being declared the loser, while the rest were removed from the fight with a single decisive blow.

As of yet, none of the lone fighters had won any of these matches. It didn't look like Aaron was going to be the first. Though he had lasted longer than most, he had already been struck three times and managed to strike down only two of his opponents. The match had been going for roughly thirty seconds.

When the match started, Aaron decided the best way to make any progress was to forgo defense and try and knock them out as quickly as possible to even the numbers. He began with those he knew were the weakest fighters. Now, with two left, Zachery was his next target. Zachery preferred to fight with a longsword in one hand and a parrying dagger in the other. This dagger boasted a wider guard. Its ends rose in a curve that was meant to catch an opponent's weapon so the wielder of the dagger could twist it in any direction to open an opportunity for an attack.

Aaron swung in a downward arc toward Zachery. The clash of their wooden swords sent vibrations along his arm. The heavier and wider broadsword that Aaron wielded in addition to Aaron's strength caused Zachery's arm to buckle when they connected. Aaron placed his shield in front of him and threw all his weight into it, slamming into Zachary with full force, sending him reeling back. At the same moment, Aaron lifted his sword and swung for his opponent's shoulders. He nearly made contact, but Griffon intervened and managed to place her great sword in front of Aaron's blade long before it reached Zachery. She used the larger and heavier sword like he had, forcing Aaron's sword down to the ground until the tip buried in the slush.

Aaron didn't have time to pry his sword away as Zachery recovered his balance and jabbed at Aaron's gut. He barely managed to keep his shield in front of him and block the first strike. Then Zachery managed something Aaron hadn't expected. He turned the parrying dagger in his hand around to hold it in the reverse grip that Daniel was accustomed to and got the blade around the back of Aaron's shield. With the wide, curved guard gripping the rim of Zachery's shield, he used it like a hook and pried Aaron's protection to the side and out of the way.

Aaron tried with all his strength to keep the wall of iron-banded wood between them, but Zachery didn't need to move his shield much, he only needed to hold him in place. With Aaron unable to back away with one arm gripping his sword and the other locked in place, Zachery easily brought his sword up into Aaron's gut to bring the match to an end.

"Very good!" Obadiah said. "Excellent use of your dagger, Mr. Thorn, and Ms. Hart, I'm glad to see you're finally learning to be more cooperative with your partners." Griffon beamed at the compliment as Obadiah turned to Aaron, who had doubled over and was breathing heavily. "Mr. Cross, exceptional performance as always."

Griffon and Zachery placed their sparring weapons onto the nearby racks before stepping back into line with the others. Aaron followed after he had caught his breath. They stood and waited for Obadiah's next command. The instructor looked up and down the line, considering his next choices, before pointing to another five that included Robin. The other four headed into the ring while she started to don her set of armor. Aaron watched the fight with half interest.

He'd begun wondering how his family back in Dalisia was doing since the New Year had begun, especially after he'd received a letter from his father, which he still couldn't bring himself to open. It sat on a shelf in his wardrobe. Every day, when he retrieved or put away his gear, he would glance at the letter, reach for it, and then pull back before closing the doors, leaving it unopened. He felt sure he knew what was written inside.

It would be a plea for him to come home, to stop what he was doing and to rethink his foolishness. But just like the days leading up to his departure, Aaron would ignore his father. His grandfather had been a Dragon Guard and Aaron had always greatly admired and respected him in spite of the whirl of rumors in Dalisia about the Order and the things they did or were doing. Aaron had loved the stories about his grandfather's adventures, chasing what he had deemed "outlaws" through cities or forests. Only now was able to connect the dots that the outlaws were in fact Disciples.

The knowledge gave the stories a new light in his eyes, and only further cemented the idea that coming here had been the right thing to do. Aaron's father, Ryan Cross, had never taken his own father seriously. In his Ryan's eyes, Aaron's grandfather was just an old man with a foggy memory who had never been around when he was a child. In the end, that was the real reason Ryan hated the Dragon Guard. It had nothing to do with the rumors and everything to do with a man he considered a poor excuse for a father.

Aaron's train of thought was broken when Obadiah shouted at Robin: "Ms. Woods, you better start taking this seriously! Fight back!"

Aaron's attention was snapped back to the fight between Robin and the other fighters. None of them had been eliminated yet, which was odd for how long the fight had been going. Robin seemed to be avoiding every swing that the others threw at her while at the same time grabbing them and throwing them off balance and to the ground, without ever hitting them. She seemed to be treating the fight like nothing more than an annoyance, and treating her opponents as a cat would a mouse.

When Obadiah again shouted at Robin, his face turning red, she seemed to roll her eyes before going on the offensive. During their combat exercises, she had often seemed to be holding back. Out of all the wardens, she was the only one to go with a bladeless weapon, a quarterstaff to be exact. Its name derived from the process of cutting a chunk of hardwood into quarters, and then refining it into a staff. It was surprisingly durable and stood at a total of seven feet, a foot taller than Robin.

This was the first time Aaron had seen Robin actually use it. She struck out with the end of the staff, hitting one of her opponents in the gut with surprising speed, making him stumble back and gasp for air. She ducked below the swing of a girl's sword and brought the staff around in a wide swing, making the others around her back away as she brought it all the way around. The staff hit the girl in the ribs, hard enough to send her off her feet and roll sideways.

Before her other two opponents could move in, Robin gripped the staff at its middle and brought it into an upward arc into another attacker's chin with enough force to send his head snapping backwards. He fell onto his back, unconscious. Her final attacker swung her sword at Robin's shoulders, but she easily dodged the blow by leaning back. The girl had panicked and swung too early and from too far away. Now Robin advanced on her. She gripped her staff with both hands and spun it quickly in front of her, making the girl back further away. In a blur of motion so fast that Aaron wasn't able to follow it, she whipped the staff around and smacked the end of it against the girl's throat.

It all happened in the span of about fifteen seconds. The courtyard fell silent. It was the first time anyone had won one of the matches so quickly and with such ease. It was also the first time any of them had seen Robin actually take a fight seriously, if that was her taking it serious. Aaron wasn't sure since the entire time she looked almost bored. Obadiah was the first to snap out of his stupor. He ran over to the fallen trainees and went about inspecting them one by one to see if they were severely injured. Without being asked, Aaron and Zachery did the same. After a moment, Obadiah instructed several of them to help the injured trainees to their feet and take them to the apothecary in the keep for aid. When they were gone, he turned to Robin, who simply stood with her staff resting on her shoulders and a look of indifference on her face.

Obadiah spoke in a tone that made Aaron fear the man more than he had ever thought possible: "What in Edaren were you thinking?"

Robin raised an eyebrow. "Taking it seriously," she said. "Did you not want me to do that?"

Her question and calm tone seemed only to infuriate Obadiah further. "I will deal with you in private. Everyone else is dismissed!"

Aaron quickly left the courtyard with Griffon and Zachery in tow. They didn't want to be anywhere near Obadiah when he scolded Robin. They headed toward the barracks to remove their gear and wait for the other sects to finish their training for the day.

"So." Aaron was the first to break the rather tense silence. "That was unexpected."

"I had no idea she could do that," Griffon said, sounding awestruck. "She just moved...so fast."

"She didn't hesitate at all," Aaron said. "She could kill someone, hitting them in the throat like that."

"Can we talk about something less awful? Like how I'm getting better than Griffon?" Zachery said. He placed his hands behind his head and smiled at her.

She shoved him hard in the side, making him stumble. "Not even close."

Aaron nudged him with his shield. "You are getting better, though. That was a new trick with the dagger."

"Daniel showed me that, actually."

Since their sect training had started, Aaron hadn't seen much of Daniel. They left at different hours of the morning and were both gone all day. When they returned, more often than not one of them would already be asleep. Usually Aaron, as Daniel seemed to have more training during the night. Aaron couldn't wait for the day when they were all finished with their training and could head out together on assignments. He couldn't imagine fighting alongside anyone but his friends.

Griffon bit her lip. "So, is anyone else surprised at how well Robin can fight? I know we went over this, but she's really good."

Zachery crossed his arms and leaned on her. "Sounding a bit jealous, aren't you Griffon?"

She was quiet for a moment before whispering to herself, "I want to beat her."

Zachery was clearly disappointed she hadn't taken his bait. "Well," he said, "I can honestly say that she went a bit overboard."

Aaron shook his head. "She seemed bored, like it wasn't even a challenge for her." The whole thing left a bad taste in Aaron's mouth. To change the subject, he turned to Griffon and smiled. "How's Clara been?"

She shrugged. "Couldn't be happier," she said. "She loves the political and history portions of her training. She's so longwinded on some subjects; I can't get her to shut up when I want to sleep."

They reached the barracks and split off to remove their gear. When they stepped through the door, Aaron noticed that Daniel hadn't returned yet. He'd been vague about the nature of his training. No matter how much Aaron asked, he kept it to himself. On the few times Daniel had mentioned something relating to his training, it had never seemed to make sense. When asked for clarification, he always answered with "Don't worry about it" before changing the subject. Shaking his head, Aaron opened his wardrobe and started to place his gear on the rack located inside. When he was finished and about to close the doors, his eyes drifted to the sealed letter. He debated once again if he should open it. Just as he was about to walk away, he heard the door open and Daniel stepped through.

Aaron glanced at the letter again. "Still haven't opened it?" Daniel asked.

Aaron shook his head. "I don't think I want to know what he has to say."

"He might have changed his mind about you coming here," Daniel said. "Either way, it's been sitting there and it's clearly bothering you. I think you should open it."

Aaron bit his lip and considered it. Daniel was right. It was driving him crazy. After several seconds, he grabbed it before he could change his mind. He sat on the edge of his cot, broke the wax seal binding it closed, unfolded it, and started to read.

Aaron. My son, you must come home. The Dragon Guard is not what you think it is. As of late there have been an increasing number of murders in Dalisia, all linked to members of the Dragon Guard by eyewitnesses. Even those who have been assaulted and survived their ordeal aim their accusations at the leather-clad members of the Guard.

What reason could they have to kill a baker, a clothier, a beggar, and a member of my own guard? It does not bode well for our family to be associated with these rumors and I urge you to consider what we know about them and those that were once one of them. Use your judgment and come to the right conclusion.

I fear that if these incidents do not stop soon then there will be no choice but for the Edaren Council to intervene with the force of the Royal Army. My position on the matter has already been brought into question due to your most recent attempt to punish me for some unknown slight by fleeing the city to join those mercenaries and by sending that commoner to our home with a letter signed by you and sealed by our own family crest to demand payment.

I fear I cannot stall the proceedings for much longer. If you choose to stay with those people then I will have no choice but to officially revoke your status of nobility and as my son. For your own safety, you must come home.

—Representative of Dalisia and the 1ˢᵗ Seat of the Kings Council, Ryan Cross

Aaron read the letter over and over again. Regardless of whether or not the allegations were true—and Aaron was sure that they weren't—if the Edaren Council intervened, it wouldn't be peacefully. There had always been tension between the council and the Dragon Guard due to the fact that the council had no real authority over the workings of the Dragon Guard unless they flat out broke a law, which infuriated them to no end.

"Well?"

Aaron looked up from the letter and saw Daniel looking at him expectantly. "Uh, it's nothing really. Just asking me to come home...like I figured."

"I'm sorry, Aaron. I know it must have been hard to leave. But I'm sure they can handle the shop without you."

He was confused for a moment before he remembered what he had told everyone. "Right," he said, "I'm sure they can manage."

Daniel looked at him with concern. "Are you okay, Aaron? Was there something else in the letter?"

He stood and shook his head, faking a smile. "Nothing else, and yeah, I'm fine. I just remembered I had something to ask Obadiah. I'll be back."

Aaron rushed out the door and into the snow before Daniel could reply. He went into the keep, through the kitchen, and up the staircase as quickly as he could. He hadn't told anyone aside from the captains and the commander that his father was the Dalisia councilman, though he was positive Claudia knew. When people knew who he was, he didn't like how it made them look at him. Like he was someone who inherently thought he was better than them. It instantly made them despise him, made them think they knew how he thought about them. When he was younger, he'd had friends in the city, but the moment they or their parents found out who his father was, they suddenly didn't want to be around him anymore. It was as if they were afraid that if they made Aaron angry, something bad would happen to them.

It really wasn't an unfounded fear if he looked at the history of council members. Too often, when someone offended a council member or someone in the member's family, the offender would be hurt by a decision of the council, whether by way of a home, land, or business eviction. Or even criminal charges. Having grown up on the side of manipulators, Aaron knew how backwards and corrupt they really were. Council members cared very little for the fate of the cities they were meant to represent. Since they rose to their positions by majority vote, they stayed in office by way of blackmail and buying those votes. The people who were expected to do everything they could to improve others' lives instead turned around and abused their power simply because they had it and didn't want to lose it.

Aaron's father had been a fisherman who made his fortune in Quiver Lake. During his life he made many connections and lucrative trade agreements with merchants and dealers all over the city, not all of which were entirely legal. Then he used those connections to buy votes and blackmail his less-than-respectable partners into buying him yet more votes. When all was said and done and he was the newly elected councilman, he backed out of the deals he had made. Anyone who came forward to say as much was quickly sent to prison for one reason or another.

Aaron thought back to the letter and the wording his father had used. His position had been questioned. This meant that he might not be on the council much longer due to Aaron joining the Dragon Guard and the murders that had been happening. His father was now linked to the Order, which in turn would give his political enemies an excuse to accuse him of orchestrating the attacks and send him to prison. This would open a seat on the council. They would then be free to elect a new member for the seat that would benefit them more than Aaron's father currently did.

As much as he disliked his father and the things he did, Aaron didn't want to see him in jail, at the very least for the sake of his family. Asking Aaron to use his judgment to "come to the right conclusion" was simply a way of saying that the only right choice was what his father had said, and that he should see it as such. With a deep sigh. Aaron reached the door to the commander's office, knocked several times, and waited. He only hoped they weren't in some sort of meeting.

Commander Hall opened the door and smiled. "Mr. Cross," he said. "Is something the matter?"

Aaron was slow to answer. "Uh, I'm not sure yet."

"I'll do what I can to help," Hall said. He motioned for Aaron to enter.

Aaron stepped though and handed Hall the letter. "I don't know how much of this is true," he said, "but I thought you should see it either way."

Frowning deeply, the commander took the parchment and quickly read through it. When he finished, he had a look of concern mixed with anger. "Thank you, Mr. Cross, for bringing this to my attention. I am sorry to say that this is not a new problem. But the news of the Royal Army is a rather...alarming development."

"It's not true, is it? The baker and the others?"

"Mr. Cross, I can assure you that these claimed deaths are not our work," Hall said. He stroked his chin while reading the letter again before glancing back up at Aaron. "Again, I thank you for bringing this to my attention. The captains and I will see what we can do about these claims. Rest assured that the chance of an invasion by the Royal Army is rather slim."

Aaron moved to the door but paused before leaving. "For what it's worth," he said, "I don't believe you would order these types of things without reason, whatever it might be."

Hall smiled slightly. "It is worth quite a lot, actually. Now if you'll excuse me, this has given me a lot of work to do."

Aaron was ushered out the door and back down the stairs. He walked the same path as before back to his barracks room. By the time he returned, the sun had set and everyone was asleep, trying to recover from another long, grueling day. He sat on the edge of his cot and mulled over everything. He doubted his father would have bothered sending this letter had it not been for Aaron's use of his signet ring to authorize a payment to Captain Andrews at Navia. He knew his father would receive it and see it as Aaron not being totally serious about striking out on his own. He would see it as Aaron still needing his father's support. The man truly infuriated him sometimes. With a deep sigh, he swung his legs onto the cot and laid his head down to try to get some sleep. Instead, however, he lay in the dark for the next several hours, tossing and turning. Finally he was on the edge of sleep when moonlight suddenly filled the room, brighter than before. He shifted in the cot and saw that Robert had opened the door and was stepping through the threshold. He was heading outside fully geared. *Odd,* Aaron thought. If Alan or any of the other scholars had risen to leave with him, Aaron would have written it off as an early morning training session. But no one else stirred. Curious, he planted his feet on the cold stone floor before striding toward the door.

He would have opened it had it not been for the furious whispering on the other side that he could only just hear. He glanced through the window next to the door and could barely see the back of Robert to one side as he spoke with someone. Aaron knelt and pressed his ear to the door.

"Why not? We have enough!" Robert said.

He could easily tell that the next voice was Robin's: "But not what we came here for!"

"How do we know they'll even tell us? Even if we stayed and finished the training, it might not be open information."

Robin was starting to sound angry. "We were sent to find out where those mutts are," she said, "and I'm not leaving until we do!"

"But now we know that Argera is still *alive,* and I have the recipe for flash powder, both of which are far more valuable."

"If we don't come back with what we were told to find, she'll kill us."

"Well," Robert said, "maybe we could stay longer if you hadn't tried to kill four people in a *sparring* match. They're suspicious of us now. They know something is off about you and us by association." Robin didn't respond. "Look," Robert said, "if I leave, which I am, you two have to come. They're going to be checking on the ranger in Silvum now. They'll know we forged her report during our recruitment."

"Fine. But it's on your head when we get back."

They stopped speaking. Aaron waited for several seconds before standing and looking out the window. All he saw through the foggy glass were tracks in the snow heading for the front of the keep. Now, with his concern and curiosity piqued, he went back to his wardrobe and quickly put on his boots before making for the door and the cold court-yard beyond.

He shuffled through the moonlit snow, following three sets of tracks. Several things ran through his mind, none of which made sense at the moment. He reached the corner of the keep, stopped just short of it, and peeked around to see Robert, Robin, and Lace at the gate. They stood before two Dragon Guards, both wardens who were clearly unhappy to be seeing the three of them outside the barracks in the middle of the night. Robert and Robin were speaking to them while Lace stood off to one side. They seemed to be exchanging heated words, though at this distance Aaron couldn't make them out. Robin threw up her hands and backed away from the guards. A moment later, Robert did the same.

Then something happened that Aaron wasn't sure he'd ever be able to explain. The snow around Lace started to move away from her. The best way he could ever describe it was that it flowed outward from her like water. She crossed her arms as if warding off the cold air and started to shake violently. The snow moved farther and faster away from her until there was a perfect circle around her, clear of snow. The Dragon Guards drew their swords. It looked as if they were about to shout an alarm, but they were too late. They were lifted by an unseen force and slammed against the iron-banded gate with enough speed that Aaron couldn't follow their movement.

Nothing had touched them. When they struck the gate, they made no sound, though the gate shuddered aggressively from the impact.

Aaron still saw nothing touching them, but whatever the force was, it held them firm against the gate where they were pinned, lifeless. The Dragon Guards had released their weapons, but they never fell to the ground. They simply hovered next to their hands. Lace began to cry into her hands as the two Dragon Guards slowly sunk towards the ground, leaving a trail of blood along the gate. When they were only a foot off the ground they were dropped into the snow with barely a sound.

It took several seconds for the guards on the other side of the gate to open the manway to investigate the disturbance. When they came through, something pushed them to the ground with such force that even from where he hid, Aaron could see them twist unnaturally and slam into the stones beneath the snow, where they remained, unmoving. Robin grabbed Lace by the wrist and dragged her over the corpses and through the manway, followed closely by Robert.

"I need you to explain it again, exactly as you saw it happen."

Captain Samantha Coe stood in front of Aaron with a look of furious concern on her face. Aaron sat on the steps outside the keep with Captain Coe and Commander Hall in front of him. Around them, a dozen or so scholars were looking over the area where Lace had done...whatever it was she did. A few rangers with wardens stood guard outside the gate to ensure that no one disturbed the area. After Robert and the others left the keep, Aaron had been unable to move for several minutes out of pure fear. He had no idea what had happened but he *knew* it was far from natural. After Aaron had mustered his courage, the first thing he did was go into the keep and alert the first Dragon Guard he could find.

Now, with the sun barely cresting the horizon, the keep was on full alert. Aaron had explained everything in as much detail as he could twice over. Now he was finishing his story for the third time.

Coe turned to Hall and rubbed her temples. "How did we let this slip?" she said. "How did we let Disciples into our fold?"

Hall shook his head and stroked his beard. "This was years in the making. Ezekiel cross-referenced everything North sent him from the interview and nothing in Silvum indicated this. Everything he found pointed to a normal family, normal life, and a normal relationship with the townsfolk. Every answer they gave during their interview lined up with what Ezekiel knew."

"We'll have to send a group to Silvum. We have crosscheck with Claudia, Austin, with everyone," Coe said. "We have to know everything that they learned while they were here, *everything.*"

Hall was about to reply when he glanced sidelong at Aaron, who still sat quietly listening. "We'll finish discussing this later," he said. He faced Aaron. "Mr. Cross," he said, "I think training will be postponed for the time being. Please inform the others as they wake."

With that, Aaron was ushered away from the scene. He made his way back to the barracks. Rather than step inside, he paused at the door. He suddenly felt dizzy. He realized he hadn't slept in over twenty-four hours. He considered letting the others find out what had happened on their own so he could get some sleep, but just as he was about to step inside, the door opened in front of him. It was Alan.

"Oh, Aaron," he said. "Are you okay?"

Aaron shook his head. Less than an hour later, they all sat in the dining hall of the keep awaiting their morning meal as Aaron recounted what he'd seen and heard the night before.

Zachery raised an eyebrow once Aaron finished the tale. "So..." he said, "how'd she do it?"

Aaron stared blankly at the table. "Nothing touched them...it's just not possible."

"It sounds like magic to me." Zachery said.

"Oh, please," Griffon scoffed.

"What?" Zachery said. "Like it sounds so crazy? There's a lot in this world we thought wasn't possible before we came here."

"Magic isn't real." Griffon said. She turned to Clara. "Is it?"

Clara shrugged. "I mean...maybe?"

"You can't be serious."

"Well, think about it," Clara said. "Disciples worship a High Dragon and Claudia did say they were able to do amazing things. Who says what they could do wasn't magic and that it isn't something Cadent taught them?"

Daniel shook his head. "Whether or not what they did was magic," he said, "I still can't believe there were three Disciples right here in the keep."

Clara shivered. "I sat next to Robert during Claudia's lectures."

"He said something about flash powder," Aaron said. "Do you know what that is?"

"It's a really dark-red powder scholars put in the ingera," Clara said. "It's what makes them explode. Claudia said it's a Dragon Guard secret, and she just taught us how to make it."

"Well, I've seen what those things can do," Aaron said. "No wonder they thought it was so valuable."

Daniel ran a hand through his hair. "What about that mutt comment? What was that supposed to refer to?"

Zachery shrugged exaggeratedly. "Whatever it was," he said, "it is well above us, so for the time being I just want to focus on getting some food."

CHAPTER TWENTY-FIVE

13ᵗʰ of Landring, 28ᵗʰ year of the Fourth Age.

IN THE LATE night darkness, Daniel dashed past trees, leaped over logs, and barreled through the underbrush of Highwood Forest. He glanced behind him and noticed the others were falling behind, so he slowed his pace enough that he was still slightly ahead of them but well within their sight. To his right he saw a flash of flame, followed by a shadow darting overhead, accompanied by the beating of wings. He slid to a stop beneath an overhang in the side of a hill just ahead of him. Aaron and Clara quickly followed suit.

Aaron adjusted the armor on his forearm. "Are you sure this is the right way?"

Daniel lowered his hood and scanned the sky above them through the trees. "I'm sure," he said.

Clara looked around. "I still don't know how you can tell where you're going when it's so dark," she said.

"Intuition, I guess," Daniel said.

"So how are we supposed to get to it without being seen?" Clara asked.

"It's in the clearing," Daniel said, "so we're not."

"You didn't mention that part."

Aaron rubbed the stubble on his chin. "We'll figure it out," he said. "For now, let's get to the edge of the tree line and see what we've got to work with."

The three of them left the overhang and started through the trees again. Now that they were further into the forest, it was far more difficult to navigate in the dark, even for Daniel. More than once, Clara and Aaron fell so far behind that Daniel lost sight of them and had to double back. When they finally reached the tree line, they saw Argera circling the fort in the middle of the clearing. At the top of a flag post at the center of the fort hung a bell.

"So how are we going to do this?" Aaron asked. He spoke in an almost inaudible whisper.

Daniel watched the dragon crane her head toward the edges of the clearing as she flew. She kept her eyes on the trees, waiting for someone to make a move.

Daniel played with the frayed edges of his scarf as he spoke. "Let's wait here," he said, "and see if another group makes a go at it. If nothing happens, we'll think of something else."

So wait they did. This was as much a test of patience as it was a race. The goal was to be the first to ring the bell atop the fort, and they had until sunrise to do it. Each team was comprised of three members, one from each sect. Due to the fact that there was an offset of rangers and scholars to wardens, graduates from previous years filled in the missing members. They only acted as fillers and let the actual trainees come up with the plans and give the orders. Argera was tasked with knocking the teams out to prevent them from reaching the bell.

Daniel reached up and made sure the smoke pouch was still tied to his shoulder. This pouch was meant to produce a thick, black cloud of smoke when Argera tagged them with a stream of fire—a controlled stream, of course. Dragons were able to regulate the temperature and width of the fire they breathed, so she wouldn't use her full force. The smoke would indicate they were out of the race. What little force she did use was not enough to penetrate their armor and clothing, which like all Dragon Guard attire had been made with scorch weed fiber and extract, giving them a flame-resistant quality. If they were exposed to a full stream of fire from a hostile dragon, however, it would do little to save them. While they would be mostly protected from the fire itself where they were covered, at least for a period of time, the heat alone would be more than enough to kill them.

After over an hour and a half of stillness, Argera started making wider circles to try to find them. Most teams were likely hiding farther back from the tree line. Daniel knew most had to be well hidden and that the waiting would go well into daylight, which would in turn end the exercise until they tried again tomorrow night, as had been the pattern for the last several days with no winners.

Someone would have to start the final leg. "This isn't working, it's just a repeat of the last few days," Daniel said. "We're going to have to make the first move if we want to finish this before sunrise."

"What move is that?" Aaron asked.

Daniel scanned the trees and picked out a good spot to make a run for it—two touching trees, one bent from weight and the other uprooted. "See those crossed trees?" he said. "I can make a run for the fort from there while you two feign an attempt from here, which should also prompt some of the other teams to head out. Hopefully Argera will be too distracted with everyone else giving me more time to make it up there."

"Better than sitting here all night," Aaron said. "How long do you need?"

"Give me two hundred dragons, then break cover."

Without waiting for conformation, Daniel started into the trees, all the while counting in his head: *One dragon, two dragons, three dragons...* He went around the clearing to the other side and crouched behind one of the crossed trees. *One hundred sixty nine dragons, one hundred seventy dragons...* He watched the area where Clara and Aaron waited and kept counting. When he reached a hundred ninety-two, he saw them jump the fallen tree in front of them and make a run for the fort. He gave Argera ample enough time to notice and dive toward them before he raised his hood and darted from cover.

It took only moments for other teams to use the opportunity to start their own sprint. He had hoped as much and was thankful it was working. He saw to his right another ranger make a run for the bell from the same side of the clearing as he was. It was Jane. She was as fast if not faster than Daniel, which meant that it was nothing more than a race now. Argera started launching thin lines of fire at the others but it took her only moments to notice the two of them and see they were far closer than anyone else.

She leaned into a sharp turn and dove after them over the open grass. With her wings spread to their full length, she was on them quickly. She shot a stream of fire at Daniel as she passed overhead, but it was narrow and easy to dodge with a quick leap to his right. But it had cost him speed. Jane pulled ahead. He pushed himself harder and tried to catch up with her, but Argera had turned around to make another run, which meant she would aim for Daniel first since he was closest. He heard and felt the beat of her wings before he saw the shadow or the light of the fire.

Without being able to see her, he had no way of knowing which way to move to avoid the fire stream, or if he needed to move at all. So he did the only thing he could and dove to the ground the moment he saw light. The fire went clean over and scorched the grass in front of him as she continued past him. He stood and started for the fort again. He saw Jane had done the same as Daniel during Argera's second pass, but she was already up and running again. There was no way he would make it before her.

But he wouldn't have too. The only rule stated at the start of the night was they were to be the first team to ring the bell by any means they could employ. Griffon charged at Jane just as she was about to reach the doorway and shoulder checked her, knocking her into the wall with enough force to make her slump to the ground groggily. Now that Griffon had stopped Jane, he was able to close the gap between them. If he could manage to get around Griffon and get to the ladder before her, his team could still win. The problem with that, however, was that Griffon was now waiting for him. While he was faster than her, she was the better fighter by leagues. He would be forced into one unless he was lucky. He was nearly on her and was preparing to try to dash around her when he saw something that unsettled him. She smiled. Then he knew why. A flash of fire to his right came so quickly that he had no time to dodge.

Argera had waited until she was within feet of Daniel. Even as he dove to the ground, with a single puff, she sent flames splashing over his shoulder with just enough fire to cause the pouch to react and spew black smoke into the air. When he rose and looked back at the fort doorway, Griffon was already gone. Moments later, he heard the bell ring out across the field. With a sigh, he fell backwards to lie in the grass. He looked up at the dimming stars while he waited for the rest of the trainees to make their way over.

Argera landed with a heavy shake and a whirlwind next to the fort. "Well, wasn't that fun!" the dragon said. "Excellent work, Ms. Hart!"

Jane groaned and stood, bracing herself against the wall. "You got lucky, Hart."

"You're right," Griffon said. "I was worried I was going to have to hit Daniel. But then I saw you." Griffon crossed her arms and smirked.

Jane quickly stepped up to look Griffon in the eye. They were close to the same height, though Griffon was wider in her warden armor. They glared at each other for a moment before Jane huffed and turned away in irritation as the rest of the teams assembled around Argera. The dragon lay on her belly and crossed her forelegs in front of her as the Dragon Guards that had been filling in for missing members bid farewell before starting back to Vigil to attend to their duties.

Argera raised her head to get a good look at them all. "It seems many of you have forgotten that dragons can see in the dark," she said. "You did not pick your cover appropriately when moving through the forest. That aside, you have all shown drastic improvement. Should you ever have to run from a hostile dragon, you will probably survive." She rose to her feet and spread out her wings. "Now, your instructors expect all of you in the library at noon. Return here tomorrow at sunset for our next exercise."

With that, she knocked several trainees off their feet with a heavy gust of wind as she leaped off the ground with a single flap of her wings and spiraled upward until she was above the dark clouds and out of sight. Daniel had never been able to see the direction she went but he assumed it was somewhere remote. With chatter rising up throughout the group, they all started back toward Vigil. As they walked, Daniel fingered the pommel of his sword. It was still odd, feeling the orange-etched steel at his side. Ever since Lace and the others had "left," things at Vigil had been much tenser. All trainees were now required to always carry a weapon and while Dragon Guard steel was lighter than normal, it was still heavy enough to be noticeable.

Griffon nudged Daniel gently. "I really am glad I didn't have to take you out," she said.

"I am too," he said with a smile. "It looked like it hurt."

"I may have gone a little overboard."

Zachery removed the burned smoke pack from his shoulder and tossed it to the ground. "A little?" he said. "I saw it from the tree line after Argera tagged me and even I felt it."

Daniel was playing with the frayed edges of his scarf when Aaron tapped him on the shoulder. "You're doing it again," Aaron said. "What's wrong?"

Daniel looked down at his fingers holding the black cloth and let go before he started talking. "I'm fine. Just thinking about an exercise Austin gave us, trying to figure it out before tonight."

"You guys seem to get a lot of puzzle-type exercises."

"He says it makes us better strategists. It teaches us to look at things from other angles, find patterns, and how to exploit them when we do."

Alan leaned toward him. "Any way we can help?"

Daniel knew that Alan loved puzzles. As much as he would appreciate the help, he shook his head and smiled. "Pretty sure that would qualify as cheating."

Aaron nodded slowly and took off his gloves. "So how's your sword-play now?' he asked. "We haven't had a chance to spar for a while."

"About the same, actually," Daniel said. "Maybe a little better one on one, but I'm still nowhere near your level."

"Doesn't Austin have you guys do any kind of combat training?" Clara asked. "Even scholars still do some with Claudia."

Daniel bit his lip as he thought over his answer. Austin did have them go through combat practices, but none of it was the straightforward tactics Obadiah or Claudia would teach. He still didn't enjoy the darker side to his training. Learning where you could cut someone to make them bleed out in less than a minute. Discovering how to break someone's arm or leg with minimal effort. Learning the weak points in the armor worn by city guards across Edaren and how to spot and exploit a patrol schedule. Knowing how to make people look as if they died naturally. He hated every bit of it.

Daniel realized he hadn't answered the question yet. "Not the kind of training you would think," he finally said.

They made good time through the forest. When they approached the northern gates of Vigil, the sun had barely crested the horizon. The guards at the manway nodded to them politely and let them pass without question. They walked the stone path through the killing field and through the second gate, where the rest of the group quickly split in every direction while Daniel and his friends paused. They had just under an hour before they were meant to be at the library.

"Well, what should we do now?" Alan said with a yawn.

Zachery stretched his arms above his head. "I don't know about you guys," he said, "but Jonathan should be making breakfast soon and I don't like missing one of his meals."

Griffon shrugged. "I could eat."

They all agreed that getting some food after their long night would be the best idea and started up the street toward the keep. The city was still quiet in the early morning, with only a few people walking the streets, while merchants and shopkeepers began opening their doors. It was a calm and cheerful atmosphere, with the newly risen sun casting a golden hue over the city and its walls. Daniel liked the city during the morning and night, but it was far too crowded for him at any other time. Too many people in too tight of a space.

He felt especially claustrophobic during midday, when the majority of people were walking the city. It was even worse during the Autumn's End Festival. He preferred the woods where it was quiet. That was where he felt at home the most. It made him feel like he was back at Sapella with the Arrow just through the trees, waiting for him to dip his feet in the cool water during the summer. He sighed and glanced around. He watched a woman and what he could only assume was her daughter walking down an alleyway. The daughter had vibrant pink flowers stuck in her hair and a small, cloth doll she held by the arm.

He glanced to the other side of the street and watched a man stumble out of the local bar, clearly still drunk from the night before. The man shielded his eyes from the rising sun with a look of confusion on his face. The man stumbled up the street and before falling to his knees and getting up again. Daniel shook his head and shifted his gaze back to the other side of street. He stopped walking and stared at the alleyway. Sitting on the ground was the doll that had been held by the girl. He looked up and down the length of the street. When he didn't see the girl or the woman, he started toward the doll.

"Daniel? What's wrong?" Alan said, stopping while the others continued on.

Daniel knelt and picked up the doll. Again he looked around, thinking he might have missed them, but when he still didn't see anyone his mind started going through possibilities. The closest intersecting street was too far away for them to have made it and gone out of sight in the short time he'd looked away. Even if they had, there would be no reason for the young girl to leave the doll behind. He studied the alley. It was barely wide enough for three people to walk side by side. It didn't go straight through to another street and the turn ahead was still too far off for them to have gone around it at the pace they had been walking. He felt foolish, but at the same time he had a sinking feeling in his gut.

Alan appeared next to him. "What's that?" he said.

Daniel handed the doll to him. "Alan," he said, "can you wait here for a minute?"

Alan looked awkwardly at the doll. "Why? What's wrong?"

"I'm not sure yet. Just wait here for me."

Daniel stepped into the alley while Alan leaned against the wall, watching him curiously. He really wasn't sure what was wrong, but something felt off. He instinctively pulled his hood up as he rounded the corner. The alley turned a second time and then a third until it opened up into a slightly wider space with two more branch-offs. Daniel would have thought the space was perfectly normal if not for the single man standing at the far end next to a wooden door. He was dressed plainly in a simple tunic and trousers and was flipping a coin, which he dropped several times.

Daniel had gone through enough training to know a guard when he saw one. The man looked to be unarmed, but Daniel knew better than to assume he had no weapons on him or within easy access. He would have once again assumed nothing was wrong here, that maybe the man was guarding a gambling den, which was frowned upon to be sure but not illegal—except for the small, pink flower half buried in the dirt of the alley halfway between Daniel, and the door.

Austin had taught them that following your instincts in situations like this was always the right way to go. Even if your suspicions turned out to be false, it was always better to be wrong about something than to ignore the possibility of something terrible happening that could be stopped. At the moment, Daniel's instincts told him he had to find a way through that door. He doubled back and found Alan still waiting for him at the entrance.

"Alan," he said, "I need you to do something for me."

The younger trainee raised a single eyebrow. "What is it?"

Daniel motioned for him to follow as he started down the street and turned onto a connecting road. He knew the area well enough to know there was a small store here that sold cheap clothing. He purchased a tunic that would fit Alan, as well as a small pack, before continuing down the street. They found the entrance to another alley. After making his way down and back to ensure it led to the same area as the previous alley, Daniel handed Alan the tunic and pack.

"There's a man just through this alley," Daniel said. "I need you to take off your armor and put this shirt on over your black."

Alan raised an eyebrow. "Why do I need to do that?"

"I need you to get his attention and find a way to make him follow you. If he sees you in armor or in solid black, he'll know you're a Dragon Guard trainee and won't follow you."

"Why wouldn't he follow me?"

"He wouldn't. Just trust me, I can tell."

Alan shrugged. He removed his leather armor, stuffing it into the pack, before pulling the tunic over his own. "So how do I get him to follow me?"

Daniel patted him on the shoulder, "You'll figure something out," he said. "Just give me a minute to get ready."

Alan nodded as Daniel darted off down the street and into the original alley. He reached the annex and crouched low in the shadows, just out of the man's line of sight. Alan took longer than Daniel would have liked, but after a few minutes he appeared, trailed by two other boys slightly younger than he was.

Daniel hadn't expected this. He wondered how Alan had managed to enlist their help. A smile crossed his face as he watched the three of them dart into the alley, holding sticks like swords. They were in the middle of a mock fight with one another. It was a decent cover. Not one Daniel would have thought of, but it fit their age well enough.

The guard at the door started shouting at them: "Hey! Go somewhere else. You aren't supposed to be back here!"

They paid no attention to him. Alan ran from one of the boys, then reeled back with his stick back as if he was about to swing at the boy. At the last moment, he pivoted and struck the man hard in the shoulder. The man quickly attempted to grab Alan by the tunic, but he missed and stumbled before one of the other boys hit him across the back, while the other jabbed him in the ribs. The man went to his knees. His face flushed with anger as he rose and started to chase after them.

They led him out of the alley, Alan turning and taking occasional swings at the man as they ran. Daniel tried his best to keep from laughing. He would have to be sure to thank Alan, but for now he had to hurry before the man lost interest in them and returned. He ran to the door and tried the handle. Thankfully, it was unlocked. He stepped inside, then quietly closed the door behind him. He found himself in a long, empty hallway that dead ended with only two doors on the left wall. He kept low and took slow, soft steps toward the first door. Daniel placed his ear against the wood and listened carefully. Hearing no sounds, he carefully tried the handle and found this too was unlocked.

Daniel gently pushed it open and was disappointed to see a storage room with boxes and barrels stacked along the walls. A quick inspection determined there was nothing out of the ordinary. He moved on to the second door and found it was the same as the first. He frowned and looked around the hall. There were no other doors in sight. After a moment, an idea popped into his head. It was a longshot, but he still had the feeling that something was wrong. He had to at least try.

Methodically, he started lightly rapping his fist against the wall opposite the doors. He made it halfway down the hallway when the sound suddenly changed from a solid thud to a hollow echo. He smiled and traced out the general shape of a doorway by the sound of his knocks. It was a false wall. He stepped back and leaned against the opposite wall. These types of doors were commonly released by a single lever or button that, when pushed, would move a series of iron rods and gears to release the lock, allowing it to swing or slide open.

The problem was finding the trigger. He felt around the area of the door, looking for a section of wood that seemed loose or out of place. With no luck near the door, he decided to try further down. He walked toward the dead end, running his hand over the rest of the wall as he went. Again he had no luck. With an irritated sigh, he stepped back to the false wall to start over. But he paused when his second step caused a board beneath his foot to creak lightly. He took his full weight off of it, then tapped his foot a few times as an idea formed.

Daniel knelt down and started pulling at the floorboards. He tried nearly every one until finally, when feeling along the gaps of one near the first storage door, he felt a small gap just large enough for his fingers. He slipped them in and felt resistance when he lifted. He continued to lift until he heard a light, metallic click beneath him, followed by a series of louder clicks accompanied by grinding in the wall. He smiled to himself as he stood. Austin had told him many times before that investigations like this were one part skill and three parts luck. He counted this as the first part of luck.

CHAPTER TWENTY-SIX

13th of Landring, 28th year of the Fourth Age.

DANIEL PUSHED THE panel open and carefully peered inside. In front of him was a long, spiral staircase that was poorly lit and smelled like rot. He put a hand on his sword before he started to climb down, carefully placing his feet to ensure he made little to no noise. He counted every step to try to judge how far down he was actually going, but he lost count when he heard voices below him. He froze. Were they coming closer or moving away? After a few seconds, the voices faded. He decided it was safe to proceed. When Daniel reached the bottom, he found himself in a long, stone tunnel lit with lanterns. Several side passages along its length were either closed off with a gate or simply caved in.

He carefully made his way forward and stopped just before the first open side passage. He pressed himself against the wall and peered low around the corner. It opened up into a room that had at least a dozen beds lining the walls and nothing else in sight. The other three rooms he checked were identical. Curious. Perhaps it was a smuggling den? Though this number of beds in such a place seemed unnecessary. With the puzzle no closer to being solved, he moved further into the tunnel. There were no more side rooms or passages. After a few minutes, the tunnel opened out onto a balcony. Daniel made his way to the edge, taking cover behind a pillar. What he saw was equally confusing and terrifying.

The balcony overlooked an open room that to him, resembled a church hall. It was lit with braziers in the corners and a chandelier hanging in the center. A white, stone altar sat near the far wall. The woman that had been walking with her child was atop it. She seemed to be unconscious and was tied to the corners of the altar by her wrists and ankles. Her forehead was marked with a rune carved into her skin. At least two dozen figures dressed in white robes with hoods pulled over their heads faced the altar, their hands clasped in front of them. Behind the altar stood another figure dressed in a similar robe. An oversized Black Hand print surrounded by strange symbols stretched across the figure's heart.

This couldn't be real. There was no way he'd stumbled onto a gathering of Disciples. Right under the Dragon Guard's nose. But there it was. It couldn't be any clearer. The woman was obviously in great danger, but as much as he wanted to get her out of there, he knew there was no way to do it with so many cultists in the room. That alone might have been one of the most shocking things to him, the sheer number of them. He knew there were Disciples in Edaren, that there were hundreds, if not more, of them across the nation. But he never thought he would see this many in one place, especially in Vigil.

The man behind the altar started to speak in a language Daniel didn't understand. He strained his ears and caught a few words he recognized, such as Cadent, Verhova, and several other old-tongue words he'd heard before from Claudia but didn't know the meaning of. The figure then withdrew a jagged, wicked-looking sword from beneath his robe and raised it above his head. He spoke a few more words before pointing the tip at the woman's stomach. The figure paused for what seemed like a lifetime before he released the blade.

But it didn't fall. It seemed to hover motionless above her as the man lifted his arms and spoke several more words in a rising tone and pace. Suddenly the man stopped, allowing both silence and the sword to hang in the air. Daniel watched with a sick fascination. It was magic. The man let the silence persist for a moment longer before with a swift motion he dropped his arms. The blade followed suit with unholy speed and buried itself into the woman's chest. Daniel turned away and had to take a moment to compose himself before he was able to turn back. The man had removed the blade and was letting the blood drip off the tip and onto her forehead.

Beneath him, Daniel heard a door open. The crowd parted as two more hooded figures approached the altar, each holding a long, iron rod attached to a collar worn by a large, grey wolf. The animal had clearly been beaten and abused to the point of being mindlessly rabid. It snapped and snarled at everything around it and foamed at the mouth as they led it to the altar. It was quite strong, as the two cultists struggled to keep a grip on the bars that held it in check. What purpose did the wolf serve? Only when it was closer to the light did Daniel see that painted along the animal's sides were more runes and symbols similar to the one on the woman's forehead.

Several more Disciples stepped up and gripped the iron bars along with the other the two. Now with two people on each of the rods they were able to reach the altar and lift the wolf by the neck so that it hung there, kicking, growling, and howling, from the iron collar. Then they slowly lifted it over the woman. The apparent leader lifted his sword again. Daniel turned away before he saw the end result and glanced from one side of the balcony to the other. There were two paths out of the room, the way he had come and another open doorway to his right. He made his way to the doorway, keeping low and away from the light and edge of the balcony.

He went through. Once he was away from the ritual room, he stood and quickened his pace. He had only gone a few steps before he heard the woman scream along with the wolf. The two sounds didn't seem right. They didn't seem *separate*. The screams continued for several moments. Underneath the sound he barely heard the man chanting again. He had to find the little girl. That was what he had to focus on right now. He had to ignore what was happening to her mother behind him. He couldn't do anything for her. But he had no idea how he was going to find the daughter or if something had already happened to her. He was suddenly overcome with a feeling of uselessness. What if she had been the first one to be used in a ritual or something worse? He would be down here for nothing, and at the moment he didn't even have an escape plan.

Daniel pushed that thought out of his mind and focused on the task before him. *One thing at a time.* He thought as he moved deeper into the poorly lit tunnel. Every door he tried was locked. When he put his ear to them, he heard no sound within. He would have picked the locks but he didn't have his tools. Even if he had, he didn't have the time to open every door. He was on the verge of giving up until he placed his ear to one door. The sound within was so quiet that he almost missed it. He had to hold his breath to ensure it wasn't just his imagination as he pressed harder against the wood. Someone was crying.

It had to be the girl. He tried the handle even though he knew it was locked. He needed a key and he had no idea where it would be or if he had time to find it. Daniel gritted his teeth. Even though his mind screamed at him not to, he turned and kept going down the passage. If he couldn't find the key, maybe he could find something else that would help him open the lock. He tried door after door. Some were unlocked, but when he did a quick search of the rooms behind them he came up empty. The whole time he heard high-pitched screams and wailing echoing behind him.

None of it sounded like the woman or the wolf. It sounded like something else. He knew he'd heard it before but his fear fogged his mind and he couldn't place it. Every scream sent chills down his spine. It made him sick to know what was happening behind him and that he couldn't stop it. He found another door unlocked and stepped inside. It appeared to be an apothecary shop, much like the one in the keep. There were tables against the wall and plants he recognized that grew only in the dark, like shadow bloom and tomb root. A quick scan failed to reveal any key or something he could pick the lock with.

But what Daniel did see intrigued him. On the table closest to the door was a small pile of dark red powder atop a cloth square. He grabbed a pinch with his fingers and smelled it. Flash powder. The trainees had been shown a sample after Robin and the rest had left to ensure if they ever saw any outside of Dragon Guard hands they would know it right away. To find it here meant the Disciples were making it. There was only a small amount here, but who knew how much they had made and where else they might be keeping it. As he looked at the substance, an idea started to form. It was a foolish idea, but it was the best he had at the moment, and he had no time to come up with a better one.

Daniel wrapped the powder in the square of cloth and ran back to the door where he'd heard the girl. He knelt and carefully poured powder into the lock until about half of it was gone. Then he tightly wrapped the rest in the cloth and jammed it in as well, leaving a corner sticking out. He went further down the tunnel again into one of the unlocked rooms he'd investigated earlier. Like several of the others, this one had been lined with beds. He cut a strip from one of the blankets with his sword, then lit the cloth in a nearby brazier and ran back to the rigged door before it burned away.

He spoke into wood: "Get away from the door!"

Daniel then took a deep breath and lit the small corner poking out of the lock. As soon as the cloth caught and held its flame, he sprinted away. He didn't know how long it would take for it to reach the flash powder or how fast the reaction would be, but he knew he wanted to be out of the way when it did. He only hoped the girl had heard and heeded his warning. The biggest problem with his plan was the noise. If the Disciples heard it—and there was no way they wouldn't—they would come in full force. Without knowing if the tunnel led to a way out, he could be trapped. He should have scouted the end of the tunnel first. Now it was too late.

Daniel dove into another room. Immediately after he was through the doorway, a bright flash lit the area and a loud explosion echoed off the empty tunnel walls. He rushed back and found that the door now sat ajar, its lock warped and the wood splintered and broken. He threw it open and found the girl with her hands tied behind her back and her face streaked with tears. Her green eyes were etched in fear as he approached her.

He knelt to cut her bonds. "It's okay," he said. "I'm going to get you out of here. Just stay close to me."

She nodded hesitantly and he helped her to her feet. They ran out the door and started sprinting down the tunnel as fast as they could. If there wasn't a way out at the end, they weren't going to escape. Behind him he heard shouting and the echo of dozens of footsteps coming toward them. They were moving too slowly, so he picked up the girl and carried her. Their pace improved, but they were still going to be caught if he didn't find a way out.

Ahead of Daniel, the tunnel split in two directions. Without time to consider, he chose the right side. He sprinted through the dim tunnel, passing countless closed passages. Behind him, he heard a long, drawn-out howl. It sounded familiar yet foreign. He was sure he had heard it before. He glanced behind him and saw Disciples were following close behind. When he turned back, he felt his gut twist. The tunnel opened into an annex of several branch-offs, all blocked by iron gates. He skidded to a stop in the open space and turned to try the nearest gate. It was locked, as was the next and the next.

They were trapped. They were in a dead end below the city with no way to make it back to the surface. He'd never felt this much pure fear in his life, not when he'd been face to face with a satlis, not even when he'd been threatened by the valgret with his brother at the Arrow. Daniel didn't know what to do. He wasn't skilled enough to fend off that many Disciples. He wasn't sure he could take even one. He had the girl to protect but no way to do so. The bars were too close together for her to slip through. Even if she could, it would only delay her fate. He wasn't even questioning what would happen now.

Daniel turned back to the tunnel and saw the Disciples lining along the entry with swords drawn, the lower half of their faces were hidden by a white mask while their eyes were shadowed by the drawn hoods. At the center of their line was the man that had been behind the altar.

"Shade take you, ranger. Always sticking your noses in places they don't belong." The man spoke with calmness that unnerved Daniel. He said nothing in response as he reached behind his back and with a trembling hand gripped his sword.

The man noticed the unease Daniel showed. "You're not a ranger…you're just a trainee." He started to laugh. "Of course a novice would find us through mere happenstance and sloppy work while the veterans remain none the wiser!" He turned to face the Disciples behind him. "Search the rest of the tunnels. Ensure he's the only one down here."

Several of them ran back the way they'd come as the man stepped forward. Then he stopped. He looked from Daniel to the girl, then back again before sheathing his sword.

"I think," the man said, "that this is a prime chance to give the new blood a chance to prove itself."

He stepped back and motioned for the Disciples to stand aside as he made his way through them. He disappeared behind them all and continued down the tunnel until he was out of sight. The new blood…did he mean a new cultist? No, he said to prove *itself*. That was an unusual word and Daniel didn't think it was unintentional. He watched every one of the robed men in front of him but none made a move to step forward. Behind them, he saw movement down the tunnel, coming closer. The man returned with something following him. It was hunched over, low to the ground, walking on all fours. It stumbled as it went. After each trip, the man yanked on an iron bar he held in his hand. They came into focus as they stepped into better light. Daniel didn't understand. How was that here? Why was it here?

The valgret was covered in grey fur that seemed to be falling off in patches as it walked. Its eyes looked confused, darting everywhere to take in its surroundings. Its sides were covered in runes and markings that matched the one etched into its skin on its forehead. Every step seemed unsure. It tripped over its own feet and fell to the ground with a whimper. The man kicked it in the side of the head. It didn't react to the blow the way Daniel expected it would. It didn't snarl or growl. Instead, it cowered, like a dog scolded by its master.

The man motioned to one of the other Disciples. The cultist stepped over and undid the collar around the neck of the valgret before taking the bar and backing out of the way. The valgret seemed unsure at its new freedom. It took a step forward before looking to the man as if asking permission to continue. The man made no motion to it and instead watched Daniel and the girl.

"You don't understand, do you?" He said it more as a fact than a question. He read Daniel's face before proceeding. "You saw us at the altar. You saw the woman, you saw the wolf. You saw the runes and you heard the *screams*."

Daniel felt himself getting weaker, his fear plaguing his body as he tried to say something, do something, anything. The man was right. He saw and heard it all. He knew they connected to the beast in front of him but he didn't understand how.

The man kicked the valgret toward Daniel. "Kill him."

The valgret looked at Daniel and then at the man before taking another step into the annex. Daniel managed to draw his sword out of pure adrenaline and terror as the animal, the monster, looked at him.

"Kill him!" the man shouted at the valgret.

The valgret leapt through the air at an awkward angle. Daniel instinctively grabbed the girl behind him and threw her out of the way as the valgret collided with him, sending them both to the ground. The valgret rolled over and past Daniel. It quickly regained its footing and started after Daniel again.

Daniel rolled to the side as it leapt to where he'd been a moment earlier. He scrambled to his feet and took a practiced stance as his encoded training took over. When the valgret lunged for him again, he ducked low and darted under its arm, dragging his sword along its side as he did so. The creature howled in pain. It skidded to a stop on the ground, gripped the sides of its head, and screamed. It began writhing and rocking back and forth. The Disciples made no move to intervene and simply watched. Daniel chose to strike while it was distracted and went to drive his sword into its back, but when he got closer it lashed out with an arm, making him backpedal. He wasn't sure what to do. It was unpredictable. If he tried to get close it would simply strike out again and it had no pattern, no method to it that he could exploit. It was purely irrational at the moment.

But then it stopped. Its hands fell to the floor and it seemed to stare at the ground absentmindedly. It then lifted its head and looked at Daniel. His eyes widened at what he saw. Its eyes were different. They weren't the eyes of a valgret. They were an emerald green. They were human. They matched the eyes of the little girl. Its mouth opened and a croak escaped. Tears started pouring from its eyes as its lower jaw quivered.

Then words came, stuttering and strained. "H-help m-me."

Suddenly it screamed again and slammed closed fists against its own head. It leaned forward and howled at the ground until it started bashing its forehead into the stones beneath it. Daniel was frozen. He had no idea how to respond to what he was seeing. But it stopped just as quickly as it began. The valgret stopped assaulting itself and sat in place without moving. The hulking monster then rose and stood on all fours again. It looked at Daniel again. Its eyes were still emerald green, still human. It took several slow and careful steps toward Daniel. He wanted to move. He didn't know what was about to happen. But he couldn't make himself move. His body wouldn't listen to him.

It came face to face with him and reached for his sword. He couldn't keep his grip on it as the valgret gripped it by the blade, then turned it around to hold it by the hilt. It took several unsteady steps back and turned its eyes towards the ceiling as it lifted the blade to its own throat, just below its jawbone. Then it ran the edge deep and long across it. It fell to the ground in a heap and sat unmoving. Thick, nearly black blood ran out of its neck and pooled on the ground around it. Daniel couldn't look away. He watched as the pool grew ever larger, wetting the fur that still fell from its body, reminding Daniel of the patches of fur he'd seen on the valgret at the river.

The Disciple leader stepped over to the corpse and kicked the blade away from it. "A shame, it showed promise."

Daniel still couldn't look away from the valgret's eyes as the blood finally started to slow.

The man strode over to Daniel. He was far taller. Somehow Daniel managed to peel his eyes away from the corpse and up to the man's eyes.

"You know nothing of the forces at work here and beyond, you are merely dust to be wiped away by the Left Hand," the Disciple said.

With that last word, Daniel felt something tighten in his chest. It was a pressing weight that made breathing difficult, nearly impossible. He hunched over. He felt light headed and his vision started to blur at the edges. He also felt cold, as if there was ice in his lungs. Every breath he managed to take was accompanied by the worst and most intense, stinging pain he'd ever felt. He fell to his knees while clutching his chest and managed to crane his neck upwards to see the man's face. His eyes were black. There was no reflection in them. They were completely devoid of color and humanity. Daniel felt his heart getting weaker as his vision went nearly black.

"Avus Dalton!" A voice shouted from the tunnel.

Suddenly, the feeling in Daniel's chest subsided and the blackness of the man's eyes retreated outward from his iris revealing them to be a light lime color. Daniel took deep, wonderful, warm breaths as his vision cleared.

The man looked to the voice in the crowd of watching Disciples. "What?"

One of them ran forward and knelt before him. His robes were spattered with blood and there was a large gash across his shoulder. "Lord Avus," the kneeling man said. "There are a number of Dragon Guards sweeping the tunnels. They are nearly upon us."

Dalton sighed and withdrew a ring of keys from beneath his robe. He strode over to one of the gates and calmly unlocked it. "We're leaving," he said. Every Disciple still in the room started for the door and disappeared on the other side. Dalton strode over to Daniel and knelt down to look him in the eye. "Enjoy your days in the light, novice," he said. "There won't be many left."

Dalton made his way to the gate. With one last look at Daniel and a glance at the little girl who sat in the corner, her knees up to her face, he stepped through and closed it behind him with a resounding *clang.*

CHAPTER TWENTY-SEVEN

30th of Sanya, 28th year of the Fourth Age.

"OH, BY VERHOVA, that's awful!" Clara said. She handed the mug back to Kenneth.

He laughed loudly and slammed the mug onto the bar, sending the contents into the air. "That it is! One mug of this would get a dragon drunk!"

Claudia smiled at Clara. "He drinks it less for the taste and more for the effect."

Daniel laughed as Clara continued to shake her head. "I don't think I would ever be able to get past the taste long enough for the effect," she said.

Daniel, Clara, Kenneth, and Claudia sat in a bar on the north side of Vigil. Through the foggy window by the door, Daniel saw snow falling outside. Tomorrow would be the first official day of winter, which meant tonight was the last day of their second year at Vigil, as well as the night of the Autumn's End Festival. It had been an eventful two years to say the least. Parts of it he simply wanted to forget ever happened. Thankfully, it had been relatively quiet since his harrowing experience below the city. The underground tunnels had been in use by the Dragon Guard in the earlier years of Vigil but had been abandoned long ago and had indeed been forgotten about entirely. But now they'd been re-charted, with guards patrolling through them at all hours.

That still did not ease the nightmares that plagued Daniel. After Dalton had left him in the tunnels with the girl, Captain Coe and Claudia had found him. He didn't actually remember them leading him and the girl out, but he did remember them treating his injuries and questioning him about what he'd seen. As much as he'd wished to forget it all, he was able to tell them everything in detail. Upon further questioning, he'd worked up the courage to ask them what it was, exactly, that he'd seen. To give reason to the horrors.

They told him that valgrets were not a natural animal, that they were made, and that they weren't the only things twisted into being by the Disciples. They also told him that Dalton was a high-ranking member of the Disciples, the personal bodyguard and voice of one of the Fingers. He was called a Nail. The idea that Daniel had encountered Dalton and lived was astonishing to him. For a time after, nearly every Dragon Guard he met asked him about the incident, most simply out of concern for him. Nevertheless, having to relive even a single moment of that day was enough to make him sick. He was thankful that at least his friends seemed to know to stay silent about it. Not once did any of them press him to tell the story. They could tell he wanted to forget it all. Slowly, the chatter about the incident faded until it was no longer a relevant topic in Vigil.

Those tunnels also seemed to be the way that Robert, Robin, and Lace had been able to leave without a trace. An entrance had been found just outside the north wall of the keep in a nearby home. The tunnel had only a few branch-offs, most of which had been caved in, but the main tunnel led to an old cave that was hidden from sight between a large rock outcropping on the beach.

Clara grabbed her mug of water and downed half of it. "I feel like it's burning the inside of my throat," she said.

Claudia laughed. "It probably is."

Kenneth took another swig of the ale. "Well," he said, "what better way to celebrate Autumn's End than a mug of Silvum shadow ale? It's my favorite tradition!"

Clara shook her head. "Why is it called shadow ale?"

"It has shadow bloom extract in it," Claudia answered.

Daniel looked at Kenneth with a concerned look. "Shadow bloom is poisonous."

"Incredibly so!" Kenneth took another draw and laughed.

Daniel smiled as the warden continued to down the questionable liquid. It had been a long time since any of them had time to relax together. Claudia had been busy teaching the scholars and Daniel had been so engrossed in his own training that he'd hardly had time to see any of his friends outside of brief moments in the barracks or halls of the keep.

"Daniel, where is everyone else?" Claudia asked as she sipped her own ale, a less-intense choice.

"Aaron is sparring with Griffon, I think."

Claudia sighed. "Those two don't think of anything else."

"Alan said he would meet us here," Daniel added, "since Zachery was helping Jonathan prepare the dining hall for tonight. So he should be here any time."

Kenneth sighed happily. "Ah, the Autumn's End feast, my favorite tradition."

Clara raised an eyebrow. "I thought drinking shadow ale was your favorite tradition," she said.

"I'm a complicated man."

The last day of autumn was always celebrated across Edaren. Some smaller towns like Sapella's Crossing held simple, town-wide feasts, while larger cities such as Forge and Dalisia hosted wonderful and grand festivals full of games and entertainment of all kinds. In Vigil, the four main streets were filled with entertainers, dozens of games, and countless stalls selling toys for children, as well as many people selling homemade wares. The Dragon Guard also held a feast in their dining hall every year for their members and the people that worked in the keep, such as the kitchen staff and a few noteworthy citizens.

Claudia turned in her chair to look at the door across the room. "You and Clara should go out and enjoy the festival," she said. "There's a fire tamer just down the street. They are just mesmerizing to watch."

Clara beamed at the idea. "Oh! Daniel, let's go. I always loved watching them in Navia!"

He looked at the door. "What about Alan? He's supposed to meet us here, remember?"

Kenneth waved him off. "Just go," he said. "When Alan shows up we'll send him your way."

Daniel shrugged and stood. "All right," he said. "I've never seen one before so this should be interesting."

Clara led Daniel onto the street and into the chaos that was the festival. Colorful banners and lanterns with colored glass hung from each light post along the streets. There were stalls everywhere with everything he could think of, from food to games to clothing. They walked toward the gate. Already, Daniel was starting to feel claustrophobic. There were too many people. They passed magicians and storytellers making children laugh and musicians filling the air with a medley of dozens of sounds, inspiring people to break into dance. It all blended into one cheerful and upbeat atmosphere.

Clara sighed as they passed a flute player. "I always wanted to learn how to play," she said.

"Why didn't you?" Daniel said while sidestepping a group of children who were running down the middle of the street.

"My mother tried to get me into lessons when I was younger, but at the time I didn't want to do anything she wanted me to," Clara said. "Now I kind of regret it."

"Right, the controlling thing."

"Yeah, that." They moved to the side of the street to avoid the larger crowd. "What about your mother? Have you heard from her or anyone else since you left?"

"Just after ranger training started, my mother and Connie both wrote me a letter."

She raised an eyebrow. "Connie? You've never told me about her."

Daniel felt his face flush slightly. "Uh, yeah, she's a friend of mine from home. I've known her since, well...forever."

"Oh. Well, lasting friendships are hard to come by, so that's good to hear." Clara sounded slightly disappointed.

Daniel furrowed his brow. "You okay?"

"Yeah, I'm fine." Clara pointed ahead and smiled widely. "Look! There's the fire tamer!"

She darted forward and started to push her way through a circle of people. Daniel saw over their heads the occasional whirl of fire. He picked up his pace and caught up with Clara at the front of the circle to watch the show. The fire tamer was a young woman. She had short, white-blonde hair that reflected the light of the fire. Her clothes were bright red and embossed with gold inlay, the design of fire working its way up her limbs. Each hand was gloved in gold cloth.

The woman held a long pole with a blazing fire at each end in each hand. She spun them in circles and tossed them in the air with effortless grace before catching them again and continuing to weave trails of light. Behind her, a young man sat beside a few open linen bags just below the small stage, barely visible to the crowd. The girl tossed both poles into the air. At the same moment, the young man reached inside one of the bags and tossed a handful of powder at the two poles. When the powder hit the flames, a bright flash of blue blinded everyone for a moment. When they looked back, the flames kept the ocean tint for several moments before fading slowly back to their true color.

The woman continued the show for several minutes. Four more times, the boy changed the color of the flames. When the show was finished, everyone clapped and cheered enthusiastically while the woman bowed, a smile crossing her sweat-soaked face.

Clara clapped by far the most. "Oh, I just love it!" she said. "The way they use the stardrop pollen to change the color of the fire is so beautiful!"

Daniel laughed. "It was beautiful," he said. "Never knew the pollen could do that."

They were about to leave when Alan came out of the crowd and nearly bumped into them. He crossed his arms and glared. "There you are!" he said. "I was worried I would have to walk around by myself. Why didn't you wait at the bar for me?"

Daniel smiled. "Sorry," he said. "Clara wanted to see the fire tamer."

"You wanted to see it too!" Clara said.

Daniel was about to reply when he was cut off by a loud and long tone from a war horn. All around them, performers stopped their acts. The music was cut short and every conversation ceased. The whole city held its breath. After a moment's pause, the tone sounded a second time. Daniel felt his heart drop. Not a sound was made. At first he wasn't sure what he should do. It seemed so out of place and he was hopeful that it was a mistake, that maybe what they thought was a horn was something else entirely. No one moved. No one dared even consider the worst as they all waited in petrified silence for nearly a minute. It was common knowledge what the signal meant. They all hoped it was a mistake.

Then across the city he saw a slight glow over the horizon, then another, followed by several more. Each steadily grew brighter until a fireball crested the wall and landed in the south side of the city with an echoing crash as it no doubt rolled and crashed through buildings and any other structure in its path, crushing countless people along the way.

A trebuchet or a catapult. He wasn't sure which had launched the fireball. It didn't matter. Moments after it struck the ground, a massive explosion echoed across the city, followed by a plume of fire and debris as a wave of force rolled out from the source. A second fireball hit the ground and it followed suit, shaking the ground and causing buildings to collapse in clouds of dust as it exploded. The crowd looked on in stunned silence for several moments, but that quickly changed. Like a wave spreading outward from the south of the city, screams filled the air.

Suddenly it didn't matter what Daniel thought he should do. The crowd decided for him. All around him, people started to run in the opposite direction of the chaos. In their rush, no one stopped to consider those around them. They shoved others out of the way and to the ground. Many had no chance to rise again as they were trampled under the panicked crowd. Daniel and the others were shoved aside and nearly thrown to the ground themselves, but Daniel managed to grip Clara and

Alan by the wrists and forced his way sideways through the crowd and into an alley to get them out of harm's way.

Alan's voice shook as he spoke: "What's going on?"

Daniel didn't answer as he racked his brain trying to decide how they were going to get to the keep. They didn't have their weapons or their armor. In times like this, they were supposed to head for the keep to prepare the defenses. For a moment he almost laughed to himself. He'd never imagined that arming to prepare to defend a city would be at the forefront of his mind, but here they were. The two long draws of the war horn was the warning of an attack. It sounded so out of place after the years of peace that no one knew how to react. There hadn't been a war in Edaren for hundreds of years.

Clara answered Alan with a reassuring tone, despite the tremor it held: "I don't know, but we'll get to the keep and we'll be just fine."

Explosions still echoed out from the south. Daniel saw an ever-growing glow as the city started to burn. The south. That meant this was an attack from the sea, which meant they were most likely being struck by ship-mounted trebuchets, which thankfully indicated they were relatively safe as long as they stayed on the northern side of the city. The range of the siege weapons would be limited due to the height of the cliff and wall. They had to get to the keep as quickly as possible. They had to get their gear. The problem was that every citizen was heading away from the flames, clogging the streets.

He turned and looked at the alley extending behind them. "We'll have to go through the alleys."

Alan looked at the way they had come. "Wouldn't the main street be faster?"

"Not with all those people."

Clara had her hand over her mouth as she looked at the steadily brightening glow of fire, her voice barely audible over the cries of the city: "This can't be happening."

Daniel placed a hand on her shoulder and started to lead them through the winding alleys toward the keep. All around them, he heard people screaming and the occasional explosion of fireballs that had been launched into the city. The alleys were empty of people, though it was still taking them far longer than Daniel would have liked under the circumstances. They rounded a corner and entered an annex that diverged into four different paths. He was about to run right through to the other side when a door leading to one of the buildings ahead burst open. He didn't know why he skidded to a stop and pulled the others into one of the alleys and out of sight. Maybe it was the fact it had opened so suddenly or it was just his reflexes. Maybe it was the sudden and terrible feeling he had the moment he saw it open and he hid out of pure fear. Something told him that if whoever was coming out of that door saw them, it would not end well. Clara was about to speak but he motioned for her to be quiet. The fear that crossed his face made her push herself harder against the wall in hopes of staying hidden. He leaned out just enough to get a look around the corner and saw that his fear was justified. Seven figures robed in white. Disciples of the Left Hand. He recognized the robes instantly. The plain design and the hand print and runes on their hearts were unmistakable.

While the Disciples stood in the alley, Daniel felt his pulse quicken. All sound around him was drowned out save for his own heart beating in his ears. The Disciples were waiting for something to come through the door. Time seemed to slow down as the first clawed hand crossed the threshold. Then the first figure was out, followed by a second, third, and fourth. Valgrets, five of them, hulking and covered in that familiar matted fur and sickly grey skin. Daniel moved back around the corner and got as close to the wall as he could. His heart was beating so loudly in his ears that he felt it was a miracle they weren't already discovered.

Alan, sandwiched between him and Clara, took a breath to speak. Even though Daniel knew it was only going to be a whisper, he covered Alan's mouth with his hand. Clara leaned forward slightly to see Daniel's expression. The color drained from her face when she saw how terrified he truly was. A voice from the alley caught his attention and he strained to listen.

It was a woman. Her tone was smooth. The sound sent chills down his spine.

"Are the Numen ready?"

"They're waiting in Highwood Forest," a girl answered. Her voice sounded familiar but Daniel couldn't place it. "When the signal is given they'll come."

"Good," the woman said. "Take your hounds and push the citizens toward the gates. Eliminate any Dragon Guard in your path. Your sister shall do the same from the east."

The girl sounded distant and sad, like she wasn't quite there. "Yes, mother."

Daniel heard the valgrets take off at a run, their claws scraping against the stone as they went until the noise faded to nothing.

When they were gone another person spoke, a man with a hoarse tone. Daniel recognized it immediately: The man from the tunnels, the one whose eyes went black. "Are you sure she can handle this, mistress?"

The woman laughed coldly. "I have no doubts that she can kill anything that tries to stop her."

"I don't doubt her abilities, mistress. It is her willingness to use them."

Her tone took a darker turn while still keeping its calmness. "You forget your place, Dalton."

"Of course. I apologize."

She was quiet for a moment, as if listening to the sounds of the city fall apart. "Come," she said. "Let us advise Gotef on his next course of action."

Daniel wanted to move but his limbs felt like they were made of iron. He heard the door close and waited for several minutes, too afraid to risk moving. Finally, he forced his body to obey him and rose. Clara and Alan followed his lead. When they were on their feet, they moved down the alley, away from the annex. When Daniel was sure they were far enough away that they wouldn't be heard if any Disciples were left behind, he nodded to Clara and Alan. The three of them started to run.

CHAPTER TWENTY-EIGHT

30th of Sanya, 28th year of the Fourth Age.

ARON MADE HIS way up the steps of the guard tower on the south side of the keep wall. He wore his warden armor and had an orange-etched kite shield strapped to his arm. Thankfully, nothing else had happened after the barrage of fire aimed at the city's south side started. He had been in the courtyard with Griffon when the first of the fireballs struck the city, but the Dragon Guards in the keep had responded the moment the second tone sounded from the horn. The organization had been fast and rather astounding to Aaron. Rangers had started combing the south of the city to bring whatever wounded they could to the keep for medical attention by the scholars, while the wardens gathered the city watch to begin preparing the outer walls for the inevitable attack.

He exited the door at the top of the tower and made his way to the captains and commander, who argued amongst themselves. Obadiah and Austin were off to the side, along with all fifteen trainees who had been inside the keep when the attack started. Aaron stood next to Griffon and Zachery and leaned toward Griffon.

"What's happened so far?" he asked.

She shrugged. "Nothing yet. They're just arguing."

Captain North pointed toward the north side of the city. "We have to get those people into the keep," he said.

Hawk scoffed. "If one of those flash powder charges landed inside our wall," he said, "you'd kill the lot of them."

Coe shook her head and nodded toward the south. "None will ever make it this far," she said. "They're barely clearing the wall as it is."

North glared at Hawk. "They're going to try to break in," he said. "Those explosions are driving everyone out of the south side as they try to get as far away from the danger as they can. That means they'll try to get to the gates, which also means they're going to bottleneck there. With the number of ships reported in the water and those already beached we're outnumbered to such extremes I almost want to laugh at the absurdity of it. Those civilians are being herded like cattle for slaughter and we do *not* have the numbers to protect them at the gates."

Commander Hall looked at Hawk sympathetically. "He's right, Hawk," Hall said. "They're herding them. We can't let them clog the gates or wander the city blindly when the true battle breaks out." The commander scratched his chin. "Captain Coe, take a third of whatever wardens we have available and head to the east gate. Send another third to the north and west as well. Try to send the civilians here. We'll start funneling them into the tunnels below the city. You have full command over the eastern defenses, get them setup for when they breach the outer wall, hopefully we can delay them long enough to finish bringing the civilians to the keep."

She nodded and crossed her arms over her chest. "Yes, commander." Coe motioned to the wardens with them on the wall and rushed past Aaron and the others.

Obadiah stepped up and saluted. "Commander," he said, "where shall we place our trainees?"

The commander looked at them all crowded behind Obadiah. They all had terrified and nervous expressions on their faces and they knew it.

"Are you sure they're ready for this?"

Obadiah nodded so slightly that Aaron almost missed it. "They have to be," he said.

Hall looked sidelong at Austin and said, "Can they manage?"

Austin considered his answer briefly. "Does it matter? They will or they won't."

Hall nodded. "Split the wardens and rangers between the east and north gates," he said. "The west will most likely be the entry point, so keep them away from there. They can at least help keep the ballistae loaded for stragglers and splinter groups. The scholars can help tend the wounded here in the keep." Hall turned to the other captains. "Hawk, you take command of the west gate. North, you get your namesake."

The captains both nodded and started toward the tower while Obadiah quickly split Aaron and the others up into their groups. Aaron was chosen to go with North, while Zachery and Griffon were with Hawk. They made their way back down the tower and across the courtyard to the gate. Nearly every Dragon Guard not already out in the city was making his or her way through. Aaron had never seen so many fully armored and armed Dragon Guards in one place. In the dining hall, they had been in only their black. It was truly something to behold. The glowing glint of etched steel gave him hope for the fight that was to come in spite of the overwhelming numbers against them.

They were about to part ways when Griffon gripped Aaron by the arm. "Be careful," she whispered.

He grabbed her wrist and squeezed it reassuringly.

Zachery smiled weakly at Aaron. "Try not to die."

Aaron patted him on the shoulder before he turned and followed the group heading north. As they were leaving, he glanced behind him. The keep was outlined by the glow of the fire in the city beyond it. He would have thought it was beautiful if it hadn't meant so many were dead because of it. Before he knew it, Jane fell in beside him as they ran. People were still pouring down the streets like a river as they tried to escape the sea of fire behind them. Even for the large group of Dragon Guards, it was slow going as they ran past and around bodies while trying to avoid trampling civilians and helping those that had fallen to the ground.

"I can't believe this is really happening," Jane said.

Aaron didn't know the girl well. She tended to keep to herself for the most part. But at the moment, it didn't matter. They were both dumbstruck by the horror and equally confused about the reasons behind it.

He shook his head as he thought out loud: "Why would Krida attack us? It doesn't make any sense. Besides, I thought they fought each other too much to organize like this."

"It could be land, religious reasons, or just for the thrill of it," Jane said. "Could be anything. Does it really matter why?"

Aaron gritted his teeth. "I guess not."

As they ran down the street, Aaron saw the mass of people growing thicker at the front of the gate. They were shoving each other and fighting to get as close to the gatehouse as possible, while all around them city guards tried to calm the panicked citizens and direct them to the keep.

North stopped just outside the mass and looked across. "We're going to have to force our way through the crowd if we want on the wall," he said.

He ordered them to wait and went up and down the back of the mob and gathered every city watchman he could find. He returned with eight, all of whom carried a shield. North organized his team as best he could with people still pushing past and the frantic crowd growing larger. He placed nine of them in an arrowhead formation, their shields raised in front of them like a wall. The rest would walk behind them to help push through.

North addressed them over the roar of the crowd: "Keep your shields up. We aren't trying to hurt anyone, but they're afraid. They won't be thinking straight or listening to reason. Just keep moving toward the gatehouse and they'll move aside if we push hard enough."

They started forward. Aaron was next to the point guard. North was behind him with a steady hand on both their backs. The moment Aaron came to the first person in the crowd he felt the resistance. Out of fear of hurting the man, he didn't put all his weight or strength into the shield.

He regretted it immediately as he started to fall back while the rest of the formation continued on.

North pushed harder against Aaron's back, using his own strength to keep Aaron upright and steady. When Aaron had his footing again he resolved to keep his weight pressed forward. North was right. They weren't going to move unless they made them. Aaron understood how they felt. He was just as afraid as they were. The difference was that he was a Dragon Guard and he had to do everything he could to keep them safe.

They managed to push through the crowd to the gatehouse in only a few minutes. North had them line their shields up as a wall between the door and the crowd so that when it was opened, the people wouldn't try to force their way inside in another attempt to get to safety. Thankfully, when the guards unlocked and opened the door, they were able to get inside and lock it again without incident.

North addressed the city guards that had opened the door: "Gather everyone you can and get them on top of the inner wall. I'll have my wardens start getting people away from the inner gate."

The closest guard seemed confused. "Inner, sir?" he said. "Are we not manning the outer wall?"

North shook his head. "We don't have the time or the manpower at the ready. We're too scattered to form a cohesive defense of such a vast area. We need to focus our forces on the inner wall to make sure we aren't spread too thin."

The guard nodded and went up a set of stairs leading to the top of the wall.

North turned to the trainees. "When we are on those walls," he said, "you do *exactly* as you're told. No exceptions! Do you understand?"

They nodded. North led them up the stairs, where they were immediately directed to carry crates of bolts to the nearby ballista lining the walls, as well as to load their first shots. Aaron took a moment to glance at the ballista and its stand as he helped crank the thick tension wire back on one of the devices. It was a circular wooden pad built into the wall itself, mounted with two wooden sets of triangle supports that allowed it to angle up and down while the pad let it pivot from side to side. The combined effort of the city watch and the Dragon Guards made quick work and after nearly an hour the northern section of wall was loaded and ready for battle.

With the job finished, North called out to the trainees and the city watch: "All right, head down to the masses below and start escorting them to the keep!"

Aaron was more than happy to follow the order, though Jane seemed to disagree. "What?" she said. "Why?"

"Because the Kridens have amassed outside the gates," North said, "and I'd rather not have a bunch of fresh-out-of-the-keep novices here to break the flow and organization of battle at a crucial moment."

"That's not fair!" Jane said. "Give us a bow or put us in the murder holes above the gate. Something. This is our city too. Let us help!"

"I gave you an order," North said. "Now *go!*"

Jane was about to protest again, but was cut off by a noise that drowned out the sounds of the screaming and panicked people below them. It was a chant, the chorus of a thousand voices speaking as one from across the killing field and over the wall. Slowly, the panicked people at the gate took notice of it. They quieted to listen as a new, eerie peace settled over the city. Everyone focused on the thousands of Kridens chanting in unison.

"Geieg, Geiod, Geiacht!"

They repeated the words over and over again. Each time they started again, it sent new chills down Aaron's spine. He didn't know Kridic. No one in Edaren did as far as he was aware, but he knew it meant something terrible. He and Jane were frozen in place, simply listening and looking at the wall across the killing field, dreading what the words could mean and hoping whatever it was would never breach the walls protecting them. Then a fresh horror washed over every man and woman on the walls of Vigil.

In the distance over Highwood Forest, a dragon rose out of the trees. It was still a fair distance off, but that only made its size more apparent. The dragon was at least twice the size of Argera. Its scales were dark, void of blue, its secondary color blacker than the night sky. The Kridens continued to chant as the dragon came ever closer with amazing speed.

Soon it was upon them. It spread out its wings to slow and stop as it landed on the gatehouse of the outer wall with enough force that the wall Aaron stood upon shook and shuddered.

The dragon paused in place and simply listened to the chant of the army behind it before letting out a long, thunderous roar. Aaron feared the sound would deafen him as he lifted his hands to cover his ears. When it finished, Aaron's ears were ringing. By the time he lifted his eyes, two new horrors were rising from the forest. One was a sickly, copper dragon with an orange secondary color. Alongside it was a ruby red beast, its secondary color grey, like forged iron. Both seemed about the same size as Argera. They quickly closed the gap between the forest and wall before splitting off from one another, landing next to the gatehouses of the east and west sides respectively.

The cries of the Kridens changed. Those outside the north gate chanted Geiacht, while the east proclaimed Geieg, and the west praised Geiod. Aaron realized the Kridens had been chanting the names of the dragons.

Geiacht stepped down from the gatehouse and stood just inside the outer wall in the killing field before turning to the gate. It lifted its forelegs and dug its claws into the iron-banded wood of the gate.

Aaron couldn't look away from the beast before him. He imagined the other two were performing similar actions as the three of them roared as one. Then, with incredible strength that seemed effortless, Geiacht tore the gate apart and threw the remains into the killing field. They crashed and rolled over the ground before coming to a stop at the base of the inner wall. The moment the way was open, the dragon stepped off the path. Kridens started pouring through the gate, never once straying from the stone road. In a perfect line headed for the second gate.

North broke from his stupor and shouted orders: "Pivot sixty and rotate accordingly! Aim for the dragon! Don't let it take to the sky! Keep it grounded!"

The guards started to pivot the ballista to aim toward Geiacht. All Aaron could do was watch in horror as the dragon leapt into the air, making the effort moot long before they'd moved the devices even half as far as they needed to. With speed that seemed unnatural for its size,

Geiacht landed on the gatehouse of the inner wall, making the structure crack under its weight and causing everyone on the wall to fall to their knees. The people crowded around the gate screamed and started to run in all directions at the sight of the mythical creature long thought gone.

The people trampled each other as they tried to move in every direction, stopping anyone from going anywhere. Aaron watched as the underside of the dragon's neck and jaw started to glow. Slowly, it brightened from a dull red to a blinding white as the fire and heat built up inside. Aaron glanced around the city. Even from that distance, he could see the other two dragons were mimicking the larger dragon. With another unified roar, they bathed the defenseless people below them in flames.

The fire burned so bright and hot that Aaron had to turn his back to the flames in an attempt to stop the burning sensation that was spreading across his skin. Then, just as quickly as it had come, the fire vanished. The scalding heat remained thick and heavy in the air, making it a struggle to breathe. Aaron knew his clothes were already soaked with sweat. Even the fire-resistant metal of the etched, steel shield he carried was warm to the touch. He turned around to see the dragon step off the wall into the city. Aaron slowly rose and glanced around to see Jane and North near him, as well as a few of the city guards, alive and well. Unlike this small group, though, most of the Dragon Guards had stood on the wall and been too close to the dragon. They now lay atop the wall, writhing in agony. Their proximity to the heat alone had burned them horribly.

Jane and Aaron looked at each other, then ran to the edge of the wall. The courtyard below was empty and charred black. Not even a corpse remained in the aftermath. The dragon turned toward the gatehouse and, just as at the outer wall, it gripped the wood of the gate with its claws and tore it free, making the gatehouse around it shatter and fall into a pile of rubble, taking burned guards with it as it fell.

Geiacht stood on its hind legs and tossed what remained of the gates into the city, crushing buildings beneath their weight. Then, its job apparently done, the dragon spread its wings and leaped into the air, leaving the chaos it had created behind as it slowly spiraled into the layer of smoke above the city. Aaron and Jane simply stared into the black stones below them, unsure how to react. Aaron was furious that the creature had done such a thing but terrified it had the power to do so. He wanted nothing more than to run to the keep and hide away. Yet he also wanted revenge for every person that had been caught in the inferno. The conflicting emotions threatened to cripple him until he heard a strong voice break though the sound of his own heartbeat and his racing and scattered thoughts.

"Everyone down into the rubble! Form a line and protect the survivors!" North was shouting and breaking everyone out of their terrified stupors.

Aaron looked past the black stones to the buildings and streets around them. There were indeed still survivors, though most of them seemed to be just at petrified as he had been moments earlier. They were unable to move as the horde of Kridens marched down the path of the killing field, adding to their fear. Aaron turned to Jane and saw that she was already moving. He balled his hands into fists. Instead of thinking about what had just happened, he focused on what he needed to do and drew his sword.

CHAPTER TWENTY-NINE

30th of Sanya, 28th year of the Fourth Age.

DANIEL, CLARA, AND Alan were moving far too slowly through the alleyways. They were still on their way to the keep but had made barely any progress. They'd had to backtrack several times to avoid running into Disciples and valgrets. The city was crawling with them now. They were using the tunnels to get inside without any resistance and emerging from every opening. Daniel assumed that meant whatever patrols had been down there when the attacks started were dead. Now, with the appearance of three dragons over the city gates, Daniel wasn't sure what they were going to do.

When the dragons were spotted, the citizens had started retreating from the gates. This managed only to clog the streets more than before. Now that the gates weren't a sign of safety, people ran in every direction, almost guaranteeing that staying on the street would mean death by trampling. Several people had thought as Daniel and taken to the alleyways, but they were quickly cut down by valgrets or cultists. Without their weapons, Daniel, Clara, and Alan couldn't protect them.

Every corner had the risk of leading the trio to something they didn't have the means to deal with. They had been going for nearly an hour when they reached another dead end and took the chance to catch their breath.

Clara slumped against a wall and placed her head in her hands. "What are we supposed to do?" she said.

Daniel shook his head as he paced back and forth. "We just have to get to the keep."

"Daniel, we've barely moved!" Clara said. "We can't even get back on the main street. We're surrounded. I'm pretty sure we've been at this spot before."

"I know! What else do you want me to say?"

"I don't know. I...I just..."

They both went silent. Daniel stopped pacing and walked over to sit next to her while Alan slumped into a corner, an empty expression on his face. He reminded Daniel of Jeremy. That same look had been on his brother's face when he and Daniel had slept in the forest so very long ago. The memory brought a smile. He hadn't thought much about his family. Now that he was, he realized how much he truly missed his brother. He had always been with Jeremy, though more often than not he'd wished he wasn't. Yet now he wanted nothing more than to see him and his mother again.

Alan's voice was quiet as he spoke in the silence: "Do you think Zachery is okay?"

"Yeah, I'm sure he's fine," Daniel answered, attempting to sound confident. "He's probably up in the keep right now."

"Do you think we'll be okay?"

Daniel felt his heart skip. "Yeah, I'll make sure of it," he said. He faked a smile.

Silence hung in the air again. Several times, they heard the flap of dragon wings and saw a shadow pass overhead, but they were too afraid to look up to see the actual beast. They couldn't bring themselves to move. Daniel felt helpless and he knew Clara and Alan felt the same. They were trapped with no clear way out. They knew their goal but it was out of reach.

Then Daniel heard something, a low and guttural growl that brought back memories of Daniel's jump from the falls in Sapella's Crossing. It made him remember the woman being changed in the tunnels below the city, made him remember the choked plea for help and the blood that pooled on the stones. The valgret stepped around the corner and turned to look at them. It bared its teeth as it slowly approached, staying so low that it was almost crawling across the ground. Daniel, Clara, and Alan jumped to their feet and huddled together in the middle of the dead end, their backs against the wall. The valgret growled again. It was moving cautiously. Daniel knew that they were smarter than they looked. He guessed that it recognized their black clothing as a sign of danger. Daniel slowly slipped a finger under his left sleeve and gripped a metal ring. He pulled it carefully over his index and middle finger.

Even though none of them carried weapons, there was one thing Austin had told the ranger trainees to always have on them since it was easily hidden and light enough that Daniel often forgot he was wearing it—a dart launcher worn around the wrist and forearm. It was a single-shot weapon that fired a dart covered in a fast-acting poison. It would cause a target to quickly fall into a deep sleep before breathing stopped altogether.

The ring, which was now looped around his fingers, was attached to a thin wire that ran through several small, iron loops to keep it secure. It was then tied to a pin holding a coil of steel in place. When the pin was pulled, the coil fired the dart through a cylinder that ended at the wrist joint. Its range was less than ideal and the dart's ability to penetrate dropped quickly with distance. Daniel would have to wait until the valgret was close to compensate for the thickness of its hide.

The valgret was about ten feet away. It started to advance faster. Daniel wasn't very proficient in aiming with the launcher, so he waited until he was sure he wouldn't miss. He wasn't even sure if the poison would work. It was much larger than any human and the dosage was meant for an average-sized person. If anything, Daniel hoped the dart would at least slow the valgret down enough to let them escape.

He watched the muscles in the creature's shoulders and legs, waiting for it to tense, signaling that it was about to pounce. He let it get a few steps closer before he raised his arm and aimed. The valgret took a step back at the motion, so Daniel waited. It had to be just a little closer before he could be sure the dart would pierce. Then the beast tensed and leapt for them, so fast that Daniel almost didn't have time to react. He balled his hand into a fist to tighten the wire over his knuckle, then flexed his hand down by bending at the wrist while keeping his arm straight to pull the pin and release the dart.

He missed.

The dart went wide, past the valgret's chest. The creature tackled the three of them. They rolled with it across the ground. The three trainees came to a stop as the valgret continued rolling past them. It jumped to its feet while they were only starting to rise. The creature reached for Clara, but Daniel managed to stand quickly enough and charged into it with his shoulder. All he did was push it backwards slightly and delay it.

Clara started to back away as the valgret growled at Daniel and reached for him. He jumped back and out of the way just as its claws swept past his face. He felt himself hit the wall as he was backing away and scolded himself for not taking note of his positioning. It was about to charge for him when it stopped and sniffed the air. It whirled and focused on Alan, who was just starting to rise. Alan's forehead was bleeding. The valgret could smell the blood.

Daniel looked on in horror as the valgret ran to Alan and grabbed him by the neck. Daniel wanted to move, wanted to run over there and make the creature release Alan, but his legs wouldn't listen to him. He wanted to scream but his voice stuck in his throat. Everything he wanted to do he couldn't manage. An overwhelming wave of fear washed over him as he watched something he knew he couldn't stop no matter how much he wanted to. The valgret stood at its full height and lifted Alan by the neck until he was at eye level. Daniel thought he saw the monster smile as it drove a clawed hand into Alan's chest.

Alan never made a sound. His face never showed the pain he must have felt. His expression was frozen in pure terror as the valgret released his neck and let him fall to the ground, limp. Daniel couldn't look away from the lifeless form of his friend. He never heard Clara scream. He didn't see the valgret turn toward her and slowly make its way over. He never heard it laugh when it stopped in front of her and prepared to do it all again.

But he did hear the familiar voice, quiet yet clear, in the chaos of the city: "Stop."

He turned to the voice and saw a woman in the white, hooded robe of a Disciple, her face hidden. The valgret turned and looked at her expectantly, its head tilted to one side and ears up.

The woman spoke again and he still couldn't place the voice: "Come."

At the single word, the valgret bounded over like an excited puppy before bowing low in front of her. She reached out and started to pet its head. It lifted itself higher to push into her hand. It was a sight Daniel hadn't thought possible. The woman stood, still quietly petting the monster, as Daniel and Clara looked on in confusion.

The hooded figure spoke again, this time in a shaky voice: "Do you know what it's like to grow up hating everything about yourself?" The more she talked, the more Daniel was sure he knew the voice. She continued as she knelt down in front of the beast, still giving it affection like a loved pet. "To grow up alone and then be taken in, and shown how to do these... *things*... that make you physically sick? To forever after have these *voices* in your head, always whispering these awful things to you?"

Daniel took a hesitant step forward. His legs shook and he was afraid they would give out under his weight. He tried to keep his eyes on the woman, but his gaze was drawn back to Alan as blood pooled around him on the stones.

She spoke again in a whisper. "Please leave. I don't want anyone else to die."

Clara had managed to stand. Tears streamed from her eyes. Her voice quivered as she spoke the name that had been eluding Daniel: "Lace?"

The woman didn't look at her but Daniel saw her hand tense at the name. She stopped petting the valgret.

Daniel took another shaking step forward. "Lace," he said, "what are you doing here?"

She took her hand away from the valgret, lowered her hood, and turned to Daniel. He saw tears in her eyes. "I don't know anymore."

Clara moved closer and raised a hand as if to help her stand. "Lace," she said, "just come with us and we can fig—"

"Get away from me!" Lace shouted. The stones beneath her cracked.

Daniel and Clara both took several quick steps back as a wave of force sent the dirt and dust around Lace away like a ripple in water.

She saw them retreat and placed both hands over her face. "They're *talking* to me again! I don't want to hear any of them, but they just keep talking, and talking, and talking all the time!"

Daniel and Clara exchanged glances as Lace started rocking in place, mumbling to herself. The valgret seemed to be growing tense as it looked back and forth between Daniel and Clara while slowly standing.

Lace looked up at the sky as her rocking ceased. "I just…I don't want to hurt anyone anymore," she said. She looked back at the valgret and started to stroke its nose, making it relax slightly. "Please, just go."

As much as he wanted to figure out what she was talking about, *who* she was talking about, Daniel knew that if they stayed here much longer, whatever Lace was doing to keep the valgret in check wouldn't last. He started toward Clara. The moment he moved, the valgret focused on him and tensed its muscles.

Daniel gently placed a hand on Clara's shoulder and started to lead her away. "Come on, Clara," he said. "We have to go."

She looked at him and started to cry again. "We can't leave Alan."

He felt as if his heart was about to physically break with his next words: "We have to."

Clara resisted for a moment before letting Daniel lead her out of the dead end and back into the maze of alleyways. When they were about to round the corner, he looked back one last time and saw Lace was openly crying into her hands. The valgret watched her, its head tilted to one side.

CHAPTER THIRTY

30th of Sanya, 28th year of the Fourth Age.

GRIFFON SWUNG HER great sword in a wide sweep and knocked the Kriden's axe to the side as he tried to bring it down on her, causing the weight of his own weapon throw him off balance. He recovered quickly and roared something in Kridic before charging at her and swinging wildly side to side. She backpedaled and tried to block the blows, but the man's strength was far greater than her own. Each blow sent vibrations down the blade and up her arm, making her tremble and nearly forcing her to drop her weapon. He swung downward again, pinning her sword to the ground under the axe head. He raised a bare fist to strike her, but he was stopped short. An arrow struck him in the center of his chest, followed quickly by a second arrow to his throat.

The Kriden took another two steps toward her before falling forward onto the ground at her feet. She glanced behind her and saw a group of four rangers firing into the horde of Kridens pouring through the west gate. All the rangers save for the trainees had been sent to the south of the city to rescue whatever civilians they could. If these four were here now, then their efforts there were clearly over. She wasn't sure if that was a good sign or not. Griffon's job when she had arrived with Captain Hawk had been to lead the civilians to the keep, along with a large group of the city watch. But shortly after they'd begun, the Kridens had started chanting.

When the dragons appeared over the gates and their necks began to glow, everyone panicked. People fled in all directions, getting seemingly nowhere while Griffon and several others were able to escape by taking cover in nearby alleyways and buildings. That didn't save them all, as the fire spread like rushing water and spilled into the alleys like canals, burning many of them into nothingness. Griffon and her small group barely survived by taking cover inside a nearby building with the door closed. The rest of the civilians that had escaped the wave of flame were now heading up the street toward the keep as Dragon Guards and the city watch that had survived tried to stem the tide of attackers pouring through the newly destroyed gate.

Thankfully, the rubble of the gatehouse had reduced the size of the opening, creating a bottleneck that slowed the assault. In spite of this, the forces of Vigil were still being pushed back by the never-ending flow of bloodthirsty southerners. The Kridens seemed to have brought their entire nation to war. The three dragons hadn't rejoined the battle yet. They seemed content to simply circle the city. Griffon was glad they didn't have to deal with them, at least for the time being. How the Kridens could have aligned with a trio of dragons was beyond her. With those creatures on their side, she couldn't see how they going to win this battle, even with the Dragon Guards' reputation and prowess as ancient dragon slayers.

Griffon turned to her left and saw Zachery trying to dodge an over-sized flanged mace. He ducked under a wide swing and lunged forward, driving his dagger into the Kriden's unarmored gut, burying it up to the hilt. Before he could pull it free and strike again, the Kriden gripped Zachery's wrist and threw him to the side, sending him skidding across the ground. With the giant's back now to her, Griffon charged at him and with every ounce of strength she had, she swung in a downward arc at the back of his neck.

The blow was solid, breaking bone and killing him instantly. The Kriden fell to the ground, ripping the sword from her hands as he did. She planted a foot in his back and managed to pull it free before running to Zachery and dragging him to his feet.

He was bent over, trying to catch his breath. "Thanks," he finally said.

She placed a hand on his shoulder. "Let's stay together."

He nodded and retrieved his dagger before they both looked out across the scene of battle. When the battle started, the two of them had been positioned at what was now the back line and told to stay put. They were out of the harshest combat and tasked to deal with any attackers that might slip through the front line during chaos. The Kridens were much stronger than any of the trainees. Out of all them that had come to the gate, Griffon and Zachery were the only ones still standing.

The rest had fallen one by one. Now the back line was only the two of them, the newly arrived rangers, and a handful of the city watch who Griffon hadn't seen in the last several minutes. She glanced back again at the rangers as they let loose arrow after arrow into the thick crowd. She turned to the body of the Kriden at her feet.

She was somewhat stunned. She had expected to feel something the first time she killed. Obadiah had said as much during their training, had said that the first time one takes a life a small part of their own goes with them, making one feel almost unclean. But Griffon didn't. What she felt was anger. She supposed it was because of who they were, what they had done, and what they were surely planning on doing. The fact was, they were here to slaughter anything and everyone they could. So perhaps anger was what she was supposed to feel.

From somewhere in the mass of bodies ahead of them she heard Hawk shouting orders with a voice that carried across the battle and the noise: "Fall back! Fall back to the keep!"

She and Zachery looked at one another before they turned and started running up the street as the forces of Vigil retreated. The two of them they were quickly overtaken by the majority of the defenders and ended up in the middle of the pack. Griffon glanced behind her over the sea of men and women and saw something odd. The Kridens weren't pursing them. Instead, they seemed to be walking casually toward them, as if for them there was no rush to finish what they had begun. Confused, she turned her eyes forward again as they ran. When they were finally close enough, the gates of the keep slowly opened to allow them inside.

They filed in as quickly as they could. Roughly twenty minutes later, everyone was inside and the gates closed behind them. Griffon and Zachery split from the larger portion of the crowd and sat next to the northeastern guard tower to catch their breath and gather their thoughts in a brief moment of peace. The sky which was now covered in a thick blanket of smoke that blocked out the stars. The Kridens had stopped firing their siege equipment long ago. It wasn't needed anymore. Half the city was on fire and the flames were quickly spreading to the rest. Griffon didn't want to admit it, but at this point she didn't think it was possible to save Vigil.

"Griffon." Zachery nudged her and nodded toward the gate.

Through the crowd, she saw Daniel and Clara speaking to Captain Hawk. When they were finished, the three of them made their way toward Griffon and Zachery until Hawk split off and went into the tower. Daniel and Clara continued heading for them. They looked haggard. Neither had armor or weapons and both were covered in dirt. Griffon was over-joyed to see that at least they had made it to the keep, mostly unharmed. But her joy quickly vanished when she saw their faces. They stopped a few steps away. Their eyes were bloodshot and puffy. Something had clearly happened, an idea that was confirmed when Clara started to cry.

Daniel took another step forward but kept his eyes on his feet. "Zachery...I..." Tears started to stream down Daniel's cheeks, leaving trails in the dirt and ash.

"What happened?" Zachery asked, fear evident in his tone.

Daniel's voice cracked as he spoke. "Alan...I couldn't stop it...Zachery, I'm so, so sorry."

Griffon was dumbstruck. His meaning was clear but she couldn't accept it. There was no way this could happen. She refused to believe it and started to look at every face in the courtyard, hoping that she would see him, hoping she would see Alan. Zachery said nothing for several moments. He simply stared at Daniel.

When he did speak, it was quietly. "Where is he?"

"We had to leave, Zachery...I'm sorry, we couldn't stay there."

Zachery stuttered as he spoke. "You...left him behind?" He was quiet for another moment. Then he struck out with his fist, punching Daniel in the jaw knocking him to the ground. He was shouting now as his tears flowed. "You left my brother out there! You let him die and then you left him!"

Daniel didn't rise. He just stared at the ground without saying a word. Griffon looked around them. Several people were glancing in their direction. After a stern look from her they quickly turned their attention elsewhere.

Zachery was quiet again. He sounded distant, like he wasn't really there anymore. "What happened to him?"

Clara wiped at her tears. "It was a valgret. There was nothing we could do, Zachery I'm so, so sorry. We almost died too. We had to get out of there as fast as we could."

After a moment of looking at the ground, Zachery turned and walked away. None of them tried to stop him or go after him. They knew it would do no good and chances were he would only lash out again. Instead, Griffon walked the remaining few steps between her and her other two friends. She pulled Daniel to his feet and gripped them both in an embrace that she didn't want to break. After a few moments which seemed to last an eternity, she let them go and the three of them sat with their backs against the tower, not saying a word.

Griffon wasn't sure if she should cry. She knew Alan well enough, but in spite of that she didn't feel the tears rising. She was saddened by his loss and she felt awful for Zachery. He'd lost his brother. Daniel and Clara had been there when it happened and just by looking at Daniel and hearing his words, she could tell he felt guilty. But in spite of all that, she didn't cry for her friend even though she wanted to. They sat for several more minutes in silence until the gate opened again. They all watched as people filed in. It was open for only a minute before it closed again. There were so few still alive.

Thankfully, Griffon could see a familiar face among them: Aaron. His face glistened with sweat. The few areas where they could see the black beneath his armor were ripped. Several spots of skin were cut and bleeding. After a moment, he spotted them and jogged over, pulling them all into a hug as soon as they were together. "Thank Verhova you guys made it," he said.

Griffon stepped back and held him at arm's length. "What happened?" she said. "Why didn't your retreat sound sooner?"

"After the dragon tore the gate away and flew off, North led everyone down over the rubble of the gatehouse. It took a long time to get the survivors out of there. Part of the gate blocked the main road, which slowed everything down. The Kridens...they just came pouring through so fast."

"Where's Jane? She was with you, wasn't she?"

Aaron nodded. "She was with North just a second ago." He looked away from Griffon to Daniel. Aaron clearly hadn't noticed the state his friend was in until now. "Daniel?" he said. "What's wrong?"

Daniel kept his eyes downcast. "Alan didn't make it."

Aaron's tone suggested he didn't want to ask his next question: "What happened?"

"We were in the city. We got cornered and we..." Daniel sighed. "I let him die. I couldn't save him."

Aaron gripped his shoulders and pulled him closer forcing Daniel to look him in the eyes. "It's not your fault."

"You weren't there."

"That doesn't matter," Aaron said. "I didn't have to be. I know you, and if there's anything you could have done, you would have done it."

Griffon was about to affirm Aaron's statement when they heard Captain Coe atop the wall, shouting orders at those gathered below. "Soldiers, get on the walls, now!"

Aaron released Daniel and looked at him and Clara. "You guys better go get your gear."

They nodded and without a word and headed for the barracks. Aaron and Griffon turned into the tower and made their way up to the top of the wall. They walked over to the captains and the commander who all stood above the gate with Kenneth, their instructors, and Jane. They were clearly arguing. Their expressions showed fury. Griffon felt the tension in the air thicken with each word. She was genuinely worried that they would break out in a fistfight.

North was gesturing toward the people below. "We *can't* send those people into the tunnels when there are valgrets, Disciples, and who knows what else down there!"

Coe jabbed him in the chest with her a finger. "Then you can explain to them that the plan is to sit here and wait to die. The tunnels lead out of the city, which means they lead to their safety. This was our original plan and there's no time to come up with another."

"We have new information," North said. "Now we know the Disciples are using the tunnels to get inside the city, which means they have control of them. Control of the very place you say will lead to their safety!"

"Then send a few squads in and clear a path," Coe said. "I will not let these people simply wait for death!"

"Would you instead send them into its arms?"

"Enough!" Hall shouted so loudly that they both took a step back from him and each other. "Neither option is ideal, but Coe is right. Worst-case scenario is we all die here in the walls of the keep. Best case is we manage to get the civilians out. Obadiah, take two squads into the tunnel through the Quin home. Most of its side passages are sealed off, so it should be clear and a straight shot to the shoreline."

"Yes, commander," Obadiah said. He turned to make his way to the tower, giving Griffon and the others a reassuring nod as he passed.

"Kenneth, Claudia, start preparing the civilians for evacuation," Hall said. "Get as many siege ladders as you can and get ready to set them over the walls so we can avoid taking people through the gate. The moment Obadiah returns with a confirmed clear, start sending the civilians over and down."

"Right away, commander," Kenneth said. He and Claudia both saluted before following Obadiah.

Griffon looked out over the city as Hall issued commands to the other officials on the wall. The outer edges of the city were now burning, along with the entirety of the south side. To the north, the Kridens were gathering not far from the keep. Griffon could see several valgrets moving among their ranks, along with the telltale white robes of the Disciples, which stood out against the dark-clad tribesmen. There were thousands of them, and they all wanted nothing more than to slaughter everyone in the city.

Griffon turned to look inside the keep. So few were left to defend it, not nearly enough against such a force. There were maybe two hundred civilians, the rest either dead or trapped in the fires, unable to make it to the keep. Vigil, the home of the Dragon Guard, had fallen in less than a night.

Without even realizing it, she voiced her thoughts: "How could this have happened?"

Hall heard her. He let his gaze follow hers as people ran about the wall preparing whatever defenses they had left.

He stepped up to stand by her. "We used to have ships patrolling the sea in case of a naval attack," he said, "but we got arrogant with the cliff as a natural defense. We used to keep the tunnels open for storage and patrolled to evacuate the city at times like this, but we sealed those off and forgot about them due to a lack of manpower. We used to do a lot of things that could have prevented this. But we got complacent and comfortable behind our walls. Comfort breeds weakness."

CHAPTER THIRTY-ONE

30ᵗʰ of Sanya, 28ᵗʰ year of the Fourth Age.

DANIEL STRAPPED ON his second vambrace and checked his wardrobe for the third time, ensuring he hadn't missed anything. He wouldn't be caught unprepared again. No one else would die because he couldn't save them. He checked the gear he wore yet again; he would be ready for anything. His longbow was strapped to his back, unstrung, the string in a pouch at his belt. His dart launcher was now reloaded with six spare shots at his belt, along with a case of twelve throwing knives and his short sword at his lower back, just above his quiver. His spare knife rested against his collarbone, hidden beneath his scarf. He ran through the rest of his gear quickly and was satisfied he had it all.

He was about to turn and head out the door when he glanced at his cot. Sitting atop it was *Hidden Efforts*, still open from his reading that very morning. He reached down and placed a hand on his logbook. Every ranger had one in a case that hung from his belt, opposite his weaponry. It was meant for keeping notes when out scouting or spying in the cities. He didn't know why but he removed the logbook. He slid the history book into its place, thankful it fit, before running down the rows of cots to the door.

Daniel stepped out and paused to take in the surroundings. Just beyond the door, several scholars treated dozens of people lying atop blankets laid out across the ground. Most were horribly burned by the fire on the south side, while others suffered from broken limbs and unsightly gashes. He heard shouting from the gate and turned to head that way. At the southeastern tower, he began climbing. When he reached the top, he saw Hall shouting orders to the city watch as they ran this way and that.

"Get the ballistae in position! I want them ready when those dragons return!"

Daniel saw that Clara had already made her way here and now huddled with the few trainees that remained. A total of eight stood to one side and watched as several guards angled and loaded ballistae along the walls. Daniel knew they kept such things in storage so they must have just been brought up. It was clear they hadn't been used in years as even now they were covered in a heavy layer of dust. After several minutes of silence and just as the last of the ballistae were readied, the horde beyond the walls began to chant again.

"Geieg! Geiod! Geiacht!"

Everyone froze in place. They all knew that this was what had brought on the dragons before. They knew it would again.

Hall turned to Captain Hawk. "What are they saying?"

Hawk closed his eyes and listened as the chant was repeated again. "Deity...or god, more closely. That's the first part of each word, but the second I'm not quite sure." He paused. He let the chant pass three more times before he continued: "Geiacht is god of war, I believe. Geieg is of death...the other one I have no idea. They are clearly names."

North looked out over the army beyond. "They think the dragons are gods?"

As the chant finished again, the three dragons dropped from the sky above the north gate and landed with a thundering crash in the city, sending plumes of ash and dust into the air. Their appearance was sudden and greeted with roaring cheers from the amassed army. Slowly, the main road began to clear as the Kridens moved aside to make a path for the largest dragon, the one with scales that seemed nothing but a void of blue that was nearly black.

Hall shouted at those staring dumbstruck at the beast: "Load the spread shot!"

It took only a few moments for the Kriden to move off the main road. When the last Kriden stepped aside, the dragon began to run. Daniel knew enough of tactics after his time here that this was an action meant to intimidate, to show the power the dragon had, that an army would literally part before it. He knew that this was something to enforce the faith of the Kridens, and crack the faith of the Dragon Guard. He was certain that this was something orchestrated by the Disciples.

The Kridens chanted again as the beast ran: "Geiacht!"

The name echoed from the throats of the Kridens in a terrible unison with the rumbling steps of the dragon. It closed the distance rapidly, its neck already aglow with a readied wave of fire. It was halfway to them when it leapt off its feet, spread its wings to their full length, and glided toward them. Daniel couldn't figure it out. Hall should have given the order to fire the ballistae by now. Instead, he simply stood and waited.

Geiacht was about to reach the gate when through the smoke and ash above came Argera. She had her forelegs out in front of her, claws spread wide, her mouth already spewing a stream of flames as she collided with the much larger beast. She ripped into Geiacht's wings and they both crashed to the ground and rolled through buildings, sending up dust and causing debris to fly as they went. They barreled through the Kridens at the side of the roadway, crushing them beneath their scaled bodies. When at last they stopped rolling, they quickly separated from each other. Argera leapt away from Geiacht and perched atop a row of buildings, cracking the roofs beneath her weight.

The other two dragons were about to start forward when Geiacht shouted to them in what Daniel assumed was Kridic. Geiacht's voice was unnervingly deep and gravely. Whatever it said caused the other two to take a step back and wait. Argera and Geiacht began circling one another, with Argera having to step over the gaps between buildings to continue her path while Geiacht simply crushed the structures beneath his feet when he encountered resistance.

Hall took advantage of their momentary stalemate to issue another set of commands: "Ballistae, angles between ten and forty-five, pivot between zero and fifty! Get me a war horn, now!"

It took those standing at the cranks a moment to realize what Hall was telling them to do before they started to turn and angle the devices to varied points between the specified degrees. Daniel had no idea where it came from, but the next thing he knew Hall had a horn in his hand and raised it to his lips. He blew three rapid short tones, followed by another three drawn-out calls. He had no idea what they meant, but Argera clearly did. She started to run toward the keep diagonally. Geiacht reacted and tried to cut her off.

According to what Daniel knew of dragons, males were usually larger and stockier than females. Geiacht dwarfed Argera in size. But she wasn't deterred as she leapt toward him and gripped his neck with her teeth. He tried to pry her off, but they fell to the ground and started to roll and tumble together. Daniel couldn't tell what was happening. All he was able to see were flashes of silver scales against blue, along with teeth and claws as they bit and slashed at one another.

Hall paced the wall and yelled, "Ballistae, wait for my mark, then release at will!"

The call came sooner than Daniel expected as Argera pushed off the back of Geiacht and took to the air with two hard flaps of her wings. The moment she was clear, Geiacht started to spread his wings.

"Release! All release now!" Hall shouted.

Every ballista on the wall chorused with a heavy *thud* as the strained arms were released, launching the projectiles forward. But they weren't the usual heavy, iron-tipped bolts. These were bundles of six smaller bolts linked together by a net of thick ropes. The ropes were dotted with jagged shards of metal. When they reached Geiacht, the nets caught on him as the bolts flew past and tore through the thin membrane of his wings until the net stopped them. They fell on the other side of the dragon and tangled together. The beast fell to his side, trapped in a mass of rope and metal that ripped his wings apart with every movement.

The dragon arched his neck as best he could to angle a stream of fire at his own side in an attempt to burn the ropes away, but when the flames dissipated, the ropes remained unscarred. Daniel smiled in spite of himself. They were made from scorch weed. Now, with Geiacht immobilized, Argera attacked again. She dove straight toward him. At the last moment, she spread her wings to ease her fall as she slammed into him with a resounding crash, sending a cloud of ash into the air.

The larger dragon's neck flared. He attempted to send another plume of fire toward Argera, but her smaller size let her easily duck and dash out of the way as the ropes hindered his movement. As the stream subsided and before he could manage to find her again, she reached out with her forelegs and gripped his upper and lower jaw. They wrestled for a moment as she strained to keep his head still and pry his mouth open wider. As they struggled, Argera's neck began to glow. She held back the flame until his mouth was steady and opened wide in her grip. Even from where he stood, Daniel could see Geiacht's eyes widen as he realized what was about to happen.

With a thundering roar, Argera filled Geiacht's throat with fire that traveled through him and incinerated everything within. Geiacht thrashed in the mass of ropes for only a moment before falling still. Argera released his head, letting it fall limply to the ground, and leaped onto his side. She paused as she inhaled again and sent another stream of flames into the air with a triumphant roar that caused those upon the keep walls to cheer and shout. Even the city watch could tell the dragon was fighting for them, and while they couldn't understand the reasons, they welcomed the results.

Their celebration was quickly cut short by the challenging cries of the other two dragons at the edge of the city. Argera turned to them and bared her fangs as the two of them did the same. They locked gazes. Seconds later, the two Kriden gods began to run through the city. They leapt over buildings and climbed across rooftops as their necks lit up with the familiar glow. Argera answered with another roar as she jumped from the corpse of Geiacht and charged toward them. It took only moments for the three to meet.

Argera let loose her fire before they met, making the two skid to a stop as their view was obscured. She leapt forward and through the flames to collide with the red dragon who, based on the chanting from the Kridens when the gates were destroyed, was called Geiod. They tumbled for a moment before Argera ran a claw over its eye, making it roar in fury. They came to a stop with Argera on top, but before she could strike again, the other dragon, Geieg, barreled into her side and sent her flying through neighboring buildings. She slid to a stop. Just as the other two were about to tackle her, she spread her wings to their full span and with a single flap began to fly out of their way.

But Argera hadn't been fast enough to gain any distance. As she rose, Geieg lifted his head and gripped her tail with his mouth. Her momentum lifted them briefly off the ground, but she didn't have the strength to lift them both. While she was frozen in the air, Geiod unfurled his wings and leapt onto her back. Argera crashed to the ground under the extra weight and Geieg quickly joined his red brother atop her, pinning her down. Geiod bit down on Argera's neck, piercing the softer scales and causing a steady flow of blood. She cried out and struggled to get out from under the two, her legs digging into the ground in an attempt to find purchase.

Geieg repositioned himself near her back and gripped where her wing met her body with his forelegs while planting his hind legs solidly on her side. Then he started to pull. Argera appeared to feel it immediately and thrashed under the two in vain. Then it happened all at once. The bone snapped. Her scales spread apart as the skin beneath them ripped, along with the muscles and tendons that held it all together. Argera's wing was ripped away.

She didn't roar. She *screamed*. Geieg fell back as the anchor it had been holding released. With the weight lessened, Argera managed a burst of strength and rose with astounding speed. She reached for Geiod with her forelegs and pulled the dragon beneath her. She gripped him on the neck where his head connected and bit down until she crushed bone, sinew, and muscle in her jaw. The Kriden dragon let loose a garbled cry as blood started to fill its throat and mouth. But Argera didn't relent. She released and lifted a clawed foreleg. Stiffening and flattening her claws like a blade, she was about to drive it down into the dragon's neck to sever it where she had weakened it.

But Geieg had recovered from his awkward fall and now on his feet. He let loose a wide torrent of fire. Unbalanced by her missing wing, Argera wasn't able to move out of the way and took the full force of the scorching heat. Even beneath the scales of a dragon lay vital organs and sensitive skin that, like any fighter donned in plate, would be cooked inside from the heat if exposed long enough. Cooking Argera had apparently not been the intention of the dragon, however. The short burst of fire simply blinded her, allowing Geieg time to charge. He barreled into her, his wings beating furiously and his forelegs spread out to embrace her. With incredible strength, he lifted her into the air.

But the extra weight prevented Geieg from reaching the height he clearly wanted. His initial momentum carried them well above the wall and the buildings below, but he was finally forced to drop Argera. She landed hard and rolled through the buildings before sliding to a stop. Slowly, the Dragon Guard defender rose from the debris and dust, but she stumbled with her first step. Argera shook her head and seemed to struggle to stay upright. She was losing this fight.

Hall knew it. He gave his next order to Austin: "Order the evacuation. We need to get everyone out of the city."

"We haven't received word from the squad sent to clear the tunnel," Austin said. "There could be more Kridens down there."

Hall narrowed his eyes. "Then tell Kenneth and Claudia to keep their weapons drawn. Get everyone out... *now*."

Austin nodded, suddenly seeming sheepish under the commander's gaze. "Very well, commander."

He ran along the wall to the tower. Daniel turned back to watch the battle of dragons. Argera had managed to stay on her feet and now faced a relentless onslaught from the Kriden gods. They stood to either side of her and were ducking in and out of her range, biting and clawing at her whenever she presented an opening, which was frequent with her injuries. The lack of balance made Argera almost defenseless. She was slowly being ripped apart. Her silver and white scales glistened red in the firelight. With each blow, weakened scales were torn away and the skin beneath shredded. Geiod lunged for her again when her attention was turned and gripped the back of her head with his jaw. He then yanked her back and started to drag her through the rubble of the city toward the keep. When they were roughly fifty feet away, he skidded to a stop and threw her toward the keep walls.

The men and women still on the wall scrambled to get out of the way of the dragon as Argera crashed into the stone, cracking it and crushing those that had been to slow to run. Geiod roared furiously as Geieg dashed past and leapt onto Argera's upturned belly, digging his claws into her chest and burying them up to his knuckles. Argera screamed again. She gripped the dragon's head and clawed at his eyes. They rolled, shattering the ballistae on the walls as they headed for Daniel and the others. All of them started to run toward the tower to avoid being caught in the conflict.

There was a flash of fire behind them as they ran. Hall was the first to reach the tower. He threw open the door and ushered everyone in and down the stairs before heading in himself. Daniel was just behind Clara as they raced down the stone steps. They had gone down only a few when the dragons crashed into the tower, shattering the top and sending debris down on top of them. Most of the larger, more dangerous chunks were knocked aside as the dragons went past and back into the city. Then Daniel noticed a blur at the top of his vision. Without thinking, he grabbed Clara by the hair and yanked her toward him.

He caught her as she fell back just in time to avoid a mass of stone bricks and wooden supports as they fell onto the stairs where she'd stood less than a moment before. The rubble broke through, shattering the stairway and leaving a eight foot gap in the stairs.

The two of them stood stunned for a moment until Daniel heard North shout at them from behind: "No time to gawk! Jump!"

The tower shook as the dragons battled and roared beyond. Daniel knew North was right, so he set Clara back on her feet before jumping the gap in the stairs to the other side. Had this been flat ground there was no way they'd all make the jump, but the downward angle let him clear the gap easier. He landed solidly and turned to motion for Clara. She hesitated a moment before leaping the span to him. She barely made it as one foot touched down at the very edge. Daniel reached out and gripped her arm before she fell backwards.

He pulled her onto and past the ledge and the two of them continued down the stairs. North easily cleared the gap and started after them. They finally reached the bottom of the tower to see Hall and the others waiting at the doorway. All they could hear were dragon roars and the sounds of their battle raging around them. Hall pushed open the door. As he did so, Geiod crashed against the keep in front of them.

He roared and as he tried to right himself, Argera clambered over the keep wall and leapt into him, clawing and biting at him with fury. Behind her, Geieg quickly followed. He grabbed her tail with his mouth, dragging her off his companion. Argera managed to retain her balance and whirled to face him. With a roar, she charged into him, slamming him into the keep wall.

While Argera seemed to be getting better at compensating for her missing wing, she was still on the losing end of the battle. The dragon was a mangled mess. Blood poured from dozens of wounds all along her body. One eye was entirely gone. Her second wing had no membrane left, leaving her looking frail and skeletal. In addition, she was clearly weaker from the blood loss and pain. Her blows carried little weight and the other dragons quickly shrugged them off.

Daniel and the others crowded around the doorway. As they did, Daniel realized it was only them left. There were no city guards and no other Dragon Guards with them. Only the commander, three captains, and the five trainees remained in the keep. The rest had been thrown from and crushed upon the walls when the battle reached them. If any others still lived, chances were they were making their way for the tunnel in the south of the city along with Claudia, Kenneth, Austin and the civilians.

"How is she still fighting?" Aaron said. He sounded awestruck and terrified at the same time.

Coe drew her swords. "It's not the first time she's had the odds stacked against her," she said.

Jane peered around the corner of the doorway as Argera raked her claws over the eye of Geiod. "I'm glad she's with us," she murmured.

Hall adjusted the straps on his shield as he spoke: "She won't be for long if we don't even the odds."

Jane peered at him. "How," she said, "are we supposed to do that?"

"*You* aren't," Hall said. "You and the other trainees are heading for the far side of the keep. If there are any remaining civilians help them get over the wall and into the tunnels, then evacuate yourselves."

"What will *we* be doing in the meantime?" Hawk asked, sounding like he knew the answer and wasn't looking forward to hearing it.

"We're going to kill a dragon."

CHAPTER THIRTY-TWO

1ˢᵗ of Eren, 29ᵗʰ year of the Fourth Age.

DANIEL THOUGHT HE'D misheard Hall for a moment. He wondered if the sound of his heartbeat in his ears had drowned out the words. But when Hall continued and Daniel heard the confidence in his voice, he knew he'd heard correctly.

"You all need to make a run for it the first chance that arises, under-stood?" Hall said as he drew his sword and looked at each of them in turn.

Aaron nodded. "Yes, commander."

Hall nodded before looking at his captains. "Coe, Hawk you're both with me," he said. "North, get back up the tower onto the wall."

Coe crossed her arms. "Are we doing what we did in Volignis?"

"As closely as we can, yes."

North groaned as he turned back toward the stairs. "Verhova save me," he said, "I just got down the bloody thing."

Hall watched him go for a moment, and then signaled for Hawk and

369

Coe to exit the tower. Before following them, he glanced back at the fresh trainees. "First chance," he said. "As fast as you can."

They all nodded. Hall ran across the open courtyard to the corner of the keep. The three dragons battled just beyond in full view. Argera's situation remained unchanged. She was caught between them, being cut apart by tooth and claw.

Jane inched closer to the door. "How are they going to do this?"

Griffon rose slightly to peer over Jane's head. "They've clearly done it before."

The three Dragon Guards reached the corner and began conferring with one another. After a few moments, Hawk stepped into the open and threw an ingera at the copper dragon, Geieg. Daniel lost sight of the small orb the moment it left the man's hand, but he saw the result of it when it struck the back of the beast's head. It exploded into a dark glob of paste that stuck to the dragon instantly. Smoke poured off in a thick pillar, making the beast flinch, shake his head, and growl deeply. The dragon whirled around. When his eyes landed on the captain, he started toward him in a rage.

Geieg took only a single step before an arrow whistled through the air and embedded itself halfway into the dragon's eye. The sudden pain caused him to lurch to one side and slam into the keep. He lifted a claw to dig at his eye, trying to pull the arrow free. While he did so, Coe charged around the corner and past and around the dragon's other foreleg. She drove one of her blades upward under the scales on the backside of its leg, leaving the sword plunged into the dragon. Geieg reacted instantly, sweeping back his leg to strike at her, but she was already letting herself fall onto her back, allowing the leg to fly over and past her. She rolled backwards and onto her feet.

Coe dashed back to the corner of the keep as Geieg attempted to put his weight back on his foot. He had obviously given up on the arrow lodged in his eye. But when the dragon tried to use the leg crippled by the sword, he growled and lifted it off the ground in pain before charging after Coe at a hobble. Daniel could tell a tendon on the leg was nearly, if not already, severed. She was already halfway down the length of the keep with Hawk by the time Geieg finished rounding the corner. When he snaked around the corner, Hall was waiting for him. The moment the dragon curved his long body around, Hall dashed forward, just behind his forelegs, with his shield raised.

He charged at the blade lodged in the dragon's leg and with a solid *clang* slammed his etched shield against it. The sword skewed at an awkward angle, causing the dragon more pain as he ensured the muscles and tendons were indeed cut. Geieg again tried to strike his assailant, but Hall was already past and continuing to run until he came to a stop with the keep wall at his back. The dragon saw him, but hampered by his inability to use one of its legs, he chose to employ fire instead of pursuing him. Geieg's neck flared white briefly before he let loose a stream of burning death. Hall dropped to his knees, placed his shield in front of him, and lowered his head behind it just as the stream hit him.

The fire hit the shield and spread away and around Hall, with the keep wall further redirecting it away from his body. The dragon maintained the stream. As it did so, Daniel saw Hawk on the far side throw something into it. Again, Daniel couldn't keep track of it for long, but just after it left the captain's hand there was a brilliant and deafening explosion in front of Geieg's face. The dragon's own flames had set the ingera off right before his eyes. The stream of fire stopped immediately as the dragon whipped his head back, roaring in pain and frustration. The moment the fire was clear of him; Hall stood and blew several quick bursts on his war horn.

Argera, still battling Geiod, heard and again understood the signal as she glanced Hall's way. She tried to peel away from her own attacker who, without the aid of his ally, seemed fairly matched against her, even in her crippled and ragged state. Argera leapt back and turned toward the wall. With the aid of her one wing, she managed to leap onto it before climbing over and into the city beyond. Geiod quickly followed after her, leaving the path to the siege ladders at the north wall clear.

Daniel watched them go. The moment the red tail vanished over the wall, Aaron spoke: "Now's our chance. Let's go!"

Clara and Jane started sprinting across the expanse. Daniel and Aaron hesitated, as Zachery still sat on the stone floor of the tower. Aaron reached for Zachery's hand to lift him to his feet.

"You okay?" Aaron asked.

Zachery nodded and stood on his own. "Let's just get out of here," he said. He shouldered past Daniel and started running.

Daniel glanced at Aaron, who simply gave him a reassuring smile before the two of them started after the rest. Daniel saw another flash of fire to his right, but steeled himself to continue on with his eyes forward. He didn't know how the fight between their leaders and Geieg would end and wasn't sure he wanted to. The five trainees quickly covered the distance to the far wall and to the waiting ladders.

There were no more civilians or guards near them, so the group climbed as fast as they could. When they stood on the wall and looked out over the city, it too sat barren, with no life in sight. Without a word between them, they started down the second set of ladders. When they all reached the ground, they huddled together. They had no idea where to go.

"Which house was the entrance in?" Griffon asked.

Aaron was the only one to attempt an answer. "Hall had said the Quin home, I think, not that it helps us much."

Clara shrugged and looked down the length of the road. "Let's just walk," she said, "and see if we find any trace of where everyone went."

"There were at least two hundred people, not counting guards," Aaron said. "So they had to leave some kind of trail behind." He started to walk without waiting to see if anyone else would follow.

All was silent around them. The sounds of the dragons behind them had faded until they were only a distant, infrequent whisper. The inferno had burned through the area and moved on the northern side of the city, leaving only ashes and embers behind. Only the remnants of homes remained, as well as traces of those who had dwelled here. Ash covered the ground like snow.

Several times they had to walk slowly and gingerly around a gathering of charred remains. Daniel had to focus to ensure that his eyes remained forward. He didn't want to look at the smallest of the corpses, children who must have been barely old enough to walk on their own. He felt bile building in his gut and that familiar tingle in the back of his throat. The smell of burning skin was all around them. It only grew stronger the further they went into this side of the city.

Aaron was at the head of their group. When he stopped walking, everyone followed suit. He seemed to be staring at something farther down the main road. A figure was hunched over next to another figure lying on the ground, unmoving. Daniel had only just realized what both were when the valgret lifted its head from its meal to swallow.

"Hide!" Daniel whispered.

He pushed Griffon and Jane to the closest side road and out of the creature's field of vision. Aaron and Zachery followed quickly and ducked behind a half-fallen wall. Daniel felt his heartbeat quicken. He could hear it in his ears, drowning out every other sound. He knew there was never only one valgret. It was just a question of where the others were. Daniel was at the back of the line that sat against the wall, so he moved further down, allowing more room for the others. They all knelt on the ground, their eyes on Aaron at the front of the line as he carefully peered around the corner and down the road at the monster. None of them saw the figure approach behind them.

Daniel felt a hand on his shoulder. His senses went into a panic. Without thinking, he reached behind his back and gripped his short sword. As he turned, he drew and swung it in a single, practiced motion. Austin leaped back, just out of range, before dashing forward and placing a hand over Daniel's mouth. The rest of the group turned to see what exactly had happened. Austin raised an eyebrow at Daniel who, now realizing who it was, nodded lightly. Austin let him go and peered at the scarf around his own neck. The scarf showed a slice along the neckline.

"Well," Austin whispered, "at least you took to the training." He motioned for all of them to follow. "Come on."

They went through several more side streets and alleyways. After a few minutes, though still moving, they finally felt secure enough to speak.

"What are you doing in the city?" Aaron asked Austin. "I thought everyone was in the tunnels."

"They are, except for Claudia, Kenneth, and me. They're guarding the entrance. I was on my way to report to the commander when I found you."

"The captains and Commander Hall were...trying to kill one of the dragons," Aaron said.

"Well then, two down, one to go."

Clara crossed her arms. "You think they can do it?" she asked.

"I know they can," Austin said. "It's just a question of what happens to them afterwards."

Austin had them stop just outside a home that seemed largely unharmed by the blaze. He knocked on the door four times before turning the handle, then waited another few moments before pushing it open and stepping inside. They followed him in and shut the door behind them. The moment he was inside, Daniel felt a wave of relief pass over him, which was only reinforced when Kenneth stepped through a door on the other side of the room.

Kenneth smiled wide, strode across the room, and placed a hand on Daniel's shoulder. "Glad to see you made it through, lad."

Daniel smiled back. "Me too."

Kenneth's eyes took in the rest of the group. "Well," he said, "let's get out of here while we can, shall we?"

He led them to the room he'd just come from. Inside, Claudia stood with sword in hand next to a slab of stone that had been removed from the floor; it now sat diagonally over part of a hatchway that revealed a set of stairs leading down into the earth. Claudia smiled wide at each of them as they stepped past her and down. Kenneth had Aaron and Zachery help him slide the slab back over the opening before moving to the front and leading the way.

The stairwell was longer than Daniel would have guessed, but then so was the spiral staircase he'd gone down during his last trip into the catacombs of Vigil. The memory sent shivers down his spine, so he pushed it aside and instead focused on the barely visible form of Kenneth in front of them. After nearly five minutes of descending in the dark, a flicker of torchlight appeared ahead of them. Shortly after, they stepped into a brightly lit annex, a square room with two tunnels leading out, one blocked by a heavy iron gate that was locked and rusted. The other tunnel featured a similar gate, though it hung wide open with a torch set into a wall mount next to it.

Claudia gently pushed past everyone and stood next to the open gate. "How about we all take a moment to catch our breath?" she said.

Kenneth crossed his arms. "Catch our breath?" he said. "We've barely–" Claudia's glare apparently made him reconsider his words. "Ah, well, uh...yes, that descent was rather taxing."

Claudia began checking each of them for injuries. When Daniel said he was fine, she gave him the same glare she'd given Kenneth and he quickly acquiesced. Daniel smiled as she stepped away from him and began looking over Griffon. He'd forgotten how intimidating the scholar could be—in a loving way, of course. Kenneth stood to one side of the gate, his arms still crossed, watching her do her work.

Austin, however, was pacing. His eyes were focused on his feet and he tapped his finger on his chin. He was clearly eager to get out of the city. Yet Daniel sensed there was something more. After spending so much time with Austin, he knew many of his mannerisms. The ranger was nervous.

When Claudia finally finished, Austin turned to the open gate. "We better get moving," he said. "We need to get out of these tunnels, I don't fancy the idea of the city coming down on top of us."

Daniel sighed and stood. His whole body felt weak and heavy. It was a struggle to move. But in spite of the fatigue, he still managed to follow through the gate.

"How long is this tunnel?" Clara asked.

Kenneth answered from the front. "Quite long. It goes all the way to the other side of city, then comes out on the beach a short distance from the harbor."

Daniel heard Aaron behind him. "Did Obadiah ever report back?"

Austin shook his head. "No. Chances are that when we had to start sending people down, he was on his way back and got pushed back out. Knowing him, he's probably leading everyone away now."

"How many people made it down here?" Aaron asked.

"By my count," Claudia said, "it was seventy-four city guards, nine

Dragon Guards not including ourselves or Obadiah's squad, and two hundred fifty-six civilians."

Daniel felt his heart skip with each number. There were so few left. Besides their team and Obadiah's group, out of the entire population of Vigil only three hundred thirty-nine remained. The Kridens had wiped out the entire city in hours. He wondered if there was anything else that could have been done to save more people, something to counter the sudden appearance of the dragons that burned so many away. He wondered if there was something that might have saved Alan.

That line of thought quickly brought him back to the scene in the alley, his failure to stop the valgret, and then Lace appearing. He was still trying to figure out what had actually happened. She had seemed so distraught and confused. Her behavior simply didn't make any sense to him. How had she had cracked the ground and soothed the monster? There was no explanation he could come up with that didn't lead back to magic. Magic like what Dalton had done to him. The magic that had stolen his breath and made it feel as if his heart had been in a vice, about to explode.

He was still lost in his own thoughts when he ran into Griffon, who had stopped walking. He looked past her and saw that the others had stopped as well.

Austin sniffed the air several times. "Does anyone else smell that?"

The air was heavily tinted with a scent much like iron. Which meant blood. For the smell to be this strong, there had to be a lot of it.

Jane was the first to voice it: "Blood."

Kenneth drew his sword slowly. "That's not a good sign."

Everyone else drew their own weapons. Daniel removed his bow and grabbed his string from his belt. He looped it over one end, then placed the same side against the ground and planted his foot against it to anchor it against his shin, with the curve of the bow resting against the back of his thigh. He pushed the arm of the bow forward and down, bending it far enough to pull the other loop of the string over the hook. He released it, letting it bend back into shape and pulling the string taunt. He tested it before grabbing an arrow from his quiver. Jane also strung her bow and nocked an arrow.

Kenneth looked back over the group to direct them. "Claudia takes the rear," he said. "Austin and I will have the lead. Everyone else get between us."

They took their positions. Austin grabbed a hand axe from his belt before starting forward again with Kenneth at his side.

Clara's voice quivered as she spoke: "It's probably Disciples, right? Ones that the forward squad killed to clear the way?"

No one answered. They all hoped that was the case, but Daniel felt it was unlikely due to the strength of the smell. He just hoped it wasn't as bad as he envisioned. He was uneasy about everything he was seeing. The tunnel was identical to the one he'd been in several months ago, poorly lit with wall sconces and carved from solid stone. The only difference was that the smell of mildew and rot that had been present previously was now being overpowered by the metallic odor of blood. His mind flashed to the image of the valgret holding his sword as it died in a pool of its own blood. Then it went to Alan being held by one of the monsters as life left his eyes.

Daniel felt himself shaking. He was soaked with sweat and shivered as the images kept flashing through his head. His hearing was being drowned out by his own heart again. He snapped out of it only when he felt a hand lightly touch his shoulder. He turned to see Clara behind him, concern clearly evident on her face. He faked a smile and turned back around. He had to focus. He pushed everything out of his mind and concentrated on the feeling of the bowstring against his fingers.

He wasn't sure if it was his imagination, but Daniel thought that aside from the smell of blood there was another scent that was altogether out of place. It was musky, almost like sweat, but more pungent. It was familiar to him but he couldn't place it. They all kept walking in cautious silence. No one wanted to speak for fear of alerting some unseen force in the dark. In addition to the new underlying scent, the smell of blood grew steadily stronger with each step. After several minutes of walking it began to make Daniel feel sick.

Austin stopped ahead of them and whispered: "Oh, no."

Daniel and the others at the back stepped forward to see what had caught his attention. But before he had taken even two steps forward, Daniel felt his feet nearly slip out from under him. He glanced down and saw that he stood in a large puddle of blood. It seemed to have flowed toward them from ahead. He pulled his eyes away and made his way forward to look past Kenneth and Austin. What he saw caused his stomach to turn. He had to move away from the others and vomit.

The tunnel walls and floors were soaked with blood. Bodies lay across every inch, as far down the tunnel as he could see. Every one of them was maimed beyond any possible recognition, with limbs missing and sections of flesh stripped away entirely. The first dozen before them wore the armor of the city watch, followed by corpses wearing the simple clothes of the citizens of Vigil. Daniel's heart sank. The Dragon Guard had thought this tunnel would be a safe passage to evacuate the citizens, but North had been right. The Disciples controlled the tunnels once again.

Daniel thought of Hall and the other captains. They'd remained above to stall and hopefully kill the dragons. Yet even if they succeeded, chances were high that they would die in the city above. Their sacrifice at this point meant nothing. The ones they had been attempting to buy time for were already dead. Every citizen in Vigil was dead. The last of them lay here before Daniel.

Aaron's voice cracked with fear: "What happened to them?"

Kenneth started forward, stepping carefully over corpses as he did. "I've never seen carnage like this," he said.

Daniel retreated further from the smell and looked back the way they had come. He felt lightheaded and braced himself against the wall with one hand. Clara had her eyes closed and her arms crossed, her back to the carnage, as she stood even further than he was from the group. She was shaking.

Jane whispered behind him: "They look like they were trying to run away."

"That they do," Austin said as he knelt beside one of the bodies. "Every one of them."

As much as he wanted to keep his eyes off of the massacre, Daniel turned and looked at the scene in front of them. Most of the bodies lay face down, toward them.

Claudia had a hand over her mouth. "What would they be running from?"

"Whatever it was," Austin said, "if they were running from it, than that means it was coming this way. It was probably waiting at the exit, until they were far enough into the tunnel that even if they ran, it wouldn't matter."

"Which means," Kenneth said, "it most likely reached the annex before we descended."

"Since it didn't come out the hatchway," Austin said, "that means it most likely went back the way it came. This could be very good for us...or more likely, very bad."

Claudia placed a hand on Clara's shoulder to gently lead her back into the middle of the group. "Let's hope for the former," she said.

Austin nodded. "Either way, we need to keep moving."

Clara turned to him with wide eyes. "You mean through...that?"

Claudia looked her in the eyes. "Clara," she said, "it's the fastest way out of the city. I know it will be difficult, but you have to keep going."

After a few moments of hesitation, Clara nodded. Claudia stood behind her with a hand on each shoulder as the group started to walk. Daniel wanted to keep his eyes straight ahead and off of the bodies, but that wasn't always possible. They all had to look at their feet to ensure they wouldn't trip. While most of the bodies lay face down, many were face up. Their expressions were twisted in terror. Each one reminded Daniel of Alan. Each time the young boy's face flashed through his mind, Daniel felt a little weaker.

The group made steady progress. After ten minutes, they were still stepping over bodies, with more ahead of them. There seemed to be no end to them.

Jane sounded calmer than Daniel would have expected. "Did any of them make it out?" she asked.

"At this point," Austin said with a heavy sigh, "I don't think so."

Clara was nearly whimpering. "So, all of Vigil is...?"

"No," Kenneth said, his tone strong in spite of the situation. "We're still alive."

Despite Kenneth's words, they all knew what the true answer was. The entire city had been overrun and burnt to the ground in less than a night. Daniel wasn't even sure he and the other survivors would be able to make it out. If whatever had done this was still down here, how would they be able to handle it? The farther into the tunnel they went, the more the second scent started to overpower his senses. He knew what it was but he couldn't bring it to the forefront of his mind.

Kenneth seemed to finally notice it himself. "What is that odor?" he asked.

"I've been trying to figure that out," Austin said. "It seems... familiar."

Claudia furrowed her brow. "It's definitely out of place down here."

"Smells like an animal of some kind," Jane said slowly as she too tried to place the source.

That was what triggered it in Daniel's mind. It was an animal. He had smelled it hundreds of times in the forest around Sapella's Crossing. "It smells," he said, "like an elk."

Kenneth sounded confused. "An elk? Why in Edaren would an elk be down here?"

Austin was at the head of the group. He stopped walking. "An elk," he said. His look of concentration slowly turned to fear. "We have to get out of here now."

"Why?" Kenneth said. "What's..." He stopped speaking, as if a realization had come over him.

Seemingly in answer, a cry echoed through the tunnels. Daniel recognized it immediately as the sound of a bull elk, a long and drawn-out bugle followed by several short and breathy grunts. Yet this was different than a standard elk bugle. It sounded hollow. It sounded wrong. It instantly made Daniel tense and reminded him of how the wolf howls had sounded as the Disciples changed it and the woman into a valgret. Into a monster.

Kenneth growled angrily as he spoke: "Shade curse it, it's in front of us!"

Aaron drew his sword. "What is? What's down here?"

"A wirvus."

"So what do we do?" Aaron asked.

Austin took a deep breath, "Hope it's not directly in front of us. We can't go back into the city and this is the only way out of the tunnels that isn't collapsed or exits into the city itself. If we're lucky it's in one of the side passages and we can pass right by it without even seeing it."

"If it's not?" Jane asked hesitantly.

"Pray."

They all started running down the tunnel in the direction of the elk bugle. There was no point now in worrying about being heard. Even if the creature hadn't been able to hear them before, it would have been able to smell them. They were jumping over bodies as they ran. Several times, Daniel slipped in the blood that soaked the floor. Each time he landed, he stumbled forward and placed his hand on the wet ground the catch himself.

A wirvus. Their lessons had covered the creature only briefly as not much was known about it. The main takeaway had been that if they ever encountered one, they should run. The circumstances didn't matter. They just had to get away from it. Daniel and the others kept sprinting, but the tunnel seemed to have no end. They were clearly beyond the city walls, so they had to be nearing the exit. Unless the wirvus had been leaving or as Austin had said, in a side tunnel, they would run into it at any moment.

They all came to a stop as a silhouette appeared in front of them. They watched as it slowly came closer, inch by inch. When it moved next to one of the wall sconces roughly twenty feet away, Daniel could finally make it out in detail.

If it had been standing at its full height the beast would have easily been ten feet tall, with antlers adding another two. But with the low ceiling of the tunnel, it was crouched. All four limbs were long, thin, and frail. The fingers on its arms were narrow, the skin missing at the tips so they melded into the long nail-like talons seamlessly. Its torso was humanoid and gaunt, every bone visible beneath the taut grey skin which was dotted with patches of dark brown fur that seemed to be falling off of it. The back was deformed into a large hunch with its spine bent in unnatural angles. Its head was in the shape of an elk displaying grey and dead skin.

Its teeth that were jagged and sharp, as if they'd been broken at their midpoint. Its eyes were sunken in and entirely void of color. In addition, the wirvus seemed to continually twitch. Constant tiny movements beneath the skin that were almost unnoticeable made it seem... wrong, as if it didn't belong in reality, as if it were a hazy dream almost forgotten but still on the edge of recollection. It looked at them curiously, tilting its head to one side, then made a sound almost like a squeak. They were all frozen in place. None of them wanted to move for fear of provoking it.

Slowly, Austin backed up to stand next to Daniel. "Daniel," he whispered, "go for the left eye. Jane, take the right."

Daniel took several moments to register the order. When he did, he nodded and drew back the string on his bow. He brought the string to his cheek and let his nose rest on it to properly aim down the length of the arrow. The wood was flexible, so drawing and holding the shot was manageable for quite some time, though the more malleable wood meant the shot had less power behind it. But at this distance it wouldn't matter. He just hoped he could hit his mark. He had been far from the best archer among the trainees.

Claudia reached into her bag to withdraw an ingera. She addressed Clara as she did. "Get one ready," she said. "We need to bring this down fast."

Clara nodded. The wirvus continued to look at them and squeak curiously.

Kenneth placed his shield in front of him and stood ready to be the wall between them and it. "Wardens," he said, "up front and low."

They took their positions as everyone waited for Austin's command. His signal would set all events in motion. Austin lifted his arm and balled his hand into a fist. He would try to poison the monster with a dart. Daniel had no idea if it would actually help. More than likely neither did Austin. As far as anyone knew, a wirvus had never been killed before. There had only been a handful of sightings and fewer survivors. But they all had the same story. An unstoppable beast that would tear through any resistance, piercing steel and ripping men apart with no effort while shrugging off anything thrown at it.

It lowered its head slightly and gave another short squeak as it stared at them.

Finally, Austin gave the command: "Now."

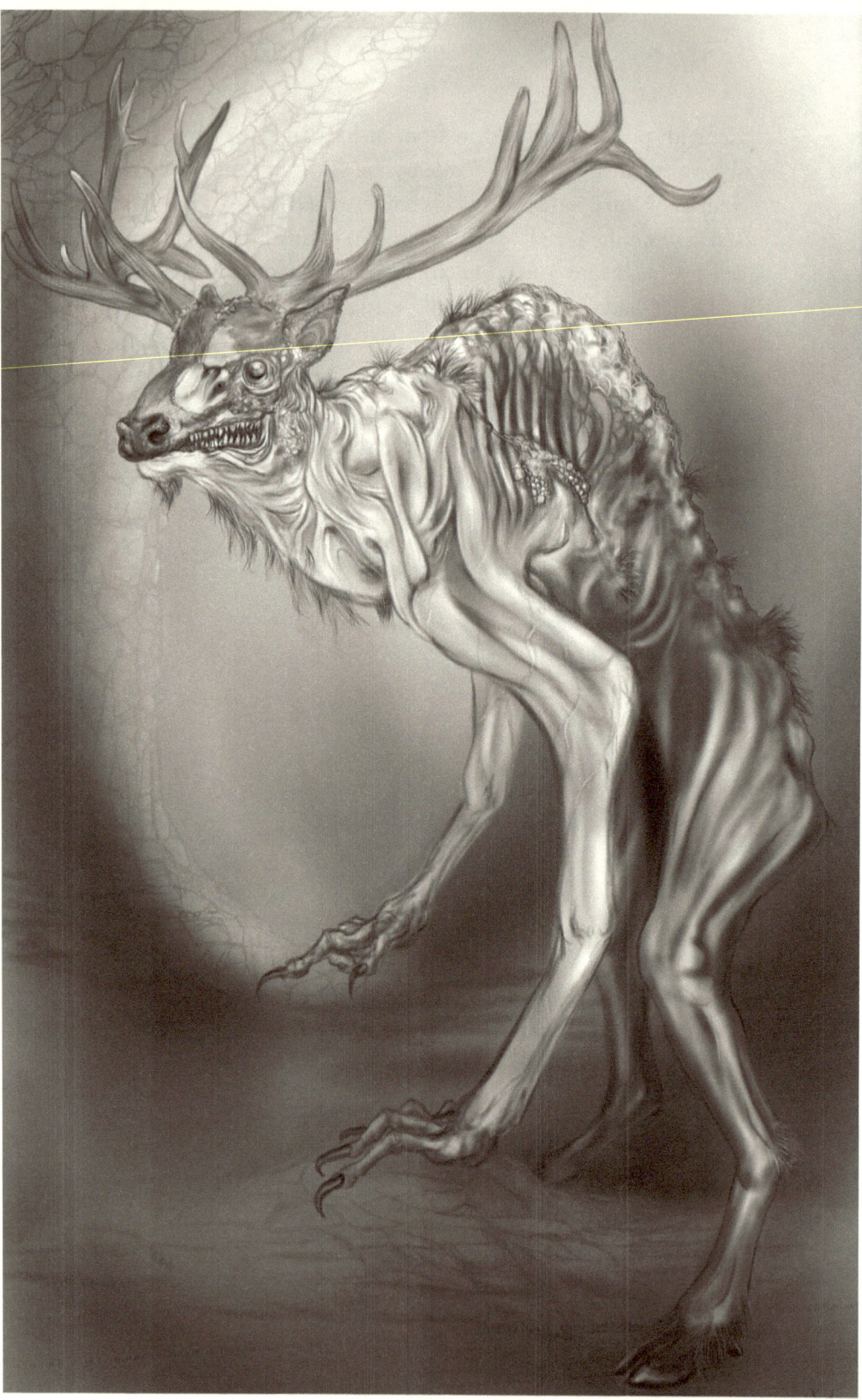

CHAPTER THIRTY-THREE

1st of Eren, 29th year of the Fourth Age.

ALL THREE ARCHERS loosed their shots. Daniel's arrow was on the mark while Jane's went high and clattered harmlessly against the beast's antlers. The monster screamed at them as it reached for its eye. Meanwhile, Austin's dart managed to hit it in the shoulder, but it was to no avail. It simply bounced off its skin and fell harmlessly to the ground. With jittery motions that looked like a nightmare come to life, the wirvus moved toward them at an alarming speed.

Claudia and Clara both ran the fuses of their chosen ingera across the spark stone at their belts. When the fuses lit, they threw them in one smooth motion so they landed in front of the wirvus as it came at them. Had it not been for the size of the tunnel, the creature would have surely reached them by now. Since it was forced to crouch, however, it moved slowly enough that by the time it reached the orbs, the fire had burned to the flash powder stored inside their centers, creating an explosion right beneath it.

Each orb had a different concoction inside. One exploded into a cloud of dark mist, while the other burst into globs of fire that stuck to the walls and the torso of the wirvus, continuing to burn. The sudden fire and choking mist caused the beast to reel back and scream again. It flared an arm forward in an attempt to ward off the pain.

Kenneth shouted, "Keep firing!"

Daniel and Jane broke out of their trance and each nocked another arrow. They didn't bother to aim for the eyes while the creature was thrashing around. They fired and nocked another and then another as quickly as they could, but each arrow simply bounced off the creature's hide with no effect. It didn't even seem to notice their attack as the fire on its body started to subside, leaving the flesh underneath simply charred and blackened but otherwise unharmed.

"It's not working! What are we supposed to do?" Griffon growled.

Kenneth shouted as he raised his shield higher, "Stand your ground, lass!"

Clara took a step back. "Shouldn't we head back to the city?" she said. "There has to be another way out!"

The wirvus shrieked at them, cutting off any further discussion. The sound was loud enough that Daniel had to cover his ears. When it subsided, his ears still rang loud enough that no other sound could be heard. The wirvus charged at them. When it was close enough it lashed out with a clawed hand at Kenneth. The size of the tunnel restricted its movement so that the swipe was clumsy. Kenneth was able to duck beneath it and swing his sword as the arm went over. The blade bit into the beast's skin, but not enough to do any more than simply irritate it.

"Back up!" Kenneth shouted.

The group complied without hesitation. Arrows did nothing to help and the scholar ingera couldn't be used in such close proximity without endangering all of them. Zachery jabbed at the creature's chest with his longsword as he retreated, but the point didn't bite into the skin. The hide was far thicker and stronger than Daniel would have thought possible, given how frail it looked. The wirvus grabbed the sword by the blade and ripped it from Zachery's grip before throwing it against the tunnel wall. It then used its forearm to slam into Kenneth's shield and Zachery's chest, sending them both to the ground in a heap.

Claudia used their newfound distance to throw another ingera directly at the wirvus. The thin shell shattered on impact, spreading thick, black ooze across its face and neck. It shrieked and clawed at its face, attempting to peal the ooze away, but only managed to spread the substance to its hands. Daniel didn't know what the ooze was made of, but it sizzled loudly and caused the wirvus to thrash against the confines of the tunnel. It seemed to be the same type of ingera that Hawk used on the dragon previously, but the skin of the wirvus did not offer the same protection as dragon scales. Austin helped the wardens to their feet while the creature was distracted. They all started to back away—save for Kenneth, who took a step forward.

"Get ready to run past it," he said. "I'll keep it distracted."

Austin looked at him, dumbfounded. "Past it" Are you mad? We need to run *away* from it!"

"Where?" Kenneth said. "Back into the city and into the maw of a dragon and a horde of Kridens and cultists? Forward is the only way out. You know that."

Daniel felt a new wave of sorrow wash over him. He was about to protest, but Claudia spoke his thoughts for him. "You'll die."

The wirvus resumed its approach in spite of the ooze still burning away its skin.

"Not if I kill it first."

The creature was only a few feet away when it suddenly reached with an arm for Griffon. Kenneth placed his shield in front of her, but the creature's bony fingers went right through it and embedded in Kenneth's forearm. Daniel was stunned. It pierced Dragon Guard steel with ease. Kenneth didn't cry out but simply gritted his teeth and grunted against the pain. He tried to pull the wirvus toward the wall to open a pathway. With his free arm, he raised his sword and chopped at the creature's face, driving it back to the stone bricks.

"Go!" he shouted.

Kenneth's efforts weren't in vain as the beast moved to the right of the tunnel as Kenneth pulled on its arm and chopped at its face. Claudia pushed everyone forward, but the size of the passage barely allowed them room to pass. They had to duck under the creature's back legs as they hurried by. Zachery snatched up his sword as they passed. When they were on the other side, Daniel glanced back. The wirvus lifted the arm attached to Kenneth, its hand still stuck in his shield, and slammed him against the wall. Kenneth's head jerked back and hit the stone as the hand of the wirvus slid free of the shield.

Yet Kenneth continued to fight. He lifted his sword again and jabbed at the creature's good eye. Even in his stunned state, he was able hit his target. When the blade pierced, the beast screamed again. In pure fury, it slammed Kenneth against the wall again and again with increasing force. Kenneth released his sword so that it hung awkwardly from the creature's eye socket. It then let Kenneth slump to the floor. The huge warden was alive but dazed.

In spite of the urgency to leave, Daniel felt rooted in place. He sensed a hand on his shoulder. He didn't know whose it was, only that it was attempting to drag him away. But he continued to watch even though his mind and body urged him to move. Kenneth struggled to his feet. With his battered arm, he slammed his shield into the blind creature's head, making it jerk to one side and dislodging the sword from its eye, sending it bouncing across the bodies littering the ground. The wirvus struck out blindly, slamming its hands and arms into the spot where Kenneth had been.

But Kenneth was moving. He rolled to the side and grabbed a fallen city guard's sword before rising again. Apparently unable to see, the wirvus was digging its claws into each nearby corpse to ensure everything in the area was dead as it searched for its still-living prey. It started to make its way toward Daniel and the others, but as it did so a clanging echoed in the tunnel. There was no other sound to be heard. Each clang felt like a stab into Daniel's heart.

"Over here, you Shade-cursed freak!" Kenneth shouted as he slammed his sword against his shield.

The wirvus turned in the tunnel as quickly as it could toward him before resuming its terrifying crawl. Kenneth was too weak to run, so he stood his ground and waited for the beast. Daniel felt himself moving again. He couldn't bring himself to look back when he heard Kenneth scream in fury, or when the scream was cut off and fell silent.

Daniel ran after the figures in front of him through eyes blurring with tears. He stepped over bodies and tried to avoid looking into their lifeless faces as they stared up at him. They all slipped in pools of blood several times as they ran through the dark. The wirvus bugled in triumph behind them. He heard it resume its pursuit. It was a scene out of a nightmare, being chased by some un-killable monster through an inescapable tunnel full of death. But this was a nightmare he wouldn't wake up from. Now he doubted that any of them would live through this.

In spite of it all, Daniel managed to turn his eyes behind them to see that the wirvus had already closed the distance. It moved with the same sporadic and twitching motions as before, which only added to the nightmarish feel of the situation. It didn't matter that it was blind. It was a straight passage, so it was only a matter of time before it reached them. As they ran, Clara reached into her bag and pulled another ingera out. She lit the fuse on her belt and dropped it into the mass of bodies. Daniel glanced back and saw it explode as the wirvus passed over it, again sending out more fire. But this time the beast paid no mind to the flames and kept up its pursuit. It was angry now. Daniel could see the air before its mouth and nose fog as it gasped in its hurried and frenzied state, hungry to reach its prey.

After only a few more moments, it was close enough to try to grab at them. It reached for Daniel's head, but he ducked under its hand and kept running. Then the inevitable happened. Jane lost her footing. She slipped in a pool of blood and wasn't able to regain her balance before falling. Daniel and Zachery had been the only two behind her and when she fell, they tripped over and past her. Daniel pushed himself up and looked behind him at Jane, who lay atop several bodies and struggled to rise as the wirvus stopped directly over her, its nose and mouth just above her, smelling the air.

Jane rolled onto her back and froze in fear. The monster opened its mouth wide and bore down, ripping chunks from her flesh as she screamed loud and long before being cut silent as the creature finally bit on her throat. Daniel's eyes were wide in horror. He felt Zachery grab him by the arm, lift him to his feet, and force him to resume their run. Daniel glanced over his shoulder and saw the creature lift its head, its mouth still dripping blood, before it screamed again, spewing bits of flesh, and resumed its pursuit.

"I see the way out!" Austin called from the front of the group.

Daniel strained his eyes. At the end of the tunnel was a ladder.

"We have to deal with the wirvus!" Claudia shouted. "If we get out in the open with it we're finished!" Austin didn't look back as they ran. "How?"

Daniel knew Claudia was right. The only reason they'd lived this long was thanks to Kenneth and the confines of the tunnel, which slowed the wirvus down enough to let them stay just out of its reach. Out in the open, the beast would be able to move freely, which meant it would be twice the speed they were if not faster. Even without its sight, it could track them by smell and hearing alone. If it shrieked above ground, surely the Kridens or Disciples would hear and quickly bear down upon them. They would have no chance. Yet they also had no way to kill it.

Claudia reached into her bag and pulled out another ingera before coming to a stop. "Austin, get everyone up the ladder!" she said. She took the bag from her shoulder and held it in one hand.

Daniel passed her and stumbled to a stop before turning to her. "Claudia," he said, "what are you doing?"

"Go, Daniel! I'll be fine!"

He felt a hand grip his shoulder again and turned to see Austin moving him down the tunnel toward the exit as the others continued past. "You heard her," he said. "Let's go!"

"We can't leave her!"

"Shut up and go!"

With a hard shove, Daniel was forced to keep moving while he continued to look behind him at Claudia. She stood in front of the creature as it steadily came closer. It stopped just in front of her and smelled the air. She stood defiant as it caught her scent and pressed its nose against her cheek, taking long and deep sniffs. Then it screamed in her face. Without hesitation, she drove a hand into its mouth. It bit down, severing her hand at the wrist, then lifted its head to swallow as she screamed in pain and fell backwards.

The wirvus screamed again and was about to go after her a second time, no doubt spurred on by the smell of her blood. But something happened. It stopped. It lurched in place for a moment, then started to thrash around the tunnel while clawing at its own chest and stomach. It shrieked the most horrifying and hollow sound Daniel had ever heard. The sound of its cry made his breath catch in his throat. The wirvus knelt down and slammed its head against the wall while ripping chunks out of its own gut.

Daniel tore away from Austin, ran to Claudia's side, and helped her to her feet. He led her away as the wirvus kicked and swung its arms and legs in a blind and painful flurry. Austin ran over and together with Daniel they got Claudia to the ladder, where she started to climb while clutching her bloody stump to her chest. Austin started up next before Daniel followed. He glanced back at the creature. It had finally managed to reach into its own stomach. All Daniel saw was fire burning away its insides as it slowly sank to its knees before falling forward and going still.

He turned and started to climb. When he reached the top, he found himself in a short, narrow crack in the rocks with the stars above him. The space was just barely large enough for him to climb through and stand up straight. Through gap he could see the hints of the ocean beyond. He turned sideways and shimmied his way forward between the two rock walls. He stumbled out of the crag and onto the shore. He'd nearly landed on top of a body. It took him several seconds to realize who he was looking at. His heart lurched again. Obadiah stared up at him with a blank expression and blood pooled beneath him in the rocky sand. Daniel realized it was soaking his hands. He jumped backwards into the rock where he struggled to breathe. His heart beat so fast he feared it would leap out of his chest.

The area around them was littered with bodies, just like in the tunnel. Snow was falling and had begun to hide the carnage with a blanket of pure white. Daniel shook his head, trying to shake away the death he saw in his mind every time he blinked. He wanted to snow to fall heavier and quickly hide everything in front of him. He again felt a hand on his shoulder. It was Griffon, pulling him onward. Her face was downcast and she kept her eyes on her feet. They all went as quickly as they could down the length of the beach, away from the city and into the cover of the nearby trees, with Claudia being supported by Aaron and Austin.

Daniel looked at the water and for the first time saw the fleet of ships the Kridens had used to reach Edaren. Hundreds of them were anchored in the water, with at least twice as many skiffs lining the docks along the cliff. Daniel saw several people silhouetted against the stars on the ships, but none of them seemed to notice the survivors of Vigil as they made for the forest just past the city. When they were far enough into the trees, they stopped. Clara reached into her bag and started treating the mangled spot where Claudia's hand had been minutes earlier.

Daniel sat down next to a tree and stared through the foliage toward the city walls. He could see the tower at the center of the city rising over the walls, with the red dragon, Geiod, perched atop it. He sat calmly, looking out over the city as it burned around him. There were no more Kridens on the outside of the walls as far as Daniel could tell. Those that weren't on the ships were more than likely sweeping the city. He imagined their lack of presence outside was either due to the fact that they didn't think anyone would escape the city or that they didn't care. Daniel guessed the latter.

Whoever did manage to escape would pose no threat to them at this point. Vigil was finished. The Dragon Guard was wiped out save for a ranger, a wounded scholar, and a handful of novices who hadn't even finished their training. Daniel looked at each one of them in turn. Clara was still treating Claudia. Griffon was looking toward the city with her hands balled into fists. Aaron stood next to her, his arms crossed. Austin was pacing off to one side and Zachery was staring absentmindedly into the trees. They were all broken. They finally weren't running from something or fighting for their lives, which meant it was a moment for everything that had happened to fully sink in.

Kenneth and Jane had fallen below. Obadiah was dead. The captains and the commander had fought with and, as far as Daniel was aware, killed Geieg, the copper dragon, but they had more than likely fallen in doing so. With Geiod atop the keep tower, that had to mean that Argera too had fallen. Alan had died in the city right in front of Daniel while he stood there, unable to do anything to stop it.

He looked at Zachery again. He hated that he hadn't be able prevent what had happened to his brother. It was his fault. It was something his training hadn't focused on, to face an enemy head on. Daniel was trained to kill the unaware and unarmed before they knew he was even there, from the shadows and at a distance. He looked down at himself. His armor, clothes, and hands were covered in dried blood. None of it was his. Suddenly, in a type of panic, he frantically dug into the small snow-drifts beneath the trees and tried to clean his hands, to try to wash it all away, hoping that maybe it would clear the memories from his mind.

"Now what do we do?" Griffon spoke with a shaky tone through gritted teeth.

Austin stopped pacing and sighed deeply. "I'm not sure," he said. "I need time to think."

Aaron looked at him in shock. "Think?" he said. "You want to take time to *think* about it?"

Austin glared at him. "Aaron. What would you have us do? Charge into the city to die?"

"No, of course not! But we don't have time to think. We have to do something now, while we can!"

"We'll head further into the forest," Austin said. "There are a few small caves we can take shelter in for the night. We have to rest."

Griffon stepped up to Aaron and put a hand on his shoulder. "He's right," she said. "We can't just act for the sake of acting. We need a plan."

Aaron looked at the ground and balled his hands into fists. "Fine."

Austin stepped over to Claudia and lifted her to her feet, placing her arm over his shoulder to steady her. Clara did the same on her other side. Without another word between them, they all headed deeper into Highwood Forest.

Their pace was slow. Every step was more challenging than the last. It was made all the more difficult by the constant, distant glow of Vigil burning behind them. Images of the city kept flashing through Daniel's mind. The bar with Kenneth seated beside him. The training field behind the keep, the library with Clara and Alan seated across from him, the commander's brilliant glass window behind his desk. All of it gone, in the hands of the Disciples and their Kriden army. He wanted to wake up. Every time he blinked, he wanted to open his eyes to the see the shoddy wooden shelf above his cot and the slight glow of sunlight shining through the small windows at the end of the barracks.

But it never happened. He only saw the empty eyes of Alan. The jagged teeth of the wirvus. The dragons as they ripped Argera's wing off and the fireballs cresting the city walls. Suddenly he felt very sick. He staggered to a tree and braced himself against it as he vomited into the fresh snowfall. Everything after that point was hazy. Before he realized it, they were sitting in a long, narrow, rock and dirt cave. The entrance was blocked by shrubs and a broken tree. He noticed everyone looked the same as he did—beaten down and heartbroken. They'd lost everything in a single night. Austin sat across from Claudia near the entrance, where they talked to one another in whispers, Claudia wincing in pain occasionally as she gripped the bandaged stump of her arm. Not long after, Daniel fell asleep.

Daniel was shaken awake by a hand on his shoulder. In a moment of panic, he tried to strike out with his fist. Austin caught his wrist and held him firmly until Daniel calmed.

Daniel nodded to him, signaling that his head was clear. "Sorry."

Austin smiled and patted his shoulder. "Good reaction time," he said. He sat down next to Daniel. When he was settled, every eye was turned to Austin.

The first to speak was Aaron: "So? Do we have a plan?"

Austin rubbed a hand over the stubble on his chin. "We do," he said.

"But none of you are going to like it." They all exchanged glances. "The fact of the matter is, this isn't just a grudge against the Dragon Guard. This isn't an isolated attack. They're not going to stop with Vigil."

Clara's voice cracked as she spoke. "What do you mean?"

"I mean they somehow brought what looks like the entire fighting force of Krida to our doorstep. An army of this size won't stop at a single city. They want to take over all of Edaren."

Claudia sighed. "Krida is not known for its mercy," she said. "They will slaughter everyone. They do not take prisoners."

Griffon leaned forward, nodding. "We have to warn the king and the Council, the Royal Army."

Austin shook his head. "It's not just a matter of warning the Royal Army," he said. "We have to warn everyone. Every city, every farm, and every village between us and Dalisia."

"How are we supposed to do that?" Clara asked.

Daniel sighed. He knew the answer. Austin was right, he didn't like it.

"We have to split up," Daniel said.

Aaron shook his head. "No. No way. Not after everything that just happened. We can't abandon each other."

Daniel agreed with him to an extent. But thinking about the situation, Daniel knew they had no other choice. They had no idea how many, if any, other Dragon Guards survived. They had to operate under the assumption that they were all that was left. That they were the only ones that knew what was coming.

Claudia strained to sit up against the wall. "This isn't us abandoning one another," she said. "This is about more than us. Whoever we don't warn dies. That is the fact of what is happening now. We can't afford to leave a single home, a single family, behind to be washed over by the Kridens."

They were all quiet for a long while, letting the truth of it sink in. Daniel glanced to the faces of each of his friends and his mentors. If they really did this, he wasn't sure he would see them again.

Griffon sighed. "So," she said, "how do we do this?"

Austin crossed his arms. "There are seven of us," he said. "We have to warn Dawnstone and Navia. They're the closest cities and one of them will be hit next." He looked at each of them. "So three will go to one and four to the other."

"Who goes where?"

"Claudia and I discussed this during the night. Clara, Griffon, and I will head for Navia. Clara's mother works for the councilman, so hopefully we'll have an easier time convincing them of the threat with you there. The rest of you will head for Dawnstone. It's the closest and Claudia needs proper care for that wound. After that, you'll head down the river to Silvum and then to Grey Gate. We'll meet there and decide what to do next."

Aaron shook his head. "How do you expect us to convince the council member of each city that Edaren is being invaded," he said, "when the rest of the nation thinks the Dragon Guard is nothing more than a joke?"

Austin sighed. "I don't know."

Claudia smiled at him. "We'll find a way."

Daniel looked to the entrance of their small shelter. Sunlight had started to shine through the foliage and illuminate them. None of them were really prepared for what was coming. It was a war now, they knew that, but it still didn't feel real. Austin was the first to make his way out into the forest. Aaron followed next. The rest slowly filed out behind him, with Daniel stepping into the ever-deepening snow. It was winter now. The journey would be hard, almost impossible. They would be lucky to live through the cold.

Austin glanced up as the snow fell, shielding his eyes against the rising sun. "We'll head for the Crossroads," he said. "Hopefully, there, we can get some horses and warn everyone about what's coming."

Clara crossed her arms against the chilling wind. "What if they don't listen?" she said. "Or help?"

"The best we can do is give them the message," Austin said. "What they do after that is up to them."

Give them the message. It made what they were doing sound so simple. But this would be what decided if Edaren stayed standing in the coming battles. It would be what decided the fate of thousands upon thousands of people. Daniel just hoped they would make it in time. Krida already had a head start. It had struck the first blow. This would be the chance to gear up for a counterattack.

Instinctively, Daniel reached down, placed a hand on his sword, and felt his grip tighten around the hilt. This was far from over.

www.ingramcontent.com/pod-product-compliance
Lightning Source LLC
Chambersburg PA
CBHW050859250626
47155CB00001B/33